Praise for Shirley Wells's

Presumed Dead

"I almost felt as though I was right there witnessing some of these conversations, leaning forward in my chair to see what witnesses would say.... The interrelationships between the people in the town are almost as intriguing as the mystery itself and the author lets readers piece together images of Dawson's Clough in bits and snatches. The setting is most definitely not a generic one, and it gave the story a brooding mood which matched Dylan Scott's character well indeed."
—*All About Books*

"The characters' lives are all interwoven, and as you read along, you wonder just who hated Anita Champion, a happy-go-lucky woman, enough to want to harm her. There's no end of suspects, several guilty parties, and no real hope for a happy ending when the mystery is solved. Ms. Wells keeps you turning those pages, though! I look forward to reading more of Shirley Wells' work."
—*Journey of a Bookseller*

"Excellent read, worthy of a five-star rating. Shirley Wells does an incredible job of writing a fast-paced thriller that will have you guessing until the end.... The quick pace of this book will keep you up at night, wanting to find out what the next page holds."
—John O. Raab, editor of *Suspense Magazine*

SHIRLEY WELLS

Shirley was born and raised in the Cotswolds, where her headmaster wrote on her school report—*Shirley is content to dream her life away.*

Years later—as an adult living in Cyprus—it dawned on her that this wasn't necessarily a bad thing and that fellow dreamers, in the guise of fiction writers, had been getting away with it for centuries.

A move to the Orkney island of Hoy followed and, during the twelve years she spent there, she wrote short stories as well as full-length romantic fiction for U.K. women's magazines.

She's now settled in Lancashire, where the Pennines provide the inspiration and setting for her popular mystery novels. She and her husband share their home with an ever-changing selection of deranged pets, who often insist on cameo roles in Shirley's novels.

When she isn't writing, Shirley loves reading (anything and everything), listening to live music, watching TV, eating chocolate and drinking whiskey—though not necessarily at the same time. She's also a season ticket holder at Burnley Football Club and can often be seen in the biting wind and pouring rain cheering on her favorite team.

And she's still content to dream her life away.

Presumed Dead

SHIRLEY WELLS

Recycling programs for this product may not exist in your area.

ISBN-13: 978-0-373-06239-3

PRESUMED DEAD

First North American Publication 2010

This edition published by arrangement with Harlequin Books S.A.

www.CarinaPress.com

Printed in U.S.A.

Presumed Dead

Acknowledgments

Many people have helped bring my story to life
and I thank them all.

Everyone at Carina Press
has worked exceptionally hard on *Presumed Dead*
and for that I am extremely grateful. In particular
my gratitude goes to my editor, Deb Nemeth, who
has not only offered encouragement and sound advice
but has also made the whole process great fun.

Living with a writer isn't easy,
and my heartfelt thanks go to Nick for making sure
I don't starve and for not minding that the word
housework doesn't figure in my personal dictionary.

It's been a real team effort. Thank you.

CHAPTER ONE

"DICKHEAD!" Dylan yelled as the driver of a blue Ka changed lanes and almost took off his nearside wing.

A female driver—no surprise there—put up her hand by way of apology and tossed back long dark hair. If Dylan had his way, women would be banned from the bloody road until they could prove themselves less emotional and less hung up on life's minutiae.

Bev was the same. She saw driving as a means of inspecting people's curtains, or drapes as she'd taken to calling them. It never occurred to her to look where she was going. Added to that, she was too emotional to be allowed behind the wheel of a car.

She could be a real drama queen at times. A teacher, her subjects were English and drama, and she tended toward the theatrical.

"You're nothing but a drunkard, Dylan Scott. A drunkard and a bloody loser!"

It had been a month, almost to the day, since she hurled those words at him, and he was still smarting. Still miffed, too. Damn it, if she must throw abuse at him, she could at least make it *accurate* abuse.

He was not a drunkard. He'd been a bit tipsy on the night in question, admittedly, but he was far from a drunkard.

The words *pots and kettles* sprang to mind and, if he hadn't been the type to prefer a quiet life, he would have reminded her of the time she'd been out with her mates only to come home and pass out in the hedge by the front door. Or the night they'd celebrated their wedding anniversary and she'd thrown up in the back of that taxi.

During almost fourteen years of marriage, she'd been drunk far more often than he had.

He hated it when she had one of her moods on her, and this was her worst yet. She'd come round, she always did, but meanwhile, life was hell.

Just when they should have been decorating the house for Christmas, she'd thrown him out. Efficient to the core, she'd even found him alternative accommodation. He was now the penniless tenant of the smallest flat in the land.

"It's got two bedrooms," she'd said, "so Luke can come and stay."

"That's a bedroom? I thought it was where I was supposed to keep the Hoover."

"You're going to get a Hoover?" She'd laughed at that, the sarcastic, angry laugh he loathed. "My, wonders will never cease. And do you know what a Hoover does exactly?"

"Oh, very droll."

He'd talked, cajoled, begged and pleaded, but he'd still spent Christmas and the New Year in the smallest flat in the land…

He felt as if he'd been sitting in his car for days rather than hours and, according to his sat nav, he still had forty miles to drive. The strong wind was increasing, buffeting his car.

The countryside was growing more picturesque and, if he'd been in the mood to enjoy it, it might have been a pleasant journey. He wasn't in the mood to enjoy anything. He wanted to be at home, his own home. He didn't want to be anywhere near Devon.

If Bev hadn't thrown him out, he wouldn't be. But she had. Ergo, he needed money. With the marital home *and* the smallest flat in the land to pay for, he needed to work.

The need for cash wasn't his only reason for visiting Devon, however. On Thursday evening, he'd answered a ring at his door to find that his worst nightmare had become reality. Just when he thought things couldn't get any worse, he'd seen his mother, suitcases at her feet, standing on his doorstep.

"Beverley's thrown you out," she'd said, as if this might be news to him, "so you'll need me now."

"Mum, I'm fine. Really, I can—"

"Nonsense. Take my cases through, Dylan. Beverley said you had a spare room going begging."

"Of course it's not going begging. It's full of junk—stuff I haven't unpacked yet." He took a breath. "Really, Mum, I'm fine. And you'll be very uncomfortable here. It's too—small. Too—awful."

"Nonsense. I've stayed in worse than this. Remember when we were out in Istanbul?"

Dylan hadn't been born at the time so he couldn't be expected to remember. That hadn't stopped her going on—and on—about the year she'd spent in Istanbul with a bunch of her hippy friends…

As he slowed for a sharp bend, Dylan wondered if life could get any worse. He was thirty-eight years old, he had no job and little hope of getting one, his wife had thrown him out, his mother had moved in, and he'd had to hunt through a pile of laundry currently lying in front of his as-yet-unused washing machine for the shirt he was wearing.

Ever the optimist, though, at least he had escaped his mother for a couple of days and, at two hundred pounds a day plus expenses, looking into the disappearance of Holly Champion's mother would pay rents, mortgages and every other damn thing for a few weeks.

In fact, given that Holly Champion had literally begged him to help her, insisted she wanted no one else, there was nothing to stop him charging two hundred and fifty a day plus expenses.

Better still, perhaps they could do a swap. Dylan would kill for a mother who did a thirteen-year vanishing act.

You'll need me now.

What nonsense was that? She wouldn't do anything useful. She had cleaned that spare bedroom meticulously, but the rest of the flat had been deemed Dylan's responsibility. As yet, she hadn't so much as made him a sandwich. Feminism had a lot to answer for.

The roads were deserted, and narrower, as he neared the coast. According to his sat nav, he was less than a mile from Verdun House now.

"Destination in two hundred yards," the computerised voice said.

"What? You have to be kidding."

There was nothing visible. Tall hedges sided a narrow road that was little more than a rutted track.

"Destination," the sat nav announced.

"Bollocks!" He scowled at the instrument. "And now I'm talking to a bloody computer!"

Dylan stopped the car. On his left, a tall hedge shielded the view. On his right was a small lane and a sign informing people that space was available on Blue Skies Caravan Park.

Perhaps he would be able to find someone who could give him directions for Verdun House.

He drove into the site and parked outside a mobile home that showed signs of life. At least, there were fresh flowers in the window. He got out of his car, strode up to the door, lifted his hand to knock and then spotted the small sign next to the step. Verdun House.

Verdun House, home of Holly Champion, was a blasted mobile home.

What in hell's name was wrong with people? It wasn't a house. It was barely a home. It was a caravan that was too idle to move.

A smiling woman in her mid-twenties dashed toward him from a neighbouring mobile home.

"Mr. Scott? You found me then. Come inside."

"This is really—I mean—you're Holly Champion?"

"Yes." A tiny frown creased her brow. "Is something wrong?"

Everything was wrong. If one thing was horribly clear to Dylan, it was that someone who lived here, on this caravan park that would be a resting place for wrinklies and maybe hordes of holidaymakers in season, could not afford two hundred and fifty pounds a day plus expenses.

"I didn't realise you were so far from the beaten track," he said, and it sounded lame even to his ears.

"It's not so far." She stood, hands on hips, to look around her, then pointed in an easterly direction. "The village is only three miles away."

"Ah."

"Cute car, by the way."

His car was not cute. It was a 1956 registered Morgan in Daytona Yellow with seventy-eight thousand miles on the clock. His pride and joy, yes. Cute, no.

"Thanks," he murmured with a sigh.

"Come inside." She led the way into the miniscule glorified portacabin.

"You'll want a drink after the journey." She got that right. "Tea or coffee? I'm sure I have coffee in."

To Dylan, a drink came in a pint glass and was cold. However, he guessed the nearest pub was three miles away. Who the hell could live with no pub within walking distance?

"Coffee, please. Instant's fine," he said, as she reached for a grinder.

"I don't have instant."

As she dealt with the coffee, he studied her more closely. At first, he would have put her at five feet ten, the same height as himself, but then he'd spotted the shoes she was wearing. Bright red, they had killer heels of about five inches.

She saw him looking at them and grinned. "Shoes are a weakness of mine."

"Ankles will be another, I imagine."

Slim and attractive in a well-scrubbed, natural way, she had long fair hair hanging down her back, and she kept tossing it away from her face as she reached for the milk—skimmed, he noted with an inner grimace—or took a mug from a cupboard. Her legs were clad in worn but clean denim jeans, and a sweater in every colour of the rainbow almost touched her knees.

"Please, sit down." She gestured to one of the two wooden stools at the small bar.

Amazingly, she'd managed to cram a fridge, washing

machine, cooker and three cupboards into what would laughingly be described as the kitchen. The small patches of visible wall space were white, broken only by two framed pencil sketches of horses. Colour came from a bunch of flowers at the window and a bright red hand towel hanging near the fridge.

"Thanks." Silently apologising to his aching body, he perched on a stool. She put a mug of coffee in front of him, then a small jug of milk and a sugar bowl, all in chunky pottery.

Dylan helped himself to three spoonfuls of sugar and added the milk. He loathed skimmed milk. "Aren't you having one?"

"I rarely drink tea or coffee. I prefer water." She smiled. "It's better for you and it's cheaper."

Sod it. He'd escaped the ageing hippy he called Mother to spend time with another resident of Planet Zorg.

"Thank you for coming," she said. "I appreciate it. I really do."

The only reason he was there was because he needed to escape his mother. That and the cash, of course, and there was no way she could afford two hundred and fifty quid a day.

"I've only come to talk," he said. "And first, I want to know two things—how you came to find me and why you think I can help."

"Okay." She sat, elbows on the narrow counter, her expression earnest. "I read about you on the internet. You found that missing schoolgirl, Carol Turner."

"Carol Turner? But that was years ago."

"Eight years." She nodded. "I was seventeen."

Only eight years? It seemed a lifetime ago.

"On the internet," she said, "they quoted you as saying you would never have stopped looking for her. I wanted someone like that to discover the truth about my mother."

"Since then—" He broke off, knowing there wasn't an easy way to explain. "Well, let's just say that a lot's happened in my life."

"I know. You spent five months in prison for assaulting Thomas Brookes and you were dismissed from the police force."

The simplicity of her words brought a reluctant smile to his face.

"I was beaten up while trying to arrest a violent criminal," he corrected her, "and then found myself on an assault charge. I was found guilty—if I'd known, I would have used far more force—and then spent the next five months being beaten up by scum in prison."

He tried not to think of those days. From a detective sergeant with a bright future to an ex-con in double-quick time. "So how did you find me?"

"I searched the internet and there was a small piece from a newspaper. It was published about eighteen months ago. From Hero to Outcast, the headline ran. You'd been—"

"Kicked out of a pub. Drunk and disorderly."

"Yes."

"I paid the fine."

She smiled. "That's all right then."

"So what makes you think I can find your mother?"

"Perhaps you can't. All I know is that, for years now, I've been determined to learn the truth—determined to *try* and learn the truth. If anyone can help, you can."

"But I've no real experience—"

"You found Carol Turner."

"Yes, but I was a police officer then. I had all the resources at my disposal. Now, I'm definitely *persona non grata*." That wasn't strictly true, but he could count his friends in the force on one hand.

"You're a private investigator now. It said so in that newspaper article."

"I am registered, yes, but all I've done is a bit of insurance work."

"Then this will make a pleasant change for you."

The way his life was going, having his testicles removed without anaesthetic would make a pleasant change.

"Employing someone—anyone, not just me—is expensive," he said. "No one can afford to work for nothing."

"Please don't imagine this is just a whim, Mr. Scott." She stood and Dylan suspected she would have paced the floor if there had been any to pace. "I left school and put myself through university." She held her head high. "While there, I did a paper round in the mornings and bar work at nights and weekends. Since then, I've worked five days a week as a primary school teacher, three nights a week in the village pub, and Sundays at the golf club. I don't smoke or drink. I buy my clothes from charity shops. Except my shoes, of course." She paused, her face pink. "What I'm saying is that, for years now, I've saved every penny possible so that I can employ someone to look into my mother's disappearance. I'd like that someone to be you."

Dylan hadn't meant to insult her by mentioning money.

He supposed he should be flattered by her faith in him, but if—and it was a huge if—he took this job, how the hell would he feel taking money from someone who dressed in stuff from Oxfam?

"Tell me about your mother," he said.

She peered out the window at the leaden January sky. "Let's walk while we talk. It'll be lovely on the beach."

"Walk?" It wasn't raining—yet—but the wind was strong enough to rock her home on occasion.

"Don't you walk?" She sounded concerned for his health.

"It has been known," he said, resigned to battling with the elements.

"Do you have a coat?"

Of course he had a coat. When you drove a 1956 Morgan with seventy-eight thousand miles on the clock, you accepted that you were likely to spend a large portion of time hanging around waiting for breakdown vehicles. "In the car."

She pulled on a thick blue coat, courtesy of Oxfam he assumed, and, much to his relief, slipped off those shoes and exchanged them for walking boots. Once outside, Dylan dashed to his car and grabbed his overcoat from the passenger seat.

"Lead on," he said when he'd locked his car.

She strode out toward a grassy bank. Dylan followed and was breathing heavily by the time they reached the top. He really should think about taking up running again.

"There." She spoke with satisfaction and Dylan could see why.

Below them was the beach. As far as the eye could

see, from east to west, a pebbly beach had its edge lapped by a wind-whipped grey sea.

"Very nice," he said.

A couple were walking with their arms linked and a scruffy black dog running at their heels, three kids were kicking a football around, unsuccessfully because it was blowing everywhere but where they wanted it to go, but, other than that and a few dozen gulls trying to make themselves heard over the roar of the wind, it was deserted.

"I think of this as my garden," she said.

"Easy maintenance."

"Very easy." She laughed.

Walking on the small pebbles was hard work, but Holly Champion didn't seem to notice.

"My mother liked a good time." She kept her hands deep in her coat pockets, and raised her voice to compete with the wind. "We lived in Dawson's Clough, Lancashire, above the hairdresser's where she worked. One Saturday night, thirteen years ago, she went out, as she did every Saturday night, and never came back."

She bent to pick up a pebble. "It was the twenty-ninth of November, 1997, and she was thirty years old. I was eleven at the time and I was taken in by her sister, Aunt Joyce. The police were called but—" She pulled a face. "They weren't interested. They believed she'd gone off with someone and left me to my own devices."

"What made them think that?"

"The fact that she used to stay out overnight, I suppose."

"When you were eleven?"

"From when I was about eight." She gave him a rueful smile. "But she wouldn't have gone off like that. No way.

If she'd been going anywhere for longer than a night or two, she would have taken me with her."

Better to believe that, Dylan supposed, than accept you were an unwanted tie. "I'll need to think about it before I decide whether or not I can help, but take me through the day she went missing. Everything you can remember."

"Okay. As I said, she worked in the hairdresser's below our flat in Dawson's Clough. She was working that Saturday, and she was busy. I know because I was there. I used to help out on Saturdays—sweeping up, making the tea and coffee, putting the towels in the washer or dryer, stuff like that."

"Shit!" Dylan missed his footing and went over on his ankle. "Sorry. Carry on."

"The shop closed at five-thirty and it would have been about six o'clock, maybe six-thirty when we got upstairs to the flat." She smiled at a memory. "She gave me two pounds for helping out. I suppose she'd been given a lot of tips. It wasn't long till Christmas, you see, and customers would have been going to office parties and suchlike."

"She didn't own the shop?"

"Oh, no. Sandra Butler owned it. Mum was paid a wage and was allowed to keep her tips. Just the two of them worked there."

"Okay. So when you got back to your flat?"

"Mum went straight in the bath and I made us beans on toast. Funny how you remember the small things, isn't it?" she said. "Anyway, when we'd eaten and washed up, Mum went to her bedroom to get ready for her night out."

"What did you do?"

"I went with her." She spoke as if it were the most natural thing in the world. "I always tried on her shoes or her jewellery while she put on her makeup. She was beautiful.

"I'll show you photos," she went on, as if she needed to prove that last comment. "On that particular night, she wore her hair up. Hair like mine, she had. She was wearing a calf-length red dress with high-heeled red shoes. As always, she wore lots of beads and bracelets. Her jewellery was just cheap stuff, but she loved it. Her one weakness was jewellery, and mine's shoes.

"She left the flat at about eight o'clock. A hug, a kiss, a warning not to open the door to strangers, a whiff of perfume, and she was gone." She took a breath and stopped to gaze out to sea. "I never saw her again."

Dylan, too, gazed at the horizon.

"Do you know where she went?" he asked at last.

"Yes. She met up with three friends. They went to a pub near the salon, then on to a club. They split up and she—she just disappeared."

"I see."

They walked on in silence until a few spots of rain fell.

"We'd better head back," she said.

She walked tall with her head held high. A proud young woman, she'd find it difficult, if not impossible, to accept that she'd been abandoned.

"Right," Dylan said when they were back at the caravan park, "I'll go and check into a hotel and—"

"Oh, no. I'm paying and a hotel is—well, it's a dreadful waste of money when I have a spare room. It's all ready for you."

Dylan shook his head. "I'll stump up for a hotel."

One with a decent bar. "I need to give this some thought and I think better alone. I'll call back in the morning to let you know what I decide. You need to think, too. If I decide to work on this, it's going to cost you a lot of money."

"I realise that." She proffered her hand. "I'll see you tomorrow morning then, Mr. Scott. And thank you."

He shook her wind-chilled, slender hand. "It's Dylan."

"Holly."

"About eleven o'clock? Or is that too early for a Sunday?"

She seemed to find that amusing. "Eleven's fine."

IN HIS HOTEL room, with a good meal and a half bottle of fine red wine inside him, Dylan lay back on the bed, hands behind his head, and went through the pros and cons of working for Holly Champion.

There were a few pros. He needed the cash. It would pass the time until Bev welcomed him back to the marital home. He wouldn't have to share the smallest flat in the land with his mother.

There were plenty more cons, though. He didn't like the idea of taking money from Holly Champion, and he didn't fancy a trip to the arse-end of Lancashire. A missing-person case had to be one of the most mind-numbing jobs imaginable. Holly had too much faith in him when it was extremely unlikely that, after thirteen years, he would discover anything new. The police had looked into it and, if they hadn't come up with any answers, it was unlikely Dylan would. In short, the job simply didn't excite him.

He'd tell her he wouldn't do it.

And do what? Drive back to his mother? To the smallest flat in the land? To a pile of laundry and a mountain of bills?

Pleased that he'd had the foresight to stop off at the off-licence on the way to the hotel and buy himself half a bottle of brandy, he took a glass from the bathroom and poured a small measure.

If it wasn't for his mother, he'd go straight home. The laundry and the bills he could cope with. But his mother—

He loved her dearly, but only when she was in her home in Birmingham. Thanks to caller display, he could ignore ninety-five percent of her phone calls, just as he'd ignored three while walking on the beach with Holly, but he always felt guilty.

Life would be a damn sight easier if he had half a dozen siblings or if he had a father to shoulder some of the responsibility. But there were no siblings and no father.

Vicky Scott had drifted through the sixties wearing bells around her neck and flowers in her hair, chanting "Love and peace," so Dylan supposed it was little wonder she didn't know the identity of his father.

She'd named him after Bob Dylan. She still idolised the singer, but her life had changed. With her old hippy friends settled and enjoying children and grandchildren, she was becoming a reluctant recluse.

On arrival at his flat, she'd tried to persuade Dylan to take a holiday with her.

"Everyone's so boring these days," she'd said. "Let's go and paint Athens red."

Convincing her that the Greeks might not want their town decorated hadn't been easy. It had involved hours of her expressing her amazement at having produced such a boring son and then, much worse, her amazement that, given the nightmare of actually giving birth, she'd managed to survive producing a son at all. There was nothing new in that. Long before his own son was born, Dylan could have got a degree in gynaecology.

If he went home now, she'd blame the lack of lentils or spinach or whatever her latest food fad was for making him staid, old before his time or any one of a variety of insults she had for him.

Going home before she was bored enough to return to Birmingham wasn't an option. It really wasn't.

Which meant that, given the crock of shit that called itself his life, he had little choice about taking this job.

CHAPTER TWO

SITTING OPPOSITE HOLLY Champion the following morning, on those wooden stools crammed into that tiny kitchen, Dylan noticed the dark circles around her eyes. It hadn't dawned on him that she might have a sleepless night waiting for his decision. He should have been flattered, but he felt like a thief. In all likelihood, he would steal her hope and reduce her bank balance to nothing.

Again, she was dressed casually in jeans and a purple sweater. Her shoes, however, were far from casual. This morning they were lime green. Still ankle-breakers, though.

"Before I say anything," he began, "I need you to understand a few things. First, it's quite probable that I won't learn anything."

"I realise that."

"Second, if a miracle occurs and I *do* find out what happened to her, it's not going to be good news. Nothing I tell you will be good news. Either she'll be dead or she'll have abandoned you. Do you understand that? You will be paying for bad news."

"She may have had an accident. Amnesia or something."

"No." Dylan shook his head. "You've seen too many films. It doesn't happen in real life."

"Okay. I'm prepared for bad news."

Dylan doubted that. "Either she got a better offer—I don't know, some bloke who didn't like kids offered to take her away from it all—or she got blind drunk and fell in the sea—"

"In Dawson's Clough?"

"All I know is that it won't be good news."

"But it could be news. It could be the end of my not knowing."

Dylan couldn't argue with that. "Third, it's going to cost you money that you don't have for this bad news. I charge—" Damn it. "I charge a hundred pounds a day plus expenses."

"Really?" To his amazement, her face brightened at that. "I was expecting more."

Shit, shit and sodding shit.

"The expenses will be crippling," he said. "There will be hotel bills, food bills when I'm away from home, probably paying for information, mileage charges—"

"Yes, yes, I realise that."

"Think of the mileage, though. You'll be paying me to drive from London to Dawson's Clough. It would be far cheaper to employ someone local."

"I realise that, but I want *you* to do it."

"Right, you're sure you still want to go ahead?"

"Wouldn't you, if it was your mother?"

"No. I'd console myself with a vision of her happily shearing sheep in Australia and thank my lucky stars."

She laughed at that. "You would not!"

"You don't know my mother."

"What's wrong with her?"

"What's wrong with her is that she's currently living with me. And whereas most mothers would be cleaning, washing, cooking and stuff like that, mine will be smoking a joint and looking through brochures for adventure holidays."

She spluttered with laughter. "She sounds wonderful!"

"I'll let you borrow her for a couple of years. Now, enough about my mother. I need to know about yours. You said you could give me photos?"

"Yes, I've sorted out a lot of stuff. Come with me."

Dylan followed her through a tiny sitting room that housed a sofa, a TV, a large painting of horses galloping along the shoreline, and very little else into a bedroom that made his spare look palatial. On top of the single bed was a stack of paperwork.

"Photos." She handed him about thirty old snaps. "They're not brilliant, I'm afraid, but you never assume you'll need one for...this."

Dylan sat on the edge of the bed and glanced through them. Each one showed a beautiful, laughing young woman who enjoyed posing for the camera.

"You're right. She's beautiful."

"Yes."

Stunningly beautiful, Dylan thought, gazing at the photos in turn. Long fair hair and very dark eyes. Tall and slim. High cheekbones. Small nose. Wide, sexy mouth. The longest legs he'd ever seen. Always laughing.

He looked through them again. He was right. In every snap, even when the camera had caught her unawares, she was laughing.

One photo in particular claimed his attention. In it, Anita Champion was holding a young toddler, presumably her daughter, in her arms. On her face was an expression of pure joy that you seldom saw.

"That's an old one," Holly said, "taken when I was about eighteen months old, but I like it."

Dylan could see why.

"The most recent one was taken a few weeks before she vanished." Holly hunted through another pile of stuff. "The photographer from the local paper was at a charity dinner in Dawson's Clough and I liked it so much, I bought a copy out of my pocket money. It shows her—ah, here it is."

"Good God!" For the first time, Dylan felt the stirrings of interest.

The photo showed Anita Champion in whispered conversation with none other than Terry Armstrong.

"Do you know him?" Holly asked.

"I know *of* him." As would most coppers or ex-coppers. "When did you say it was taken?"

"About a month before Mum vanished. There was a big dinner dance in Dawson's Clough. I've no idea what it was for or even how Mum came to be invited, but I remember her excitement. A reporter from the local paper was there and, although this was never published, they had a display in the office window with about fifty pictures of the event. I liked this one."

"Did your mother know Terry Armstrong?"

"I don't know. Why? Who is he?"

Dylan gazed at the photograph. It looked as if the couple were sneaking two minutes together. Perhaps two minutes to arrange a rendezvous. Or two minutes for Anita Champion to end their affair. Or blackmail him…

Dylan couldn't be described as an expert on relationships, but they looked close.

"Terry Armstrong." His mind was racing. "A Londoner. East End villain. It's said he has several members of the police force on his payroll." It was also said that he was a cold-blooded killer, but Dylan kept that to himself.

"Are you sure?"

"I'm sure. His face will be familiar to one hell of a lot of coppers."

What had taken Armstrong to Dawson's Clough? And what was the connection between him and Anita Champion?

"What happened to your father?"

"He walked out on us when I was three years old," Holly said in a matter-of-fact way. "Mum said it was no surprise. Said it was a relief really. They'd both been kids when they got married. And they only married because Mum was expecting me."

"You don't keep in touch?"

"I don't remember him. I haven't seen or heard from him since I was three."

She didn't seem bothered about that. Perhaps this obsession she had for discovering the truth about her mother pushed out everything else.

"My mother's birth certificate. Hairdressing qualifications—" she handed over the certificates, "—medical card, dental appointment that, of course, she never kept. Cards she sent on my birthday and suchlike—oh, I know you don't want those but I thought her handwriting—"

"Yes. Thanks."

"Her diary for that year. There's not much in it—

mainly birthdays, working days, reminders to pay the rent—that sort of thing."

She left the room for a moment and came back with a sheet of paper. "Here are names of everyone I can think of who knew her back then. I know it's a long time ago, but—"

"It is." He looked at the list of names. Holly was nothing if not thorough. Against every name was a physical description, relationship to her mother—usually *acquaintance*—and approximate age. "You do realise that you could do all this yourself? You could see these people and ask them about your mother."

She shook her head. "I remember at the time how everyone was convinced she'd gone off with some man. Even her friends believed that. It hurt."

It would. But it was probably true.

Two hours later, a box full of paper in his arms, Dylan was walking to his car. "I'll be in touch."

"Thank you."

It was Dylan who should have been thanking her. Not only was she the answer to his current financial problems, she had given him something to think about. He was curious about the beautiful young woman who had vanished on that November night thirteen years ago. He was even more curious about her relationship with Terry Armstrong.

Perhaps, after all, this wouldn't be as dull as he'd thought.

"Dylan?"

He already had his hand on the car's door. Another car was slowing to a stop not far from his.

"Yes?" He walked back to her.

"If you've time for a quick character assassination

of my mother, Aunt Joyce is just the woman to do it." She nodded at the car, her expression surprisingly grim. "My aunt and uncle, Joyce and Len."

Joyce, when she got out of the car, wore an expression very similar to Holly's. Len was the only one with a smile. He was late forties, Dylan supposed, with thinning dark hair.

"Hello, love." Len hugged Holly, then held her at arm's length. "It's so good to see you."

"You should have phoned," Holly said.

"She wanted to come and see what had happened with—" Len nodded toward Dylan. "Is this him?"

"Yes. This is Dylan Scott. Dylan, my Uncle Len and my Aunt Joyce."

"Pleased to meet you both."

Dylan's hand was shaken by a smiling Len. It was then, somewhat reluctantly he thought, shaken by Joyce.

"You're going ahead with it then?" Joyce asked.

"Dylan has agreed to try and find out what happened to Mum, yes," Holly said. "Shall we go inside? Dylan, can you spare a few more minutes?"

"Of course."

He wouldn't miss this for anything. Several things were puzzling him. For example, how, when presumably Joyce and Len had taken Holly in out of the kindness of their hearts, there was so much animosity between aunt and niece. And how this surly, dour-faced woman could be Anita Champion's sister?

With four of them inside Holly's home, the health and safety experts should have been on full alert. Holly refused to sit down so Joyce and Dylan took the sofa, and

Len perched on one of the stools he'd carried through from the excuse for a kitchen.

Joyce's face still hadn't managed a smile. She had hair that, unlike her sister's long blond locks, was a greying brown colour. It was lank and uncared for. Her face bore no traces of makeup. Her skirt was brown, and the jumper she wore beneath her brown jacket was also brown. Everything about her was dull and drab. And brown.

"You must have been close to your sister," Dylan said.

"No."

If he'd told her she was the ugliest woman he'd ever clapped eyes on, and it was possibly true, he couldn't have insulted her more. "Oh, I thought that, as you took Holly in—"

"I've never shirked my responsibilities, Mr. Scott. We had no children, Len and me, and we'd never wanted any. But as I said, I've never shirked my responsibilities."

"I see." He saw why there was little love lost between the two women. Holly had been a "responsibility" from the age of eleven, it seemed. "Did you see her often? Anita, I mean?"

"Twice a year, maybe. We had nothing in common."

"We were glad to have Holly." Len smiled at his niece. "She was as lovely then as she is now. We're very proud of her."

"Holly doesn't want to hear this," Joyce said, "but Anita was only interested in two things. One was Anita, and the other was men. You're probably thinking it was unusual for a woman to go off like that. Not in Anita's case, it wasn't. She thought nothing of leaving Holly alone for a weekend while she stayed with some man or other."

"A weekend is one thing," Dylan said, "but to vanish completely—"

"Before we moved down here," Joyce said, "Anita asked if we'd mind Holly for the weekend. I can remember it as if it was yesterday. She was supposed to collect her on the Sunday night because it was Holly's first full day at the primary school on the Monday. Of course, Anita being Anita, she didn't turn up, did she? It was left to me to take the kid to school. Do you know how long Anita was gone?"

"Er, no."

"Then I'll tell you. Almost a fortnight!"

"That's—"

"Typical of Anita. She was the most selfish person I ever knew. From the moment she was born, she thought the world owed her something."

"You were—how old when she was born?"

"Five."

"She can't have been all bad," Dylan said. "After all, she gave Holly a very happy childhood until she disappeared."

"Children are easily fooled. A child doesn't understand right from wrong. If a child is having fun, it's happy. It doesn't care about education, financial stability or anything like that. Do you think Anita would have put Holly through university? Never in a million years."

"Aunt Joyce," Holly said, "it's my decision to try and find out what happened to Mum. If you have anything useful to tell Dylan, then please do so. I'm very grateful for all you and Len have done for me over the years, but slagging off Mum isn't going to help, is it?"

"Of course it's not," Len said with a stern glance at his wife. "Mind, there's not a lot we can tell you, Dylan, because we didn't see much of Anita. I was offered a job down here and so we left Lancashire when Holly was six. It's such a long journey that we didn't go back very often. Then Joyce and Anita's parents died, so we saw even less of her. On the rare occasions we went back to visit my sister or brothers, we'd call on Anita, maybe go out for a drink with her even, but no more than that."

"It was enough," Joyce said. "More than enough."

"You knew Anita's father then," Dylan said. "What was he like?"

"Ian was a smashing bloke," Len said.

"Too good for her."

Dylan was longing to slap Joyce. She was like a snake, spitting malicious venom with every breath. But not as good looking. In fact, given her looks, her sour grapes had probably been present since the lovely Anita had entered her world.

"We were at their wedding, of course," Len went on, ignoring his wife again. "It was only a small do, at the local registry office, but—"

"She only married him because she was expecting," Joyce said.

"Even so, she was happy that day." Len smiled at Holly as he spoke. "She looked an absolute picture and she didn't stop smiling. She wanted everyone to be happy with her."

"When she disappeared," Dylan said, "was there anyone special in her life? Apart from Holly, I mean. Anyone she'd met recently? A new man perhaps?"

"There was never anyone special in her life." Joyce's tone was scathing. "She was too selfish. Even Holly, her own daughter, wasn't special. If she had been, she'd never have gone off and left her, would she?"

"We never heard of anyone," Len said, "but we hadn't seen her that year. We'd had a card from her the previous Christmas with her usual scribbled note, but that was all. We hadn't been to Lancashire that year, you see."

"Can you tell me if she ever mentioned a man named Terry Armstrong to you?"

"Not that I recall." Len looked to Joyce for confirmation.

"She wouldn't have mentioned her men to me," Joyce said. "She'd have got pretty short shrift if she had. She had a daughter. She shouldn't have had time for men."

Dylan wondered if Joyce was religious. It often seemed to him that, the tighter a person clasped the Holy Word, the more un-Christian they became…

"If she'd been in any sort of trouble, would she have come to you for help?" Dylan addressed his question to Len, who was more helpful, but Joyce answered anyway.

"Money, you mean?"

"Any sort of help."

"I doubt it," Len said, and he seemed to regret that. "We just didn't have the contact."

"I see. So how did you find out that she'd gone missing?"

"The police came to see us," Joyce said, "wanting to know if we'd heard from her. Well, of course we hadn't. But as I say, I wasn't going to shirk my responsibility. Family is family no matter what. We went straight to Dawson's Clough and fetched Holly."

"It wasn't quite as straightforward as that." Len spoke with the patience of a man well used to clarifying his wife's snappy remarks. "As Holly was only eleven, the police soon had social services involved. We thought Holly might go to her dad but Ian hadn't seen her for 8 years—"

"She couldn't even remember him!" Joyce spoke as if Holly wasn't there.

"She couldn't." Len's smile for Holly was warm. "Holly didn't want to go to Ian, and social services thought it would be less traumatic for her to come to us."

"Because we could give her a decent home life." Joyce threw back her shoulders. She would have made a good drill sergeant. "Ian didn't even have a job at the time. Besides, he'd made it clear how much she meant to him, hadn't he? For all he cared, she might not have existed."

"And, of course," Len said, "we all assumed it would be short-term. We thought Anita would be back."

"*You* might have." Joyce clearly hadn't.

Dylan wanted to get away from these depressing people. Or Joyce at any rate. There was nothing she could—or would—tell him about Anita's disappearance.

As soon as they'd run out of conversation, he got to his feet. "Time I was off. It's been good to meet you both."

Holly walked with him to his car. He guessed that she, too, needed to step away from them for a few moments.

"Your aunt bears no resemblance to your mother," he said at last.

"No." She laughed at that, but it was a laugh heavy with despair. "None whatsoever. You'll be in touch?"

"Of course."

"Thanks." She looked back at her mobile home and grimaced. "I'd better not shirk my responsibility any longer. Thanks again, Dylan. I'll look forward to hearing from you."

CHAPTER THREE

AT A LITTLE after two o'clock the following afternoon, Dylan sat in a small and shabby unisex hairdresser's in Dawson's Clough where the windows dripped condensation. Apart from a lady under a huge dome-shaped dryer, he was the only customer.

The salon was in a street of old three-storey stone properties, some residential and some business premises. Nearby was a fish-and-chip shop, an Indian restaurant, an art shop and a baker's.

Thanks to a hassle-free run up the M1 and the opportunity to race up the M6 Toll road, the drive had taken him under five hours, and that had included a quick stop at Keele Services for petrol, coffee and a sandwich. He'd clocked the journey at two hundred thirty miles, so hadn't done too badly.

Lancashire brought with it an unexpected feeling of déjà vu. Until the age of four, he and his mother had lived on his grandparents' farm in the county. That had been west Lancashire, though, and Dawson's Clough was as far east as you could go. Besides, when he'd been dragged from the farm to Birmingham, kicking and yelling loud enough to wake the dead according to his mother, he had been far too young to register anything. Yet there was a familiarity about the buildings cast from local stone and the unmistakable accents.

As a teenager, Dylan had been on a school trip to

Blackpool. They'd messed around in the amusement arcades and dutifully seen the famous illuminations. He couldn't remember Lancashire as being anything special, though. Today, with a watery sun doing its best, the scenery amazed him. The towns—rows of terraced houses scattered around the long-silent cotton mills—ended abruptly and the Pennines rolled on seemingly forever.

He supposed this corner of east Lancashire could be bleak when mist or snow covered the hills, but now, it was stunning.

"Would you like to sit here?" a woman called to him.

"Thanks." He took his seat in front of the mirror. "Just a trim, please. Not too short."

He assumed he was speaking to Sandra Butler. Her name was outside the shop and on several framed diplomas inside. Heading toward fifty, she was about the right age, too. She was reed-thin and shapeless, with a pinched face. Her hair, long, dark and streaked with red, didn't look to be in good condition. Dylan expected hairdressers to have glossy, bouncy hair, but hers was dull and dry.

"This takes me back." He smiled as she picked up her scissors. "I was a salesman covering this area—oh, it would be fifteen years ago now—and I used to call at this very shop for a trim. Did you work here then?"

"I did. I've owned it for twenty years this year."

"Really? I know I always got good service at a good price. You can't ask for more than that, can you?"

"I like to keep my customers satisfied."

"To tell the truth," Dylan said, "I was hoping to—well, it's a long story, but I remember another woman who worked here. Anita Champion, her name was. Daft really, but we went out together a couple of times and I was hoping she'd still be here."

The scissors stopped midair for a moment or two.

"Anita? Blimey, you're going back, love." The scissors were idle but her hands weren't. Lancastrians, it seemed, still needed their hands to talk, a legacy from life in the cotton mills when the noise made conversation impossible. "You're out of luck anyway. She's long gone."

"Oh? I don't suppose you've any idea where she is now?"

"Nope. She did a runner. Didn't turn up for work one day and I didn't get so much as a sorry on a postcard."

"Really?" Dylan feigned surprise. "That doesn't sound like the woman I remember. I thought she enjoyed working here."

"So did I." The scissors had to be still again. "We got on well at one time. She even had the flat above the shop." She pointed toward the first floor. "A good wage, plus her tips." Sandra Butler's lips tightened. "It just goes to show. Took me for a right fool, she did."

"She had a young daughter, didn't she?"

"She did, but that wouldn't stop her. She thought nothing of leaving that kid to fend for herself. An eleven-year-old in that flat alone—" She shook her head at the very idea. "A selfish bitch, that's what Anita Champion were."

"What happened to her? The kid, I mean."

"Got taken in by Anita's sister. She and Anita were chalk and cheese. Anita looked out for herself and didn't care a jot for anyone else. As I found out to my cost."

"What exactly happened?" Dylan asked.

"How do you mean?"

"Anita didn't turn up for work one day, you say?"

"It were a Saturday night." The scissors were idle. "Four of them went out on the town. I would have gone with them but my boyfriend of the time, Eddie, were home on leave from the army, and we wanted time on our own, if you know what I mean."

After a sharp nudge in the shoulder, Dylan assured her he did.

"There were Brenda, Yvonne, Maggie and Anita. They all met up in the Commercial, that's the pub round the corner from here. Then they went on to Oasis, a club. It's closed down now, but we had some times there, I can tell you. Anyway, Yvonne could never hold her drink so she went home early, but that's the last any of them saw of Anita."

"What did the police make of it? I assume the police got involved? After all, she could have had an accident or something."

"When she hadn't turned up after a week or so, the police asked a few questions, but what were the point? If she'd had an accident, the hospitals would have known about it." Those scissors, held tight in hands that moved erratically as their owner spoke, came dangerously close to his eye. "Looks like you'll have to forget that drink, love. She's long gone."

"Hmm." Dylan shifted in his seat. "It's not quite that simple. The thing is—it's embarrassing really, but I was only twenty-four and she'd have been almost thirty. We had a bit of a fling and, yes, I know I was a fool, but I gave her a ring that had belonged to my mother. Emerald. Antique. I was really hoping—needing—to get it back."

Sandra Butler shook her head at such stupidity.

"You and dozens more, love. She were always after men—always getting what she could from them. Believe me, if it were valuable, she would have sold it years ago."

"Oh? Did she have money problems?"

She laughed at that. "Course she did. It used to burn holes in her pockets."

Snip, snip, snip.

She brushed loose hairs from his collar. "Right. Seven pounds fifty, please."

Dylan eyed himself in the mirror and was relieved to see she'd done a tidy job.

"I'm in a bit of a predicament, aren't I?" He stood and took his wallet from his pocket. "I don't suppose you could tell me where her friends are—the three people she went out with that night? Or her daughter? I have to find Anita."

"You won't do that."

"I can at least try."

"I don't know where her daughter is. Like I said, she were taken in by Anita's sister and they lived down south somewhere."

"What about the friends she went out with that night?"

"They'll only tell you what I have."

"They might remember something else. Be able to give me some clue perhaps."

She looked at him for long, long moments. It was an odd look, as if he were a horse she was thinking of buying at market.

"Yvonne still lives in the Clough," she said. "I can give you her phone number, if you like."

"Would you? I'd be extremely grateful."

"Not that she'll tell you anything else." She took one of her business cards from a pile and wrote down the number without having to look it up. "There you go."

"Thanks. And if you hear anything—" Dylan grabbed one of those cards and scribbled his own name and mobile number on the back, "—would you give me a ring?"

"What's that? Dylan?"

"Yes."

"Look, I haven't heard anything in the last thirteen years, so I ain't going to hear anything now, am I?"

"Probably not. Anyway, thanks." He handed her a ten-pound note. "Keep the change."

"Aw, thanks. And good luck, love!"

CHAPTER FOUR

SANDRA HAD A quick glance at Mabel, decided that another five minutes under the dryer wouldn't hurt her, and headed for the stairs.

"Won't be a minute, love!"

Once upstairs, she picked up the phone and tapped in Yvonne's number.

"Yvonne, it's me. I can't stop, I've got Miserable Mabel drying to a frazzle, but you'll never guess what. Some bloke's just been in and he were asking after—well, you'll never guess."

"Then you'd better tell me, hadn't you?"

"Anita Bloody Champion!"

Silence met her statement. Sandra wasn't surprised—it had been years since any of them had mentioned that name.

"You still there, Yvonne?"

"Yes. Course I am. You took me by surprise, that's all."

"It took me by surprise, too. Can you believe it? After all these years?"

"What did you tell him?"

"What do you think?" Sandra demanded. "I told him that she went out with you three one night and vanished. Said I'd have gone too but that my Eddie were home on leave."

"God!"

"He were desperate to find someone who knew her. Preferably someone who were with her on that last night."

"What? Oh, no!"

"What could I do? I tried to put him off, but it were looking suspicious."

"Christ!"

"He's all right. Nice enough to look at, the right side of forty, good tipper. He told me he had a bit of a fling with Anita and gave her a ring—another bloody sucker for a pair of legs and tits by the sound of it."

"Please don't tell me you gave him *my* name. Please!"

"I had to. It would have looked as if we had something to hide if I hadn't. I gave him your phone number, not your address. Anyway, he's okay. As I said, he's not bad looking really. Just under six feet, dark hair, not overweight. Clothes are a bit creased, but nice enough. As you're on your own now, you can get him to take you out for a meal or something."

"Bloody hell, Sand! And what am I supposed to tell him?"

"The truth. Anita vanished, remember?"

There was another long pause.

"I can't talk to him," Yvonne said. "Why the hell did you have to give him *my* name? The very thought of that night makes me want to throw up."

"She vanished, Yvonne. She went off with some bloke, like she always did—and usually one of our blokes at that—and didn't come back. That weren't our fault, were it?"

Yvonne didn't answer.

"I'll have to go," Sandra said, "or Mabel's hair'll be dropping out. I'll ring you later, okay?"

"God, Sand, I wish you hadn't done this. I really do."

"Yeah, well, I'll speak to you later."

YVONNE REPLACED THE receiver and strode to the kitchen and the drawer where she kept her emergency ciggies. If this wasn't an emergency, she didn't know what was.

What in hell's name had possessed Sandra to give this bloke her phone number? Why pick on her?

Of course, as far as Sandra was concerned, it was just a joke. She had no need to worry because she hadn't been there that night. She'd sent the rest of them to do her dirty work.

Damn. She had cigarettes but no lighter.

She switched on the electric hob, pulled her hair back from her face, and lit her cigarette.

Why now? She inhaled deeply and had to perch on the kitchen stool as a wave of nausea hit her. It was early, but she needed a drink. A cigarette always went better with a drink.

She poured herself a vodka and took a swallow.

Why now? Why, after thirteen years, was some stranger sniffing round after Anita?

Once the nausea had worn off, the cigarette and the vodka calmed her a little. Sandra was right. Anita had vanished and they knew nothing about it. There was nothing to worry about from some ex-boyfriend. God, she thought with a snort of laughter, if all Anita's exes crawled out of the woodwork—

She almost fell off her stool when her phone rang. A

quick look at the display showed her that someone was calling from a mobile. It must be him.

She couldn't answer it.

Then again, it might be about the job she'd been interviewed for last week. They wouldn't call from a mobile though, would they?

It rang out until the machine clicked on. No message was left.

Now she didn't know if she should have answered it or not. If it was about that job, they'd call back. They wouldn't not give her the job just because she'd been unable to take the call. She'd spent years working in an estate agent's office and she could do the job backwards. Besides being smart and intelligent, which was more than could be said for the gum-chewing girl sitting in the office when she'd gone for the interview, she had a knack for selling houses.

Her spirits lifted somewhat. Perhaps, after all, she had a job lined up. God knows, she needed it.

Seventeen years of marriage down the toilet, just like that. It hadn't been a great marriage, but it still hurt. No doubt countless other women felt the same when their husbands left them for a younger model. Now, Ken had two step-kids and a baby on the way. That's what hurt most.

She wasn't going to dwell on that. Far better to think of the financial mess she was in. Ken had paid off the mortgage, thank God, but he'd made it clear he wasn't going to pay the bills for ever. She desperately needed a job.

She couldn't help thinking that if Sandra was the friend she claimed to be, she would have let her work in the salon on Fridays and Saturdays instead of employing that spotty sixteen-year-old. Yvonne had no intention of begging, though, especially to be a glorified skivvy to Sandra.

The caller would try again and she would have to answer it. Even if it was Anita's ex, it was no big deal. Her, Maggie and Brenda—they didn't know anything. They'd gone for a night out, as they often did. Anita had been chatting up some bloke, as she always did. They hadn't seen her since. That was all there was to it.

It was no big deal.

Shortly before six o'clock that evening, the phone rang again and, this time, with a voice that shook, she answered it.

"Yvonne Yates?" a man asked.

It was him. She knew it. "Yes?"

"Ah, you won't know me. My name's Dylan Scott and I spoke to Sandra Butler—the hairdresser, you know?"

"Oh?"

"Yes. She said I should chat to you. It's a bit embarrassing, to tell the truth, but I need to find Anita Champion."

Yvonne's hands were sweating so much, she half expected the phone to slide from her grasp. "Oh? Well, I'm sorry, but I've no idea—"

"I know, but you might be able to help. Might we talk perhaps?" At her hesitation, he said, "Tell you what, I'm staying at the Pennine Hotel. I don't know what you have planned for this evening, but I hate dining alone. Perhaps you could join me?"

Damn it, why not? It was no big deal and, God knows, it was ages since she'd been out. Ages since she could afford it. She'd skipped lunch, there was nothing in the cupboards or the freezer, and, according to Sandra, he was all right. Not bad looking and a good tipper, she'd said.

"Okay."

"Great. Thanks so much. About seven-thirty?"

"Fine."

It was no big deal, she reminded herself yet again. Let some other sucker buy the drinks for a change.

CHAPTER FIVE

THE PENNINE HOTEL was on Market Street, the road that sliced Dawson's Clough in two. A solid stone building, erected in 1865 according to the plaque above the entrance, it looked very grand indeed from the car park. Inside, it showed signs of wear. The carpets, once a rich blue, were threadbare in places, the lift creaked from old age, and several light bulbs needed replacing.

Dylan's bedroom was freezing. A massive old radiator beneath the tall sash window was hot to the touch but was having no effect on such a large, high-ceilinged room.

The bathroom didn't even have a radiator. A small brown stain in the wash basin, an ill-fitting toilet seat, a huge white bath, several thick towels, but no radiator.

He sat on the bed, then got up to drag a chair close to the radiator, and phoned the marital home, ready to reason with Bev.

"Mum's gone out," Luke thwarted those plans, "so Cathy's stopping with me. We're having a game on the Xbox." He lowered his voice to a whisper. "She's rubbish, Dad."

"Girls are. So where's your mum gone?"

"Dunno, but she changed her dress three times before she left. Must be important."

A Monday should be a drink with the girls at one of their homes. She wouldn't change dresses for that. She'd wear jeans, ready for an evening of chocolate, wine and gossip consumption.

"Perhaps she's gone to the cinema with Lucy." But she'd wear jeans for that, too.

"No," Luke said. "Lucy just phoned."

"Oh."

"Will you be back for the match on Saturday?" Luke clearly had more pressing things on his mind.

"I will. Tell your mum I'll call round about eleven."

"Great."

With his son happy, Dylan pushed all thoughts of his wife's date from his mind. Besides, it wouldn't be a date. She was probably going to a school function. Bev would be missing him as much as he was missing her. She'd soon come round. She always did.

He tapped in another number.

"Dylan?" Holly Champion answered on the third ring.

"The very same. I've nothing to tell you, I'm afraid, but I'm about to have dinner with Yvonne Yates. She's on your list, but I wondered what you remembered about her."

"I remember her well, probably better than any of Mum's friends. She used to dote on me, and was always buying me presents. Mum said it was because she hadn't any children of her own. She thought Yvonne was lonely. I quite liked her, probably because she made me laugh. She used to get drunk and fall over a lot. That's funny when you're a kid."

Dylan hoped she wouldn't fall over this evening. "Anything else?"

"Not really. She was always smartly dressed. She worked at the local estate agent's, so I suppose she had to be because she used to show people around the expensive houses. Her husband, Ken, was always chatting up Mum. Sorry, but I can't think of anything else."

"Right. Okay. If I learn anything, I'll be in touch." He had to ask. "Are you still sure you want to go ahead with this?"

"Of course."

"Right."

"Do you have a clean shirt for your dinner date?" she asked, and, forced to smile, he looked down at a small stain on the pocket.

"I'll buy a couple tomorrow..."

Dylan left his room and went downstairs to the bar. It was much warmer there, thanks to heavy velvet curtains that shut out the night and a pile of logs blazing in a cavernous fireplace. A few leather armchairs were arranged around the fire, but Dylan sat at the opposite end of the room on a stool by the bar.

Half an hour later, his pint of beer almost finished, he saw a brunette walk in, look at those present and wander toward him.

"Mr. Scott?" she asked.

"Dylan." He offered his hand. "And you'll be Yvonne. Thanks so much for coming. Now, what can I get you to drink?"

"A vodka, please. Vodka and tonic." She sat on the stool next to his and put a small black handbag on the bar. "I feel as if I'm here under false pretences. There's nothing I can tell you about Anita. She just vanished, you see."

"So I gather." The barman put their drinks in front of them. "The thing is, I really need to find her, and I'm hoping you might remember something—anything—that could help." He chinked his glass against hers. "Cheers."

Slim but shapely, Yvonne Yates was an attractive woman. She would have been even more appealing if she hadn't looked so stressed.

"In any case—" he remembered his manners as well as his need for information, "—it's a rare treat for me to have such an attractive dinner companion."

While he offered a silent apology to Bev, Yvonne's eyes, dark and green, sparkled at the compliment.

"Are you married?"

"Separated." Thanks to Bev's latest strop, that was technically accurate. "You?"

"Divorced." She couldn't quite meet his gaze. "It was finalised last month."

"Ouch. I'm sorry about that."

"It isn't the end of the world, is it?"

Gaunt, weary-eyed and tense, she looked exactly like her world had ended.

"Of course not. His loss is another man's gain. But let's not talk of marital problems. Are you hungry or would you like another drink first?"

She downed her vodka and put the glass on the bar. "Let's have one more, shall we?"

Dylan needed to watch her. Unless he was mistaken, that hadn't been her first drink of the day and, with her senses blurred by alcohol, her memory would be worse than useless. Anyone would struggle to remember the events of thirteen years ago. Drunk, it would be almost impossible.

She grabbed her drink from the barman and Dylan decided it was time for business.

"Let me tell you why I'm here. As I said, it's a little

embarrassing. About fourteen years ago, I was a salesman covering this part of the country. I used to call at your friend Sandra's, to get my hair cut. Anita Champion used to do it and we fell into conversation. I was away from home and—" He shrugged in a man-of-the-world way. "One thing led to another and we had a brief fling. I was twenty-four and she was almost thirty. I thought it was serious." Another near-perfect man-of-the-world shrug. "Fool that I was, I gave her a ring that had belonged to my mother. An antique emerald. My father wants it back and—well, the truth is, I'm in deep shit. I need to find Anita Champion or her daughter."

She'd listened without commenting or showing any surprise whatsoever. Dylan assumed Sandra Butler had already spoken to her.

"I wish I could help," she said, "but I can't. I've no idea where she went."

"That evening, the night she went missing. Could you tell me about that?"

She nodded. "Me, Maggie and Brenda met her in the Commercial, the pub round the corner from her flat. She lived above Sandra's hairdressing salon then. We had a couple of drinks there and then went on to the Oasis. That was a club on Pennine Way, but it closed down about ten years ago."

"How did you get there?"

"Sorry?"

Dylan guessed her speech had been rehearsed and his question had thrown her.

"Did you walk? Catch a bus? Take a taxi?"

She frowned at the seemingly pointless question. "We walked. Why?"

"I'm just trying to picture it. And how did Anita seem?"

"Fine. The same as usual. Laughing, happy, out for a good time."

"And when you arrived at the club?"

"We split up. You know how it is. A chap asks one of you to dance—you meet up with someone you know and have a chat with them. I saw Anita dancing with one man. Then, the next time I saw her, she was dancing with another. That was it. I didn't see her again."

The barman interrupted them. Their table was ready.

When they'd settled in the dining room, studied the menu and placed their order, Dylan came back to the point of the evening. "The men Anita was dancing with that night—did you know them?"

"No."

"Did she seem happy to be with them?"

"Of course. That was why she went out. To flirt. Us three went out for a few laughs. Anita went to get a bloke or two."

Such bitterness, Dylan thought, surprised.

Their soup arrived and he concentrated on small talk for a while. He chatted about the area, complimented her on her appearance, told her she must have been much younger than Anita, which pleased her immensely, and watched her slowly relax. She still picked at her food, but she did relax slightly.

"More wine?"

Giggling, she wagged a finger at him. "You'll get me tipsy."

She was already tipsy.

"We're both consenting adults." He winked at her.

Eventually, he managed to steer the conversation back to important matters. "What did you think when Anita vanished?"

She looked at him blankly.

"Presumably, you had all planned to get a taxi home at the end of the evening? You must have been—annoyed, I suppose, that she didn't tell you where she was going?"

She thought for a moment. "It was nothing out of the ordinary. Men were like moths to a flame where she was concerned and she was—well, no offence, but she'd sleep with anyone."

"None taken," he said. "I've come to realise that. She was a right slapper, wasn't she?"

"She was." She warmed to her theme now. "Everyone knew what she was like. Good God, she even slept with—" She broke off and took a huge gulp of wine.

"She even slept with?" Dylan asked.

"Anyone. Young, old—she didn't care."

Which wasn't even close to what she'd been about to say. "I remember she was talking about—oh, what's his name?—a big noise—club owner down in London."

"I've no idea." She seemed genuinely puzzled.

"Oh, it'll come to me. He was a wealthy bloke. Ah, Terry Armstrong. That was his name"

"The property owner?"

"Could be." He could be into anything.

"I know him. Well, know of him," she said, "but Anita didn't have anything to do with him. There's no way she could have known him because he wasn't around back then. He moved up here from south somewhere."

So Terry Armstrong was living in Lancashire. Well, well.

"Perhaps it was my mistake," Dylan said. "Or perhaps it was wishful thinking on her part. Let's face it, if she was out for all she could get, he'd got a lot."

"Someone like him wouldn't have looked twice at her."

Ah, but he had. Dylan had the photograph to prove it.

"And as I said," she added, "he only moved up here six or seven years ago. She couldn't possibly have known him."

"Perhaps I'm wrong. Forget I mentioned him. Tell me what the rest of you did that night. Did you take a taxi home and assume she'd turn up the next day?"

"Yes. Well, I wasn't feeling well so I went home before the others."

"Oh?"

"I'd had too much to drink," she said. "I told Maggie and Brenda I was going, and they both waited outside with me till the taxi arrived."

"I see." Dylan was still wondering what had brought Terry Armstrong to Lancashire. "Would Anita have gone off with a stranger? After all, she had a young daughter waiting at home for her, didn't she?"

"Holly, yes." Her face softened. "Poor kid. Anita didn't deserve her."

"You got on well with her daughter?"

"I liked her, yes. But I do get on well with children. I always have."

"Do you have—?"

"No." Another gulp of wine. "No, I couldn't have any of my own."

"Ah, I'm sorry." Was that the cause of her bitterness?

"You learn to live with it. Do you have any?"

"A boy," he replied. "Luke. He's eleven going on thirty. He's a good kid. The best."

"Like I said, Anita thought of no one but herself. No one was surprised that she went off." She smiled another of those pinched little smiles. "I'd love to help, really, but I've no idea where she went or who she went with."

Dylan resorted to socialising for the remainder of the meal. Small talk wasn't his forte, but he knew he had to make an effort. While they lingered over a second coffee, he decided that, as he'd bought her dinner—at least, Holly Champion had bought her dinner—complimented her and flirted with her, he was owed some information.

"I'm sorry to have to drag all this up after so long," he said. "It can't be pleasant for you, and I'm sure you were questioned for weeks by the police."

"They asked a few questions, yes."

But not enough. "I bet they did. They always do, don't they? When there's a child involved, I mean."

She nodded, but didn't comment.

"What did they ask you about?"

"The same as you've asked about, really. They just wanted to know what had happened that night. We couldn't tell them anything, though, could we? I mean, we don't know." She glanced at her watch. "It's time I called a taxi."

"I'll get the barman to do it," Dylan said. "Look, I know I'm being a damn nuisance, and I know it's unlikely anyone can help, but—well, I'm pretty desperate. Do you have phone numbers or addresses for your friends Maggie and Brenda?"

She looked at him, considering, then, with a hint of defiance in her voice, said, “Sure.”

She took a black diary from her bag, tore a page from the back, then looked through the A-Z sections for the two addresses. “Sorry, but I don’t have phone numbers for either of them. Just addresses. And for all I know, they might have moved. We don’t keep in touch.”

“That’s okay.”

Ten minutes later Dylan stood outside the hotel in the biting cold, waving her off. She’d promised to keep his phone number and call him if she thought of anything else, but Dylan knew he wouldn’t hear from her again.

So that was that. He had nothing to tell Holly Champion, nothing at all. Except for the fact that Yvonne Yates knew more than she was saying.

CHAPTER SIX

PANDEMONIUM ALWAYS RULED when Maggie donned her coat and boots. She didn't even have to reach for the leash before Tess, her bouncy, two-year-old golden retriever, began yapping like a lapdog and leaping around as if she were on springs.

This morning, with the doorbell chiming at the exact moment she reached for the leash, the dog almost went into orbit.

"For God's sake, Tess!"

Maggie tried to open the door to the porch without letting Tess out, but the animal was having none of it. A spider plant went flying from the table, and compost scattered everywhere.

She'd chosen a retriever because everyone agreed they were calm, sensible, reliable dogs. What had clinched it perhaps had been seeing blind people guided along the streets by gentle retrievers who didn't put a paw wrong. Despite attending training classes at the town hall, Tess was still liable to head into the path of oncoming buses.

Maggie yanked open the front door and Tess, deaf to all commands, launched herself at the stranger. Her paws almost reached his shoulders as she tried to lick his face.

"Tess, get down. Now!" Maggie yanked her back by the scruff of her neck.

"Sorry about that," she said, although if this man was trying to sell her something, it served him right.

"No problem." He brushed hairs from his jacket as if being molested by dogs was an everyday occurrence. "Mrs. Waters, is it? Maggie Waters?"

"It used to be. I'm Maggie Gibson now. Tess, get down! Down!"

Tess finally contented herself with weaving between their legs, her tail wagging with the sheer joy of the moment.

"My name's Dylan Scott. I spoke to Yvonne Yates last night and she gave me your address."

"Oh?"

There had been a time when Yvonne and Maggie had been friends but, now, even the birthday and Christmas cards had fizzled out. They might bump into each other in town a couple of times a year and go through the "Lovely to see you" and "We must get together sometime" routines, but that was all.

"Yes," he said, "I'm trying to find Anita Champion or—"

Maggie felt every last drop of blood drain to her feet. She was aware of his voice, as if coming from a great distance, but she couldn't take in a word.

Anita Champion. She hadn't heard that name for years. Didn't want to, either.

She bent to grab Tess's collar and fasten the leash, more in an attempt to hide her shock than anything else.

"Hasn't she told you I'd be in touch?" he was asking.

"Anita?"

"Er, no. Mrs. Yates. Yvonne."

"No." How could she, the bitch? How could she give this stranger her address? "No, she didn't. We don't keep in touch."

She had to get rid of him. No way was she going to relive—

"Who are you?" she asked.

He didn't look like a police officer, but you couldn't tell. These days, all coppers, teachers and doctors looked young and scruffy. Not that this man looked either. She'd put him at late thirties. His clothes were good quality if a little crumpled. But if he was a policeman—

It didn't matter who he was. She didn't want to speak to him or anyone else about Anita Champion.

"I'm sorry but, as you can see, I'm on my way out." She checked Tess's leash. "I'm sorry you've had a wasted journey." That must be his car. An old yellow sports car.

"I'll walk with you," he said, much to her disgust. "Perhaps we can talk as we walk?"

Maggie didn't know what to do. What *could* she do? She couldn't forcibly throw him from her path. Nor could she refuse to speak to him.

With fingers that shook, she locked the front door and shoved her hands in her pockets. It was sunny, but the wind still carried that icy chill with it. She was glad of it, though. Glad of the chance to take in huge gulps of air.

"Who are you?"

"Dylan Scott." He fell into step beside her. "Years ago, about fourteen, I knew Anita Champion. We had a bit of an—well, a fling, I suppose you'd call it."

Was there a man who hadn't?

"The thing is, I was a stupid young fool, and I gave

her a ring. An antique emerald. It had belonged to my mother and wasn't mine to give away." He rubbed his hands briskly in front of him. "But I thought it was going to be marriage, kids, the works."

Funny, but he didn't look that foolish. Still, youth was a dangerous thing. Few people knew that better than Maggie did. At eighteen, she'd married Dave and imagined her life would be one long romance.

"I need to find Anita or her daughter," he said. "As I mentioned, I saw Yvonne Yates last night and, although she told me all about the night Anita went missing—"

"Then I hope she told you I wanted no part in it."

He stopped mid-stride and Maggie cursed her quick tongue.

"Tess, heel!" She gave the leash a sharp tug.

"No part in what?"

Now what did she say? "What did Yvonne tell you?"

"Just that the four of you went out for the evening, that you split up at Oasis, and that none of you saw Anita again."

"That's true enough."

"So what was it you wanted no part in?"

"Oh, the evening, that's all." They reached the park gates and she bent to free Tess from her leash. "I didn't want to go out that night. They were heavy drinkers and I wasn't. That's all."

Although his hands were deep in his coat pockets now, he didn't seem to mind the cold wind or the drizzle that had started.

"I see," was all he said.

Tess was running free, oblivious to anything other than the park's scents and the wind-blown leaves. The dog would be expecting to spend an hour here, maybe more. Usually, Maggie enjoyed the woodland walks and the sculpture trails, but today she strode on, wanting this ordeal over.

"Do you still keep in touch?" He broke the silence. "With the other women, I mean?"

"No."

They had for a while, but whenever they'd got together, talk had invariably turned to Anita. It hardly made for fun times.

"Did you get on well with Anita?" he asked.

"Yes. Yes, I suppose so. I had nothing against her."

"What about her daughter?"

"Holly? Oh, I liked her. Animal mad, she was. Longed for a pony, or even a dog or a cat. But that was out of the question, of course."

"Because of Anita's work?"

"There was that. Holly had school, too. She was a bright kid and into every activity going, so it would have been left to Anita to look after. But it was the money mainly. Anita lived from day to day. If she worked more hours or got more tips, she spent it all. It never occurred to her to save something for a rainy day."

"Did she have serious financial problems, do you know? Big debts? Someone chasing her for money?"

"Not that I know of, but it wouldn't surprise me."

"Can you think back," he said, "to anything Anita might have mentioned? A man who was special? A place she longed to go? Family and friends she was close to?"

"No." The reply was too abrupt, but she couldn't help herself. She wanted to forget Anita Champion. She wished the woman had never existed. "There was no one special." She knew she had to tell him something. "As for family, there was only her married sister. Joan or Joyce, something like that. Young Holly went and lived with her when—when it became obvious that her mum wasn't coming back."

Maggie began to relax a little. She'd told the truth, and she could talk about Anita. It was in the past. Almost forgotten. Life had moved on.

Back then, she'd been a twenty-six-year-old who had dreaded going home to a husband who would shower her with kisses or punches depending on his mood. Or, more accurately, depending on his alcohol consumption. She had escaped all that. The divorce had come through five years ago, almost to the day.

Last year, she'd married Ron, a gentle, caring, steady and reliable man. That made him sound boring, but he wasn't. There was a difference between steady and boring. He had a good job, leaving her free to work four mornings a week at the rescue centre. Ron had his two boys, but they were polite adults and made no demands on them. Maggie had Tess. Life was good. It was uncomplicated.

"And no one's mentioned her since?" Dylan Scott asked.

"No. Well, the police got involved for a while afterwards, but that was all."

"No one came looking for her?"

"No. Not until now. You."

It was the truth. Today was the first time in over twelve years that she'd heard Anita's name mentioned by anyone other than Yvonne, Brenda or Sandra. And that was fine by Maggie.

Her first instinct on seeing Dylan Scott had been to

look up Yvonne's phone number, assuming she hadn't moved, and give her what for. It was a damn cheek giving her address to strangers. What did it matter, though? No harm had been done and she had no wish to speak to Yvonne.

They were soon exiting the park and heading for home. Maggie couldn't get there quickly enough and was relieved when they turned into her road.

She stopped by his car and offered a regretful smile "I'm sorry I haven't been able to help."

"Not at all. You've been very helpful." He reached into his pocket and wrote his name and mobile number on a page he tore from a notebook. "If you hear anything, or think of anything else, will you call me?"

"Yes, of course I will. Well, goodbye, Mr. Scott." She left him standing by his car.

Taking her keys from her pocket, she strode up to her front door. She turned, smiled, waved, and then let herself inside.

Damn. She'd forgotten the mess from that spider plant. It would have to wait a few minutes.

With Tess unclipped from her leash, and with her own coat and boots removed, Maggie went to the kitchen, tore that scrap of paper into tiny pieces and dropped them in the bin.

CHAPTER SEVEN

THE LARGE ESTATE was a mix of modern townhouses, semi-detached and detached properties, and the roads had been named after birds—Kingfisher Rise, Swallow Drive, Heron Road. You certainly couldn't accuse the planning departments of lacking imagination, Dylan thought.

Brenda Tomlinson lived at number four, Nightingale Avenue, a detached house with a neat front garden. At least, if Yvonne Yates was to be believed, she lived there.

No one answered the door but curtains twitched at the house opposite so Dylan dashed across the road, cursing the steady rain, and rang the doorbell.

"If you're looking for Brenda or Tom," an elderly grey-haired woman said, "you're out of luck. They've jetted off to Corfu."

"Ah. No matter." At least he had the right address. Courtesy of a small canopy above her door, he was sheltered from the rain for the moment, too. "I'll catch them when they get back."

"A week on Tuesday."

"It's all right for some."

"If that's what appeals." She sniffed. "It's not my cup of tea. All they'll get in Corfu is a jiffy tummy. Foreign food? You can keep it." She pulled a face. "Still, live and let live, that's my motto."

Dylan very much doubted that. "Be nice to see some sunshine, though." Although the wind had dropped and the temperature had risen slightly, it had rained solidly since two o'clock this morning.

"You don't see much sunshine when you're confined to bed with food poisoning."

"True. All that hanging about at airports, too. It's not for me." He nodded at Brenda's house. "Been before, have they?"

"Always jetting off somewhere. Three foreign holidays a year. They always have a fortnight about now, a week in June and another in September."

"Very nice. Well, nice if you can afford it."

"He's a car salesman," she said, as if that explained everything. "Still, I suppose you'll know that."

"No. It was Brenda I was hoping to see. We've not met, but a friend gave me her address. She knew an old friend of mine—Anita Champion."

The woman looked blank. "You'll have to come back a week on Tuesday then."

"I'll do that. Thanks. And I'm sorry to have bothered you."

Dylan drove back into Dawson's Clough, parked the car, grabbed his big black umbrella and went for a walk round.

He'd done the same yesterday, after his meeting with Maggie Gibson, and he still needed to get to know the town. It was much bigger than he'd imagined, and an odd mix of old and new. The cotton industry had brought prosperity to the area and, with the looms now silent, the mills were either in various states of disrepair or had been renovated to provide fully-serviced luxury apartments. The pedestrianised shopping centre had been revitalised, yet the buildings around its perimeter looked old, tired and forgotten.

Tesco loomed large in front of him and he decided to have a coffee and a sandwich while he thought of the best course of action. He needed to talk to Yvonne Yates again and, as he would be the last person she wanted to hear from, he would have to use all his charm.

He was shaking excess rain from his umbrella, about to walk in the store, when he saw a sign. Two shirts £10.

He inspected them and wondered how much profit there could be in selling what looked like good quality shirts at that price. Perhaps it was down to sweat shops and child labour. Surely Tesco wouldn't go along with that?

With four in his hands—two blue, one maroon and one grey—he double-checked they were a sixteen-and-a-half collar size and carried them to the till.

If he did nothing else, he would get the washing machine working at the weekend. Perhaps his mother could do it while he took Luke to the match. Fat chance. She would be too busy meditating or practising her tai chi, whatever that was.

He didn't want to think about his mother, though. He wanted to know why Yvonne Yates and Maggie Gibson had lied to him. What were they hiding?

A coffee and a sandwich later, his new shirts on the passenger seat, he sat in his car and called Yvonne's number.

She answered almost immediately.

"Yvonne? It's Dylan. Dylan Scott."

"Oh, yes?" She sounded guarded.

"Yes. Two things. First, I must apologise for my

behaviour. A delightful dinner companion and all I did was talk about another woman. I can't believe I did that. I'm so sorry."

"That's okay." Slightly less guarded.

"Second, I'm going home on Friday and I wanted to make amends. Would you have dinner with me tomorrow night? If I promise not to drone on about other women?"

"Well—"

"I can't blame you if you say no."

"Er, no. I mean, yes. Yes, okay."

"Really? Hey, that's brilliant. Tomorrow, I'll be the perfect gentleman. Promise."

He'd even wear a clean shirt. A new clean shirt.

"I'll look forward to it," she said.

Perhaps this time, he needed her tongue loosened by alcohol.

"Shall I come to your hotel again?" she asked.

"If you like. Then we can go on somewhere else. You choose. I'll be ready and waiting at six."

She laughed. "See you about seven then." The connection was cut.

Dylan drove back to the hotel and left his car there. It was time to go to work.

Broad Lancashire accents were all around him—some people sounded as if they had never been outside Dawson's Clough. There must be plenty of people who could remember the Oasis club and, more important, Anita Champion. All he had to do was find them.

And the best starting place was the pubs. God, it was a tough job.

By nine o'clock that evening even Dylan, who dreamed of living in a pub, was keen to get back to his hotel and his bed.

He'd started in the Commercial, dark and dingy with a miserable landlord and a clientele of no-hopers, then moved on to the Red Lion, where he was the only customer for an hour.

Now he was at the bar in the Pheasant, a warm and homely pub if a little jaded, where the walls were covered with old photographs of Lancashire scenes. Better still, he had finally found someone who had known Anita Champion.

"Once seen, never forgotten," his companion said. "An absolute stunner, she were."

"I know. I was in the queue of admirers. A long way back, but at least I was in the queue."

"I were more of a—friend." The man put out his hand. "Bill Thornton. Let me buy you another. Black Sheep, is it?"

"It is, yes. Thanks, Bill, that's generous of you." They shook hands. "Dylan, by the way. Dylan Scott."

After Bill had enjoyed a joke with the barmaid, a loud young girl in tight denims and even tighter T-shirt, their drinks were in front of them, two pints of Black Sheep.

"The landlord's a miserable bugger, but he does keep a good pint. Yorkshire beer, this is." Bill took a swig from his glass, savoured it, and licked the froth from his top lip. "Brewed in Masham. Do you know the story?"

"Story?"

"Paul Theakston's family had been brewing beer in Masham for—ooh, probably six generations—but then, much to Paul's disgust, it were sold off to become part of Scottish and Newcastle Breweries. But young Paul were the black sheep of the family—you get it?—and he decided to stay on in Masham and do what his family had done best, that is, brew damn good beer in the traditional manner."

"Really?" Dylan took a swallow from his own pint and decided that Paul Theakston had done them a huge favour. "It's a cracking pint."

"That it is."

"A good story, too."

Bill nodded, and concentrated on his beer.

"So you were a friend of Anita's?" Dylan asked.

"I were. I can't say there weren't times when I didn't want more, but really it were better like that. We used to have a drink together now and again. Sometimes we went to the cinema. She loved films, didn't she?"

"Yeah." Dylan nodded as if remembering happy evenings in front of the large screen with Anita.

"I remember we saw *Braveheart* three times," Bill said. "She could almost recite the script."

"Oh?" There was an old ticket for a showing of *Braveheart* in the stuff Holly had given him.

"She were a big Mel Gibson fan. Never read much, did she?"

"Not that I remember."

"Nah. She liked biographies, though. And, of course, she loved Princess Di. Read everything about her after she died."

Of course. Princess Diana died three months before Anita disappeared. Newspapers and magazines would still have been pushing the story to the front page.

Bill smiled. "She'd have been in her element with all this celebrity-this-that-and-the-other they put on telly these days."

"She would, wouldn't she? Do you remember the last time you went out together?"

"I remember all right. It were a Monday night, the Monday before she disappeared, in fact."

"Oh?" Dylan supped from his glass.

"Yes," he said, clearly thinking back. "I were off to my uncle's funeral in Glasgow the next day. I were going to be away for ten days, catching up with family, so we had a farewell drink." He looked wistful. "I didn't realise then, of course, that it really were farewell."

"How did she seem?"

Dylan respected a male perspective more than a female's. You got logic from a man whereas, so far, he'd had nothing but crap from her female friends.

"Fine," Bill replied. "The same as ever. Happy, content—the same as she always did. She made me promise to call her as soon as I got back."

"So you don't believe she had plans to—go somewhere?"

"Never in a month of bloody Sundays. I told you, she were happy with her lot. Content. She might have had a few boyfriends, more than a few to tell the truth, but she weren't daft. She liked a good time and there's no harm in that."

"None at all," Dylan agreed.

"Besides, she wouldn't have left Holly behind. She loved that kid. Holly meant the world to her."

"People seem convinced that she went off with someone."

"I know they do and they're bloody daft." Bill took a quick swallow of beer. "No way. She wouldn't have left Holly. I'm telling you, just as I told them bloody hopeless coppers when they finally decided to show some interest, that she didn't go nowhere. Willingly, at least," he added.

"What do you mean by that?"

"Exactly what I said. Look, I have no idea what happened to her, but I know it weren't good. She wouldn't have left Holly with no word."

Dylan didn't know what to make of that. Sandra, Yvonne and Maggie all seemed to believe she'd met a rich toy-boy and gone off for a better life. Bill, on the other hand, suspected something far more sinister.

A few minutes later, a chap in his late sixties entered the pub and walked up to the bar. "All right, Bill?" He looked Dylan up and down and gave him a brief nod.

"Geoff." Bill tugged on the man's arm. "You'll never guess who we've been talking about. Anita Champion!"

"Christ, that's going back a bit. Why? You've not heard from her, have you?"

"No."

Bill made introductions and Dylan decided to get another round of drinks in.

"Dylan here has come to the Clough hoping to find Anita," Bill was saying.

"You'll be lucky," Geoff scoffed. "I bet she's in bloody Brazil or somewhere."

"You think so?" Dylan asked.

"Yes. Oh, I know Bill thinks something terrible happened to her." He grinned. "But he reckons the CIA had Kennedy shot and nothing will convince him that the Yanks walked on the moon."

Dylan smiled, as was expected.

"She were a handsome woman," Geoff said,

chuckling, "but I can't imagine she were abducted by Martians."

"How well did you know her?" Dylan asked.

"Not as well as Bill. I have the newsagent's on Trueman Street, just round the corner from where she lived. She used to come in for her lottery ticket and a packet of fags on a Saturday night."

"She didn't smoke," Bill said, and Geoff rolled his eyes.

"Of course she did, man. A packet of ten every Saturday night she bought."

"She might have had the odd one," Bill said. "A social smoker, I suppose you'd call her. If she were out with the girls, she might buy a pack."

"There's no might about it." Geoff's sigh was impatient.

"When she disappeared, Geoff," Dylan asked, "did she come in that night?"

"No. Well, she stuck her head inside the door to tell me she'd been into Manchester the day before and that she'd see me next week. She'd have bought her fags in Manchester, you see."

"How did she seem?"

"The same as always. Full of life. Like a bloody whirlwind. Opened the door, shouted that she'd see me next week, and were gone."

"Did you see her after that?"

"I didn't," Geoff said. "That were the last I ever saw of her."

"What about her friends?" Dylan asked. "The night she went missing, she went out with Yvonne Yates, Maggie Gibson and Brenda Tomlinson. Did you see any of them that night?"

"No. But I wouldn't. They used to meet in the Commercial, and they'd have walked straight there from their homes. There would have been no need for them to pass my shop." He emptied his glass. "I saw Maggie a couple of days later, and she were right upset about Anita."

"Was she?"

"Yes. Upset or annoyed, it's a job to tell. Like everyone else, everyone except Bill here, she assumed that Anita had gone off with some bloke and not bothered telling anyone. Well, I mean, even her daughter, young Holly, assumed she were staying out all weekend. That's why none of us knew she hadn't got home until the Monday."

Dylan could understand why the police hadn't shown much interest. Just because Anita had stayed out for weekends before, everyone—everyone except Bill—assumed she'd met a sure thing.

Dylan might have shared that view if he hadn't been convinced that both Yvonne and Maggie had lied to him. Or at least been very economical with the truth.

One thing was certain, he would handle Yvonne with care tomorrow night. She knew something, he was sure of it, and he was determined to find out what it was.

"What about that property owner?" Dylan asked. "What was his name? Terry Armstrong? Was he one of her admirers?"

"Terry Armstrong?" Geoff laughed at that. "He weren't even living here back then. He came from your neck of the woods, mate."

"I heard he used to visit the area before he moved." But why, Dylan had no idea.

"Did he? I never knew that," Geoff said. "But even so, what the hell would he have been doing with someone like Anita? Sorry, Bill, I know she were a friend of yours, but even you have to admit she didn't move in Armstrong's circle."

"What makes you ask about him?" Bill asked.

"Just something I heard. Well, something she told me once. It made me wonder if she had a bit of a thing going with him."

"In her dreams!" Geoff laughed.

"No." Bill shook his head. "We were close, me and her. She would have told me if she'd known a bloke like that."

Dylan wasn't convinced. He hadn't seen two strangers discussing a dinner and dance or the weather in that photo. He'd seen two people with secrets.

"I suppose you knew her husband then," Dylan said. "Ian, was it?"

"A good bloke," Geoff said. "Moved to Wigan, he did."

"Married a girl from there." Bill nodded in agreement.

"Do you still keep in touch?" Dylan asked, but the pair shook their heads.

Ian Champion would be easy enough to find. At least, Dylan hoped he would. If people went missing, it was usually to avoid someone or something. A spouse, a loan, a lawsuit. Otherwise, it was easy enough to trace people.

A man was standing by the bar watching the three of them. In his thirties, Dylan supposed, with overlong dark hair, he was clearly a few pence short of a shilling. His left hand was slightly deformed and he was stooped. For all that, his clean, pressed shirt put Dylan to shame, and he was even wearing a tie.

Bill saw Dylan watching him. "Don't mind Simple Stevie," he said. "He's as mad as they come but he's harmless enough."

"He used to work at Sainsbury's," Geoff said, grinning, "collecting up the trolleys in the car park, until he were found taking them for long walks. Tried to take one up the hard shoulder of the M65." He put up a hand in Stevie's direction. "All right, Stevie?"

Stevie nodded and grunted. Then he emptied his glass in record time and shuffled, limping awkwardly, out of the pub.

"Must have been something you said," Dylan murmured.

CHAPTER EIGHT

YVONNE YATES'S CHOICE of eating place was Chang's, the Chinese restaurant on Market Street. Dylan, a huge fan of Chinese food, had been pleased about that until he'd seen the prices. Not that he was paying, it was all on expenses, but it didn't seem right that Holly Champion should have to waste her money on a liar like Yvonne.

This evening she was wearing a short, figure-hugging black dress that showed off long, shapely legs and more cleavage than was good for him. He wondered if it was for his benefit. If so, it was wasted.

"The food and the service are always excellent here," Yvonne said when they were seated.

Few things irritated Dylan more than that empty statement. It was talking for the sake of it. Presumably, if the food was crap and the service sloppy, people who had sampled the place already, like Yvonne Yates, wouldn't return, and the restaurant would go out of business.

"I adore it." She looked around her. "It's not as tacky as most of them."

"It's very nice." Crisp white tablecloths, thick red carpet, the interior devoid of the usual Chinese kitsch.

Dylan wasn't a restaurant person. He would prefer to get a takeaway and eat it, feet up, in front of the television. He had to make small talk, too, something he hated and something he was exceptionally bad at.

"What would you do if I tore my clothes off?" Bev had asked the last time they'd been out for a meal.

"I don't know." If he hadn't feared it was a trick question, he would have suggested she try it and find out.

"I wonder if you'd actually say something. You know, open your mouth and let words come out."

As Dylan had suspected, it was a trick question…

"You said you're going home tomorrow?" Yvonne broke into his thoughts.

"That's right, yes. There's nothing for me up here."

He was going home, taking his son to the match, maybe getting his washing done, doing a spot of grovelling to Bev, hopefully moving back to the marital home, and then returning to Lancashire on Monday.

"Where's home?" she asked.

"Shepherd's Bush. Well, usually. As I said, my wife and I are separated but usually it's Shepherd's Bush. Tomorrow, I'll be taking my son to watch the match. Arsenal."

"That's nice."

"Yeah." It was always the highlight of Dylan's week. Luke was the easiest person in the world to get along with, and they had fun. Until they got home, when the vocabulary Luke heard at the match often spilled out to send Bev's blood pressure through the ceiling.

"You'll be banned from going, Luke, if that's the sort of language you're listening to," Bev had said once.

"I'm sure he's heard worse in the playground." Dylan never failed to be amazed at the language some children came out with.

"I've heard worse from you, Mum." Luke's quick response had had Dylan stifling a laugh…

"So you've given up trying to find Anita?" Yvonne was asking.

"No, but I know there's nothing more to find out here. Maggie told me what happened. She said she wanted no part in it, but I suppose she would say that, wouldn't she?"

Yvonne's eyes widened to the size of ten-pence pieces. "She—she told you? Maggie did?"

"She did. I think she was under the impression that you had."

"Well!" Yvonne took a sip of her wine and shook her head in amazement. "Maggie never says boo to a goose."

"Really?"

"Believe me, she's as quiet as a mouse." She thought of something else. "And she said she wanted no part in it? That's rich. I was the one who was against it. Me! That's why I went home early. I didn't want anything to do with it."

"I suppose that the passing years have dimmed the memory. Anyway, never mind that. I promised we wouldn't discuss Anita."

As he had hoped, and gambled on, Yvonne couldn't let it go so easily.

"My memory is as sharp as it ever was, thank you very much." She squared her shoulders. "As I said, I was the one who didn't want to know. God, I'm hardly likely to forget that, am I? I quite liked Anita. In fact, if we could ask her, I bet she'd say I was her best friend."

"Really?"

"Yes. Really."

"Well, there's no need to discuss it—"

"She had her faults, but at least she was open about

them. So she'd slept with Sandra's boyfriend. So what? Eddie was a right tosser anyway. In my eyes, all it did was prove that Sandra was better off without him."

"That's just what I thought."

No wonder Sandra Butler had seemed so bitter. Eddie had succumbed to her employee's considerable charms.

"But, oh no." Yvonne was in full flow now. "Sandra wasn't going to let either of them get away with that. She wanted revenge and nothing I said could talk her out of it."

Dylan shook his head in what he hoped was a sympathetic way.

"Brenda was all for it, too. Mind, she always was a complete bitch. As nice as pie to your face but, the minute your back was turned, she couldn't find a good word to say about you."

"Really? I haven't had the pleasure. According to her neighbour, she and her husband are in Corfu."

"Best place for them," Yvonne muttered. "Of course, it was easy for her, working at the hospital I mean. I suppose things weren't so strict back then. She could get hold of anything."

Hospital? Dylan's very acceptable red wine struggled to find its way down his throat. What in hell's name had they done to Anita?

"What, um, was it exactly that she got hold of?" he asked.

"I can't remember what it was called. All I know is that it made you ill if you mixed it with alcohol."

Good God. These women—Sandra busy in her salon, Maggie walking her dog, and Yvonne downing wine and picking at chicken wings—were remarkably cool. "And did it make her ill?"

"Didn't Maggie tell you?"

"She gave me her version, of course," Dylan said, "but it seems she has a habit of stretching the truth a bit."

"Too right she does. Fancy telling you it was her who wanted no part in it. Cheeky bitch."

She emptied her glass and Dylan refilled it.

"Ta," she said. "Well, like I told you, I wanted nothing to do with any of it. As soon as they put that—that whatever it was—in her drink, I scarpered. Went home and left them to it."

So, regardless of what had happened to Anita, Yvonne was in the clear.

"I have proof of that, too," she said. "As it was still quite early, I called in at the Commercial on my way home. Loads of people saw me."

In the clear *and* with a convenient alibi.

Dylan tutted. "Maggie didn't tell me that."

"Well, it's fact. I had to phone Sandra the next day to find out what had happened."

"It sounds as if you were better off out of it." Dylan tried to sound sympathetic but it was difficult.

"Too right I was."

The waiter came to clear away their plates and Dylan endured the usual "Was everything to your satisfaction?" and "Can we tempt you to a dessert?" routine with as much patience as he could muster.

He ordered a coffee and a brandy. Yvonne, after a great deal of deliberation, which included flirting with the young waiter, settled for coffee.

Dylan had thought he might find it difficult to return to their discussion, but Yvonne couldn't let it rest.

"Do you think Sandra might have lied to me?" she asked, pulling a red serviette to pieces.

He gave her a smooth smile. "How can I answer that? I don't know what she told you."

"Just that they—Maggie and Brenda—left Anita in the alley at the side of Oasis. And that she was throwing up. But, according to Brenda, she was in the recovery position so wouldn't have choked or anything."

"I hadn't realised she was a doctor." Dylan somehow managed to keep the amazement from his voice.

"She wasn't. She was a nurse. But fully trained and everything."

Dylan was struggling to take in any of this. They had put something in Anita's drink, something they knew would make her ill, and then, when she was vomiting, they had abandoned her to her fate.

"Did it never occur to you that something might have happened to her?" he asked.

"No."

Their coffees and Dylan's brandy arrived. Now Yvonne was too preoccupied to spare the waiter a second glance.

"Well, yes," she said at last, "of course it did. But they heard someone, which is why they legged it. It was a bloke and they heard him talking to Anita. If there had been anything wrong, seriously wrong I mean, he would have taken care of her, wouldn't he?"

"We have to assume so," Dylan said, adding a dark, "if there was time."

Frightened eyes darted to his. Yvonne Yates could say what she liked but, for the past thirteen years, she had been haunted by the disappearance of Anita Champion. Presumably, all four women had.

Dylan was trying to look as calm as Yvonne, but it was damned difficult.

"I suppose all four of you have worried that revenge might have escalated to murder?"

"Murder?" Her voice was a whisper, almost too quiet to catch. "No. No, of course we haven't. That stuff, the stuff Brenda gave her, it was harmless. It only lasted a couple of hours at most."

"Did Brenda know Anita's medical history? Did she know what, if any, medication Anita was taking at the time?"

Yvonne blew on her coffee and took a sip before answering. "Probably. But either way, it didn't matter. It was only something harmless. It was just a joke."

"Not very funny as it turned out, was it?"

She began picking at the serviette again. "Anita was healthier than any of us. Nothing Brenda did caused her any harm."

"I see." All Dylan saw was the female at its most lethal. God, it was no wonder he had misogynistic tendencies. "If there really was a man trying to talk to Anita that night, does anyone know who it was?"

Yvonne shook her head. "The girls didn't recognise the voice. Well, they didn't hang around to find out."

Serviette fragments were scattered across their table like drops of blood.

"Anita brought it all on herself." Her voice was harsh. "Sandra's bloke wasn't the first. Ask anyone. Ask Alan Cheyney what she was like. It was thanks to Anita that his wife walked out."

The name Alan Cheyney was familiar.

"He's got a fishing shop on the main street," she said on seeing his puzzled expression.

"Ah, yes." Dylan had been in every shop on the main street, showing Anita's photo to staff and asking questions, but Cheyney's angling shop had been closed. He made a mental note to call again first thing in the morning.

Yvonne pushed her empty cup away. "It's time I went home." Her voice was flat and suddenly weary.

"What? Oh, no. Listen, we'll go somewhere else and I promise not to mention Anita."

"But you will. Or I will. That's how it always is. Always will be, I suppose."

There was no arguing with her, and Dylan didn't try too hard. He had learned all he was likely to, and he wanted to be rid of her.

He believed her story. He believed that the lesson they had wanted to teach Anita had gone horribly wrong. Whether that lesson had ended as murder, he didn't know.

And unless he could find the unknown man from the alley, if indeed that man had ever existed, he never would know.

CHAPTER NINE

THE FOLLOWING MORNING, Dylan called at Cheyney Angling for the third time. Today, the Back in 10 Mins sign had been replaced by a large white card that declared the shop Open.

He stepped inside and found himself in a jungle of fishing rods, reels and metal stands with dozens of small packs of hooks dangling from them. There wasn't room to swing a minnow.

"Morning." The man behind the small and equally cluttered counter had been opening mail. Bills, by the look of it.

"Good morning." Dylan inched his way forward without getting hooked. "I'm looking for Alan Cheyney."

"Oh?" A wary look came into his eyes, and he flashed a quick glance at the street.

"Is he around?" Dylan asked.

"I'm Alan Cheyney." Reluctance at revealing his identity had turned to defiance. "Who are you?"

He didn't look Anita Champion's type. Whatever that was. He was about five feet nine inches tall and his brown hair was thin. He was wearing grey trousers and an ill-fitting green sweater. He gave the impression of being more interested in catching trout than attractive women.

"My name's Dylan Scott. I've come to Dawson's

Clough to try and find a woman I used to know. Anita Champion."

Cheyney's gaze travelled the length of Dylan. He looked as if he wouldn't trust him as far as he could cast a line.

"I heard someone was asking after her," was all he said.

"Did you know her?"

"I did."

"And I suppose you're going to tell me the same as everyone else? That she vanished one Saturday night and hasn't been seen or heard of since?"

"That's about the height of it."

"Did you know her well?"

"Fairly well at one time, yes."

Dylan waited for more. There was no more. "Close, would you say you were?"

"Depends on your definition of close, doesn't it?"

He was a cagey individual.

"I heard she was responsible for the break-up of your marriage," Dylan said.

"Then you heard wrong."

"Oh?"

"Marriages break up without any help from outside. My marriage was over long before my wife caught me and Anita together."

"So you had an affair with Anita?"

"It's common knowledge. My ex-wife made sure of that."

It might be "common knowledge," but, in the same situation, Dylan couldn't imagine telling a stranger he'd had an affair without first asking a few questions. As yet, Cheyney hadn't shown the slightest interest in *why* Dylan was looking for his ex-lover.

Perhaps, as news of Dylan's interest was spreading through Dawson's Clough, Cheyney had heard the story of the love-struck idiot trying to find a ring he'd foolishly given Anita.

"How long ago was that?" Dylan asked.

"It was over about a year before Anita left the Clough."

Left the Clough. Not vanished or disappeared, but left the Clough.

"Any idea why she might have done that?"

"No."

"Odd, isn't it? Her leaving the Clough, I mean, when she had a daughter waiting for her."

"It's not the action of a normal woman," Cheyney said, "but Anita wasn't like anyone I ever knew."

"How do you mean?"

"I mean she needed to be having fun. All the time. The Clough bored her. Everyone in the town bored her."

"What's your theory?"

"I don't have one. I've no idea where she went, and I've got far better things to do with my time than invent stuff."

"I knew Anita, too," Dylan said.

"Oh?" Perhaps he hadn't heard the story of the lovelorn southerner.

"Yes. About fifteen years ago. She said something to me about Terrence Armstrong. Did she mention anything to you?"

At the mention of Armstrong's name, Cheyney flinched, Dylan was sure of it.

"No," the man said.

"Are you sure?"

"I'm sure."

"Do you know him?"

"He owns the ground you're standing on."

"Really? Ah, I heard he had a bit of property in the town."

"You heard right then. Look, I can't help you, and I've got things to do."

"Fine," Dylan said. "Thanks for your time. I appreciate it."

Walking back along the street, Dylan ran a word-for-word replay of the encounter in his head. Mention of Terry Armstrong in the past had brought blank looks and the conviction that Anita couldn't possibly have known him. Cheyney, though, had visibly flinched at mention of the man's name.

Why?

He knew something, Dylan was sure of it.

CHAPTER TEN

"Is your mum going to be in later?" Dylan asked his son.

They were enjoying the usual Saturday afternoon halftime ritual of a meat pie. Arsenal were beating Manchester City one nil and that always made the pies taste better.

"Dunno," Luke said between mouthfuls. "She's been out a lot lately."

"Has she? Where?"

"Dunno."

Dylan had hoped to worm his way back into Bev's good books, but that was going to be impossible if he couldn't see her. She'd come round, she always did but, given that his mother was still in residence and filling the place with the evil smell of scented candles, he wanted it to be sooner rather than later.

"Come on, Dad, they'll be kicking off in a couple of minutes."

They fought their way back to their seats and prepared to cheer on the Gunners.

Dylan was struggling to concentrate on the match. He couldn't rid his mind of four women who thought it acceptable to drug a so-called friend and leave her to her fate in a dark alley on a cold November night. The thought made him shudder.

Bev had her funny little ways, hundreds of them,

but she could never do something like that. Few people could.

How strongly would you have to hate someone to pull a stunt like that?

Anita's crime? She had, allegedly, slept with her employer's boyfriend. Yvonne Yates was right about one thing—it takes two to cheat and Anita had merely proved that the boyfriend wasn't worth knowing.

Dylan could have kicked himself for not learning more. Yvonne had said that Sandra wasn't going to let *either of them* get away with it. So what had happened to the boyfriend?

According to Sandra, she would have been out with the girls that night if her Eddie hadn't been home on leave. Had the others dealt with Anita while she dished out Eddie's fate?

If anyone else had wanted revenge, Dylan might have expected Eddie's clothes to have landed in the street, or a fresh mackerel to have been hidden in his car's engine. With Sandra, anything was possible.

Dylan needed to find this Eddie. Just as he needed to find the man, if indeed there ever was a man, who had gone to Anita's aid in that dark alley.

The words *haystack and needle* sprang to mind...

Dylan slapped his gloved hands together for warmth. Despite his thick coat, scarf and hat, he was chilled and, unusually, he wasn't sorry when the game ended. Arsenal had beaten Manchester City two-nil, but it hadn't been a thrilling game.

As he drove, he began to thaw out and, by the time they reached the marital home, he could feel his toes again.

"Mum's home!" Luke gave Dylan a sympathetic look.

"I'll try and put in a good word for you, Dad. And I won't repeat what that bloke called the ref," he added with a grin.

Dylan groaned. "Please don't."

"I won't. He was right, though. The bloke was a—"

"Yes, yes. He probably was, although what he does in his spare time is his own business. Let's just forget that particular incident, shall we?"

They walked inside and Dylan got halfway along the hall before a stern-looking Bev, arms folded across her very attractive chest, barred his way.

Luke wasn't put off.

"I've promised to show Dad an old Arsenal program," he said, and Dylan wondered when he'd learned to lie so easily. "I'm just going upstairs to find it."

"Don't be long then," Bev warned him.

Dylan stood facing his wife. And she faced him straight back.

"It was a great game." He decided to opt for a safe subject.

"Good."

"Yeah. We won, two nil. It was cold, though. Not that Luke seems to feel it."

She rolled her eyes. "I'll make you a coffee, Dylan, and then you go."

"Aw, thanks, Bev."

He followed her into the marital kitchen. There was something different, yet he couldn't see that she'd changed anything. Venetian blinds at the window above the sink looked the same. Kettle, tea, coffee and sugar canisters, bread bin—all were in their rightful places. The usual wrinkled apples and a couple of oranges sat in the wooden bowl. Bananas hung from the chrome tree, and the glove dangled from the cooker door.

"It used to be cream," she said on a long sigh.

"Ah. I wondered." He couldn't remember it being cream. For all he knew, it could always have been this pale green. "It looks good, Bev."

"It was nice to just get on and do it."

"You should have said. I could have done it for you."

"I did say, Dylan. I said time and time again for two years."

"Ah."

Now she mentioned it, he could vaguely remember her telling him he had plenty of time for painting.

"Thanks," he said as she thrust a mug of coffee at him.

It was time for an "I've changed—you were right—how can I possibly make it up to you?" conversation. Unfortunately, Bev had other plans.

"Here's Mum," she said as a car door was heard being slammed shut. "Right, I'm off. See you, Dylan. And don't stay too long!"

"Oh, er, right. Thanks for the coffee."

"You're welcome."

Bev was gone and her mother, someone Dylan had always got along well with, took her place in the kitchen.

She gave him a hug, then clucked her teeth at him. "You've really done it this time, Dylan."

"She'll come round, Pam. She always does."

Her expression as she patted his arm was a disturbing mix of sadness and frustration. "Don't count on it, love."

Luke raced into the kitchen, and Dylan noticed the way his son's face fell when he spotted his grandmother. As much as Luke adored her, Dylan knew the lad had been hoping for a reconciliation between his parents.

"Has Mum gone out?"

"She has," Dylan said, "so you'll have to behave for your gran."

"I always do. And don't worry, Dad, I meant what I said. I'll put in a good word for you."

"Thanks."

Dylan would talk to Bev next week. What she was doing, he suspected, was trying to make him jealous, to make him believe she had another man at her beck and call.

Come to think of it—

"Who painted the kitchen then?"

"It looks much better, doesn't it?" Pam ran a hand over the wall. "That cream was too bland with the pine units. She's thinking of doing this wall—" she pointed to the back, "—in an olive green. I'm not so sure about that. What do you think, Dylan?"

Dylan couldn't see that it would make any difference. "Best to leave well alone, I'd say."

"Yes, you're probably right."

Only when he was on his way back to the smallest flat in the land and his mother did he realise that his question hadn't been answered.

Who had painted the kitchen?

But he wasn't going to worry on that score. He was Bev's husband. He belonged with her. And with Luke. They were a family.

CHAPTER ELEVEN

ON MONDAY EVENING Alan Cheyney locked up his shop and went into the back storeroom, a huge, ugly place that had been used to hang animal carcasses when the shop had belonged to the butcher. A few hooks still dangled from the steel beams.

There wasn't much in there as he couldn't afford to buy stock, but it served as his office and kitchen. He threw himself down in a chair, put his legs on the desk and stared at the wall.

He could add up the day's takings or he could take himself off to the Pheasant and drink the meagre profit.

To hell with it, he'd have a pint and worry about everything in the morning.

After double-checking the locks and the alarm, he left the shop and crossed the road. He stood for a moment to look back at his little empire. The recently painted sign, Cheyney Angling, looked impressive. It was the only thing that did.

His brother, Pete, had called him all kinds of a fool, but Alan hadn't taken any notice. Being made redundant at the age of fifty-four had seemed like a godsend. He'd always loved fishing, and he'd thought it would be easy enough to open a shop that catered for fellow anglers' needs.

Totting up the day's takings wouldn't have taken long.

He'd sold four pounds of maggots and a fly rod for a hundred and eighty pounds. Profit for the day? About thirty quid.

He'd worry about it tomorrow.

When he pushed open the door to the Pheasant, he was surprised to see half a dozen people at the bar. Monday nights were usually as dead as his shop.

Bill Thornton and Geoff Lane were perched on stools so Alan took the one next to them.

"How's it going?" Geoff asked as Alan paid for his pint.

"It isn't."

"Wrong time of year, I suppose," Bill said. "Far too cold for fishing."

"Is it hell?" On reflection, though, perhaps Bill was right. Only the hardy, experienced anglers went out in January, and they had all the kit they needed.

Geoff grinned. "You'll go out fishing all night, mate, but other folk have brains."

"Trade will pick up in the summer," Bill said.

Alan doubted he'd survive until the summer. He was behind with his rent, two of his suppliers had refused him credit—

"Probably." He didn't want to think about it.

"Course it will," Bill said.

Would it? Alan had an online shop, but the big boys were selling far more cheaply than he could. As for a shop in Dawson's Clough, it was a waste of time. There were plenty of good fishing sites around, but angling was dying out. Kids would rather hang around street corners taking drugs.

Pete had been right. He was a damn fool.

"Tell you who we were talking to the other night,"

Bill said. "Wednesday it were. A bloke called Dylan Scott. He were looking for Anita Champion. You'll remember her, Alan."

"I do. I saw him, too. He came into the shop asking about her. Funny that, after all this time, I mean."

"Where do you reckon she is?" Geoff asked.

"God knows." Why exactly *was* Dylan Scott trying to trace her? He was posing as an ex-boyfriend, but Alan didn't believe that for a moment. "Probably married to some rich Arab sheik," he said, trying to make light of it.

"Never in a million years," Bill said.

"Here we go again." Geoff rolled his eyes, grinning.

"You can scoff," Bill said, "but no way did she walk out on young Holly."

"Bill here reckons she were abducted by aliens." Geoff chuckled.

"Aliens would make a beeline for Dawson's Clough." Alan supped from his glass. "Come to think of it, I saw a few intelligent life forms hanging around outside the library."

"I never mentioned aliens." Bill was getting irritated. "Bloody daft, you are."

"Maybe this Dylan Scott will solve the mystery," Geoff said.

"That shop of yours, Alan," Bill said. "You rent it off that Armstrong bloke, don't you?"

"Yeah."

It was odd having Dylan Scott asking questions about Anita and then mentioning Terry Armstrong. Bloody odd.

But if Alan didn't want to think about his day's

takings, he certainly didn't want to think about Armstrong. They'd only met once, and he'd seemed pleasant enough then, but when the standing order for the rent didn't go through in December, he'd sent a bloke to the shop to discuss the matter. Alan hadn't liked him at all. A big bloke, full of aggression.

"That Dylan Scott thought Anita might have known him," Geoff said. "I can't believe that, though. For one thing, he didn't live round here in her day. For another, she weren't in his league."

"Dunno. I can't imagine her knowing him." Alan wished they'd forget it. "You having another?" He opened his wallet.

Over the next pint, talk centred around the weather, the roadworks that would be starting in the summer, and the lack of facilities for kids in the town. Alan was glad of that. January's standing order for rent hadn't gone through either, and he was expecting another visit from Terry Armstrong's assistant.

No point worrying, though. If he lost the shop, he lost it. He'd get another job on the lorries. It was easier than running a business. A lot easier.

It was gone eleven when he left the Pheasant. He'd planned to have a pint, maybe two, then walk home via the fish-and-chip shop, but that had closed for the night. As the kebab shop was open, waiting for the last few stragglers to leave the pubs, he stopped to buy one of those instead.

He ate it as he walked, a few bits of meat dropping for the pigeons, and only had a small portion left when he turned into his road.

A big dark car was parked outside his house, but he paid it no attention until, as he drew level, the door was flung open, hitting him in the ribs and tossing the last of his kebab to the ground.

A tall, well-muscled man, whisky on his breath, bundled him into the car.

"We need a chat," he said, as the driver floored the accelerator and the car shot forward.

"What the hell—"

"Just a friendly chat."

"Who the hell are you?"

"Doesn't matter."

"Stop the car. Stop the fucking car!"

A fist banged into the side of his face. "Shut your fucking mouth!"

The car screeched round corners until it came to a halt by the disused rail tracks.

"What do you want?" Alan tried to get out, but the back doors were locked. "Money? I can get you money!"

The driver was soon out. It was he who opened the back door and yanked Alan out. The two men pinned him against the car.

"You've got the wrong bloke," Alan shouted.

"I don't think so. You see, a little bird told us that you've been a naughty boy," the driver said. "It seems you've been chatting up your landlord's wife?"

"What?" Alan had no idea what he was talking about.

"At the golf club. A Friday night. A couple of weeks before Christmas. Ring any bells, does it?"

"I was—" His teeth had started to chatter. "I was there, yes, but—"

"We know that. You were seen. Now, your landlord

doesn't want the likes of you pawing his wife around. Got that?"

Alan remembered the event, but nothing had happened. There had been a crowd at the bar and someone had jostled him so that he'd spilled some beer on her dress. Naturally, he'd apologised. He'd taken a handkerchief from his pocket and dabbed at the stain. She'd laughed, he recalled. Said it was lucky his mother brought him up properly, making sure he never left the house without a clean handkerchief. And that was all.

"Look, you've got this all wrong—"

"It never pays to make a fool of your landlord, you know. It made him look at you and your rent. Seems like you owe him some money. Quite a lot of money, in fact."

"Look I'll pay the rent. I said—"

A fist hammered into his face and his words were lost as a tooth flew from his mouth. Punches rained down on his head and his ribs. Alan could taste blood. Could feel himself losing consciousness.

When he dropped to the floor, he was kicked front and back.

"You've got till Friday!"

Two doors slammed and, mercifully, the engine fired into life and the car sped off into the night.

Alan lay on the ground, his face finding welcome relief on a clump of wet grass. Every time he coughed, pain shot across his chest, and he tasted more blood. There was a gaping hole where a tooth had been.

He should get up and go home, but he wasn't sure he could stand, let alone walk.

You've got till Friday.

Four days.

CHAPTER TWELVE

ON WEDNESDAY EVENING Dylan left Dawson's Clough and began the 25-mile drive to Manchester.

Monday had been a complete waste of time. After a weekend of highs and lows—the main high was spending a lot of time with Luke and the low was not seeing Bev—Dylan had returned to Lancashire in a keen, enthusiastic mood. That had evaporated as he'd spoken to one person after another and learned precisely nothing.

He'd talked to people who'd worked at the Oasis nightclub but staff there were treated too badly to stay long. They were all young, too, and although some had heard of Anita, no one remembered her.

Yesterday had been equally pointless until the evening when, nursing a pint of beer, he found someone who not only remembered Anita, but also knew and kept in touch with Sandra Butler's boyfriend, Eddie Swift.

"Well, when I say I keep in touch with him," Glyn said, "I really mean the wife does. A Christmas card and birthday cards for the kids, you know the sort of thing."

Dylan nodded to indicate that he did.

"I'll give her a call. She'll have his address."

"Really? That would be great."

As Glyn hit a number on his mobile phone, Dylan went to the bar to refill their glasses. This piece of news was worthy of celebration on two counts. First, he'd found Eddie Swift. Second, and more important, the man was alive and well and obviously hadn't suffered anything too drastic at the hands of Sandra and her devious chums.

He carried their drinks back to the table but Glyn, pen poised over a beer mat, still didn't have that address.

"I'll be home as soon as I've finished this pint." As he spoke, Glyn nodded his thanks for the fresh drink and rolled his eyes in despair. "I don't know, do I? Half an hour perhaps. An hour at most."

Dylan sympathized. He'd had exactly the same conversation with Bev many times. Women couldn't grasp that "a swift half" or "a couple of pints" were merely figures of speech. They seemed to believe they were accurate timescales that must be adhered to on pain of death.

Glyn finally scribbled an address on the beer mat and switched off his phone.

"Why do women have to make such hard work of life?" Glyn emptied his glass and took a sip from his fresh pint. "I'm not to give you this, she says, until I know exactly what you're up to. Oh, and while she wasn't prepared to give his phone number to a complete stranger, she's calling him now to let him know you'll be paying him a visit."

"I can understand that. Better to be safe than sorry. After all, I could be anyone."

"Eddie can take care of himself. He's ex-army and still keeps himself in good shape."

Hopefully, Dylan would soon find that out for himself.

Glyn's wife hadn't wanted to give out Eddie Swift's

phone number, but it had been easy enough to look it up in the phone book. Dylan had tried the number a couple of times this morning, and then again this afternoon, but no one had answered. Assuming that Mr. and Mrs. Swift worked during the day and the children attended school, Dylan had decided to drive to Manchester this evening.

The address Glyn had given him was for a modern detached house on the outskirts of the city, and it looked as if Dylan's luck was in. Two cars were parked on the drive and lights shone from within.

His knock on the door was answered by a smiling blonde. "Ah, you'll be our mysterious stalker."

"That's me. Dylan Scott. I assume Glyn's wife warned you I'd be calling?"

"She did. She also warned me you'd been drinking with Glyn so I was to watch you." This was accompanied by a laugh. "Come in out of the cold. We're just having dinner. Will you join us?"

"Oh, no. Thank you, that's kind, but I couldn't. And I'm sorry to interrupt. Would you rather I came back later?"

"Don't be silly. Have something to eat with us. There's plenty, so you won't be putting us out."

She led him through a hall and into the kitchen where a man and two children of around ten years old sat at the table eating a curry that set Dylan's mouth watering. The man stood and offered his hand. He was well over six feet tall, towered above his petite wife, and looked as if he was no stranger to the gym. "Dylan Scott, isn't it? Eddie Swift. Sit yourself down and have something to eat. Rosie always cooks enough for twenty."

"I have to." His wife laughed. "Eddie always has lots of mates calling round. They only come for a meal."

The room was as welcoming as its occupants. Postcards sent by friends and family were stuck to the fridge with magnets, magazines were scattered around, fresh flowers shared the window sills with healthy-looking plants, and schoolbags had been abandoned on the top of a cupboard. It was a room that reflected the warmth of its occupants.

The children, Flora and Harry, were polite and as friendly as their parents. They were also keen to escape to their rooms and, as soon as their plates were wiped clean, they were gone.

Rosie, meanwhile, put a generous portion of curry in front of Dylan and sat to finish her own food.

"This is so generous," Dylan said. "I feel terrible now. I've come here to be nosey and you're feeding me."

"You're trying to find Anita Champion, I hear," Eddie said.

"That's right, yes."

If Eddie had anything to hide, he would have had plenty of time to work on his story. There was nothing Dylan could do about that, though. Glyn, when prising the address from his wife, had had to repeat the old story about the antique ring. In any case, Dylan didn't think Eddie was hiding anything. He and his wife were genuine—and generous—people.

"I spoke to the hairdresser, Sandra Butler, and she said that you and she used to date at one time?"

"Eddie's got girlfriends in all corners of the globe." Rosie's eyes shone as she teased her husband, and Dylan experienced a sigh deep inside. He and Bev should be like this. They should enjoy this easy banter.

"And some are best forgotten," Eddie said. "Like Sandra Butler. You didn't tangle with her if you had any sense."

"Oh?"

"We're going back—what?" Eddie did a quick mental calculation. "Thirteen years. I was in the army and having a grand old time. I used to come home on leave, flirt with all the pretty girls, and then head back. It might sound a bit callous, but I forgot most of them. Sandra was difficult to forget, though. We went out three or four times when I was home on leave and, when I went back to my unit, she wrote me letters practically every day. The way she spoke, you'd have thought we were engaged."

"You broke her heart?" Rosie seemed genuinely concerned.

"I don't think she had a heart."

Dylan was content to eat and let Eddie do the talking. The curry was delicious—tender pieces of chicken, nice and spicy but not too hot.

"That last time I came home on leave—" Eddie skewered a piece of chicken with his fork. "Sandra assumed we'd get together and carry on as if we were practically married. I didn't particularly want to hurt her feelings so I told her I had other plans and took her assistant, Anita Champion, out instead." He gave Dylan a knowing look. "That was no hardship. Anita was something special, wasn't she?" Laughing, he grabbed Rosie's hand, lifted it to his lips and kissed it soundly. "Not as special as you, my love, obviously, but she was something."

With mock indignation, and laughing as she spoke, Rosie snatched her hand back. "You're full of crap, Eddie Swift."

"I know, but you love me all the same."

Until now, Dylan hadn't believed the perfect relationship existed, yet it looked as if Eddie and Rosie Swift had exactly that. It was difficult to imagine them having the blazing rows or the sulky silences other couples did.

"So I spent the night with Anita. She was a breath of fresh air compared to Sandra. She knew how to have fun without thinking strings were attached. In any case, she had a daughter and that's all she cared about. Unlike Sandra, she wasn't looking for a husband."

"What happened?" Dylan asked.

"Sandra found out and I have no idea how. I can only imagine she was spying on us. Well, spying on me probably. I kept giving her excuses as to why I couldn't be with her, you see. I'd tell her I'd arranged something with my mates or I had to visit my parents. I think she must have followed me and seen me with Anita."

"What did she say?"

"What didn't she say? I'd agreed to see her on the Saturday night. I was determined to get through to her that I wasn't interested. I planned to tell her she was a lovely woman, but I didn't want a relationship—you know the sort of thing."

"Would you believe I could marry such a rogue, Dylan?" Rosie didn't wait for a reply. "Let me get you some coffee."

Eddie watched his wife as she cleared away their plates and prepared the coffee.

"Sandra let me into her home and then slapped me across the face." His smile was rueful. "She was screaming like a banshee and telling me how I could fuck off because she wouldn't touch anything that had been near that slag Anita. Believe me, it got pretty ugly. I've never hit a woman but I came close that night."

Having met Sandra and her friends, Dylan knew how tempting it must have been.

"The next day," Eddie said, "I had my dad's car parked in town. I stayed with Mum and Dad when I was on leave, and I often borrowed Dad's car. Four months old it was. A top-of-the-range saloon. Anyway, I'd been round the shops and when I got back to the car, it had been trashed. All four tyres had been slashed, the paintwork had been scratched, and the word *Bastard* had been painted across the front bumper."

Dylan winced at that and knew a sudden urge to rush outside to make sure his Morgan was safe.

"I was furious." Eddie gave a small smile. "Almost as furious as my dad."

"I'm not surprised. I shudder to think what I'd do if anyone touched my car. I take it Sandra was responsible?"

"Must have been. I couldn't prove it, though. I stormed round to her house and demanded to know what the hell had possessed her to do such a thing. Of course, she claimed not to know what I was talking about. She was responsible, though. I'm sure of it."

Rosie poured the coffee and the smell must have alerted the children to the possibility of goodies. They burst into the room just as their mother was slicing a large chocolate Swiss roll. With a piece in their hands, they chattered non-stop.

"Can we watch our DVD now?" Flora wiped her mouth on her sleeve and then her hands on her jeans. "You said we could, Mum."

"I said you might be able to. That's might, okay? As in possibly yes and possibly no."

"So can we?" Harry asked.

"You may." Rosie grabbed Harry before he could escape. "You need to wash those hands first. And you Flora. Under the tap. Now."

The children laughed and splashed around enough water to bathe a small horse before racing for the sitting-room.

"Do you have children, Dylan?" Rosie asked. "Or do you have more sense?"

"I have a son, Luke. He's eleven and he can twist me and his mum round his little finger."

"Kids seem to be born with that ability, don't they? I never was. I had to do as I was told."

"What?" Eddie laughed at that. "You were spoiled rotten. Still are, come to that."

"Take no notice of him, Dylan."

Rosie gave Dylan and Eddie a large slice of chocolate Swiss roll and took a sliver for herself. She might have been dieting but she had no need to.

"The day your father's car was vandalized," Dylan said. "When was that?"

"The Sunday." Eddie's words were muffled as he tried to eat cake and speak at the same time. "While Anita was out with the girls on the Saturday night, Sandra was yelling at me and screaming like a fish-woman. The next day, Dad's car was wrecked."

"So you confronted Sandra?"

"Yes, and, of course, she denied all knowledge. She was gloating—telling me that Anita had stayed out all night so must have found someone better. At the time, that's what everyone thought. They assumed Anita had spent the night with someone. It wouldn't have been the first time. Not by a long way."

"When was the last time you saw Anita?"

"The Friday night. I asked her if she fancied going out, but she didn't. She'd been in Manchester that day and was knackered. Oh yeah, and she said she'd be out on the Saturday night so didn't want two late nights on the trot." Eddie licked chocolate from his fingers. "I could take a hint. I knew she was trying to let me know she wasn't interested, just as I'd tried, and failed, to let Sandra Butler know."

"Did you see her after that?"

"No. The next thing I knew, the police were looking for her. Not that they looked very hard. They, along with everyone else, were convinced she'd taken off with some man or other and would come back when it suited her. All the police were bothered about was making sure her daughter was taken care of."

"That's crazy," Rosie said. "No woman would leave a child alone."

"Anita would." Eddie looked at his wife as he spoke. "She'd done it before—gone off for a week."

"Good God."

If only Anita had been like Rosie. If she'd been a more responsible mother, the police would have taken far more interest in her disappearance. Anita, however, wasn't like Rosie. Nor was she like any other woman Dylan had known.

"She definitely gave no hint about going away anywhere?" Dylan asked. "She didn't mention anyone special in her life?"

"No."

"What can you tell me about her friends? I've heard

that, on the night she disappeared, she'd been out with Yvonne Yates, Maggie—"

"And Brenda. Yeah, that's right. They went out most Saturday nights and usually ended up at Oasis."

"I believe they did end up there. What are those women like?" Dylan considered telling them Yvonne's story about the way Anita's so-called friends had drugged her, but there was no point. Not yet.

"Anita liked them well enough," Eddie said. "She liked most people though. I suppose, in their way, they liked her, too. But they could be bitchy about her behind her back. They were jealous, plain and simple. While they spent money and time on clothes, hair and makeup, Anita could be dressed and ready to go out in ten minutes and still outshine every one of them. They hated it."

"Right." Dylan was trying to imagine the scenario that existed thirteen years ago. "We know Sandra Butler was out for revenge on you because you'd been with Anita. What about Anita? Presumably she'd want to put Anita in her place, too?"

"How do you mean?" Eddie asked.

"What do you think Sandra would have done to Anita? She vandalized your car. What might she have done to Anita?"

"I suppose she might have hurled a few choice words at her. But I can't see her doing anything else. Anita was too valuable to her. She was a hard worker and popular with the customers. Sandra was a money-grabbing cow—still is, I shouldn't wonder—and she'd have known that replacing Anita would have been nigh on impossible. As for possessions, Anita didn't have anything valuable. No, I expect they had a row and that would have been the end of it."

Dylan wasn't so sure. Again, he considered telling them Yvonne Yates's story about the drug Anita was given, but there was no point until he knew more about it.

"What about Anita's other friends?"

"It's a long time ago," Eddie said. "I only saw people in the Clough when I was home on leave. I used to catch up with family, drink too much, chat up the girls and then go back to wherever I was stationed. Anita knew practically everyone in the town but I couldn't give you any names." He tapped his finger against his teeth. "There was another nightclub in the Clough at the time. I'm damned if I can remember what it was called, but Anita and the others used to go there. I never went although I gather it was pretty seedy. From what I recall, the drinks were expensive and watered down and the place was raided by the police every fortnight. All the druggies hung out there."

Dylan would ask around. Plenty of people must remember it.

"Unless I'm getting confused with somewhere else," Eddie said, "I seem to think Anita was friendly with one of the bouncers there. He used to get her free drinks."

"Really?"

"Maybe. Sorry, Dylan, but I didn't go there. I'm only going by memory so I may be wrong. I was only home on leave a couple of times after that. Then I married Rosie and we spent the next three years in Cyprus."

"That's great, thanks. I can ask around."

Thirteen years was a long time. People moved on. Memory became blurred.

"It's time I was going," he said. "You've been more than generous—both with your food and your time—and I'm extremely grateful. If you think of anything else, Eddie, anything at all, no matter how stupid it seems, will you let me know?"

"Of course."

Rosie reached for a pen and a black leather-bound phone directory. "If I don't put your number in here, we'll lose it."

She wrote his name and number neatly under S and then again under D.

"Thanks. And thank you for the food. It's been a real pleasure to meet you both."

"You, too," Rosie said. "Keep in touch, won't you?"

"Yes, let us know if you find out anything. I've always been curious."

"I will."

Rosie and Eddie were showing him out when he spotted a familiar object on the small table in the hall. "School raffle tickets?"

"They're a permanent fixture in this house." Rosie laughed. "This time they're hoping to raise funds for a swimming pool."

And next time it would be to improve the sports ground. Dylan knew all about that. He swore he'd bought Luke's school four times over. "Give me a fiver's worth."

He was reaching for his wallet but Rosie waved it away. "Dylan, no. You can't do that."

"I can. I know how difficult it is to sell the things. Besides, I might win a—" He read the ticket and whistled.

"A weekend in Paris? The best my son's school comes up with is a couple of bottles of wine."

Rosie, very reluctantly, took the money from him and handed him the tickets. "Thanks."

As he left the house and the door closed behind him, the night air chilled him. Or perhaps it was more than the air.

He sat in his car for a moment and gazed back at the house. What a delightful couple. That's how he and Bev should be. Exactly like that. They would be, too. He was going to have a serious talk with Bev. It was high time she stopped acting like a child and saw sense.

Feeling much better, he fired the engine and began the journey back to Dawson's Clough.

CHAPTER THIRTEEN

ALAN CHEYNEY SAT by his bed to wait for the doctor.

When Armstrong's thugs had driven off on Monday night, he'd tried to walk home. He'd made it back into town, but then he'd passed out in the chemist's doorway. A copper had found him and he'd been admitted to A&E to have his gum, lip and a gash above his left eye stitched. Three of his ribs had been broken, too, but he was still surprised to be in hospital on this cold Thursday morning. Considering beds were at a premium, he'd expected to be discharged yesterday.

He could have discharged himself, but he was in no hurry. While the police looked for "two unknown assailants," he was safer in hospital. He'd even toyed with the idea of feigning mysterious complaints just to remain in the haven of the building.

Pete had called yesterday and, although Alan hadn't gone into too much detail, his brother had promised to lend him a thousand pounds. It wasn't enough, but Alan was grateful. It might keep Terry Armstrong off his back for a while.

Pete had also taken the week off work to look after the shop for him. It was a week of his annual leave, too, so Kath, his wife, wouldn't be happy. Alan owed him.

The door swung open and a nurse came into the ward followed by a man carrying a huge, cellophane-wrapped basket of fruit.

"Mr. Cheyney, a visitor for you."

"Me?"

Alan looked past the fruit to the suited gentleman and he felt his guts, broken and bruised, turn to mush. It was Terry Armstrong.

The last Alan had heard, Armstrong was in Florida, in the house where he spent four or five months of the year. Judging by his suntan, he hadn't been back long.

"My dear chap," Armstrong said, "I've just heard the news. As I was saying to this lovely young lady, I take it as a personal affront if anything happens to one of my tenants." He grabbed Alan's hand and squeezed it. Hard. "Here, a few grapes for you."

The few grapes would have filled a fruiterer's.

"So tell me, Alan, what happened? Two men attacked you, I heard. I suppose they thought you had the contents of the till on you. What's the world coming to, eh? Let's hope the police soon catch up with them."

Everyone in the ward, the nurse included, was captivated by this genial, charismatic man.

"Yes," Alan agreed, realising he hadn't spoken.

Armstrong pulled up a chair close to Alan's. "I can't stop, but I wanted to say how sorry I am."

"That's, um—"

"I hear you'll be going home later today. You'll be glad of that, I'm sure. Back at work soon, eh?"

"Yes."

"Hanging's too good for them. Young kids, I expect. They think the world owes them a living."

"You're right about that." Charlie, in the next bed, had been waiting for the chance to join in the conversation. "They should bring back National Service."

While Alan's stomach continued to churn, the entire

ward chatted about the youth of Dawson's Clough and what should be done about them.

When, after about twenty minutes, Armstrong stood to leave, he'd formed his own fan club.

He shook Alan's hand again and leaned in close, his breath hot against Alan's face as he whispered, "I'll have my money tomorrow. Meanwhile, keep away from my wife."

With smiles and waves to everyone on the ward, Terry Armstrong made his exit.

I'll have my money tomorrow.

CHAPTER FOURTEEN

DYLAN SAT IN Asda's cafe, eating the biggest breakfast they offered—because he'd overslept and missed it at the hotel—while wondering where to start.

Last night, driving home from Eddie and Rosie Swift's house, he'd thought again about Alan Cheyney. The man remained a mystery. From the little Dylan had managed to find out, he was a decent, honest, hard-working type. He'd been made redundant after more than thirty years driving lorries for the same company and, with the small lump sum he received, opened his not-very-successful angling shop. Divorced, he lived alone in a small semi-detached house. An eight-year-old car sat on the drive. He lived modestly.

But he'd had an affair with Anita and he rented his shop premises from Terrence Armstrong. Cheyney was linked to them both. He was also wary of answering questions.

Dylan took his small notebook from his pocket and, fork in one hand, idly flicked through the pages as he ate.

He pushed his empty plate aside and took his phone from his pocket. He hit a button and listened to it ring out three times, before it was answered by a voice so croaky it was impossible to guess at the gender.

"Pikey? Is that you?"

"Yep, still breathing. Just about. I thought I was

getting over a dose of flu but I'm not so sure now. But never mind my groans, how are you, you old bastard? Hey, thanks for the Christmas card. Pity it got lost in the post."

"Eh? You didn't get one? Hell, that'll be Bev. She's thrown one of her wobblers."

She hadn't told him he had to deal with the cards, though, and he hadn't thought about it. He wouldn't have sent many but he would have sent one to Pikey. D.S. Keith Pike was a good mate. A big bloke with a shaved head, he looked more thug than copper, but he had a heart as big as a horse's, and his wife and two daughters could do with him as they pleased. He would die for them. Willingly.

He and Pikey had worked alongside each other for three years but, unfortunately, they hadn't been together the night the call came through that ended with Dylan being put behind bars.

If Pikey had been with him, it would have been sorted. Honest to the core, Pikey wouldn't have been tempted to lie by the offer of promotion. He wouldn't have been interested in showing Joe Public that complaints against police officers were taken seriously. Nothing but the truth would have mattered to him.

"So how have you upset the lovely Bev this time?" Pikey asked.

"Oh, the usual." To be honest, Dylan wasn't sure of the specifics. A drunkard and a loser, she'd said, but he had no idea what had brought that on. "She'll come round. She always does."

"Always has," Pikey corrected him.

"Yeah, well. So how are Sheila and the kids?"

"Great, thanks. You'll have to come and see us. You must owe me a pint."

"I will." If Pikey came good on this, he'd buy him a barrel. "Tell me, do you have friends at Lancashire Constabulary?"

"I have no friends at all. Best way, mate. All they do is phone you out of the blue when they want something."

"Aw, come on, Pikey. A great bloke like you must have friends everywhere."

"Ha! What exactly are you wanting from Lancashire Constabulary?"

As he finished his coffee, Dylan told Pikey all about the disappearance of Anita Champion.

"Leave it with me and I'll see what I can do," Pikey said when he'd finished.

"Thanks, mate. I owe you."

"You do."

As he snapped his phone shut, Dylan tried not to think of the laughs he and Pikey had shared during the days Dylan had been a respected member of the police force. Instead, he tried to decide how to put the day to best use.

He was gazing out the window across Asda's car park when he spotted the unmistakable figure of—what was his name? Stevie? Had the unkind name been Simple Stevie?

Dylan finished his coffee, put mug, plate and cutlery on the tray and quickly took it to the rack. He was soon going down the escalator and heading for the car park.

For a moment, he thought he'd lost Stevie, but then he spotted him pushing a trolley toward the car park's exit. Perhaps trolleys were his friends. At least they didn't argue, beg for favours, answer back or call you cruel names.

Dylan caught up with him and put a restraining hand on the trolley's handle. "Perhaps we ought to take this back, eh?"

He spoke gently enough, but Stevie, if that was his name, looked terrified.

"It's okay," Dylan said, "but I think they like to keep them here. It could be useful having a few spares in Market Street, I know, but better not, eh?"

Stevie nodded and released his grip on the trolley.

"We'll put it there." Dylan pointed to the plastic-covered trolley park.

Stevie nodded again, then, limping awkwardly, walked beside Dylan as he pushed the trolley.

Dylan stacked the trolley with the others and removed the pound coin from the slot. "Is this yours?"

A shake of the head indicated that he'd probably pinched the trolley from an unsuspecting shopper.

"I suppose it is now." Dylan gave him the coin, which disappeared into the pocket of a black anorak.

"It's Stevie, isn't it? I saw you in the pub—the Pheasant—when I was chatting to Bill Thornton and a chap called Geoff."

Another nod had Dylan wondering if the man could talk.

"Dylan. Dylan Scott." He offered his hand which, after a brief hesitation and wiping his own hand on spotless jeans, Stevie shook.

It was too early for a beer, and Dylan didn't fancy another coffee. Stevie was the one who looked as if he needed a good cooked breakfast washed down with something hot.

After a brief inner debate, Dylan decided that getting on the right side of Stevie might be beneficial. It was often the case that quiet people—and they didn't come more tight-lipped than Stevie—had sharpened powers of observation.

"Do you fancy a cup of tea or coffee?" he asked. "Or something to eat?"

Stevie regarded him with mild surprise. "Yes," he said finally and, although it was closer to a grunt than a word, Dylan breathed a sigh of relief. At least he was capable of speech.

This was proved when, at the food counter in Asda's cafe, Stevie said to the girl behind the counter, "Big breakfast and extra toast, please."

Dylan got himself a cup of tea. They sat at a table by the window that gave a view of the car park and the town, and Dylan watched, both fascinated and appalled, as Stevie shovelled in mouthful after mouthful.

Neither spoke until the plate had been cleared and wiped clean with a square of toast saved specially for the task.

"Good," Stevie said with satisfaction.

"You're welcome." But there was no such thing as a free breakfast.

Dylan reached into his pocket and pulled out the best photo he had of Anita Champion. By now, he'd shown it to so many people that it was beginning to look creased and tatty.

"Do you know this woman?" He slid the photo across the table to Stevie.

"Yes."

"Yes? You know Anita Champion?"

"Yes."

Dylan stared at him in total amazement. Stevie spoke, grunted at least, as if it were the most natural question in the world.

"Have you seen her during the last thirteen years?"

"No."

Stupid question. Of course he hadn't. No one had.

"Did you know her well?"

Stevie seemed to consider the question seriously before answering. "No."

"Did you know her daughter Holly?"

"Yes."

"Did you know her well?"

Again, a long pause before he answered, "No."

For all the surprise Stevie showed, Dylan might have been asking him about the weather. Or perhaps he'd been warned that Dylan was asking questions. And the only person who would warn him would be the one with something to hide.

"What about Yvonne Yates?" Dylan asked. "Do you know her?"

"Yes."

This process would be speeded up considerably if only Stevie would expand on his answers. However, on this cold, wet Thursday morning, Dylan had to be grateful for anything.

"So you know the women Anita went out with the night she disappeared? Yvonne Yates, Maggie Gibson and Brenda Tomlinson?"

"Yes."

"Did you see Anita the night she vanished?" Dylan asked.

"Yes."

"You did? Where?"

Stevie thought for a moment, probably realised that yes or no wouldn't suffice, and rose to his feet. With a grunt and a wave of his hand, he indicated that Dylan should follow him.

There had been a brief shower while they'd been in Asda's cafe but, although the pavements were slick and the air was damp, it wasn't raining as they walked through the car park.

Stevie said nothing as he limped along, and Dylan was too busy thinking to talk.

They cut through two alleyways and walked along Market Street until they turned into Rose Walk and then Pennine Way, close to Dylan's hotel. Stevie stopped outside what had once been Oasis, the nightclub Anita Champion had visited on that last night.

It would have been so much easier for Stevie to simply have told him.

"You saw her here?" Dylan asked. "In the night-club?"

"No."

Stevie tugged on Dylan's sleeve and led the way to the alley at the side of the building. Halfway along, he stopped. He looked ahead, looked back as if judging the distance, then pointed to the ground at his feet.

"She was here?" Dylan asked in amazement.

"Yes."

Dylan had always considered himself a patient man, but Stevie's short answers would soon have him tearing out his hair.

"She was lying down?"

"Yes."

"She was ill, wasn't she? Probably being sick?"

"Sick. Yes."

Two words. With luck, they would soon progress to a whole sentence.

"Did you talk to her?" Dylan asked.

"Yes."

"What did you say? What did she say?"

"Taxi," he replied. "She said taxi."

"She wanted a *taxi*?" Dylan had imagined an ambulance would have been a more apt mode of transport.

"Yes."

"Where to?"

Stevie would have set off again, presumably to show Dylan her intended destination.

"Whoa. Hang on a minute, Stevie, let me get this straight. How long were you with her here?" He pointed at the ground. "Five minutes? Ten? Twenty?" he added to speed things along.

"Thirty," Stevie answered with a shrug that was perhaps intended to convey the word "approximately."

"Right. You spent half an hour with her—while she was being sick?"

"Yes." He pointed at the building. "Water."

"You got her some water?"

"Yes."

"So she drank the water and then wanted a taxi, right? Could she stand at this point?"

"Yes." Stevie hesitated for a moment, then took half a dozen paces, bouncing off one wall and then the other. "Drunk."

"Ah."

Drugged more like.

Stevie gave a sharp pull on Dylan's sleeve and, this time, Dylan followed him to the end of the alley.

Stevie pointed to a spot a hundred yards along the road ahead of them. "Taxi."

Sure enough, there were three cabs waiting on the rank.

"You walked along the alley with her? You helped her to walk along?"

"Yes."

"And you helped her into a taxi—there?"

"Yes."

"Did you go with her?"

"No."

Dylan knew a sudden urge to throw himself under the bus that trundled into view. Why wouldn't Stevie communicate? What the hell? Dylan was no psychiatrist. "Do you know where she was going?"

"Morty's."

"Morty's? Where's that?"

"Gone. Come on." And Stevie set off.

It looked as if Yvonne Yates and her merry band of vipers were in the clear. There *had* been a man in the alley and it seemed that, after all, Anita had been well enough to go on to Morty's.

Odd that Yvonne and her chums hadn't known that. Surely the local coppers would have found out and word would have spread. Perhaps they hadn't. Maybe, they, too, had been content with the idea of Anita Champion abandoning her daughter for a new life.

That was so unlikely though. No one knew of anyone special in her life, and no way would she have gone off with someone she had met that night. Anita Champion might have been all sorts of a fool, but, when it came to men, Dylan would bet she'd been wary. A good time, yes. Commitment, no.

On and on they walked. Had Dylan known the distance involved, he would have insisted they get a taxi. They had walked the length of Dawson's Clough and ended up on the Manchester Road, a wide, busy road with three-storey stone-built terraced houses on either side.

When they reached the end, Stevie pointed. "Morty's."

It was a former mill that had been converted, quite recently by the look of it, into luxury apartments with all the security imaginable. Several expensive vehicles sat in designated parking spots.

"Okay." Enough was enough. If they tried any sort of conversation at Stevie's pace, they would see in next year. "I realise you don't like talking to people, Stevie. I even sympathise. Sometimes, I'd rather not get involved myself. The thing is, though, conversation is a necessary evil. Okay? I need you to tell me all you know about Morty's—and what you know about Anita Champion's movements the night she vanished. Okay?"

Stevie nodded, which wasn't promising.

"The night she went missing," Dylan said, "what happened? You saw her get in a taxi to come here, yes?"

"Yes."

Dylan waited but that was it.

"Did you see her again?"

Stevie shook his head.

"What about her friends? Did you see them?"

Stevie was a long time answering, which meant he was probably wondering how he could condense all he knew into the fewest words possible.

"Leaving Oasis," he said at last. "The Yates woman at eleven o'clock. The other two after midnight."

It was perhaps the longest speech he had ever given.

"Where did they go?"

"Don't know."

Dylan turned his attention to the building in front of them. "What was Morty's?"

"Club. Disco. Drink. Drugs."

"When—?" What was the point? He could easily find out when the place had closed down. It would be quicker than asking Stevie. "Do you know who Anita saw that night?" he asked instead. "Do you know if she was meeting someone?"

"No."

"Did you tell the police she'd come here?"

"No."

"Did they ever speak to you about it?" Dylan asked.

"No." Stevie grinned suddenly to show a couple of gaps in his teeth. "Simple Stevie."

Officers wouldn't have questioned him for two reasons. One, he wouldn't have made a reliable witness. And two, no one would have had the time or the patience.

"Do you know who worked at Morty's?" Dylan asked.

"No."

He couldn't take any more of this. His life was slowly ebbing away.

"Tell you what, Stevie, I'll meet you at Asda tomorrow morning and treat you to breakfast. About ten o'clock?"

"Good."

With that, Stevie limped back toward town with his head down.

It had been a long, frustrating morning, but at least Dylan had made progress. He knew that Anita Champion hadn't met her end in that dark alley by Oasis. Despite being drugged by her so-called friends, she'd been well enough to make it to Morty's.

When Stevie was out of sight, Dylan, too, walked back toward the town centre. Now he didn't mind walking. In fact, he liked it. It aided his thought processes.

He went straight to Dawson's Clough's Library, a small building right in the centre of town, where a bored-looking young woman on the desk sent him in the right direction.

"The reference library is on the first floor. Take the stairs, then the second door on your left. You'll find all the old copies of the newspaper there. Sorry, but we haven't got them onto microfilm yet."

"That's okay. Thanks."

"Or it might be quicker to find what you want on the computer. Any big stories will be on the internet if you do a search."

Dylan had thought of that, but he couldn't imagine the workings of Morty's being newsworthy enough to get on to the internet. It was worth a try, though, and it would be much easier than trawling through old newspapers.

Once signed in and seated in front of a computer, the end one of a row of six, he searched for "Monty's, Dawson's Clough." Several hundred hits were thrown up, and the first told him that apartments on Manchester Road were finally offered for sale in May 2007 following problems with planning permission on the site that had once been Mortimer's, fondly known by local residents as Morty's.

An hour later, he'd discovered that in 2005, following rumours of financial problems, the owner, one Phil Mortimer, had put the club up for sale. Dylan had also gleaned that Stevie had been right about drugs being bandied about the premises.

As for Phil Mortimer, Dylan could find nothing. There were plenty of Philip Mortimers, but whether any of them was the ex-owner of Morty's was anyone's guess. Perhaps he was still in Dawson's Clough running another business. Or perhaps, like Anita Champion, he had vanished.

THAT EVENING DYLAN phoned Holly Champion and, as was usual because of the number of jobs she juggled, had to leave a message. He couldn't imagine being so obsessed with anything that he'd work all the hours God sent simply to pay someone to ask a few questions.

But she was paying for more than that. She wanted him to *find* her mother. He could only do that, though, if Anita had abandoned her daughter for a better life. Holly wouldn't want a result like that.

If he *did* find out what had happened to her mother, what would she do? Her purpose for living would be gone. Would she give up the part-time jobs and stick to teaching? Would she keep working and use her spare cash to finance exotic holidays? Would she still buy her clothes from Oxfam?

Dylan had no idea. He firmly believed, however, that Holly's obsession was unhealthy. If it were him, he'd accept it and move on. Life was too short.

Not that he was in the same position, he thought

grimly. So far today, his phone had registered four missed calls from his mother.

His hotel room was far more spacious than his own bedroom, but the freezing temperature was beyond a joke. He'd spoken to the receptionist and, after apologising profusely, she'd promised to send someone up to check it. Whether anyone had been, he had no idea.

Forgetting the cold for the moment, he lay back on the bed, hands linked behind his head, and thought about Anita Champion.

Why, when she must have been feeling like death, had she taken a taxi to Morty's? To keep a date? In the hope of meeting someone special? Wouldn't the sensible thing have been to write off the evening and go home to her bed?

She didn't strike him as a sensible woman, though. He envisaged her as impulsive, always game for a laugh or an adventure, hopeless with money, a dreamer—

For all that, he also thought of her as loyal to her daughter. Fun-loving, yes, but not to the point of recklessness, not when it came to Holly.

His phone rang. He sat up and, with fingers almost numb from cold, answered Holly's call.

"What do you know about Morty's?" he asked, getting straight to the point.

"Morty's?"

Obviously not a lot.

"It was a nightclub," he said.

"Sorry, but it means nothing to me."

"I believe your mother may have gone there the night she vanished."

"Really?"

He heard the catch of excitement in her voice, the hope that progress was being made.

"It's possible." He didn't want to raise her hopes only to dash them again. "Do you remember a chap called Stevie?"

"Stevie who?"

"Ah." Dylan didn't know his surname. "Once seen never forgotten. They call him Simple Stevie."

"That Stevie. Yes, of course I remember him, poor chap. Why do you ask?"

"He's the one who claims your mother went to Morty's that night."

"I see." Her excitement lessened slightly. "Well, I suppose he could be right, although I can't think his memory would be too reliable."

"What do you know about him?"

"All us kids grew up knowing about Stevie, but I expect the story was exaggerated over the years. Apparently his mother was killed when he was about five years old. She was walking him to school one day when a car mounted the pavement and hit her. It's said she was dragged along the road for a hundred yards. There's worse, too. Because she was holding Stevie's hand, he was dragged with her."

"Dear God!" Dylan shuddered.

"It was awful. Poor Stevie hasn't been right since. Apart from his physical injuries, and I gather his leg was badly crushed, the mental scars are unthinkable. His grandmother and his father brought him up for a while. She was a strict, no-nonsense sort of woman, so I don't believe he saw much love or affection from her. I don't know about his father. I expect he was a bit traumatised, too."

"More than likely."

"Stevie ended up in care eventually."

Dylan felt a rush of sympathy for his new friend. No wonder he didn't speak much.

"I'm surprised Stevie talked about Mum," Holly said. "When I knew him, you couldn't get two words out of him."

"You still can't."

"I think Mum liked him. All us kids called him Simple Stevie and she hit the roof one day. She said we should all thank God we weren't suffering like him and show him a bit of kindness." She sighed. "She was quite right, of course, but you know what kids are. They can be cruel."

"So can adults." Children had the excuse of ignorance. Adults like Bill Thornton and Geoff didn't. "Okay," Dylan said. "If I find out anything else, I'll let you know."

"Thanks, Dylan. I really appreciate all you're doing."

"I haven't got anywhere yet."

"But you will. You're the best."

For a long time after they ended the call, Dylan thought about that. To his wife, he was a drunkard and a loser. As far as the police force was concerned, he was no longer fit for the job because it was believed, on the say of an habitual offender, that he'd used unreasonable force during an arrest.

Yet, for some reason, Holly Champion had faith in him. He only hoped it wasn't misplaced.

Knowing he couldn't put it off any longer, he called his mother.

"Dylan, there you are! I was beginning to worry. I'll

tell you what, though, this flat of yours is growing on me. I've bought some more scented candles today and I'm just arranging them in the bathroom. Really, that's the best room in the flat—"

Dylan lay back on his bed and let her talk. No response was necessary.

CHAPTER FIFTEEN

STEVIE'S HEAD ACHED when he woke up. He was surprised to find himself in bed, and he tried to think how he'd got there and why he was still wearing his clothes.

He couldn't remember.

He tried to decide, unsuccessfully, what day it was. It didn't matter as they were all the same, but he had a notion he was supposed to be somewhere today. Was it today the Council was sending people to fit a new front door?

He got out of bed, put a hand to his aching head, and walked into the hall where he saw a brand new white door. He remembered now. Two men. One big and fat. The other was thin and moved quickly. Stevie had made them a cup of tea.

He put on his anorak and went outside. The best thing was to walk. The doctors had told him that. Said he must keep walking along the road. Said it wouldn't happen again.

He walked along to Market Street where the cars moved slowly. There were so many of them, they had no option but to crawl along. The drivers tapped steering wheels or spoke into mobile phones. Some were smoking, others yawning.

Stevie liked Market Street with its slow-moving traffic. He took a left onto Pringle Street. Cars moved slowly here, too. Some parked outside the newsagent's, causing congestion. Stevie could overtake them easily.

He kept walking until he was on the Manchester Road. The pain in his head increased with the noise of the cars. Here, the cars raced toward the M66 and Manchester. Four rows of cars. Noisy. Powerful. Smelly.

He stopped walking as he remembered. Yesterday—was it yesterday?—he'd walked along this road with the man. They had walked all the way to Morty's. The man had asked him about Anita Champion.

Breakfast. The man had said to meet him at Asda for breakfast.

Stevie cheered up. He didn't have to walk along this road, he had to go to Asda. The man had said so. He mustn't tell the doctors, though.

The man wanted to talk about Anita Champion. Stevie had liked her. She'd been kind to him. Once she'd given him a sandwich. He'd been sitting on one of the benches in Moors Park and she'd come to sit beside him.

"Isn't it a lovely day, Stevie? I wish I didn't have to go back to work this afternoon. I could quite happily sit here all day."

She was always smiling. Talking and laughing, too.

"Do you want a sandwich? Cheese and onion?" She opened a bag and offered him one. "You may as well take one. I won't eat all these."

So he took one of her sandwiches. It was good. Thick crusty bread and slices of cheese with thickly chopped onion, it was delicious. He could remember that. He could remember a lot of things.

"What about you, Stevie? What are you doing today?"

"Walking."

"Oh? That's nice. Where are you going?"

He had no idea. The destination wasn't important. "Doctors say so. Say I must walk by the cars."

"Oh, Stevie, I'm sure they don't mean every day." She had looked appalled. "I expect that was years ago, after the—accident. It'll be like falling off a bike, when they tell you to get straight back on again. It's so you're not afraid to do it."

Stevie wasn't afraid to walk by the cars. It made his head hurt, but that was because of the noise and smell. He wasn't afraid.

He'd stood and brushed a few breadcrumbs from his jeans. The pigeons would be along for those.

"Walking," he'd told Anita, and he'd set off for the main road.

The man wanted to talk to him about Anita Champion, but Stevie couldn't remember. He could remember her getting in the taxi that night, and he could remember walking up to Morty's. He hadn't actually seen her there, though. But he wouldn't have. He must have walked there and straight back. He couldn't remember doing so, but he must have because he could remember her friends—those women—leaving Oasis.

But that was all. The next thing he remembered was waking up in his bed the following day.

He was at Asda's store before nine o'clock. As he took the escalator to the cafe on the first floor, he could smell freshly baked bread. The man wasn't in the cafe, though, so Stevie went outside again.

The trolleys were lined up by the dozen, each chained to the one in front. If they let him walk with one of those, he would be fine. All he would hear was the satisfying, comforting squeak and rumble of the wheels. He wouldn't hear the cars and his head wouldn't hurt so much.

He walked across the car park, back and forth, sometimes using the zebra crossings, occasionally stepping straight between the rows of cars.

"Morning, Stevie!"

"Morning, er—"

"Dylan," the man said. "My name's Dylan Scott. Remember?"

"Dylan."

They walked inside and took the escalator to the cafe.

He liked the man. Dylan. He would remember that.

He liked the breakfast, too. His plate held an egg, two sausages, three rashers of bacon and a portion of mushrooms. On another plate, he had two slices of toast and two individually wrapped chunks of butter.

The man had a pot of tea. "I've had breakfast," he said. "At the hotel. It's included in the cost of the room."

Stevie had never been inside a hotel.

"So," the man said as Stevie tucked in, "have you thought of anything else? Is there anything you've remembered about the night Anita Champion went missing?"

"No." He couldn't remember. He'd tried, but he couldn't.

"What about Morty's? Was there a bouncer working there? Did someone get free drinks for Anita?"

Stevie couldn't remember. No, he was sure he hadn't known anyone who worked there. "No."

"I spoke to Anita's daughter last night, Stevie. You

remember Holly, don't you? She remembers you. She said her mum liked you."

Stevie felt his mouth curl into a smile at that. He couldn't help it.

"Yes." He remembered Holly. It was nice that she said Anita Champion had liked him.

The smile vanished. He wanted to remember, but he couldn't. Anita Champion had got into the taxi, he knew that, and he could remember walking up Manchester Road to Morty's. He must have turned round and walked back into town, but he didn't remember doing so. He could remember seeing those women, three of them, leaving Oasis. One of them, Yvonne Yates, had left early. There had been something wrong between the other two. They had been angry about something.

What had happened, he worried, between the time he walked up to Morty's and the time he was outside Oasis?

"Who used to go to Morty's, Stevie? You must know that. You know Anita Champion went there. You must know others who did."

But Stevie didn't. His breakfast was finished and his head was hurting. He didn't know. Couldn't remember.

He shouldn't be here. He should be walking along the road. The doctors had said so.

"Must walk."

He limped out of the cafe, down the escalator and across the car park.

"Must walk," he reminded himself.

CHAPTER SIXTEEN

AS HE DROVE on the M65 to Blackburn, Dylan wondered why the gods had it in for him. What had he ever done to anyone?

His wife had thrown him out, his mother had moved in, he was penniless—well, he would be if it weren't for Holly Champion's faith in him—and now, as if that lot wasn't enough, he was on his way to meet the copper from hell.

Pikey had phoned him that morning, soon after Stevie's abrupt exit from Asda's cafe.

"You'll never guess," he'd said, laughing.

"Then I won't bother. Out with it."

"The senior investigating officer on the Anita Champion case was none other than your friend and mine—are you ready for this?—Frank Willoughby."

"What? Oh, no. You're kidding me."

"Nope. I knew he hailed from Lancashire—hey, it's a small world, isn't it?"

"Small and full of shit," Dylan groaned. "Of all the coppers in the world—"

"He's retired now so perhaps he's mellowed."

"Fat chance."

"I told him you'd like a word and he was more than happy for me to pass on his number. Said he'd look forward to hearing from you."

"Look forward to kicking me in the bollocks, more like."

Dylan and Pikey had experienced the dubious pleasure of working under D.C.I. Frank Willoughby when he had been sent down to the City on an undercover job. He was a damn good detective, Dylan acknowledged grudgingly, but he was a bastard to work for. Nothing they did was right. Nothing.

Every day had started with a bollocking for some misdemeanour or other. They had all prayed for his stint of duty to end.

"Soft fucking southerners" had been his favourite description of Dylan and Pikey.

There was no getting out of it, though. As he'd been the senior investigating officer on Anita Champion's case, Dylan had to talk to him. For all he knew, they might have gathered all sorts of info.

So he'd phoned him.

"I'll be out for an hour or so," Willoughby had said. "About three would suit me best." He'd given Dylan his address and that had been that. The conversation hadn't been long enough to tell if he had mellowed or not.

With the aid of his sat nav, Dylan found the address fairly easily and stopped his car outside a solid detached house with a huge well-maintained garden. Very nice.

It was precisely three o'clock, so Dylan might earn a Brownie point for punctuality, another of Willoughby's foibles. Either way, he would treat himself to a few pints if he managed to escape with his testicles in the right place.

He walked up the driveway, prodded the doorbell and heard a deep bing-bong echo through the interior.

Then he was face-to-face with Frank Willoughby.

It was getting on for sixteen years since they had worked in the same building, and Dylan was taken aback by the change in the man. He looked much older and, amazingly, almost frail.

"Well, well, well," Frank said. "I never thought I'd see you north of Watford Gap. You'd better come in."

"Thanks." Dylan was led down the hallway, through the kitchen and into a conservatory—heated, thank God—where several newspapers and an empty coffee mug suggested that Frank spent a lot of time in there.

"How are you, Frank?"

"Can't complain. You?"

"About the same."

Frank must be heading toward sixty, Dylan guessed, but he looked older. His skin had a greyish tinge to it. His hair was still the same, though. Short, thick and dark.

"Retirement agreeing with you?" Dylan asked.

"Not particularly, but I had a heart attack a couple of months back, so any sort of work is off the agenda for a while." He gave Dylan a searching look. "Retirement agreeing with you?"

"Not particularly."

"Better than being inside, though?"

"Yeah, better than that."

It had been too much to hope that Willoughby hadn't heard about his spectacular fall from grace and dismissal from the force.

"You're driving so you won't want a proper drink, will you? Fancy a cup of tea?"

"That would be great. Thanks."

While Frank clattered around in the kitchen, Dylan admired the view of the hills from the conservatory.

"Nice spot," he said when Frank put the tea things on a wicker table.

"It is, yes. Now, sit yourself down."

"Thanks."

"Pikey seems to be doing well for himself," Frank said.

"So it seems, yes."

"He's a good copper."

Sixteen years ago, Pikey had been another soft fucking southerner, but Dylan refrained from saying so.

"He tells me you're looking into the disappearance of Anita Champion," Frank went on.

"I am, yes. Her daughter's asked me to see what I can find out. I'm surprised that more wasn't done at the time."

"There was no money. Isn't that what it always comes down to?"

"Not where you're concerned, no." The copper Dylan remembered wouldn't have let a minor detail like resources affect an investigation.

"A month later, a child was abducted," Frank said. "We were busy working on that. It was more important than chasing a grown woman across the country."

There were two large slices of what looked to be homemade fruit cake on the tray, and Dylan helped himself to one.

"Is that what you thought? That she was swanning around the countryside?"

Frank let out his breath. "Not really."

His answer surprised Dylan. "So what *did* you think?"

"We all hoped she would turn up, obviously. But there was no evidence of foul play, none at all, so there was nothing we could do, was there? Besides, we launched a massive search for Janice Bright, the missing child, so we would have found a body if there'd been one to find."

"Not if the perp had buried her in his cellar." Dylan took another bite of cake. It was heavy and moist, just the way he liked it. He'd skipped lunch, too, so he was starving.

"And whose cellar should we have searched?" Frank asked. "She had no enemies. There was nothing to suggest she hadn't just taken off."

"Leaving her daughter behind?"

Frank shrugged at that. "What have you learnt so far?"

"What makes you think a fucking soft southerner like me has learnt anything?"

Frank smiled at that. "Even soft southerners make good coppers. Sometimes."

"This one didn't. This one was dismissed from the force."

"Yeah, I know. And I was sorry to hear it. Really sorry."

Dylan's head flew up. He'd imagined Frank would think a filthy cell the best place for him.

"I've arrested dozens of scumbags in my time, Dylan, and they don't take kindly to it. I could have been in the same situation myself, many times. Any copper could."

"Thanks. I appreciate that." He did. More than Frank could know.

"Come on, then. Tell me what you've got so far."

"Probably nothing. How about you tell me what you know?"

Frank smiled like an experienced hand indulging a young rookie. "I know we weren't called in until over a week after she went missing."

"Why was that?"

"Because everyone, her daughter included, assumed she'd met up with someone—a man—and would return when it suited her."

"Her daughter was only eleven!"

"Yes, I know." Frank put his hands together and rested the tips of his fingers beneath his chin. "So what do I know? I know she went out with friends, as she often did on Saturday nights. They started at the Commercial, went on to Oasis and then split up—as they often did—and, although she was seen dancing with a couple of unidentified men at the club, she was never seen again." He shrugged a little sheepishly. "As I said, we were busy with other things. We put out an appeal for information, but nothing came of it."

"So you closed the case? Just like that?"

"Of course not. The case is still open, but you can't follow leads that aren't there. She was a grown woman, Dylan. We made sure her daughter was okay. That was our main priority." He leaned forward and picked up his cup of tea. "So what have you found out?"

"Anita Champion slept her with her employer's boyfriend, one Eddie Swift. To teach her a lesson, the other girls—and I imagine Sandra, her employer was behind it—put something in her drink. God knows what. One of her friends, Brenda Tomlinson, was a nurse at the time so, presumably she could have got hold of anything. She's on holiday so I haven't managed to speak to her yet. Anyway, this had the desired effect and Anita was later seen by two of those friends throwing up in the alley outside Oasis. They heard a man go to her aid and then they scarpered.

"The man, Stevie—God, I still don't know his surname. He's a few pence short of a shilling and they call him Simple Stevie. According to him, he stayed with her for half an hour, got her some water from the club, and then walked with her to the taxi rank. He saw her get in the taxi and he knows she was intending to go to Morty's. Morty's was a—"

"Shit hole," Frank said. "We used to get called out to that place most weeks."

"Mm. Anyway, that's the last time she was seen as far as I can tell. But I've only just found out about that, so I'm going to find—or try to find—people who worked there."

"Right."

"Eddie Swift reckoned that a bouncer at a nightclub used to get free drinks for Anita."

"I'm impressed." Frank nodded at the other piece of fruit cake. "You have that. I'm supposed to be watching my weight."

Dylan was more interested in Anita Champion, but he was also starving, so he grabbed the cake.

Frank, meanwhile, left the room for a few moments and returned with a phone. He tapped in a number, then had a good chat with his caller.

Dylan's patience was about to expire when he heard Frank say, "Tell me, mate, what was the name of that bouncer at Morty's? The big ugly bugger we arrested?… Ah, yes, that's it…Can you think of anyone else who worked there?…Oh?…Did he indeed?"

When the call ended, Frank returned the phone to

the other room and came back with a pen and paper in his hand.

"Now then." He wrote quickly. "Colin Bates was a bouncer at Morty's. Ugly sod. We had him on an ABH charge. The bloke who did the disco for years was a flash prat by the name of Sean Ellis. He was crap at his job, but got to keep it because the ladies liked him. And, of course, you'll know that Phil Mortimer owned the place?"

"Yes."

"He and his wife run a nursing home now." Frank grimaced at the notion. "There must be more profit in waiting for death."

Dylan took the paper from him. "Thanks for that, Frank, I appreciate it. I owe you."

"You owe me nothing, lad. But you'll keep me informed, will you? It'll give the old grey cells—" he tapped his head, "—something to work on."

He was lonely, Dylan realised with a jolt. What about the attractive wife they'd met once? Who was baking fruit cake? "How's your wife?"

"Ex-wife. Married three times, divorced three times. Not a great track record, is it? How's your wife?"

"Bev's fine." Dylan's reply was automatic. "Well, to be honest, she's throwing one of her wobblers at the moment. She'll come round, she always does, but in the meantime, it's a damn pain. You know what it's like, Frank."

"I should do." Frank sighed.

"Don't tell me you've put your hand to baking."

"Ha. That's Esme, my next door neighbour. She's taken to mothering me since the heart attack. But don't worry, fending her off gives me something to do."

Dylan was surprised to find himself liking Frank Willoughby. Who would have believed that? Retirement and a heart attack had softened his one-time boss. Or perhaps Frank had always been a likeable sort of bloke. He'd been hard on his underlings, but perhaps that went with the job.

"There's something else," Dylan said.

"Oh?"

"This." Dylan took the photo of Anita Champion and Terry Armstrong from his pocket and handed it over.

"Christ! Where the hell did you get this?"

"From her daughter. It was taken four weeks before Anita vanished. The first of November, to be precise. Holly bought a copy from the local paper."

"Taken where?" Frank asked.

"Dawson's Clough. The Town Hall. It was a charity dinner. I've no idea how Anita came to be there, though. No idea how Armstrong came to be there either, come to that. I've looked it up in the local paper but there's no mention of either of them."

"Armstrong's wife came from round here," Frank said. "She's as hard as he is, but she likes to be seen to be doing the right thing. They've been living here for about eight years now. Maybe it got too hot down in the smoke for him. Maybe he's content to reap the rewards now."

"Hmm."

"But how the hell did someone like Anita Champion come to be with an evil bastard like him?" Frank didn't wait for an answer. "You'll do well to look very closely at Terry Armstrong."

"I intend to."

One thing was certain, if Armstrong's name had

come to light during the original investigation, Lancashire Constabulary would have found the resources for a very thorough inquiry.

"So how are you liking Lancashire?" Frank asked as he was showing him out.

"It's okay. Beautiful in parts. It's just—"

"The bloody awful weather." Frank chuckled. "Always raining."

"Yeah."

"Ah, well, we're all waterproof." He nodded at Dylan's car. "Very nice."

"I restored it myself. So far—" he touched the wooden trellis on the wall, "—it hasn't missed a beat."

"Good for you!"

Dylan suddenly felt awkward, and he had no idea why that was. "Well, thanks again for your help, Frank. I'll let you know if I find out anything else."

"I'd like that. I'm usually here. You have my number anyway."

"I have." Dylan shook hands with him and then walked smartly to his car.

He fired the engine and took off without a backward glance. There was something sad, even a little pathetic, about ex-D.C.I. Frank Willoughby that unsettled him. Perhaps it was the knowledge that, unless he did something constructive with his life, Dylan would end up exactly the same.

CHAPTER SEVENTEEN

MOORSIDE RESIDENTIAL HOME stood at the end of a long curving driveway. A large stone building, it was a couple of miles from Dawson's Clough, alone on top of the hill and, even on a damp Monday morning, looked impressive.

Dylan yawned as he drove into the car park. He'd had an early start that morning and hadn't slept particularly well over the weekend.

In fact, apart from the six hours he'd spent with Luke, having a few laughs at the bowling alley, his weekend had been a waste of time.

Instead of getting his washing done, he'd sifted through the papers Holly had given him. Most of it appeared to be junk, but there were two old and often-handled Valentine's Day cards, both signed *Guess who?* in the same hand, which intrigued him. Dylan wished he *could* guess.

There were cinema ticket stubs, old lottery tickets, a bookmark made by Holly, dental appointments card, magazine cuttings. Dylan had been through it all a dozen times looking for clues…

There were several vehicles in the car park and Dylan pulled up between a gleaming Mercedes and a black Porsche. Ending your days at Moorside wouldn't be a cheap option, Dylan presumed, so the cars might have belonged to relatives. And if this *was* a highly profitable venture, as Frank Willoughby believed, Phil Mortimer would be able to afford the best.

He walked into a thickly carpeted reception area where a young girl in a spotless white uniform looked up and gave him a bleached white smile.

"Hello, there, I was wondering if I might see Mr. Mortimer for a couple of minutes."

Dylan hadn't wanted to phone in advance because he preferred to catch people unawares. Given time, they perfected their stories. However, it was a hit-and-miss way to operate, and often resulted in Dylan being told the person in question had just left for a fortnight's holiday.

"Is he expecting you?"

"No, but as I only need a couple of minutes—"

"Just a minute, Mr.—?"

"Scott. Dylan Scott."

Still smiling as if she were auditioning for a toothpaste commercial, she lifted the receiver, waited a moment and then said, "Phil, a Mr. Dylan Scott would like to talk to you. May I send him through?" A pause. "Thank you."

She replaced the receiver and emerged from behind her desk. "This way, Mr. Scott."

Dylan was led along a hallway where large black-and-white photographs adorned the walls. One he recognised as *The Singing, Ringing Tree*, Burnley's stunning panopticon, a sculpture of galvanised steel pipes that sat high above the town on Crown Point. Another was of Lancaster Town Hall.

His companion knocked on a door and Dylan was ushered into Mortimer's office. Easy peasy, he decided with satisfaction.

"Thanks for your time." He shook the man's hand. "I'm not trying to book a place here," he added in a jokey manner, "but I'd like to pick your memory, if I may."

"We're fully booked for the foreseeable future, so that's just as well. As for my memory, that's passable. How can I help?"

Judging by the excess flab around his girth, Phil Mortimer lived well and spent too much time sitting in his chair. He was mid-fifties with dark hair turning to grey, and a scar close to his left eye. His stomach hung over grey trousers and his white shirt strained at the buttons. There was a gold chain (expensive) around his neck and a chunky Rolex (*very* expensive) on his wrist.

After a brief hesitation, Dylan decided to trot out the somewhat well-worn story of the antique ring. It made him look like a love-struck fool so people opened up more. If he said he was working on the case for a client, it would be too official. People would be wary.

He rattled off his story, watching Mortimer's eyebrows rise higher with each word.

"I need to know what happened to that ring," he finished. "And to do that, I have to know what happened to Anita Champion."

"Gosh." Phil Mortimer leaned back in his executive leather chair, hands linked behind his head. "I haven't thought of Anita in years."

"You knew her well?"

"Not as well as I would have liked to," he said with a wink.

"She was something, wasn't she?" Dylan injected an air of wistfulness into his own voice.

"Stunning. The men fell at her feet, and the women stabbed her in the back at every opportunity."

Not literally, Dylan hoped. "I've been asking around, and I believe she went to your club on the night she vanished. Is that right?"

"Really? I couldn't say. It's possible, of course. We're talking—what?—ten, twelve years ago?"

"Thirteen. It was the twenty-ninth of November, 1997."

"Was it really? How time flies."

"Did the police ask questions at your club at the time?"

"Not as far as I can remember. They put an appeal on TV and the local papers mentioned it, but, no, I don't recall them asking about her at the club. Presumably, if anyone had seen her there that night, or anywhere else for that matter, they would have told the police."

"Presumably, yes. But you don't remember her being there that night?"

"Sorry." He shook his head. "Mind you, I couldn't say for sure if I was there that night. I had good staff so I wasn't there every night."

"I see. Yes, someone said she was friendly with the staff—well, the DJ, Sean Ellis, and one of the bouncers, Colin Bates."

"Bates?" Mortimer rolled his eyes. "I fired him. It soon became apparent that he enjoyed his job too much. Short on brain, but handy with his fists."

"Do you recall Anita being friendly with him?"

"I can't say I do. No."

"What about the DJ, Sean Ellis?"

"A born flirt." Mortimer smiled. "He was good for business. The ladies loved him. He could charm honey from bees when he tried." He winked again, which Dylan found slightly disconcerting. "I expect Anita was friendly with him all right. Not that I ever heard anything."

"Is he still in Dawson's Clough?"

"He is. Not that you'd recognise him these days. The charm's gone, I'm afraid. Knocked out of him by a blonde who managed to drag him to the altar. Has half a dozen kids now and spends all his time propping up the bar at the Red Lion."

Dylan knew the pub. He'd spent an hour in there. Alone. He would have to call again and meet up with Sean Ellis.

"Who *did* Anita spend time with at the club?" he asked.

"You'd make a good policeman." Again Mortimer spoke in that false, jokey manner of his.

"I used to be one."

"Oh?"

"Yes." Dylan wasn't going into detail. "Which would make you think I could find Anita, but I'm drawing a blank. I'd be grateful for names."

"I wish I could give you some." Mortimer shook his head. "Sorry, but I can't think of anyone. People went there, usually when the pubs closed, and either stayed or moved on. They chatted, they drank, they danced—"

"Took drugs?"

Mortimer's good mood dropped a notch. "A few might have. You try to run a clean place, but there are always a couple who get through the net."

"Of course. Do you remember the last time you spoke to Anita?"

"Yes. It was when she cut my hair. That must have been three or four weeks before she did her disappearing act because I turned up at the shop expecting a trim, only to be told that she hadn't shown for a week."

"Were you surprised?"

"Well, yes, of course. She was totally irresponsible, but she'd never pulled a stunt like that before. I assumed she'd see sense and return home." He shrugged. "She never did, though. Now—well, who knows? She could be anywhere."

"Dead or alive." Dylan watched the other man's expression carefully.

"Gosh, yes, I suppose she might even be dead now," Mortimer said as if the thought had struck him for the first time.

"Or she could be soaking up the sun in the Caribbean."

"Far more Anita's style."

Dylan stood up. "Thanks for your time, Mr. Mortimer. I appreciate it."

"You're more than welcome." Mortimer also rose to his feet to shake Dylan's hand. "I'm sorry I can't help."

"Don't worry about it. It was a long shot anyway." He indicated the room in general. "This must be a change for you after the club. Quite a career change."

"Not really. My wife was a nurse, so with my management experience it was an obvious choice."

"Ah, I see. Well, thanks again."

Dylan left the room and deliberately headed toward the double doors at the end of the hallway. He found himself in a day room where several residents gazed at a large-screen television. Waiting for God, Dylan thought.

Still, there had to be worse places to wait. As these homes went, Moorside was the height of luxury.

He had a good look round on the way out, but it didn't help. What had he expected? To see Anita Champion watching the latest Hollywood blockbuster?

No. People like Anita, people with spirit, wouldn't last five minutes in this place. She might be dead or alive, but she wasn't the type to wait for God. She would have to be dragged, fighting all the way, to her celestial resting place.

THE RED LION was worse than Dylan remembered. Judging by the decor, the pub hadn't seen a lick of paint or a duster since the smoking ban became law.

On this visit, he wasn't the only customer though. A couple in their late sixties were sitting at a table in a dingy corner saying nothing. They simply sat and gazed ahead, occasionally drinking.

The other plus point was the price of the beer. It was almost fifty pence a pint cheaper than the other pubs in Dawson's Clough. Even that wasn't pulling in the customers, though. Unsurprisingly, there were no guest ales and certainly no Black Sheep on offer.

Dylan had almost finished his pint and was unsure if he could face a second when another customer came in.

"Sean," the barmaid greeted him. "Thought you were giving us a miss tonight. The usual?"

"Yeah, a pint of your finest, Beryl."

Was this Sean Ellis? Anita Champion would be forty-three now, and this man looked to be around the same age. Maybe a couple of years older.

He was running to fat. Even his face looked pale and

bloated. Tight black jeans were held up with a thick black leather belt. On top was a blue sweater and a black jacket that was shiny at the elbows. Two earrings, small gold hoops, dangled from one ear.

Dylan emptied his glass, walked up to the bar to stand beside him and ordered another pint.

His companion meanwhile was already halfway down his drink.

Dylan stared at him until he had his attention.

"Sorry," he said, "but do I know you? There's something familiar—"

"I don't think so, mate."

"I'm sure I recognise you. Mind, it's probably from ages ago. I spent a fair bit of time in Dawson's Clough about fourteen or fifteen years ago."

"Oh?" His companion looked more closely. "Ever go to a club called Morty's?"

Dylan slapped a hand to his forehead. "That's it! You were the DJ there!"

"Sean Ellis." He nodded and almost broke into a smile.

"You were good. Damn good."

"Yeah, well." The smile broke through.

"I had some great times at Morty's," Dylan said. "I bet you'd remember the girl I was seeing at the time—well, not seeing as much of as I wanted to, if you get my drift. Anita Champion."

"Anita? Christ, yeah, I remember her all right."

Everyone did. Yet no one seemed interested in where she was now. "Actually, that's why I'm back in Dawson's Clough. I'm trying to find her. Or her daughter."

"Haven't you heard? Did a runner, Anita did."

"I heard about that, yes."

"She's not been seen or heard of for years. Ten years probably."

"Thirteen."

"Yeah, probably."

"Can I get you a drink?" Dylan asked.

"Sure. Anyone can get me a drink. I'm not proud. Thanks." He swigged the last dregs from his glass and banged it on the counter. "Beryl, how about we have some music? It's like a bloody graveyard in here."

Beryl obliged by hitting the button on an old CD player, and the Pogues began belting out "Bottle of Smoke."

"That's more like it." Sean tapped his hands on the bar in approval.

Dylan paid for their drinks and was wondering how best to bring the conversation back to Anita when Sean spoke.

"Anita Champion. Christ, I haven't thought of her in years. They don't make 'em like that any more."

"They don't."

"We had some fun, me and her."

"Oh?"

"Yeah."

Dylan waited but Sean had been transported to a better place.

"She dumped me for some other bloke," Dylan said at last. "Perhaps that was you?"

"Nah." Sean took a long swallow of beer. "She were—oh, about eighteen when me and her got it together. I weren't her first bloke, neither. God, she could drive a bloke insane with that body of hers."

"Don't I know it." Dylan wondered about the Valentine's Day cards that Anita had kept for years. "Together long, were you?"

"No. It were just—well, when we fancied a bit of the other, if you know what I mean."

Dylan nodded.

"Mind," Sean said, "that were my choice, not hers. I weren't a one-woman bloke. Couldn't see any sense in that. I mean, I like listening to the Pogues, but that don't mean I don't want to hear a bit of the Killers now again. D'you get my drift?"

"Absolutely. She seemed the same, though. She could pick and choose. I never got the impression she wanted to settle down."

"Not with you maybe. She'd have married me all right."

Would she? Or was Sean Ellis all talk?

"Have you never married then?" Dylan asked.

"Yeah, I got married all right. She were pregnant so I had to do the decent thing, didn't I?" He nudged Dylan and grinned. "Not that I'm saying I'm a one-woman bloke, mind. As I told you, I can't see much sense in that."

Dylan could see sense in it. And if Sean Ellis had been married to Bev, he would have seen the sense in it, too. Fortunately, Dylan had never wanted to stray, but he couldn't even begin to imagine Bev's reaction if he had.

Dylan *was* a one-woman man. Which was why he was struggling to cope with this strop Bev was throwing. Many men would have taken it as an open invitation to find pleasure elsewhere. They would have a grand old time tasting forbidden fruit until it was time to go home. Not Dylan.

"She—Anita, that is—mentioned something to me once about that property owner, Terry Armstrong. Do you remember him?"

"His name's in the paper sometimes." Ellis frowned. "What did she say about him?"

"I can't remember exactly. It was enough to make me think that she and him might be having an affair or something."

"It can't have been the same Terry Armstrong. He's only been here for six or seven years."

"Eight. But I gather he used to visit the area before he lived here."

"Yeah? Perhaps she did know him then."

"It's probably nothing."

"She were hard to resist," Ellis said.

Dylan could believe that it would take a stronger man than Terry Armstrong to turn her down. "You never heard anything? Never saw them together?"

"God, no. I never heard of the bloke till he came up here and started buying up loads of houses."

"As I said, it was probably nothing."

"The bloke's worth millions." Ellis sounded envious. "That's what happens though. Money goes to money."

It does when you'll do anything—including having people killed—to attract it. "Seems to."

"Her daughter," Ellis said, "Anita's daughter, I mean, went off with Anita's sister. They lived down south, I reckon."

"Yes, I heard that."

"I bet she's a looker now, too."

Oh yes, Holly Champion was a looker. She had the same features as her mother, and yet there was something missing. Holly usually looked serious, whereas her mother had laughed a lot, enjoyed life to the full. It was her devil-may-care attitude that had added to Anita's attraction.

"I heard," Dylan said, "that Anita was in your club the night she vanished. In Morty's."

"She were." Ellis stared into what was left of his pint, which wasn't much, presumably thinking back to that evening. "She were as pissed as a fart." He grinned at the memory. "I mean, she were usually drunk at the end of an evening, but that night she were totally out of it."

"Oh?"

"Yeah. Odd, now I come to think of it. She were really hammered, yet I don't remember seeing her look happier. She were excited. Real excited."

"Was she?"

"Yeah. I remember that. Mind, she only stopped for a quick word—requested a record, can't think which one—and then went off to dance with some lucky bastard."

"Did you recognise him?"

"Nope."

"Did you see her later in the evening?"

"I caught a glimpse of her a couple of times, but nothing more."

"The lucky bastard she was dancing with, did she seem to know him well?"

Ellis laughed at that. "How could you tell? She were draped all over him, but that weren't unusual. Besides, she could hardly stand, so she'd have to lean on him a bit."

At least Stevie had been right. Anita *had* been at Morty's that night.

Dylan found it comforting to hear that she'd been happy. Excited even. Perhaps, after all, she *had* taken off for a better life.

"So you never saw Terry Armstrong at Morty's?" Dylan asked.

"No." He downed his beer. "He has a place in the States, you know. Can't blame him, can you? If you had money, would you hang around here?"

"Probably not."

Dylan had learned all he was going to from Sean Ellis so, after buying the man another drink, he left.

That was okay, though. At least he knew Anita had been at Morty's. He was still on her trail.

She'd been excited. And Ellis had said he'd never seen her look happier. Why?

CHAPTER EIGHTEEN

MAGGIE HADN'T SLEPT properly for several nights, ever since Dylan Scott had called on her, in fact. When she did fall into a restless sleep, her dreams were disturbing. In one, Anita had been waving to her. In another, a policeman had been standing behind her and, when she'd spun around to look, it had been Dylan Scott.

Ron had been asking her what was wrong, but she hadn't been able to tell him. Instead, she'd invented excuses about being too cold to sleep. Mind, that wasn't a real lie. The temperatures had dropped, an easterly wind had sprung up, and every forecaster was predicting heavy snowfalls.

Anita was a ghost from her past, and she saw no need to dump any of that on Ron. He was a quiet, easy-going chap who wouldn't understand how she had escaped her brutal pig of a husband every Saturday night for a few drinks and some laughs with the girls. He wouldn't understand that, compared to Dave's violent temper, the girls' outrageous behaviour had been a welcome relief.

She couldn't say she had ever really enjoyed their company, but their high spirits had brought some warmth into her cold life. They had been daring, they'd flirted with all and sundry, and Maggie had suffered endless teasing from them. Maggie the Mouse, they had called her to her face. Much worse to her back, she suspected.

Yet she had been too grateful to step out of her real life for a few hours to care.

Ironically, the only one she had come close to liking had been Anita.

Sandra had been loud and hard, always boasting about her ability to "train" her men. She'd been forever telling Maggie that she must face up to Dave. "Christ, girl, you've got a bloody frying pan, haven't you? Hit the bastard with that!" Sandra hadn't trained Eddie, though, had she? He'd jumped into bed with Anita at the first opportunity.

Yvonne had been okay on the rare occasions she was sober. She was everyone's friend until their back was turned. Then, the cruel insults flew. She had been vain, probably still was, and Maggie shuddered to recall the tantrum she'd thrown when Anita had turned up one Saturday night wearing an identical dress. Of course, the fact that Anita could have wowed the catwalk in a bin bag had only fuelled Yvonne's anger. Anita had always been the one to turn heads and Yvonne had hated that.

As for Brenda, Maggie had loathed her. There was a cruel streak stamped right through her like Blackpool Rock.

She had once nursed Maggie's elderly neighbour through his last days and had moaned to Maggie about him "always pissing himself when I'm on duty." The poor man had been terminally ill, for God's sake. She was a nurse, what did she expect? Mr. Johnson had been a kind, friendly, independent man who had deserved her respect, deserved to end his days with dignity.

Maggie had loathed Brenda for such cruelty. She wouldn't allow her to nurse a dog.

In fact, she wished to God she had never got involved with any of them.

Now, she couldn't stop thinking about that man, Dylan Scott. She couldn't quite believe the story he'd given her about having a fling with Anita. Anita had never mentioned him. Jewellery had been her passion, and if a man had given her a valuable ring, or a cheap one come to that, she would have flaunted it.

Could it be that Dylan Scott was a police officer trying to catch them out? Were they, after all these years, under suspicion?

Maggie had torn up his phone number but she could call the Pennine Hotel. Even if he'd checked out, they would pass on a message.

Did she want to talk to him, though?

If she got it off her chest, she might sleep better. And really, she'd done nothing wrong. She had panicked, as had Brenda, but that was all.

He would ask why they hadn't called for an ambulance, and Maggie had no answer to that. How she wished she'd behaved differently thirteen years ago. She hadn't, though. Maggie the Mouse had gone along with it all, as she always had.

CHAPTER NINETEEN

EARLY ON WEDNESDAY morning Dylan was driving toward Blackburn and Brenda Tomlinson's home. According to her neighbour, she and her husband should have returned from Corfu yesterday.

It was a bitterly cold day with snow flurries blowing in on an easterly wind. At least it made a change from rain, and it was very picturesque where the snow had settled.

Dylan didn't think he would learn anything new from Brenda, but it wouldn't hurt to have a chat. And of the three women who had been with Anita on that last night, Brenda had to be the most interesting. It was she, after all, who had allegedly procured the drugs.

By the time he pulled up outside her house, a blizzard was blowing. It stung his eyes as he dashed for the front door.

"Yes?" A hefty woman with bleached hair and wearing mock combats answered his ring.

"Mrs. Tomlinson?"

"Yes?"

"I'm sorry to bother you," Dylan said, "but I've been talking to friends of yours, Yvonne Yates and Maggie Gibson. It was Yvonne who gave me your address."

"Oh?" She looked as friendly as a seriously pissed-off Rottweiler.

"Yes, it's a long story, I'm afraid, but I'm trying to find Anita Champion. Or her daughter."

Despite her time beneath the Corfu sun, her face turned the colour of the snow that gusted into her hallway. She looked down at it. Then she looked up and down the road, presumably checking to see if any of her neighbours were watching the exchange.

"You'd better come in," she said. He had expected the door to be slammed in his face. Judging by her scowl, it wasn't only a door she wanted to slam in his face.

"Thanks." He wiped his shoes on the mat and followed her into the kitchen, where a noisy washing machine was in full spin mode.

She hit the Off button and the machine juddered to a stop.

"I really am sorry to bother you," Dylan said again, "but I need to find Anita and you're my last hope. As I said, I've spoken to Yvonne and Maggie, but they can't help."

"I can't, either." Her eyes were blue and cold, like chips of ice.

"I thought not." He smiled. "Now, the last time you saw her, she was lying in the alley at the side of Oasis. Is that right?"

Outrage registered on her face but was quickly masked. He could see her mind ticking over. Why had the idiots told him about that?

"That's right. She never could hold her drink."

"I gather you were the one who obtained the—well, whatever it was that made her ill?"

"Look, I don't know who the hell you are, but I think you should leave."

"It's okay." Dylan held his hands in front of him in a

placatory manner. "I'm not bothered about that—I just wondered if you'd heard from her since, or if you know where I might find her daughter."

"I've no idea where she went—where either of them went." This came through thin red lips.

"I've heard there was a man about—when Anita was lying in the alley," Dylan said. "Is that right?"

"Yes."

"You've no idea who that was?"

"No."

"I'd like to find him. Presumably, he stayed with her until she was well enough to go home—or go somewhere—under her own steam?"

Brenda Tomlinson simply shrugged.

"How long would that have been, do you think?" Dylan asked. "What did you give her? I mean, was it fast-acting? Long-lasting?"

"Are you a copper?"

"Good God, no." Dylan laughed at the very notion. "I'm just a damned idiot who fell for Anita. One of the many. I was stupid enough to give her a ring, one that wasn't mine to give. I need to find her."

As he'd hoped, she relaxed slightly.

"I don't care what you did to her that night," he said. "Believe me, she's not my favourite person."

She let out her breath. "I was nursing back then and we wanted to teach her a lesson—"

"Because she'd been fooling around with Sandra's boyfriend?"

"Yeah. Well, it was easy for me. I got a couple of laxative tablets and we put those in her drink. They gave you the shits, of course, but they were safe enough. They just made you sick if you mixed them with alcohol."

"I see."

"She'd have been okay within a couple of hours."

"Unless she had a medical condition you didn't know about, I suppose?"

"She had the constitution of a horse. She could eat like a pig and never put any weight on."

Unlike Brenda, who looked as if she just ate like a pig.

"Ah, well." Dylan smiled genially. "You'll have nothing to worry about then."

"Nothing at all. We slipped something in her drink, that's all. That's not a crime, is it?"

"Actually, yes, it is."

"It didn't hurt her. If it had, she'd have been found in that alley, wouldn't she? Now, if there's nothing else—"

"Thank you. You've been most helpful."

As Dylan walked back to his car, he shuddered. It was difficult to believe there were such women in the world.

He would stake his life on Yvonne Yates and Maggie Gibson having spent all these years worrying about Anita's fate. He very much doubted if Brenda Tomlinson had spared her a second thought.

Either way, Dylan had no intention of putting her mind at rest by letting her know that Anita had been well enough to get to Morty's.

DYLAN WENT STRAIGHT back to Dawson's Clough and his hotel.

"There's a message for you, Mr. Scott." The receptionist handed over his key and a square of paper.

Dylan's first thought was Bev. His spirits soared as he

imagined a reconciliation, then plunged as he panicked about Luke being involved in an accident. The message wasn't from Bev, though. Of course it wasn't. She would have called his mobile.

Instead, Maggie Gibson had tried to contact him. She had asked him to phone her before five-thirty today or between eight-thirty and five-thirty tomorrow.

Dylan was curious and, as it was a little after twelve, he called the number she'd left.

"Ah, Mr. Scott." She sounded nervous. "I wondered if you'd discovered anything? About Anita, I mean?"

"Nothing at all. I don't suppose you've remembered anything—?"

"Can we meet?"

"Of course." Now, Dylan was really intrigued.

"Are you at the hotel? I could be there in twenty minutes."

"Yes, of course." Before he could say more, the connection was cut.

Dylan spent most of those minutes gazing out his window at the now steadily falling snow. It was years since he'd seen real snow. If it was snowing at home, he and Luke could build a snowman. But that was unlikely. Snow fell on the Pennines. It avoided London.

He was beginning to feel affection for this part of east Lancashire, and that surprised him. It was very much a what-you-see-is-what-you-get sort of place. No airs. No pretence.

He loitered in reception for a couple of minutes, looking at tourist brochures and deciding he'd pay Towneley Hall a visit before he left the area, and when Maggie Gibson walked through the hotel's revolving entrance door, he was there to meet her.

"Would you like to go through to the lounge?" he asked. "We can have tea or coffee?"

She nodded, but looked nervous. "Tea would be nice."

Dylan escorted her to the lounge, saw her seated in a sofa by the window, and went to the bar to order tea for two.

When he returned, she had removed her coat. Today she was wearing black trousers and a blue blouse. It was easy to picture her in Wellington boots, though, and hard to imagine her hitting the town with the likes of Anita Champion, Yvonne Yates and Brenda Tomlinson. She must have been like the sparrow among the birds of paradise.

"You have me intrigued," he said as he sat opposite her.

She gave him a long, appraising look. "Are you a policeman?"

"You're the second person to ask me that today. No, I'm not a policeman."

She visibly sagged with relief.

"The first person was your friend, Brenda Tomlinson."

She said nothing, but the expression on her face told Dylan that they weren't friends. He wondered if they ever had been.

"What did she tell you?" she asked.

A young Polish girl brought the tea to their table.

"Milk and sugar?" Dylan asked.

"Just milk, please."

Dylan poured, put a cup of tea in front her, and leaned back in his chair. "Brenda couldn't tell me anything."

"I don't suppose she could." There was heavy sarcasm

in her words. "She was a nurse back then, as you probably know. A cruel nurse who cared nothing for her patients. Not that that's relevant. Anyway, Sandra found out that Anita and her boyfriend—that's Sandra's boyfriend—had, well, you know. So Brenda came up with the idea of making Anita pay. Like I said, she was cruel. So when we all got to Oasis that night, Brenda put something in Anita's drink."

Dylan said nothing.

"Within—well, certainly within the hour, Anita was complaining of a bad headache and nausea. Yvonne went home at that point, but I stayed because—" She attempted to lift her cup but her hands were shaking too much. "I suggested to Anita that she go outside for a breath of air. I went with her."

"Go on," Dylan said.

"I sat with her for a while, and she said she felt a bit better. She still had a headache, though, and I said we ought to call a doctor. But Anita didn't want to make a fuss so we went back inside." She let out her breath. "Brenda had a go at me for fussing over her. She said that, if I told Anita what she'd put in her drink, there would be worse, much worse, put in mine."

"Having met her, that doesn't surprise me."

"Yes, well, Anita felt better and had another drink. Then she felt nauseous again and I went outside with her again. She couldn't stand—God, I was terrified. I ran into the club to tell Brenda. She insisted there was nothing to worry about but agreed to have a look at her."

Her hands were still shaking, but she managed to pick up her cup this time and take a small sip before returning it to the safety of the saucer.

"We were walking up to her when we heard someone—it was a man's voice and he was saying something to Anita. Brenda grabbed my arm and pulled me back to the club. All the while, she was threatening me, telling me that I should keep my mouth shut."

"I see."

"I did," Maggie said. "I've kept my mouth shut ever since. But that was the last time any of us saw Anita, and I've always wondered—"

"If you'd killed her?" Dylan said, and she nodded, her skin as white as the porcelain cup on which she fixed her gaze.

"I should have gone to the police," she whispered. "I know that, but I was too scared."

"Of the police or Brenda?"

"I know how it sounds, but Brenda mostly. At the time, you see, I was married to a drunken bully. She'd threatened to tell him I was seeing someone else. He'd already put me in hospital twice, and I couldn't face—I just couldn't face it."

Dylan lifted his own cup and slowly, thoughtfully, drank his tea. Perhaps he could put her out of her misery. "The man you heard was Stevie—oh, hell, I still don't know his surname. Some people call him Simple Stevie."

"It was—Stevie was there?"

"Yes. He fetched her some water and stayed with her for a while. Then he saw her into a taxi. Anita went to Morty's. People—Sean Ellis, the DJ—saw her there."

"Oh. So—" A tear slid down her face. "So she was all right?"

"I think so. She was dancing. Drunk. But yes, as far as I know, she was all right."

Maggie was hanging on his every word, seemingly oblivious to the tears rolling down her cheeks.

"We knew she would have gone on somewhere else that night, but—well, she might have got ill later, a delayed reaction or something. She might have fainted or something. Fallen into a ditch. Grown confused and wandered over the moors—"

"Indeed," Dylan agreed. "And for all I know, any of those things might have happened."

Her relief faded slightly.

"But if she went to Morty's," he said, "and I'm fairly certain she did, who would she have met up with?"

"I don't know." Her voice was shaky. "She would have flirted with Sean Ellis. He was the DJ there then."

Dylan nodded.

"She wouldn't have gone out of her way to meet him, though. There was Matthew Jackson, of course. He used to go there quite often. Perhaps she was hoping he'd be there."

"Matthew Jackson?" The name meant nothing to Dylan.

"Anita was a bit tight-lipped about him, but I always thought she still had feelings for him. They'd been an item years before, but he dumped her. I don't believe she ever got over him."

"Oh?" Why had no one mentioned him?

"I always thought that was why she could laugh and joke with men so easily. After Matt, no one meant anything to her."

"Is he still in Dawson's Clough?" Dylan asked.

"No. He moved away. Him and his family."

"He was married?"

"Within six months of dumping Anita, yes. He had two boys."

"How long ago did he leave Dawson's Clough?"

"Ages ago. It wasn't long after Anita vanished. Six months maybe."

"I see." Dylan would ask Holly if she remembered him. "What do you know about him, Maggie?"

"He came to the Clough with his parents during our last year at school. He was different. He came from Scotland for a start, and he was nice-looking, clever, good at sport. You know the sort."

Dylan certainly did. Every school had one of those. They always had their pick of the girls and made the other boys feel totally inadequate.

"Anita used to hang around with him even then. He used to play her along. He loved to have another girl on his arm to make her jealous. In fact, I think she only went out with Ian to make *him* jealous."

"Ian?"

"Her husband. Holly's father."

"Ah, yes."

Because the man had been out of Anita's life for so long—eight years before she vanished, in fact—Dylan kept forgetting about him. Was that wise? Maybe he'd returned to claim what he thought was rightfully his—his wife and his daughter.

"That was a marriage doomed to failure if ever there was one," Maggie was saying. "Ian liked to settle in front of the telly every night, whereas Anita wanted to be out having fun. There's no way Anita would have married him if she hadn't been expecting Holly."

She smiled briefly at old memories. "Anita was scared to death of being a wife and mother. She wasn't the sort to settle down. The very word responsibility brought her out in a cold sweat."

Yet she'd done a good job raising her daughter. Holly was well-balanced, intelligent and hard-working.

"What did Matthew Jackson do on leaving school?" Dylan asked.

"All sorts of things. In the end, he had his own garage. It's still there now, on the industrial estate. He sold it and moved away. Someone said he'd gone abroad but I wouldn't know about that. He was a bit of a loner. In fact, I don't know anyone who kept in touch with him. I suppose people get like that when they've spent a childhood moving around."

She reached for her cup and saw that it was empty.

"More tea?" Dylan asked, and after the briefest of hesitations, she nodded.

"That would be good. Thank you."

She was far more relaxed now. Knowing that Anita Champion had at least made it to Morty's on the night in question had laid several fears to rest. The responsibility for Anita no longer lay so heavily on her shoulders.

SNOW HAD BEEN falling for most of the day, and it now lay, a couple of inches deep, on the pavements. Gritters had been back and forth, and the main roads through Dawson's Clough were a slick, dirty mix of grit and slush.

At this time of night, a little after ten o'clock, there were few people about. Taxis overtook Dylan as he walked, and a few people stood outside pubs to smoke, but other than that, he had the town to himself.

As yet, he hadn't thought any more about taking up running again. He knew he should, and he knew he'd enjoy it. He also knew that the hardest part was getting started.

His passion for walking depended on his mood. When life seemed straightforward, not that he'd experienced that for a while, the idea of walking didn't appeal. Yet, as soon as he had puzzles to fathom, he loved to walk. Usually things became clearer with every step.

Tonight, however, everything was as clear as the slush in the gutter.

Unless, as Maggie had worried, Anita had wandered onto the dark moors alone and fallen to her death, someone knew what had happened to her.

She was dead, Dylan was almost sure of it. People could say what they liked about her irresponsible lifestyle, but he couldn't believe she would leave Holly behind.

Dead or murdered?

If the latter, random, accidental or premeditated?

His imagination was running away with him. She had few friends, but no enemies that he knew of. She was a hairdresser, for God's sake.

But what about Terry Armstrong? The idea of Anita being close to someone like him was too difficult to comprehend.

If he'd had an affair with Anita, and plenty had by the sound of it, how would he have ended it? Would she have taken it lightly? Had she threatened to make a scene, to expose him, to sell her story to the local rag and tell his wife?

It was possible, Dylan supposed. Unlikely, as he couldn't imagine Anita as the vindictive type, but it *was* possible. And how far would a man like Armstrong go to ensure a woman's silence?

He shuddered as his subconscious answered that one for him.

What about Ian Champion, Anita's ex-husband? How did he fit into things? Dylan tried to put himself inside the man's shoes. If he and Bev split up, if Luke was three years old and Dylan had to live away from him, from them both—

Dylan didn't know what he'd do. He did know, however, that he wouldn't remain silent for years. Even if his marriage was over, he would have to know his child. He would have to. Most fathers would have idolised such a pretty daughter. What had made Ian Champion so disinterested?

Dylan still had to find Colin Bates, one-time bouncer at Morty's and small-time criminal. He'd regularly obtained free drinks for Anita. Why had he been so generous toward her? Had he fancied his chances? Had there been something deeper between them?

And now Matthew Jackson had been thrown into the equation. If Maggie was to be believed, he'd been the love of Anita's life. Had he sent those highly prized Valentine's Day cards?

Dylan's coat was dotted with huge soft snowflakes now. Presumably his hair was the same. He guessed, too, that his shoes would soon have an ugly water mark on them.

Walking in this weather was madness.

He stood beneath a street lamp and pulled out the photograph of Anita Champion that went everywhere with him. He gazed at her smiling face, as he'd done so many times before, but inspiration didn't strike. All he knew was that, if you were that desirable, that different, you courted trouble. There were too many jealous women in the world. And too many men anxious to protect themselves, their marriages, their reputations—

One only had to think of her acquaintances. Sandra, her employer, was furious because her boyfriend had leaped into bed with Anita. Yvonne Yates and Brenda Tomlinson were jealous of her, couldn't wait to see her fall flat on her face—literally. Maggie might have been a friend, but she was too weak to stand up to the other girls. Ian, her ex-husband, seemed totally disinterested. Matthew Jackson had enjoyed toying with her emotions…

Had Anita had any *real* friends?

There was Bill Thornton, of course. He'd been a friend. As had Stevie. Were those the only friends she'd had?

The thought saddened him. He hadn't known Anita, but he felt he was beginning to know the woman she had been. And he was certain he would have liked her and been proud to call her friend.

So what now? He could trawl the pubs again and try to talk to yet more people. He couldn't face it, though. Not tonight.

He walked slowly back to his hotel. Tomorrow was a brand new day. Tomorrow, he would find out all he could about Matthew Jackson.

CHAPTER TWENTY

FRANK WILLOUGHBY STOOD for a moment and admired his snow-covered garden. Artists and architects could do their best, but nothing could outshine Mother Nature. Other than a few marks left by birds and a neighbour's cat, the snow, and it was five inches deep on the bird bath, was untouched. It dazzled in the early morning sunshine.

He put a couple of pieces of bread and a fat ball on the bird table, then returned to the kitchen for seeds to top up the feeder. Until the thaw, the birds would stand no chance.

Such beauty had him re-evaluating life. He'd discovered that, after a heart attack, it was the easiest thing in the world to sit and vegetate. Frank had no intention of doing that. With that attitude, he might as well be in his box. The scene before him simply reinforced that.

Anyway, he had more important things than his health to worry about, and the murdering bastard currently topping his list was none other than Terry Armstrong.

Frank had first come across him years ago, when Armstrong had been ensconced in London and Frank had been sent south on one of his many undercover jobs to try and get close to the man.

Impossible. No one got close to him.

Except Pamela. Armstrong's first wife had got *too* close…

Frank had seen more than enough dead bodies during his career, but none like hers. Even now, the memory made him sick to his stomach. And if he lived to be a hundred, no one would convince him that Armstrong hadn't been responsible for Pamela's butchering.

When Armstrong moved to Lancashire, probably because there were too many other murdering bastards after him in London, every copper in the area soon knew all about him. Yet they'd never found anything to pin on him.

A couple of his enemies had been murdered but, each time, Armstrong had an ironclad alibi. He'd be smiling for cameras at a function that came with a hundred witnesses. And no one talked. Men would rather get banged up for life on a murder charge than risk upsetting Terry Armstrong. Revenge tended to come in the form of a long, slow death.

Everything Armstrong touched was legit. He made sure of that. His accountant was one of the most respected in Lancashire, as was his lawyer. To all intents and purposes, Terry Armstrong was a fine, upstanding member of the community.

The murdering bastard!

Smiling for the cameras—

"Christ!"

Frank's heart began to race. That wasn't good for him, no doubt, but it was a familiar feeling that he welcomed.

"Christ!" he said again, as he went to the house and picked up the phone. He tapped in the number, waited as it rang out, and eventually heard the sleepy voice of Dylan Scott.

"Sorry. Did I wake you?" he asked.

"You did. It's— Oh, is it eight o'clock already?"

"Closer to half past."

There was a rustling sound. "What is it, Frank?"

"I've had a thought about Terry Armstrong."

"Oh?"

"I knew the first of November, 1997 rang a bell. That charity dinner, the one where he was photographed with Anita Champion, took place on the same night that a bloke called Chris Bentley was murdered. He was as bent as they come. Had a habit of acquiring passports for anyone who was willing to pay."

"And?"

"There was a witness, and we caught Bentley's killer. Well, when I say caught, I'll amend that to found. With a bullet through his head. We never did find out who shot him."

"What's it got to do with Armstrong?"

"Maybe nothing. He wasn't a suspect. No reason why he should have been. But it has his trademark and it's made me think. You see, him and Bentley were banged up together. Same place, same time. A bit of a coincidence Armstrong being in Dawson's Clough at the time, too. According to him, he only ever visited the place to keep his wife happy. Strange him being here. Funny that he had so many witnesses that night, too."

"Interesting."

Frank's thoughts exactly. Of course, Armstrong being at a function where he knew the local rag would have cameras proved nothing.

"He's back in Dawson's Clough," Dylan said.

"Oh?"

"Yeah. He flew back from Florida last week. I was planning to call on him today."

"I've had a few run-ins with him in my time, Dylan. It might help if I went along with you to have a chat."

Silence.

Frank felt all kinds of a fool. He was no longer Dylan's boss. The man was working on a case that he was quite capable of solving on his own. Why would he want help from Frank?

"When can you go?" Dylan asked at last.

"In five minutes, if you like."

"Yeah, well, let me have breakfast first," Dylan said, and Frank was relieved to hear a smile in his voice. "I'll come over to your place in about an hour. Okay?"

"Great."

When Frank replaced the receiver, he was aware of adrenalin pumping through his veins for the first time in months. At last he had something to think about other than his health, his bloody boring diet and endless hospital appointments.

He was smiling. And who would have believed that thinking about that murdering bastard, Terry Armstrong, could cheer him up?

CHAPTER TWENTY-ONE

"CHRIST, YOU DON'T go in for comfort, do you?" Frank said.

"It's an acquired taste." Dylan had to smile. Many people admired the Morgan's classic design, but few managed to enjoy a noisy, bumpy journey. "The suspension's a bit stiff, that's all."

"You could flog this and get a proper car, you know."

Dylan slowed to a stop as the lights turned red. "This is a proper car."

Frank grunted and sat more upright in his seat.

"Terry Armstrong," Dylan said, as he pulled away. "What do you know about him, Frank?"

"I know he's a murdering bastard. He was born in the east end of London in 1957. His father and uncle were both behind bars at the time. Terry came up through the ranks, working for uncles and cousins, all crooks, until, aged about twenty, he went into business on his own."

"As what?"

"We'd say loan shark. He chose to believe he was offering a public service. He added to that with several of those tanning shops—not leather, but sunbeds and that sort of thing. A front for money laundering, we always reckoned."

When Dylan had been on the force, Armstrong had been under investigation for money laundering. They'd never got anything to stick, though. Rumours had been rife about Armstrong having senior police officers on his payroll.

"He employed a couple of thugs to make sure everyone kept up to date with their payments," Frank said. "If they didn't, they'd have a few bones broken as an incentive. We had one chap, Ross Williams, on assault. Almost murder. Of course, Armstrong pretended to be horrified and said Williams had been overzealous. Williams ended up behind bars, and his missus seemed to come into a bit of money."

"A present from Armstrong?"

"We couldn't prove that." Frank paused for thought. "Then, and we're talking 1990, maybe 1992, it became common knowledge that Armstrong's wife, the lovely Pamela—lovely if you have a passion for vipers, at any rate—was having an affair with Tom Andrews."

"Who was he?"

"Another of Armstrong's employees. Built like the proverbial brick shithouse. Another who used to collect loan repayments."

"Ouch!"

"You can say that again. Pamela was brutally murdered. And I mean, Christ, it was brutal. Slow and bloody painful. She'd have been begging to die."

Dylan put his foot down as they joined the M65 heading to Burnley.

"What happened to the boyfriend, Tom Andrews?" he asked.

"His body was found by a boatman working the Thames. He'd had the luxury of a single bullet."

"And nothing to link the murders to Armstrong?"

"Not a bloody whisper of evidence."

"As Don't Fuck With Me messages go, it was pretty clear though," Dylan said.

"Crystal."

A brief snow flurry slowed down motorists, Dylan included.

"Pamela was a nasty piece of work," Frank said, "but she didn't deserve to die like that. No one does."

"Not even Terry Armstrong?"

"Maybe. Dunno."

So where did Anita Champion figure in this, Dylan wondered. How and why had she got involved with Armstrong?

"That was 1992, yeah? So what brought Armstrong to this neck of the woods, Frank?"

"He claims it was his second wife, Susie. She originates from Preston. They met when she was nursing in London. Someone knifed Armstrong—only a warning, sadly—and he ended up being nursed by Susie. They married six months later. He claims she wanted to come home, but I reckon the heat was on in London. If someone was warning him off—well, I reckon he wanted a fresh patch."

"Was he married to Susie in 1997? When he was at that charity dinner with Anita Champion?"

"He was, but he was still living down south. He didn't move up here till 2002."

"So why did you have dealings with him up here?" Dylan asked.

"He's semi-retired now, but back then, he was still providing his public service—loans at extortionate rates. He was also buying a lot of property to let. He still owns half of Dawson's Clough."

"Go on."

"He had competition up here. Maurice Goodfellow, a misnomer if ever there was one, was in the same business. One night, an old mill he'd had converted to fancy apartments, went up in flames. Arson."

"An insurance job?"

"No. More like another Don't Fuck With Me message from yours truly," Frank said. "I'd stake my life on Armstrong being involved, but again, there was no shred of evidence. Nothing. Not a bloody sniff of it." He pointed at the roundabout up ahead. "You need to turn left here. It's only about a mile from here."

Dylan concentrated on the directions Frank was giving until he slowed the car to a stop.

"This is it?" Dylan had expected a grand place set in several acres with huge electronic gates. What he saw was a modest detached house in a cul-de-sac shared by eleven identical properties. There was nothing to indicate that its owner had amassed a small fortune over the years.

"It is." Frank smiled at his surprise. "It's just the sort of house an honest, hardworking man would own, isn't it?"

"I suppose it is."

"He still has a place in London," Frank said, "and I expect his pad in Florida is a bit more upmarket."

"We'd better see if he's available for comment."

They exchanged the warmth of Dylan's car for the icy air. It ought to be too cold for snow, Dylan thought, yet the sky looked full of it.

Dylan rang the bell and they waited a few moments until Terry Armstrong, wearing black trousers, black roll-neck sweater and quality shoes, opened the door.

He looked at Dylan enquiringly, then his eyes

narrowed as he recognised Frank. “Chief Inspector! Well, well, well. Long time no see.”

“Ex-chief inspector,” Frank corrected him.

“Ah, yes, so I heard. Heart attack, wasn’t it? Too much stress?”

“May we have a word, Mr. Armstrong?” Frank ignored that.

“Of course. You know me, always happy to help.” The man oozed self-confidence as he closed the door behind them and showed them into the lounge where the furnishings shouted money. Top-of-the-range audio-visual system, expensive leather suite, deep carpet, large signed paintings…

“So what can I do for you?” Armstrong gestured for them to sit.

Dylan sat, as did Armstrong. Frank, it seemed, would have preferred to stand, but, possibly feeling the odd one out, he too sat.

“Dylan Scott,” Dylan introduced himself. “A client has instructed me to look into the disappearance of an acquaintance of yours.”

“Client? You’re a private investigator?”

“Yes.”

“An ex-cop then. Yes, you have the look of one. Kicked out, were you?”

“As a matter of fact I was. For taking the law into my own hands. Now, as I said, I’m looking into the disappearance of an acquaintance of yours.”

“Oh?”

So very confident. Very tanned, too. Who wouldn’t be, though, if they could afford to spend half their lives beneath the sun in Florida? “Yes. A Mrs. Anita Champion.”

"Anita Champion? No, sorry. The name means nothing to me."

"She disappeared thirteen years ago, in November 1997."

"As I said, the name means nothing to me."

His performance was worthy of an Oscar.

"How's the wife?" Frank asked. "Faithful and true, is she?"

Armstrong's eyes darkened to pools of black. "She's well, thank you, Chief Inspector."

"Good. I'd hate to think of her…straying and ending up like poor Pamela."

"God, yes. Pam. It's difficult, but life goes on."

"Not for her, it doesn't."

"Sadly, no."

Armstrong said the right words, but they chilled Dylan. There wasn't a hint of emotion in his eyes. He was a big man, well muscled. Dark hair was greying, the only sign of the passing years.

Dylan produced the photo of Terry Armstrong and Anita Champion and showed it to Armstrong. "Anita Champion."

Armstrong stared at it for long, quiet moments. "Sorry, but I don't recall the woman. Odd that," he added with a thin smile, "as she's very attractive."

"Very," Frank said. "And the two of you look to be friendly."

"Chief Inspector, I come into contact with lots of people. We chat, we share a joke, and we never see each other again. I've no idea where this was taken but, judging by our clothes, I'd guess it was a function—"

"Dawson's Clough, November 1997," Frank said.

"The same night that an old chum of yours, Chris Bentley, was murdered."

"Bentley, you say?"

"You remember him all right. You did time together."

"Oh, Bentley. Yes, I heard about it, now you come to mention it."

"I'm sure you did. And this—" Frank prodded the photo, "—was taken the same night. It was at a dinner to raise funds for the local hospice."

"An admirable cause, but I'm afraid I still don't recognise the lady in question."

Dylan didn't believe him. "Anita Champion was thirty when this was taken. She had an eleven-year-old daughter. She worked as a hairdresser in Dawson's Clough. Divorced. Husband walked out eight years previous. She liked a good time. Went to the clubs in Dawson's Clough—Oasis and Morty's."

"No. It means nothing to me, I'm afraid."

"Vanished four weeks after this was taken."

"Dear me."

"People have a habit of vanishing after contact with you, don't they, Mr. Armstrong?" Frank said.

"No, Chief Inspector, they don't."

"Okay. They have a habit of ending up dead," Frank corrected himself.

"I've known my fair share of tragedy, yes."

"This, I believe—" Dylan took the photo from Armstrong, "—was taken before you lived in the area."

"If it was taken in—when did you say? 1997?—then yes, it was."

"So you had no business in the area at that time?"

"None at all, Mr. Scott."

"I've heard it said," Dylan remarked, "that no man could resist her."

"I can believe that."

"Yet you did?"

"I imagine I only had a few seconds in her company." Armstrong was the king of cool. "Any longer and I would have remembered her. Having said that, I was, and still am, a happily married man."

"Where is Susie?" Frank asked.

"Shopping in Manchester. Why?" He gave a soft but chilling laugh. "Did you think she'd been bludgeoned to death?"

"It crossed my mind."

"What a devious mind you have, Chief Inspector."

"That's what a lifetime of dealing with killers does to a man."

"I can imagine. Now, if there's nothing else—"

"No," Frank said, "but if I find you've been lying, I'll make sure you're hauled in front of a judge even if it's only for double parking."

"Double parking?" Armstrong seemed to find that amusing.

"Until I can nail you for the murder of your late wife."

"That's enough, Chief Inspector. I've tried to help, but I won't be accused—"

"Save it. We're leaving."

They were soon dashing through a light snow shower to Dylan's car.

"Well?" Dylan asked when they were inside.

"I don't know. It could be that he didn't know her."

"Mm. It could be he did, too."

"You think he did?"

Dylan sighed. "I don't know. He's such a practised liar, it's hard to tell."

"Don't I know it." Frank rubbed his hands together for warmth. "Brr. Let's get moving. And don't spare the horses."

DYLAN DROPPED FRANK off, then drove to Brightwell Industrial Estate. Having spoken to the grand total of three people who remembered Matthew Jackson, but no one who kept in touch with him, he'd decided to visit Jackson's old garage.

The industrial estate was a sprawling mass of units in all shapes and sizes with Brightwell Garage, established before the estate was even thought of, sitting at the entrance. About thirty used cars, all less than three years old, faced the road, and a smart showroom sat behind them. To the side was the service department, where a couple of cars were being worked on. A young man in overalls was busy clearing snow from the forecourt.

Dylan parked his car and was looking around him when a portly middle-aged man rushed up to him.

"We don't see many like this." He ran a caressing hand over the Morgan's bonnet.

"It's not for sale," Dylan put in quickly.

"I'm not surprised. You'd be better off going to a specialist, a classic car specialist."

Dylan knew that.

"It's in good condition," the chap said. "You should get a good price on it."

"I should. I've spent enough on it—time and money."

"A mate of mine had a Morgan. Mind, that were back

in the seventies. Thought it attracted the women." He grinned at that. "It never did."

"No?"

"He traded it in for a Lotus, if I remember right. Elise, I think it were. Had that a few months and then got himself an Alfa Romeo."

"Really? Well, I've had this—" Dylan tapped a fond hand on the roof, "—seven years now."

"You're not a family man then?" This was said with a knowing grin.

"Yes, I am, actually. We've got a Vauxhall Vectra, but my wife uses that."

"Oh, well, this is just the thing for a bit of fun driving then."

It was. Although dashing up and down the motorway to Lancashire was pushing the fun bit slightly.

"Are you looking to buy?" The man's gaze was still on the Morgan.

"No. I was hoping to talk to the owner of the garage."

"You're talking to him."

"Ah, right. Then let me explain. My name's Dylan Scott and I'm trying to find the gentleman who once owned this garage, name of Matthew Jackson."

"I'm Harry Tyler." Dylan's hand was shaken. "Now then, Matthew Jackson. The name rings a bell, but I'm damned if I can think why."

"Have you had the garage long?"

"Nine years. Coming up to ten now."

"This Matthew Jackson had it twelve or thirteen years ago."

"Ah well, I reckon he'll be the bloke who sold it to Stuart Connolly then. I bought it from him. A lot smaller it were then. Connolly didn't deal in used cars. Just did the servicing and MOTs. A decent enough bloke. Between you and me though, he could afford to be. Bought this place for a song."

"Did he? From Matthew Jackson?"

"Now that I couldn't swear to. I might be able to find out, though, if you've got a few minutes to spare."

"I certainly have. Thanks, I'd be grateful."

"In my office. Why is it you're wanting to find him?" he asked as Dylan fell into step.

"I'm a private investigator." Dylan felt something of a fraud calling himself that. "A client is trying to trace her mother, one Anita Champion, and I gather this Matthew Johnson was a friend of hers."

"From these parts were she, this Anita Champion?"

"Dawson's Clough, yes."

"Never heard of her. Mind, I only moved here when the business came up for sale. Before then I lived in Blackburn."

He spoke as if Blackburn was in a different country rather than fifteen miles down the road.

They entered the main showroom and went to a small and exceptionally cluttered back office which housed a desk, two chairs, four tall filing cabinets, dozens of car registration plates, a small monitor showing the main forecourt, a phone, piles of paperwork and a board holding car keys.

"Now then." Harry pulled open one of the drawers of a filing cabinet. "If I've got it, it'll be here."

"If it's easier, I can come back later."

"No trouble. We're quiet today." Lots of seemingly unrelated paperwork was pulled out. "I keep most things," Harry said, stating what was becoming obvious.

"You never know when it'll come in useful. I'm the same at home, tell the truth. My missus is always nagging me to throw stuff away. If I did, I know I'd need it the very next day."

"I know the feeling." Dylan could sympathize. "I was away for a week once, and when I returned, my wife had hired a skip and cleared out my garage."

"No!" Harry was so horrified, he stopped what he was doing. "Whatever did you do?"

"The skip wasn't being collected till the next day, thank God, so I managed to save a lot of stuff."

"Women!" With a disgusted click of his teeth, Harry carried on searching.

Minutes ticked by, but Dylan had nothing better to do, and any clue as to Matthew Jackson's whereabouts would be welcome. Besides, he liked Harry. He liked people who weren't afraid to talk.

"Now then," Harry said. "Here's a stock-take that Stuart Connolly did. This means we're in the right era."

Apart from stopping to take a couple of brief phone calls, Harry kept on shuffling through papers, sometimes marvelling at what he found, and occasionally deciding something should be thrown out. But naturally, it wasn't going to be thrown out during the current decade.

"Here we are. Damn it, I knew I recognised the name. I expect it stuck in my head because of the fancy French address. Now, this don't mean that your Matthew Jackson sold the place to Connolly, but I reckon he must have."

He handed Dylan a sheet of A4 paper that had various, mostly local, telephone numbers printed on it. At the bottom, in pencil, someone had written out Matthew Jackson's address.

"This were hanging up on the board there when I bought the place," Harry explained. "I kept it up for a while because a lot of the phone numbers were useful. But either they've changed or we don't deal with these people any more."

"I see. May I copy down this address?"

"Be my guest. Sorry there's no phone number," Harry said. "Funny that. I can't see the point in it. I'd sooner have a number than an address."

"Don't worry about it." Dylan copied the address with great care. Maggie had thought Jackson had gone abroad. It seems she was right. "This is great. Really. I'll soon find a number."

"I suppose Stuart Connolly kept it in case he needed to send stuff on to the bloke. I've never had anything to do with him, obviously, and of course Connolly only kept the place for a couple of years, too. I bet he retired on the profit."

"Is that why he bought the garage? As a quick way of making money?"

"I couldn't say. All I know is that Matthew Jackson, if indeed it were him, sold it cheap."

Dylan took the photo of Anita Champion from his pocket. "Do you recognise this lady?"

Harry took the old photo to the window and examined it carefully. From the lack of interest he showed, Dylan guessed he was more interested in cars than beautiful women. He couldn't blame him for that. Cars were far less trouble.

"Never seen her before in my life. Is this the woman who's disappeared?"

"Yes. Thirteen years ago. Her name's Anita Champion."

Harry shook his head. "Sorry, but I don't recognise her. As I say, I haven't been here long. Well, coming up to ten years."

"That's okay. Thanks, anyway. I appreciate your help."

Harry walked outside with him. "If you do think of selling the Morgan—" There was a wistful sigh in his voice.

"I'll let a classic car specialist deal with it," Dylan said, and Harry laughed.

"Yes, that would be best." He shook hands with Dylan. "Look after it, lad."

"I will."

Dylan gave the Morgan a few unnecessary revs as he drove away from the garage.

CHAPTER TWENTY-TWO

AT LEAST IAN Champion hadn't done a disappearing act. It had been easy enough to trace Anita's ex-husband to the small local authority estate in Wigan. Some of the houses showed signs of neglect—rusting cars on the drives, gardens untouched for years, abandoned toys and overflowing wheelie bins forming an assault course—but the four at the end, including Champion's, were well cared for.

Receiving no answer to his knock, Dylan walked round to the back of the house. Here, on a large expanse of snow-covered lawn, was a child's swing.

A man strode down the path of next door's garden. Unlike Dylan, who had a thick overcoat on, he was defying the weather by wearing a T-shirt.

"Excuse me," Dylan called out.

The man walked up to the dividing fence. He looked suspicious.

"I'm looking for Ian Champion," Dylan said.

"He'll be down on his allotment."

"And where would that be?"

"You go down to the end of the road and you'll see a post office on your left. About fifty yards past that, take a left. Keep straight for a couple of miles and you'll come to a pub, the Nag's Head. Just past there, do a right. Keep going until you see a row of sheds on your left."

"Thanks." Dylan tried to memorise the directions.

"Is that fancy car out front yours?"

So that's why he'd dashed outside in a T-shirt, to see who was snooping around.

"It is, yes."

The man nodded, unimpressed. "You'll be better off walking the last bit then."

"Right. Thanks."

Dylan returned to his car, guessing that he was still being watched.

As he drove, he repeated the directions to himself. He made a right turn after the Nag's Head and soon found himself on a narrow track that was under snow.

He reversed and returned to the pub's car park. No way was he risking his Morgan on that.

It was cold, and the snow crunched underfoot, but the sky was blue. He found the allotments easily enough. The snow couldn't hide the fact that some, most in fact, hadn't been touched for years. A few were immaculate.

A man was clearing snow from one of the plots and Dylan wandered over, careful to keep to what looked to be paths. It seemed ridiculous to be on an allotment in this weather.

"Excuse me, but I'm looking for Ian Champion. I was told he might be here."

"You were told right then. What can I do for you?"

Before Dylan could answer, a young girl, no more than three years old, came out of the shed clutching a tiny pink spade.

"Good girl," Champion told her. "You clear that bit, eh?" He turned back to Dylan with a smile. "It all helps."

The child kicked her way through the snow in bright

pink Wellington boots and began clearing a small path.

"What can I do for you?" Champion asked again. He looked fit, and his healthy skin colour suggested he liked to spend his time outdoors, but he couldn't be described as handsome. He was quite short, probably about five feet seven or eight, and the little hair he had left was mostly grey. A couple of missing teeth made his face look lopsided.

"My name's Dylan Scott and I'm trying to find out what happened to your ex-wife, Anita."

"Anita? Good God." Twice he opened his mouth to speak, and twice he closed it again. "Well!" he managed at last.

"I'm a private investigator." Dylan decided honesty was the best policy. "Your daughter, Holly, is paying me."

"My daughter?" The expression on his face was difficult to fathom. A mix of surprise and wistfulness? "Holly's not my daughter, Mr. Scott."

"Sorry?"

"I said Holly isn't my daughter."

There was no resemblance whatsoever, but what did that mean? Nothing, in Dylan's view. People said he looked like his mother, but he'd never spotted any similarities. And no one seemed able to decide if Luke looked like him or Bev.

All the same, Ian Champion's comment shocked him.

"But I thought— You were married to Anita, weren't you?"

"Oh, yes. For three years." Champion plunged his spade into the snow.

"Granddad—"

"Chloe, love, how about you build another snow castle, eh?" He strode into the shed, the girl following him, and emerged with a pink bucket. "There you go, sweetheart."

"I love you, Granddad!"

Laughing, Champion swept the child into his arms, kissed her on the cheek and set her down on her feet again. "And I love you, too."

"Your granddaughter?" Dylan asked. "She's adorable."

"Yes. Mind, I nearly had a fit when my Emma said she was expecting. Sixteen she was, only just out of school. Still, we wouldn't be without young Chloe now."

"I'm sure." Dylan watched Chloe for a few moments, but he was still coming to terms with more important matters. "You were saying that Holly isn't your daughter?"

"Anita was eighteen when she fell pregnant," he said on a heavy sigh, "and I was twenty-four. We'd been going out together for about a month and thought we ought to get married. Anita wasn't the type to settle down, but she did her best."

His gaze rested on some distant spot. "Life was okay," he said. "Not great, but okay. We both thought the world of Holly, and I suppose that kept us together."

Dylan had dozens of questions, but he kept silent.

"When Holly was three she had an accident. She was with Anita, round at Anita's friend's house. Yvonne had the dishwasher open and—and there was a knife sticking up. Holly tripped and cut her throat. She lost a lot of blood." He drew in a deep breath. "We were at the hospital when we found out that she wasn't my daughter. Blood types, you see."

He fell silent.

"You say *we* found out, Mr. Champion. Neither of you had any idea?"

"No. Well, I suppose Anita must have wondered. She must have, mustn't she?"

"Perhaps." Dylan was unsure how to answer that.

"It made no odds to me," Champion said. "I couldn't have loved Holly more."

"Then I admire you." Dylan didn't believe him. "If I found out that my son was someone else's—" He offered a shrug.

"I'm not saying I wasn't angry. I was furious at first. I felt as if I'd been taken for a right fool." The hint of a smile curved his mouth. "It was impossible to be angry with Anita for long, though."

"But you walked out anyway?"

"Walked out? Oh, no. It wasn't like that. Anita didn't want me around, you see. As soon as she knew Holly wasn't mine, that was it as far as she was concerned. She had no need for me in her life. And there was no arguing with her."

Which didn't fit with the story Holly had given Dylan. According to her, he'd walked out on his family. *Mum said it was no surprise. Said it was a relief really. They'd both been kids when they got married.*

"And you never tried to contact either of them?" Dylan tried to keep the amazement from his voice.

"I tried phoning, but Anita would have none of that. I wrote to Holly, sent her cards and things—they were all returned unopened by Anita. In the end, I gave up. You have to. For your own sanity."

Champion crossed to where his granddaughter was struggling to empty her bucket of snow.

Once that was done, she was filling it again.

"Two years later, I met Jean," Champion said, rejoining Dylan. "We had Emma, Joe and Tom." He sighed. "I put Anita and Holly from my mind. I had to. It was too painful."

"So did Anita tell Holly that you'd abandoned them?" That didn't sound like Anita. Not, Dylan reminded himself, that he'd known the woman.

Several emotions flitted across Champion's face—sadness, regret, anger. "All I know is that Anita believed it was best for everyone, especially Holly, if I had no more contact with them. Is that what Holly thinks? That I abandoned them?"

"That's what she told me."

Once again, Champion had to go to his granddaughter's aid. When he came back, he nodded back at the girl. "Chloe's the same age as Holly was when—when she had the accident."

Dylan nodded. He'd thought as much.

"How is she?" Champion asked. "Holly, I mean."

"Fine. Working hard. She's a teacher."

"A teacher? My!" He smiled at that. "She always was bright. And I expect Anita's sister, Joyce, pushed her hard. I can't say I ever took to Joyce. Still, she's done a good job raising Holly by the sound of it."

"You knew she'd been taken in by Anita's sister then?"

"Oh, yes. There was right hoo-ha when Anita went missing. The police were here wanting to know why I'd had nothing to do with them and why I hadn't been paying maintenance toward Holly. They seemed to think

I'd ducked out of my responsibilities." His eyes sparked with indignation. "I told them about the accident and how Anita hadn't wanted anything to do with me after finding out that Holly wasn't mine."

"And they accepted that?"

"They checked it out through our medical records—mine and Holly's." His eyes were moist. "It was daft really, but I'd started to believe that Holly would be coming to me. After all, my name was still on her birth certificate. But I had no job, they knew I wasn't Holly's biological father—and then Anita's sister, Joyce, stuck her oar in. Social services decided that I had no claim and that a blood relation—especially a blood relation who could offer a good, steady home life—was a better option for Holly."

"And yet you'd been her father and bonded with her for the first three years of her life."

"That's exactly what I said, but it meant nothing to them. And perhaps they were right. After all, Holly didn't even remember me." He smiled, but it obviously took a great deal of effort. "And look at her now. A teacher, eh?"

"Yes, and she's eager to find out what happened to her mother."

More than eager. She was obsessed.

"I suppose that's understandable, but after all this time—" Champion shook his head as if he felt that, after so long, it was an impossible task. "Even for Anita, it's bloody odd, though. Holly meant the world to her, and I know for a fact that she wouldn't have left her."

"A lot of people believe she did exactly that."

"No way. That's what the police reckoned and I told them it was nonsense. Anita had a reputation, I'm not denying that, but she used to play on it a lot of the time. It was almost as if she enjoyed her notoriety."

"She went to Morty's on the night in question," Dylan said. "No one's seen her since."

"Morty's?" Champion rolled his eyes. "What a place that was. Watered-down drinks. Everyone off their heads. She sometimes dragged me there, but I hated the place."

"On the nights you didn't go, who would have kept her company?"

"She knew lots of people there. Often her girlfriends—there were four of them, Sandra, Yvonne, Maggie and Brenda—would have a night out. There was Colin Bates, too. He worked there as a bouncer. Him and Anita were friendly because they'd known each other a long time. They went to school together. Matt Jackson was another who was at school with her, and another who used to fancy her." He pulled a face. "Most men did. I was a bloody fool to think she'd be content with a bloke like me."

Dylan couldn't think of anything to say that would have sounded sincere. "I've spoken to most of those people, but not Matthew Jackson. He's living in France now or so I believe."

"Is he? That's news to me. He was a mechanic when I knew him. He was a good one, but he'd always try and make a few quid here and there. You had to watch him."

Dylan nodded. "Anyone else you can think of?"

"No one special. Oh, there was Sean Ellis—"

"The DJ?"

"Yes. He fancied his chances with Anita. He used to see what was going on at the club, too. Well, he would, wouldn't he? He used to sit in a metal cage thing playing his music. He always knew who was with someone they shouldn't have been with."

Chloe was bored and tugging at her grandfather's trousers.

Ian Champion bent down and picked her up. "Her mum's working. My wife, too. I used to work for a local builder, but he's had to lay everyone off. Still, I'll soon find another job. Meanwhile, I'm number one babysitter."

"And enjoying every minute of it?"

"Yeah," he admitted. "I know they can be difficult, demanding, but they soon grow up, don't they?"

"They do. Right, I'll leave you to it." Dylan hunted in his pockets for a piece of paper, found an old receipt for a newspaper, and wrote his name and phone number on it. He really would have to get some business cards printed. "If you think of anything that might help, will you let me know?"

"I will, yes." Champion examined the paper, then put it in his inside jacket pocket. "Holly—you'll tell her hello from me?" He looked embarrassed. Awkward.

"I will." Dylan ruffled Chloe's blond curls before walking back to his car.

As he walked, he wondered if Ian Champion's story was accurate. Why would Holly say he'd walked out on them? Because it was what she'd been told? So whose story should he believe? Anita's or Ian Champion's?

Had Ian Champion walked out in disgust when he discovered that Anita had been unfaithful? He wouldn't be the first. Or the last. So why lie about it?

HOURS LATER, WHEN Dylan was back in his hotel room, he took a thick sweater from his bag and pulled it on.

Ridiculous when you had to put on more clothes when you came inside.

He was still musing about the Champions and trying to decide which of the three were lying.

Had Anita lied to her daughter? Had Ian Champion lied to him this afternoon? Or had Holly lied to him?

Dylan supposed it was no big deal. If people didn't lie, he wouldn't have a job. All the same, he didn't like to be taken for a fool.

He pulled his chair closer to the enormous radiator and called Holly Champion. He thought she might be working, but she answered within three rings.

"Dylan, how's it going?"

"Slowly." He didn't want to hurt her feelings, but hell, feelings did get hurt. It was life. And it was she who wanted the truth. "I saw—" He was about to say "your father," but changed his mind. "I saw Ian Champion today."

"Oh? Why? What does he have to do with anything?" She didn't sound pleased. Perhaps she thought he was wasting his time and her money.

"Who knows? But according to him, he wasn't the one who wanted your parents' marriage to end?"

"What? He walked out on us!"

"He claims, and I can't think why he'd lie, that your mother wanted him gone. Do you remember having an accident and going to hospital when you were about three?"

"I should do," she replied. "I've still got the scar to prove it."

"What happened?"

"I tripped over at Yvonne Yates's house," she said in a matter-of-fact way, "and landed, neck down, on the dishwasher. Or, more accurately, on a carving knife that had the blade sticking up."

"Hmm. That's what Ian Champion told me."

"So?"

"He also said that, while you were in hospital, blood tests confirmed that he wasn't your biological father."

Silence met his statement. A silence so long that, in the end, Dylan had to check if the phone line was still live. "Holly? Are you still there?"

"Yes. Yes, of course. I don't know why he'd say that."

"Perhaps it's true."

"More likely he's invented that story so he didn't have to stay with us, so he never had to hand over any money to my mother." Her voice was scathing. "People will think better of him that way. He could hardly tell people he was a piece of shit who turned his back on his wife and daughter and never bothered with them again."

Dylan was taken aback by the strength of her feelings. He'd never heard her swear, and it wasn't an experience he wanted to repeat. "According to him, he wanted to stay with you both. Also according to him, he phoned often, but your mother wouldn't speak to him. He claims, too, that he sent you letters and cards but that your mother returned them to him unopened."

Silence met this statement, too.

"Then he's lying," she said at last. She spoke far more calmly now.

"Why would he do that?"

"How should I know? You're the private investigator."

"He has a three-year-old granddaughter now. I

met her, too. She idolises him. He seems to be a happily married family man who enjoys pottering on his allotment."

"Does he?" No interest whatsoever.

"He seemed proud when I told him about you—that you were a teacher."

"Proud?" She gave a short, humourless laugh at that. "Why would he be proud? If, as he's telling everyone, he's not my father, there's nothing for him to be proud of. And as he's had nothing whatsoever to do with my upbringing, it's irrelevant anyway."

If she truly believed her father had walked out on her, Dylan supposed she had every right to feel angry. "He spoke of you fondly. And he told me to say hello from him."

"Did he indeed?" Still no interest. "Exactly why did you go to see him?"

"When people disappear, family members are usually the ones in the know. Now, while I agree that he's been out of the frame for a good many years—well, you never know, do you?"

Like everything in life, including murder, family members were always the first place to start.

"And did he tell you anything useful?" she asked.

"Not really."

"Then it was a waste of time, wasn't it?"

Dylan ran his free hand over the warm radiator. Had it been a waste of time? He didn't think so. "We'll see. But other than that, there's nothing to report."

"Well, thanks anyway. Thanks for the work you're doing, I mean. I appreciate it, I really do." Ian Champion was forgotten and she was her usual sunny self again.

"You'll get there in the end, Dylan. I just know you will."

Dylan wished he was as confident.

He wanted to press her for more information about her mother, about the possible identity of her real father—if indeed Ian Champion wasn't her natural father—but he decided to quit while he was ahead. She would be able to tell him nothing. As far as she was concerned, her father was Ian Champion, a cowardly man who had walked out on his family.

Dylan wasn't convinced. He believed Ian Champion's story.

"I'll be in touch," was all he said.

CHAPTER TWENTY-THREE

EUREKA! DYLAN HAD been hoping to meet up with Stevie, and he was pleased to see his new friend in Asda, gazing at iPod accessories.

"Breakfast?" Stevie's eyes lit up at the sight of Dylan.

"Why not?"

They took the escalator to the first floor and, when Stevie had his breakfast and Dylan his cup of tea, they sat at what was becoming Their Table.

Dylan wasn't sure what he wanted from Stevie. That was the problem, of course. With Stevie, you had to ask questions that had a simple yes or no answer. Stevie observed, he knew about people, but getting that information from him would have tested the patience of angels. Still, nothing ventured, nothing gained.

Dylan knew better than to interrupt Stevie's eating so he drank his tea and watched shoppers park their cars and stride across the slush-covered tarmac to the store. Scowling women clutched lists. The few men brought along for the Big Shop wore resigned expressions.

"Stevie," Dylan said, when his companion's plate had been wiped clean with a square of toast, "have you thought of anyone else who might have been with Anita Champion the night she went to Morty's?"

A long pause for thought. "No."

"What about Matthew Jackson?" he asked. "Did you know him?"

"Yes." So why in hell's name hadn't he mentioned him? The trouble with Stevie was that you had to know the answer before you asked the blasted question. "I was talking to Anita's friend on Wednesday, Maggie Gibson, and she said that Matthew Jackson was a special friend of Anita's."

"Yes." A smile almost broke out on Stevie's face.

"Did you see him that night? The night Anita went from Oasis to Morty's, did you see Matthew Jackson?"

Stevie thought for a moment. "No."

"But he might have been at Morty's?"

"Yes."

"Did you see Anita with him often?" Dylan asked.

"Yes."

"Anita liked him, didn't she?"

"Yes."

"What about Terry Armstrong?" He handed the photo to Stevie, who looked at him blankly. "Did you ever see Terry Armstrong with Anita?"

"Yes."

"You did? Where?"

Stevie got to his feet. "Come."

Dylan groaned. It wasn't snowing, in fact it had thawed a little, but the pavements were an inch deep in slush and, knowing Stevie, they could have a long hike in front of them. Yet what was the alternative? Conversation was impossible.

As Stevie limped out of the car park, Dylan knew a rush of guilt for his unkind thoughts. If he'd been dragged along the road with his dead mother, spent

God knows how long in hospital, then been bundled into a care home, *he* probably wouldn't feel like talking either.

They walked into the centre of Dawson's Clough. When they were at the back of the Co-op, Stevie turned into a short street of modern terraced houses. At one of these properties, number seven, he took a key from his pocket and opened the door.

"This is your home, Stevie?"

"Yes."

It was a flat, small but clean. Dylan passed a kitchen with spotless white units on his way to a sitting room that housed a well-worn suite and very little else.

He stood in that room while Stevie disappeared through another door. There were no pictures or books. There wasn't even a TV. A pile of newspapers shared a long, low glass-topped table with a phone. The sofa faced a gas fire with a gleaming brass surround. A cream rug, also unbelievably clean, sat in front of that.

Stevie returned with a large cardboard box that he set down on the rug.

He gazed at the fire for a moment, then took the decision to switch it on. Dylan was glad of that because the flat was seriously cold.

With that accomplished, Stevie opened the box.

"Good grief!" Dylan stared in amazement at hundreds, no, *thousands*, of newspaper cuttings. "Do you save everything?"

Stevie thought for a moment. "No."

But he saved *almost* everything. Local news and sport, all the hatch, match and despatch notices.

"How far back do they go?" Dylan asked.

"1974."

Dylan experienced a sudden hollow pain. "From the accident? When your mother died?"

"Yes."

The lad had been five or six years old at the time. He must have sought out the old newspapers years later. Or had someone saved them for him? Surely not. Adults would have wanted the child to forget.

The dates 1995–2002 were written on the side of the box in thick black ink. Sitting on the rug were details of anything remotely newsworthy that had happened in Dawson's Clough—for all the cuttings were from the *Dawson's Clough Journal*—over seven years.

Stevie turned the pile upside down and, quickly for him, discarded cutting after cutting.

"What are you looking for?" Dylan asked.

"Mr. Armstrong and Mrs. Champion."

"Do you think there will be anything?" It seemed highly unlikely.

"Yes."

Half an hour later, Dylan needed to answer a call of nature. "May I use your bathroom, Stevie?"

He didn't look up. "Yes."

"Where—? Oh, never mind."

The first door Dylan tried led into a bedroom. It was a large room that housed a single bed that had been pushed up against the wall, a wardrobe, a set of drawers and dozens of boxes that presumably held yet more newspaper cuttings.

The room next to that was the bathroom, and the cleanliness put Dylan to shame. The white suite was spotless and the chrome taps sparkled.

As Dylan relieved himself, he wondered how Stevie could need such an array of medication as sat on the window sill. There were bottles and boxes of pills in all sizes and colours.

He washed his hands, careful not to leave splash marks, dried them on a spotless white towel, and returned to the sitting room where Stevie was still on his knees working his way through those cuttings.

Dylan sat and watched him. Nothing was said. All was silent other than the hiss of the gas fire and the soft rustle of old newspaper.

Half an hour must have passed when Stevie suddenly grunted and thrust a piece of paper at Dylan.

It was a wedding photo, two strangers with radiant smiles. Underneath was a brief description of Matthew Jackson's marriage to Julie Carrington at St Mark's Church, Dawson's Clough.

"So this is Matthew Jackson," Dylan said.

Stevie nodded and carried on with his search.

It was difficult to tell, as most people were at their best on their wedding day, but the man looked as if he'd have no trouble at all attracting women. Perhaps he wasn't tall, perhaps his wife was exceptionally short, but his hair was thick, blond and quite long, his face perfectly proportioned and his teeth were strong and white. It would have been easy to picture him on a Californian beach or a Hollywood film set.

His wife had short dark hair and an elfin, almost vulnerable appeal with large, doelike eyes.

The cutting was dated March 1995. Anita's one true love, if indeed Matthew Jackson qualified, had married his Julie two and a half years before Anita disappeared.

Stevie continued to search and Dylan continued to watch. By two o'clock, he was starving.

"Shall I nip out and get us fish and chips or something?"

"Good," Stevie said.

The chippy was less than a hundred yards away and the Chinese lady behind the counter was soon wrapping two pieces of battered haddock and enough chips to feed the population of east Lancashire.

When Dylan got back to the flat, Stevie broke off from his task to take two plates from a cupboard, put a piece of fish and half the chips on each and place them in the microwave for a few seconds. Spotless cutlery was given to Dylan. He'd assumed they would eat from the paper but, for all his odd ways, Stevie had standards.

When they had eaten, Stevie went back to his box of paper. Less than five minutes later, he found something that interested him.

"Here," he said.

Dylan took the piece of paper. It was dominated by a photo of a crowd of about twenty people standing by a bonfire.

"Well, well."

Most in the photo were hidden beneath thick coats and hats, but it was impossible to miss Anita Champion despite the large collar on her coat and the scarf wrapped around her neck. Standing next to her, so close their shoulders were touching, was none other than Terry Armstrong.

The fireworks display had taken place on the fifth of November, 1997, just days after the two were photographed at the charity dinner, and little more than three weeks before Anita Champion vanished.

"Stevie, may I borrow this?"

"Yes."

"Thanks. I'll make sure you get it back."

"Yes."

Stevie was still sorting through papers.

"I'm setting off for home now," Dylan said. "That's London. I'll be back on Monday. I'll see you at Asda's cafe at about eleven o'clock on Monday, shall I? If you find anything else, you can bring it along, yes?"

"Yes." Stevie didn't even look up as Dylan let himself out of the flat.

Dylan was whistling as he walked back to the hotel. Terry Armstrong could say what he liked, but he'd known Anita Champion. Twice they'd been photographed together, and that was taking coincidence way too far for Dylan's liking.

CHAPTER TWENTY-FOUR

ON SATURDAY MORNING Dylan decided enough was enough. His mother was meeting a friend at the V&A and Dylan was standing in his room surrounded by enough unwashed clothes and bedding to keep a laundry business going for six months. If Stevie could exist in that soulless flat and keep the place clean, it wouldn't hurt him, Dylan, to wash a few clothes.

He made a coffee and, while drinking that, hunted for the washing machine's user manual. He knew one existed because he'd seen it when he moved in, but he couldn't find it anywhere. Perhaps he didn't need it.

The machine's door was open so he put a dozen shirts inside. One was maroon so he took that out again. He knew you weren't supposed to mix colours.

He rooted out a box of wash powder tablets from under the sink, but how many did he need? Deciding it was better to be safe than sorry, he unwrapped four and put them on top of his shirts.

Then came the tricky bit. There were a whole host of numbers to choose from on the machine. He'd checked labels inside the shirts, but they hadn't told him anything. Nothing he could understand at any rate. Then he spotted it—Quick Wash. He hit that button and the machine whirred into life.

How many times in the past had he asked Bev about her day, only to hear she'd done a couple of loads of washing? Good grief—it wasn't rocket science, was it? He'd have the lot done by lunchtime.

Satisfied that all was working as it should, he left the flat and went to buy a newspaper. He'd have a leisurely morning doing his washing and, this afternoon, he'd iron it all.

By the time he got back, the machine was in full spin mode. There seemed to be a worrying amount of foam spinning with the clothes, but perhaps that didn't matter.

When all was silent, he removed his clean shirts, filled the machine with more, put less powder in this time, and, feeling smug, sat with his feet up to read his newspaper. Oh for the easy life of a housewife.

His reading was interrupted by the phone.

"It's me," Bev said. "I have to go out tomorrow morning so I wondered if you could pick Luke up at nine o'clock instead of ten."

"Of course. Where are you going? Anywhere good?"

"Only out with— What's that noise?"

"The washing machine's just started spinning." He couldn't keep the note of pride from his voice.

"The— You're using the washing machine?" She gave a sarcastic laugh. "Good grief. You never cease to amaze me. Anyway, must dash. Thanks for that. I'll see you tomorrow. Bye."

DYLAN WAS AT the marital home at nine o'clock sharp the following morning.

Luke was pleased to see him but Bev dashed down the stairs, coat and bag in hand, and was on her way out of the door. "Behave yourselves," she said. "And don't be late back, Dylan."

Dylan watched her go with a heavy sigh. She hadn't even noticed his neatly ironed, blindingly clean shirt. Ah well, he'd see her later.

"What shall we do then, Luke?"

"Ten-pin bowling?"

"Yep, sounds good to me."

"We could have our lunch at McDonald's and go down the amusement arcade on the way home."

Dylan didn't care what they did. Luke was easy to be with and they always had fun.

The bowling was hectic, but they had a lot of laughs. Over lunch in a packed McDonalds's they discussed such weighty issues as penguins' ability to fly underwater and why Luke couldn't have a dog. The dog subject had been discussed for the past five years. They spent over two hours in the amusement arcade before returning home.

Bev was sitting at the kitchen table with a magazine open in front of her and a coffee in her hand.

"D'you want a coffee, Dad?" Luke asked.

"Yes. Thanks. That would be great."

"I'll make it." Bev shooed Luke away from the kettle. "So what have you both been up to? Have you had a good day?"

To give her credit, she always showed an interest in the time he spent with Luke.

"Brill," Luke said. "We went ten-pin bowling and guess who won? Me."

Bev smiled at that and Dylan guessed she was assuming he'd let Luke win. He hadn't.

"And we had lunch in McDonald's," Luke said.

"Really? Nice and nutritional then."

"Yeah." Luke was lucky in that her sarcasm went right over his head. "I'll make myself scarce, shall I? I bet you want to talk about grown-up stuff."

"We do." Dylan spoke before Bev had chance to argue. He could see she was going to.

Luke grabbed an apple and raced into the sitting room. The television would soon be on.

"Are you going to tell me you washed and ironed that shirt?" So she had noticed.

"This one? Yes, I did." He was still proud of his achievements but spoke as if it was nothing.

"Wonders will never cease." She laughed that laugh again and put a cup of coffee in front of him.

"Thanks." Right, it was time for a serious discussion. "Luke's right, you know. We do need to talk, Bev. This is silly. Why don't we put it all behind us and get back to normal?"

She was about to sit at the table again but changed her mind. "Dylan, I told you, I can't live with you any more."

"You told me a lot of things. Like the fact that I'm a drunk and a loser. I'm neither of those and you know it. I'm working, Bev."

"And I'm pleased for you."

"So let's try again."

"No." She sighed impatiently, as if she were addressing a four-year-old. "How many times do I have to tell you? It's over."

"And how many times do I have to tell you that I've learned my lesson—"

"This isn't about teaching you a lesson, for God's sake. This is about what I want. Me!"

"And what is it you want exactly?"

All he saw in her eyes was uncertainty. She didn't know what she wanted. To Dylan's way of thinking, that just proved she was being deliberately stubborn.

"It's more what I don't want, Dylan. I don't want to live with you anymore."

Dylan stayed for another half hour, but she wouldn't see sense. If they talked about Luke or the weather, she was fine. Anything more important, like the state of their marriage, had her changing the subject.

He left with his usual sense of frustration and wasn't in a good mood when he reached the flat.

On top of everything else, his mother showed no sign of going home. She claimed to have raced to his side because he needed her. What nonsense. Who'd spent all of yesterday washing and ironing? Not her. She hadn't so much as washed a shirt for him. Her own clothes were washed, by hand, every day. What had she done for him? Nothing.

As mothers went, however, he had always accepted that his was worse than useless. He loved her, God knows why, but she specialised in hindering rather than helping.

He decided to put stubborn wives and impossible mothers from his mind and concentrate on more pressing matters.

Holly Champion answered her phone on the second ring. "Dylan? How are you?"

"Fine, thanks. I don't have any real news, I'm afraid. I was just wondering if the name Matthew Jackson meant anything to you."

"Matthew Jackson. Um, no, not really. Well, it rings a vague bell, but I can't think why."

"I think your mother was friendly with him. They were at school together. He owned a garage in Dawson's Clough."

"No, sorry. I might have heard the name but I can't think where."

Their chat was brief. She didn't sound her usual cheery self and he wondered if she was still sulking about Ian Champion's story.

He went to bed and, two hours later, got up again. He wanted an early night because he needed to be back in Lancashire by eleven to meet Stevie. There was no point lying in bed unable to sleep, though. He may as well make a cup of tea.

The door opened and his mother, clad in the thickest, oldest dressing gown he'd ever seen, joined him.

"You having tea?" She clicked her teeth. "That's the last thing you need if you can't sleep, love. The caffeine will keep you buzzing for hours."

Dylan was far from buzzing.

"You need camomile," she said. "I'll make you one."

Ramming foul-tasting substances down his throat was the closest she came to helping.

When the pale brew was made, she sat beside him at the table. "What's keeping you awake then? Beverley?"

"No." The question took him by surprise. "She'll come round. She always does."

"What if she doesn't?"

That wasn't even worth considering. "She will."

"I still can't believe you did all that laundry," she said. "Good for you. See? You can cope admirably."

"I know I can. That's what I've been trying to tell

you." Hope sparked. "So, really, you can go home, Mum. I'm in Lancashire most of the time anyway, and I can't see myself getting to the bottom of this one very quickly."

"Oh? Is it going badly?"

"It's not going at all. But it all happened so long ago." For once, Dylan had more important matters on his mind. "Tell you what, if you wanted to go home, I could drive you up there tomorrow."

"Dylan!" She hooted with laughter. "Anyone would think you wanted to get rid of me."

Anyone would be right.

"I'm taking Luke out on Wednesday evening," she said. "We're going to the cinema. And I'm meeting up with a friend on Thursday. Don't you worry about me, love, I'm enjoying seeing a bit of life."

"Right." He knew when he was beaten.

"What about you? Aren't you enjoying getting away from the city?"

He looked at her, surprised. As it happened, he *was* enjoying the change of scene.

"You're a country boy, love." She smiled indulgently. "I'll never forget the tears we had when I dragged you to Brum. You loved it in Lancashire. Loved the farm. You must have cried for a month. Solid."

Dylan had never thought of it like that, and because the possibility of her being right was unpleasant, he simply shrugged.

"It's gorgeous around Dawson's Clough, isn't it?" she said.

"It's okay."

"Almost home for you, too."

He had no idea what she was talking about.

"You're what?" she asked. "About fifty miles from the farm?"

"About that, I suppose."

"And the farm, the countryside—it was always home to you."

He wasn't sure about that. After all, he'd been five when they'd moved to Birmingham, and he hadn't lived within fifty miles of open countryside since. He did like Dawson's Clough, though. He liked the area. He liked the pace of life, the warmth of the people, the humour, and the fact that strangers weren't afraid to strike up a conversation.

Two road signs in particular had made him smile. Someone had seen the official Lancashire—A Place Where Everyone Matters road sign and, courtesy of a can of paint, had replaced it with Lancashire—A Place Where No One Matters. Another had been changed to Lancashire—A Place Where Everyone Mutters.

"My life's here," he said. "My wife and son are here. Born here, both of them. It's where I belong."

"If you say so." She smiled, humouring him.

"Anyway, it's time I was off to bed."

"But you haven't drunk your camomile."

"You're right, Mum, I haven't. Goodnight."

CHAPTER TWENTY-FIVE

IT WAS JUST before twelve o'clock when Dylan pulled into his hotel's car park the following day. He'd had a productive morning, though.

He hadn't slept much—perhaps he should have had that camomile after all—but he'd had a good journey and met Stevie shortly after eleven. Unfortunately, Stevie hadn't found anything else, or anything he thought relevant, but that didn't matter too much because Pikey had phoned.

"Colin Bates? He's on probation for disorderly conduct at the moment and he's working at Bannister's, which is a canning factory somewhere near Accrington."

"Brilliant. Thanks, mate."

"You owe me, Dylan. And he's a mean bastard so if you have to deck him, make sure you've got loads of witnesses. Or none. We don't want you behind bars again." He cleared his throat. "Sorry, mate. Sick joke."

"It's okay. I'm not made of glass. I'm not bitter, either." Not much. "It's all water under the bridge."

"I can fax his mug shot through if you like."

"You can? That would be brilliant." Dylan had hunted through his pockets for a hotel bill and given Pikey the fax number…

He left his car, grabbed his bag full of clean clothes and strode into the reception.

"Ah, Mr. Scott." The receptionist looked at him in

the same way she might look at dog shit. "There's a fax for you."

"There is? Great."

She took it, with his key, from the rack and handed it over.

Dylan unfolded it and looked from it to her. No wonder she was a little pale.

"Handsome chap, isn't he?" he said, unable to think of anything more appropriate.

She nodded, asked if there was anything he needed and, on being assured there wasn't, went back to her work.

Dylan studied Colin Bates's photo as he took the lift to his room. A bull-headed man, with no neck at all and his hair shaved off, he would make a good bouncer. If he said you were leaving, you'd leave. It would take a brave man to argue with him. A tattoo in some sort of Celtic design formed a band around his neck. His nose was long and misshapen.

He'd be easy enough to recognise.

For the first time, Dylan unpacked his bag. Before, he'd simply grabbed what he needed from it but, in deference to his clean clothes, he hung shirts and trousers in the wardrobe and put underwear in the drawer.

With that done, he left his room, went back to his car and took off for Accrington.

Most of the snow had gone. Small drifts lay in the lee of walls, but all the main roads were clear. According to weather reports, however, more was heading for the UK.

He stopped at a filling station to ask for directions to Bannister's. He got lost, asked again at a newsagent's and got lost again. It was two o'clock before he found the factory. It was a small, ugly concrete building about five miles outside Accrington. He'd hoped to catch people having a lunch break, but now all workers were inside.

Dylan passed the time by wandering around Accrington and buying himself a coffee and a newspaper. He felt as if he was wasting time, but sometimes the job was like that. He'd wanted to visit Terry Armstrong today, but he wanted Frank with him for that and, because of a hospital appointment, his ex-boss couldn't make it.

Armstrong could wait, though.

At a few minutes to four, unsure what time the shifts were, he was outside Bannister's main gates. Waiting.

On the dot of five-fifteen, around sixty workers spewed out of huge green metal doors and descended on the gates. They were laughing, shouting and chatting like children let out of school for the long summer holidays.

As Dylan had suspected, Bates was easy to spot in a crowd. He was right at the back, deep in conversation with a younger man. If anything, he was even uglier in the flesh.

He was a big bloke, topping six feet, and broad with it. His walk, which Dylan suspected was supposed to resemble Hard-man Swagger, was close to a waddle. You wouldn't tell him that to his face, though, unless you fancied a trip to the nearest A&E department.

Most of the workers headed for a couple of waiting coaches but a dozen or so, including Bates and his chum, preferred to walk. Dylan followed at a distance.

They passed a few houses that looked as if they were waiting for the bulldozer, a small boarded-up church and a derelict mill, then came to a large red-bricked housing estate. On the lines of a rabbit warren, it made tailing anyone difficult, and Dylan was thankful when the two men headed for a pub.

The Black Bull was as hideous as Bates. A huge barn of a place with litter blowing across the car park, it boasted at least two cracked windows and one that was boarded up.

Dylan hung around outside, away from the meagre lighting, for about ten minutes, then went inside.

The interior was as unappealing as one would have expected—huge screen TV blaring out, torn upholstery on chairs and benches, empty glasses left on tables, and a bar that was swimming in spilt beer.

Dylan was glad he was driving and could only risk one pint. He only hoped he'd be able to find his car when he left. Hoped it would be in one piece as well.

Bates and his pal were standing at the far end of the bar, still deep in conversation and paying him no attention.

Dylan began staring at the pair until Bates noticed and looked as if he wanted to do something about it. Something involving violence.

"Sorry, mate," Dylan said, "but I thought there was something familiar about you. We haven't met, have we?"

Bates looked him up and down. "Nope."

"Don't suppose you've spent time inside, have you?"

"Have you?"

"Six months in Wandsworth and then Newgate," Dylan lied.

"What for?"

"ABH."

"Yeah?"

For a moment, Dylan knew he'd won respect. There were times when first-hand experience of life inside was an advantage.

Dylan had lied to Pikey. He *was* bitter, as bitter as hell, but he'd make it work in his favour.

Then he noticed Bates looking at his clean clothes and shiny shoes.

"Job interview," Dylan explained. "Some dump up the road called Bannister's."

Both men laughed at that.

"Should have guessed," Bates said. "They send us all there."

"What? You're there?"

"Yeah."

Dylan drank some beer. "I'm still sure I've seen you before. How about Dawson's Clough? I don't suppose you know the place?"

"Might do."

"Ah, got you!" Dylan grinned. "You worked at Morty's. I'm going back a bit, mind. Probably ten or twelve years. That was you, wasn't it?"

"Could have been."

"You used to get free drinks for a friend of mine. Anita Champion. Remember her?"

"I might do."

Did he look cagey? Well, yes, he did, but he was a naturally cagey bloke and it probably meant nothing.

"I'd love to know what happened to her," Dylan said. "Just vanished, didn't she? And I'd only seen her the week before, too."

"I saw her the night she went."

Now Bates was bragging. Good.

"What? Up at Morty's?"

"Yeah."

"What did she say to you? Mention anything about taking off, did she?" Dylan supped his beer, trying to look casual.

"She said a lot." Bates grinned. "She was way out of it. Pissed as a fucking fart. Kept going on about horses. Reckoned she was going to buy a fucking horse for that brat of hers."

"A horse?" Dylan laughed. "Where was she going to keep it? At her flat? Tie it to one of the hairdryers?"

"Fuck knows. She was pissed."

And drugged. "Who was she with?"

"That flash fucker Jackson."

"Oh?"

"She always had the hots for him."

"Yeah," Dylan said.

He was about to ask if Bates had told the police all this, but he knew the answer. Men like Bates only ever said two words to the boys in blue. One was "fuck" and the other was "off."

Bates's mate nudged him. "Time we were out of here."

They both emptied their glasses.

"See you," Bates said as they were leaving.

"Yeah, right. Maybe at Bannister's."

So Anita *had* been with Matthew Jackson that night. Perhaps it was time to board a cross-channel ferry.

CHAPTER TWENTY-SIX

IT WAS QUITE early, not even five o'clock, but Alan Cheyney locked the front door of his shop and went to the storeroom for a cup of tea. A total of four customers had been in the shop but, for once, he'd had a fairly profitable day.

He was still shaking, though. Had been all day.

True to his word, Pete had handed over that thousand pounds and, in turn, Alan had put it through his bank to the rent account. He was still more than four thousand pounds in arrears, but perhaps it had bought him some time.

He'd had a phone call this morning from Jason, the wimp who dealt with the lettings, and Alan had told him he'd have to give up the lease on the shop.

"Are you giving Mr. Armstrong formal notice?" Jason had asked in his usual nasal tone.

Alan had given the matter a lot of thought. In fact, he'd thought of nothing else. "Yes."

"We'll need that in writing then. You realise, of course, that you'll be liable for rents et cetera until the end of July."

"But if I move out—"

"Until the end of July." Jason didn't sound so much of a wimp now. "If you can lay your hands on the agreement, I'm sure you'll see that—"

"I've got the agreement."

"Good. Then we'll look forward to receiving the—" pause for him to sniff, as if he was struggling to use the word, "—arrears. Mr. Armstrong's a good man and he's given you until this coming Friday. Meanwhile, if there's anything else we can help you with, please don't hesitate to contact me."

Alan would have to keep the shop on and hope he could raise some money. Maybe Pete could give him another loan. He hated asking but there was no alternative. The bank wouldn't give him anything; he owed them too much.

What a bloody mess.

He still hadn't recovered from the shock of Armstrong bringing fruit to the hospital. But even more amazing was that the prat had thought Alan had been chatting up his wife.

Bloody ridiculous!

Alan hadn't spoken above five words to her. He wouldn't even have known who she was if Len, one of his mates, hadn't taken the mickey.

There was jealous and then there was Armstrong, it seemed. That beating—Alan still wasn't sure if it was for daring to speak to Mrs. Armstrong or a reminder that the rent was in arrears.

Terry Armstrong was mad. Stark, staring bloody mental.

If Alan had been in the market for a woman, which he wasn't, and hadn't been since his wife walked out, he'd have gone for something prettier than Mrs. Armstrong—

What was that?

Someone was in the back yard.

During the past month or so, a gang of kids had been

smashing windows and causing all sorts of damage in the street. That was the last thing he needed.

Just as he reached the door to investigate, it was pushed open, hitting him square in the ribs.

"Sorry about that, Mr. Cheyney."

He didn't recognise the face, hadn't seen it before, but he knew the voice. It was the one that had said, "You've got till Friday." Its owner was responsible for the state of his face and his still very painful ribs.

There were two of them, and when he noticed they were wearing black gloves, his stomach somersaulted and landed in his feet.

"It's all sorted. I spoke to Jason on the phone this morning." He waved a shaking hand toward the shop. "The phone's in there. Call him. Ask him! He'll tell you!"

"We've spoken to him," the slightly taller of the men said. "We take our orders from Mr. Armstrong, not Jason."

The other man was strolling around the storeroom, picking up fishing rods before returning them, very carefully, to their rightful place.

"I remember when this was a butcher's shop," he said.

Sod that. Alan didn't care. "Perhaps Jason hadn't spoken to Mr. Armstrong." His voice was quivering.

"Maybe. Maybe not."

Alan took a couple of deep calming breaths. They wouldn't risk beating him up again. The black gloves were supposed to frighten him, that was all.

"Have you had a good day?" the shorter one asked.

"I have." Alan dashed to the folder on the desk where a couple of credit card slips and a small amount of cash sat. "See? And all this will go straight to Mr. Armstrong for the rent."

They both looked at the chits, then the taller one put the cash in his pocket of his leather jacket. He looked enquiringly at Alan.

"If you give me a receipt for that—"

The man roared with laughter. "Hear that, John? He wants a fucking receipt."

"Dunno what he'll do with a receipt where he's going, do you?"

"I can't see it getting him through them pearly gates."

The other man picked up Alan's mobile phone. "Look at this. Top of the range. I'm surprised he can afford a flash thing like this." He dropped it into his pocket. "He won't be needing this, either."

"Right," Alan said, "you've had your little joke."

The tall one leaned into his face. "We haven't even fucking started yet!"

The other one went into the shop. Alan heard him try the door to check that it was locked. He came back, looked at Alan for a few moments, then stepped out the back door. When he returned, seconds later, he was carrying a length of thick rope. He nodded up at the steel beams where the old butchers' hooks still hung.

"That's where they used to hang the meat, you know..."

CHAPTER TWENTY-SEVEN

DYLAN HAD SCANT respect for weather forecasters and was convinced they predicted storms, gales and floods to cover their own backs. This time, however, they were spot on. Yesterday, on his way back from Accrington, he'd driven through a blizzard, and at least four inches of snow had fallen overnight. Yet more had been threatened, too, not only for Lancashire but the whole country. Fortunately, the gritting lorries had been ready, the main roads were clear, and Dylan reached Frank's house without denting the Morgan.

Punctuality was Frank's byword and he was ready to go.

They'd spoken on the phone last night, and Dylan had been tempted to ask if Frank fancied a trip to France. He hadn't, mainly because he'd known, deep down, that it would have been a gesture made out of sympathy. There was no need to drag Frank along on what could well be a wild-goose chase just because he thought the chap was lonely.

He hadn't spoken to Holly about it but, if she objected to funding his trip, Dylan would finance it. Bev had often complained that he was like a terrier with a bone and she was right. If a job was worth starting, it was worth finishing. Admittedly, he had only started this particular job because a) he needed the money and b) he needed to escape his mother and his temporary accommodation.

Now, though, he was involved. He wouldn't be able to rest until he'd discovered the truth.

As soon as Frank was in the car with his seat belt fastened, Dylan showed him the grainy but unmistakable photo of Terry Armstrong and Anita Champion at the fireworks display.

"What do you think, Frank?"

"I think the lying bastard will put it down to coincidence."

So did Dylan.

"Let's hope he had nothing to do with her disappearance," Frank added. "You wouldn't want the job of telling the daughter that her mother had met the same end as Pamela."

Dylan shuddered at the thought. "I'd lie."

He would have to. It would be bad enough telling Holly that her mother was dead. There would be no need to go into detail.

Half an hour later, they were being ushered into the warmth by an unsmiling Terry Armstrong.

"I don't have anything more to tell you." The gangster look had disappeared with the smile. Today, he was wearing a blue sweater and blue jeans

"Yes, we're sorry to bother you again, Mr. Armstrong, but something else has turned up," Dylan said.

"Like what?" He didn't bother to hide his irritation.

"Like this." Dylan kept hold of the photo. There was sure to be a copy or even the original somewhere, but he wasn't taking chances. "You being photographed with Anita Champion. Again." He thrust the photo under Armstrong's nose. "Now—" he didn't give Armstrong time to speak, "—I think you'll agree that it's no coincidence."

"How well did you know Mrs. Champion?" Frank asked.

Armstrong was calm. And why not? He had his own way of dealing with problems.

More than calm, he looked relieved, as if he'd been expecting them to ask about something else.

"I didn't." Armstrong's voice was like ice. "I'm standing next to her—if indeed that is her. It doesn't mean I knew her."

"It's a long time ago," Dylan said. "Perhaps you've forgotten."

"No."

"Okay, Terry, let's cut the crap," Frank said. "I know and Dylan here knows that you're lying. You knew Anita Champion, no doubt about it. Now, it's in your interest to tell us how well you knew her. You see, this is starting to look like a murder investigation, and you wouldn't want the police going through your business again, now would you?"

Dylan, seeing the anger blaze in Armstrong's eyes, tensed himself, ready for any stunt Armstrong might pull.

"Okay," Armstrong said at last. "I knew her. Satisfied?"

"How well?" Dylan asked.

"Well enough to sleep with her on three, maybe four occasions." Armstrong stabbed an angry finger at the photo. "It was supposed to be discreet so God knows how that bloody thing was taken."

"A bored photographer sent out from the local rag to cover the fireworks display naturally focusses on an attractive woman, I suppose," Dylan offered in a helpful manner.

"So you had an affair with Mrs. Champion?" Frank said.

"Hardly. I had sex with her. That's all. I was—still am—happily married, and I'm sure she wanted an affair no more than I did."

The photo in question had been taken on the fifth of November, 1997, a little over three weeks before she vanished. What had happened? Had Anita made financial or emotional demands? Had she threatened to expose his infidelity to his wife? Or had Armstrong tired of her and decided to silence her anyway?

"Mr. Armstrong, how would you describe your relationship with Mrs. Champion on the twenty-ninth of November, 1997?" Dylan asked.

"I wouldn't even describe it as a relationship."

"Where were you on the night of the twenty-ninth of November, 1997?" Dylan persisted.

"At home in London, I imagine."

"Any witnesses?" Frank asked.

"For fuck's sake, how the hell would I know? It's thirteen years ago." Armstrong calmed himself. "I came to Lancashire to see my wife's family and we all went to that bloody awful charity dinner. I met up with Mrs. Champion, we got chatting and arranged to meet the following day. On future visits to the area, I called her at the place she worked and we'd sneak off to a hotel for a couple of hours."

"What about this?" Dylan waved the newspaper cutting at him. "This isn't an hotel room."

"That was the last time I saw her. My wife and her family dragged me along to see the fireworks. Mrs.

Champion was there and we chatted for all of two minutes."

"About what?" Dylan asked.

A short angry laugh. "Can you remember what you spoke about thirteen years ago?"

"Probably not."

"Did you plan to meet perhaps?" Frank asked.

"No. It was only a flying visit because Susie's father was ill."

"Presumably," Dylan said, "you tried to call her on your next visit?"

"I imagine so, yes." Armstrong thought about it. "That would have been around Christmas. I heard she'd done a runner."

"I see." Dylan returned the newspaper to his pocket. "In your opinion, was she the type to do a runner?"

"Yes."

"Just walk out on her daughter?"

"In my opinion, yes."

Dylan could see the hard outline of Armstrong's fists in his pockets, but he wasn't too worried. Men like Armstrong didn't bruise their own knuckles. They paid someone else to do it for them.

"And now I'd like you both to leave." He marched to the front door. "If there's anything else I can help you with, I suggest you contact my lawyer first."

"We'll do that," Frank said.

As they walked to his car, Dylan couldn't help thinking that Anita Champion had lived life on the edge. She'd counted some highly dubious characters among her friends. Terry Armstrong, Colin Bates—they were thugs.

So what sort of man was Matthew Jackson? From

what Dylan had heard, he was a normal, hard-working bloke who'd done well enough to buy his own garage. Judging by Anita's other friends, that was sounding more and more doubtful.

He'd driven for a full five minutes before Frank broke the thoughtful silence.

"Wouldn't it be great to hear Anita Champion's version of events."

"Wouldn't it just."

"If she decided to play games with Armstrong—"

"I know."

If she decided to play games with Armstrong, she would be very lucky indeed to receive just a single bullet.

"And we'd find no evidence." Frank spoke with certainty and Dylan feared he was right. Men like Armstrong were tidy. They cleaned up after themselves.

By the time they reached Frank's house, snow was falling heavily.

"I'm thinking of taking a trip to France to see Matthew Jackson," Dylan said.

"I thought you might."

"Yeah, well, the last time she was seen, she was with him." He looked at Frank. "It's a long drive to the ferry, I have no idea if he's even living in France these days, and it will probably be a waste of time, but do you fancy coming along?"

"Me?" Frank grinned with childish delight. "I'm not totally buggered yet, so I might be able to help. Yes, count me in!"

"I'll sort it out tomorrow. Are you okay to go on Thursday?"

"Too right I am!"

BY THE FOLLOWING evening, Dylan had booked the ferry to France and he was looking forward to the trip. On the rare occasions he visited the country, he used the Chunnel. Matthew Jackson lived near Cherbourg, though, so it would be quicker, and cheaper, to take the ferry and skip the long drive from Calais.

He'd also ordered an alarm call for the morning. Other than that, he'd achieved nothing.

Dylan found it odd that, although practically everyone could remember Jackson and his wife, no one, as yet, had admitted to receiving as much as a Christmas card from him. People's memories of the couple were vague.

If it hadn't been for an off-the-cuff remark from Maggie, Dylan wouldn't have heard of the bloke. He wouldn't have visited Jackson's old garage and found his address in France, he wouldn't be planning a ferry trip…

It was as cold as ever in his hotel room. He'd make this one phone call and then find somewhere warmer to end the evening. Her number was in his book and he was pleased when she answered. "Mrs Gibson? Maggie? It's Dylan Scott. Can you talk for a moment?"

"You'll have to make it quick."

"Thanks." Presumably her husband had gone out for the evening. "It's about Matthew Jackson. After I spoke to you, I visited the garage he used to own on the industrial estate. I've got his address in France and I'm planning a visit."

"I see. But what does any of this have to do with me?"

"I was just wondering if you could tell me anything at all you remember about him." Dylan edged closer to the radiator. God, it was cold. "You said he came to Dawson's Clough with his parents from Scotland. Is that right?"

"Yes, but he wasn't Scottish. They hadn't lived there long. In fact, I gather they'd moved around quite a bit. I think he'd spent a lot of time in the Midlands—Nottingham and Stoke-on-Trent."

"And after school, what did he do then?"

"He worked as a mechanic, but I couldn't tell you where. Now I come to think of it, I think he might have worked at a couple of places. I don't know. It's a long time ago. Anyway, it wasn't long before he bought his own garage. He did very well for himself."

Why could so few people remember him? Dylan had asked dozens of people if they'd known him and, although a few had, their memories were vague.

"What about Julie, his wife?" Dylan asked. "Someone said she didn't come from round here. Is that right?"

His question was drowned out by sudden high-pitched barks. Dylan thought he heard Maggie say something, but whether she was talking to him or the dog, he couldn't be sure.

Dylan warmed his hands on the radiator as he waited for normality to resume in Maggie's house.

"Sorry about that," she said. "Someone at the door. Tess—stop that."

Were dogs supposed to resemble their owners or vice versa? Maggie and Tess didn't do a lot for either theory. Maggie was quiet and plain whereas the dog was exuberance on speed.

"You were asking about Julie." She sounded breathless. "She didn't come from the Clough and I'm fairly sure she was born in the Cotswolds. It was somewhere posh anyway. I know how she and Matthew met though."

"Oh?"

"Julie studied at Manchester University and a friend she met up with there came from this area. I can't remember the girl's name—Wendy perhaps, or was it Wilma? Anyway, Julie used to visit her and that's how she met Matthew. The other girl married an American and went to live over there."

"I see. So Matthew and Julie married, and I believe you said they had two children?"

"That's right,' she said. "Two boys. The family lived on Burnley Road—a nice semi. They seemed to be doing very well for themselves. I remember being surprised when they sold the garage and took off. It seemed quite sudden."

"It's funny, Maggie, but apart from you, hardly anyone seems to remember him."

"Oh, well—"

Dylan could feel her embarrassment oozing down the phone line. Maggie the Mouse. Of course, she would have lived in Anita's shadow. She would have envied her, longed to be like her, both in looks and in spirit. He'd bet a lot that Maggie had been in love with Matthew Jackson. And Jackson wouldn't have looked at her twice.

"I'm not sure when they left the Clough but it was only about six months after Anita vanished." She spoke quickly, probably to cover her embarrassment. "So it would have been some time in the summer of 1998, I imagine."

"He sold the garage in June 1998." Dylan knew that

much. "And you can't think of anyone who might have kept in touch with him?"

"No, I can't. Sorry."

The lack of contact struck Dylan as odd. He might not be great at keeping in touch, but only because Bev was so good at it. She still exchanged Christmas cards with a couple they'd met on holiday before they were married. It's what people did. Or what most people did.

"Okay, thanks for that, Maggie. I appreciate it." Dylan ended the call and grabbed his jacket. He wanted a drink and he wanted to get warm.

He left the hotel and walked along to the Pheasant, planning to have a couple of pints before bedtime. He would have stayed at the hotel, but the price of beer was prohibitive.

The first person he saw, sitting at the bar, a newspaper spread in front of him, was Bill Thornton. Dylan joined him.

"All right, Bill?" he said as he waited for his pint to be pulled. "Dylan," he reminded him.

"I hadn't forgotten, lad. And no, I can't say as I am all right."

"Oh?"

When they'd met before, Anita's old friend had worn a smile for everyone. This evening, the pint of beer in front of him was untouched, and he looked lost.

"Bad news," the barmaid told Dylan as he paid for his beer.

"What's wrong? None of my business, I know, but if I can help—"

"No one can help now." Bill thrust the newspaper at Dylan. "A friend of mine."

Dylan read the lead story with a growing sense of

disbelief. It told of a local businessman who had hanged himself. Alan Cheyney.

"I found out last night," Bill said, "and I still can't take it in."

Dylan couldn't, either. He didn't like it. He'd asked a few questions and then Cheyney decided to end it all. Coincidence?

"Knew him well, did you?"

"I did, yes. It's funny, isn't it," Bill murmured, "how you think you know someone? Mind, I were only thinking—not long before he were beaten up by them thugs—that he looked as if he had things on his mind."

"He was beaten up, you say?"

"He were. That would have been a fortnight ago. The Monday night it were. He were in here drinking with me and Geoff, and then some evil buggers, pardon my French, beat him up when he were walking home. Ended up in hospital, he did. Busted ribs, stitches." His anger at the attack left him on a long sigh. "And now he's gone. Dead. Bloody hanged himself. Christ, nothing's that bad, is it?"

"Depression's a terrible thing though," Dylan said.

"It is, yet I can't believe he were depressed. He's not the type. Or weren't the type," he corrected himself. "He's been through some bad times, but he's never let it beat him. First, his son were killed in a car accident. Nineteen, the lad were. No age, is it? Going too fast, of course, but then, kids do, don't they?"

Dylan nodded.

"That were years ago. Then his wife left him. Not long after that, he lost his job."

"Perhaps it all piled up."

"Must have, I suppose. Funny, though. I mean,

there can't be nothing worse than losing a child, can there?"

"No." Dylan often wondered if parents ever recovered from that. He knew he wouldn't cope if anything happened to Luke. A tragedy like that went against all laws of nature. "It's the worst thing imaginable."

"So to come through that—" Shaking his head, Bill tossed the newspaper aside.

"I spoke to him. I called at his shop to ask him about Anita Champion."

"I know. He were telling us about that when we had a drink with him. And he were talking about his business. It weren't going well. All the same, I can't see summat like that bothering him. He were one of those who'd get by. He'd driven lorries for years. It were when he lost his job he decided to open that fishing shop. We all said it were a daft idea. I mean, who goes fishing these days? But he said he'd give it a try. If it failed, he said he'd go back and get a job lorry driving."

Dylan could think of nothing to say. Bill was clearly upset, and who could blame him?

"I wonder what'll happen to his shop now," Bill said. "It were a butcher's for years. Of course, when old Sam retired, his kids didn't want to know, so it were sold. Terry Armstrong owns it now. He owns all them shops along there. Come to think of it, he owns most of Dawson's Clough."

"So I gather."

It was mention of Armstrong that made Dylan pick up the newspaper and read the report more carefully. The article was brief and mainly concentrated on the number of suicides in the area during the past five years. The forensics team would have gone over the place carefully.

If the police weren't interested in interviewing anyone, and they clearly weren't, it was a suicide.

"When you say he was beaten up, Bill, what exactly happened?"

"Just that. He were walking home from here when two blokes jumped him. They kicked him about and left him for dead. Luckily, a copper found him and got an ambulance. I expect they thought he'd got money on him. Kids today, they'll do anything for a couple of quid."

Dylan nodded at the truth of that.

Perhaps he was looking for things that didn't exist. Maybe Cheyney's links to Anita Champion and Terry Armstrong were nothing more than coincidence. Perhaps the bloke hanged himself because the business was failing. He wouldn't be the first to do that.

As sad as it was, Alan Cheyney wasn't his problem. The man had committed suicide and it was too late for anyone to do anything for him now.

Dylan's problem was finding out what had happened to Anita Champion. And hopefully, he'd learn a little more tomorrow.

CHAPTER TWENTY-EIGHT

THE FOLLOWING AFTERNOON, after a long car journey made all the more tedious by snow, Dylan and Frank were crossing the English Channel.

Dylan had nipped onto the deck for a breath of fresh air, but he hadn't imagined it would be quite this fresh. Other than the swirling white wash from the ferry, everything was grey, making it difficult to say where the sea ended and the sky began.

He'd spoken to Holly, and she'd been more than happy to fund his trip. She'd been excited, in fact, believing that Dylan was getting close to the truth.

"I expect it will come to nothing," he'd warned her, "but, as far as we know, Matthew Jackson was the last person to see your mother that night." He'd stopped himself, just in time, from saying "to see your mother alive."

It could be that Anita Champion had taken off with the love of her life and was currently buying croissants and speaking French. Dylan tried to convince himself of that. In his heart of hearts, though, he believed she was dead. Her life had been too—too what, he wondered. Joyful? She had enjoyed playing games and she had chosen dangerous playmates.

Yet he liked her. More than anything, he hoped she was alive.

As far as he knew, Matthew Jackson lived, or *had*

lived, in a small village near to Barfleur, about twenty kilometres along the coast from Cherbourg. But he could have moved long ago. According to French directory enquiries, there was no phone at the property. Maybe Jackson was ex-directory. Or maybe, and this was far more likely, something had been lost in the translation. Dylan's French was nonexistent.

Jackson might have vanished as completely as Anita Champion. If it hadn't been for Harry Tyler's penchant for hoarding, Dylan wouldn't have known where to start looking for him.

At times, Dylan felt like he was investigating the Dawson's Clough Triangle.

He hoped he wasn't wasting Holly's time and, more important, her money. His own time wasn't worth a lot. In fact, until Bev got over this strop, it wasn't worth anything.

God, he wished she'd get over it. He longed to go home. All he wanted was to climb into his own bed alongside his wife.

On that thought, with the French coastline ever nearer, he went back inside to find that Frank had given up on his crossword and was talking on his phone. Dylan checked his own phone and he, too, finally had a signal. He had three missed calls from his mother, but they could wait.

"Lancashire Constabulary," Frank said when he ended the call. "They've found nothing to suggest anything dodgy about Cheyney's suicide."

"Did he leave a letter?"

"No."

"That's odd in itself."

"Yeah. There were marks on him suggesting he'd

tried to free himself, too. But that means nothing. Hanging isn't as quick as people think. Well, it is if you get the drop right. Otherwise—" Frank grimaced. "Most people, when they realise they aren't dead, tend to change their mind and start clawing at their neck. I suppose panic sets in. Or religion."

"Maybe. But the more I think about it, the more convinced I am that Armstrong was expecting us to talk about something else on Tuesday. What if he thought we were going to ask about Cheyney?"

"Come on, Dylan. Even a murdering bastard like him wouldn't kill someone just because he was late with the rent."

Dylan knew he was right. His imagination was running wild again.

"Let's concentrate on Jackson," he said and Frank nodded.

"We don't know a lot about him, do we?"

"Aren't you the king of the understatement, Frank. All we know is that he may or may not have been the love of Anita Champion's life. He trained as a mechanic and took out a loan to buy his own business. He must have done well at that and decided to live in France with his family. Perhaps he's keeping the country's Citroens roadworthy."

"Don't raise your hopes. I expect he's just a good-looking bloke who Anita Champion fancied. There were a few of those."

"A bit of a loner." Dylan ignored Frank's comment. He was growing defensive on Anita's behalf and that was ridiculous. God knows, she wasn't a saint. "A lot of people in Dawson's Clough remember him, yet no one keeps in touch. Odd that, don't you think?"

"Not really. If I moved to France, I wouldn't keep in touch with anyone."

"Yeah, but you're a miserable bugger."

Frank grinned at the insult. "Actually, I wouldn't mind living in France. Just wish I could afford it."

"I don't think property's any dearer, is it? Cheaper than the U.K. probably. Fags and booze are cheaper. The weather's better..."

When they drove onto French soil, Dylan supposed the weather *was* better, but, that wasn't saying a lot. It was milder, the wind was gentler and there was no snow. There was rain, though, and lots of it. They had ten minutes of torrential rain followed by five minutes of sunshine followed by ten more minutes of torrential rain.

Dylan drove slowly. Very slowly. The rain was making visibility nonexistent at times, and he didn't like driving on the right and negotiating roundabouts the wrong way.

It took just over an hour to find Jackson's home—or, more accurately, the address that had been pinned to the board in Harry Tyler's office for so long.

It was still light, just about, and, now that the rain had stopped, the countryside was idyllic.

"Not bad," Frank said. "A bit flat compared to the Pennines though."

Dylan had to smile. The Alps would be inferior to the Pennines so far as Frank was concerned.

The house was large, square, and typically French, if there was such a thing. The exterior walls had been painted pink so perhaps that added to the illusion. It sat by the side of a narrow road, was surrounded on three sides by land, and boasted several outbuildings.

"*Gites*," Frank scoffed on seeing the sign welcoming visitors to the property. "Just a fancy term for bed and breakfast."

Perhaps Jackson had given up working on cars and was frying a full English or serving up a continental breakfast for visitors.

Dylan parked in the driveway and they walked up to the front door and knocked. A young dark-haired girl opened it and Dylan could tell, although he couldn't say how, that she was French.

"*Bon soir.*" She was slim, mid-twenties and, in readiness for tourists perhaps, wearing a summer dress.

"Good evening." Dylan refused to even attempt French in front of this beauty. "Do you speak English?"

She shrugged and smiled. "*Un peu.*"

"My name is Dylan Scott, and this is my colleague Frank Willoughby. We're looking for Matthew Jackson. Does he live here?" And why the hell did he have to talk so slowly? And so loud?

"Live here?" She gestured at the pink stone walls. "This Monsieur Jackson? But no."

"Ah. How long have you been here?"

"Me? Three years."

"And you don't know Mr. Jackson?"

She shook her head, and Dylan wasn't sure if she was confirming that she didn't know Mr. Jackson or if she didn't understand the question.

"Mr. Jackson—English man. One moment, please." Leaving Frank with the young woman, Dylan dashed back to his car for the photograph of Jackson.

She had a good look at it then shook her head. "I don't know your Englishman. Sorry."

"Is there anyone else here who might know him?"

"Today? No. My—how do you say?—partner? She is in Cherbourg on business all day. There is only me today. Sorry."

So that was that. They now had the whole of France to search.

Dylan scribbled down his name and mobile number and handed it to her. "Could you ask around for me? Ask people if they know Matthew Jackson?"

"I will."

"Thank you. And you'll call me if you find out anything?"

"On this number? I will."

"Your English is very good," Frank told her. "Much better than our French."

"Thank you, Monsieur Willoughby." Her smile was radiant.

Dylan and Frank walked back to the car and then Dylan drove toward Barfleur, the nearest place likely to have food and accommodation on offer.

"What do you think she meant by partner?" Frank asked. "Do you reckon she was a lesbian?"

Dylan hadn't thought about it. He'd assumed she'd meant partner as in someone who ran the B&B business with her. "Could be, I suppose."

"What a waste."

"Why? Were you going to thrust your many charms upon her, Frank?"

"Probably a bit young for me."

"Only by about thirty years, mate."

When they reached Barfleur, the rain was bouncing off the pavements, and boats were bobbing on the choppy water in the harbour.

"Have you got all the paperwork needed for driving in Europe?" Frank asked.

"It's a bit late to be asking me that."

"Have you?"

Dylan shrugged as he parked near the church. "I've got a GB sticker on the back. Well, I hope I have. It's one of those magnetic things so it might have fallen off as we disembarked."

But when he got out and had a look, it was still there.

Given the time of year, the town wasn't swarming with tourists and, within half an hour, they had two rooms for the night in a tall old house. Soon after that, they were sitting down in the one and only restaurant that was open for business.

"I suppose we'll have to go begging to the police for assistance in finding him." Dylan had no enthusiasm for that. "It's easy enough in England because everyone leaves a paper trail a mile long, but I've no idea how it works over here. And I doubt if a phrase book would help much."

"I've got plenty of contacts on the force. We'll get on to them in the morning and they can get on to the gendarme or whatever they call themselves."

Dylan was grateful. The French must leave a trail of the exact length as their English counterparts. It was just that he had no idea how to follow them in France.

They both had pizzas—huge and tasty, if not very adventurous—and, after showing Jackson's photo to everyone in the building and drawing a loss, they decided to head for the bars.

"Only one bar open?" Frank was both shocked and disgusted.

France, it seemed, closed at eight in the evening.

The bar—singular—was small and dingy, but surprisingly busy. Dylan ordered a couple of large glasses of what the French called beer.

"Gnat's piss," Frank muttered, even more disgusted, and Dylan couldn't argue with him.

They showed Jackson's photo to everyone present. There was much head shaking going on in that bar.

Later, a chap with an acoustic guitar walked in and started playing old Beatles tunes. No one paid him any attention whatsoever. He carried on playing as Dylan showed him the photo, and didn't even pause to shake his head.

Minutes later, four Englishmen came in. They were loud, full of their own importance, and did little to further Anglo-French relations. However, they were English and they boasted a smattering of French between them.

Dylan's hopes were soon dashed, though. They hadn't heard of Jackson and didn't recognise him from the photo.

Having taken the piss out of the French for an hour, they left and Dylan wasn't sorry.

He was ready for his bed and waiting for Frank to finish his gnat's piss when a man in his early thirties walked into the bar.

"Excuse me—" Dylan showed him the photo.

"Ah, *oui*. Englishman. Matt. Has a—how you say?—*bateau?*"

"*Bateau*?" Dylan frowned as he dug deep into school-day memories. "Ah, boat?"

"*Oui*. *Bateau*. Saint-Vaast."

"Saint-Vaast?"

The barman intervened at this point.

"Saint-Vaast-la-Hougue is, er, *une, deux, trois, quatre*—" He held up fingers until he reached ten. *"Dix kilometres."*

"And this man, Matthew Jackson, has a boat there?" Dylan couldn't believe his good fortune.

"*Bateau, oui,*" said the newcomer. "Er, lucky man."

"*Very* lucky," Dylan agreed.

Jackson was lucky to have a boat in Saint-Vaast-la-Hougue, and Dylan was extremely lucky to have found him without the hassle of going through official channels.

So delighted was he that he bought a round of drinks for everyone in the bar.

No one was sober, even the barman was struggling to open the till, and Dylan and Frank were soon being thanked for all that Britain had done for them during the war.

"It was a long time ago, and nothing to do with us." Dylan wasn't too drunk to feel embarrassed.

Frank nudged him. "It's because we're close to Omaha Beach. Tourists flock here. It must keep it fresh in their minds."

A couple of drinks later, and Dylan and Frank walked, or staggered, slowly back to their accommodation.

A drunkard and a loser.

Ah, but he wasn't. At this particular moment, he was drunk, but that didn't make him a drunkard. And it certainly didn't make him a loser. He'd found Matthew Jackson.

By way of celebration, he began singing. "There'll always be an England..."

SAINT-VAAST-LA-HOUGUE, a much larger town than Barfleur, was basking in sunshine at ten o'clock the following morning. A chilly wind was blowing in from the sea, leaving a salty tang on Dylan's lips, but it was a clear day and the island of Tatihou was visible. Other than a few locals strolling along with bags of bread or fish, all was peaceful.

"Let's start at the harbour, and see who's about. You are up to this, aren't you, Frank? All this walking, I mean?"

"What do you think I am? Some bloody soft southerner? Of course I'm up to it."

Frank quickened his pace, and they must have looked as if they were in training for the changing of the guard.

Dozens of boats were moored in the harbour, mainly expensive-looking yachts. Plenty of boats but a dearth of people.

"We've no idea what sort of boat he has." Dylan was annoyed with himself for not persevering with their French companion last night. "Fishing boat? Yacht? Speed boat?"

"It won't be one of these." Frank pointed to a gleaming white yacht. "They cost an absolute fortune."

He was right. Unless Johnson had been remembered by a few wealthy aunts, he wasn't going to be terribly well off. He'd let his garage go at a bargain price, wanting a quick sale, and, by the time the mortgage had been paid off, he hadn't been left with a great deal.

"He's unlikely to have a fishing boat," Dylan said. "Before Dawson's Clough, he'd lived in Scotland, but only for a year or so. Before that, Nottingham and Stoke-on-Trent. He couldn't have lived further from the sea if he'd tried. What would he know about fishing?"

Frank nodded his agreement so, as they walked, they paid more attention to the less expensive pleasure vessels.

Dylan showed the photo of Jackson to a dozen people but no one claimed to know him.

"Let's go into the town, Frank. If he spends much time here, he'll be known in the shops."

There were surprisingly few shops in the town, but lots of restaurants and cafes. Most were closed, and looked unlikely to open until the spring brought the tourists.

"Nice place," Frank said as they walked.

It was a beautiful place, tranquil compared to London, soft and serene compared to Dawson's Clough. Better still, it wasn't raining. On days like this, it was easy to forget the snow they'd left behind and believe that spring wasn't far away.

They entered a large shop that sold fishing rods, outboard motors, wetsuits and knick-knacks with a nautical theme.

Yet again, Dylan produced his photo and showed it to the young man behind the till.

"Monsieur Jackson!" He delivered a long speech. In French.

"*Parlez-vous anglais?*" Dylan asked, fingers crossed.

The assistant thought about it, much as Stevie thought about questions before answering, and then, with a regretful shrug, shook his head. "*Non. Pardon.*"

With a lot of finger pointing, Dylan asked if Jackson had a *bateau*.

"*Bateau. Mai oui.* Lucky man," he said, smiling.

As they left the store, Dylan wondered why people thought of Jackson as a lucky man. Was it because he had a boat, because he was a good-looking devil and a hit with the women, or because his wife appealed to the males among the population?

They celebrated confirmation of Jackson's existence by having a beer at a cafe overlooking the harbour. Dylan had fancied a coffee but, unless things had improved dramatically in the country since he and Bev had spent a fortnight there one summer, he knew the French couldn't do coffee. Champagne and croissants, yes. Coffee, no.

They set off again and began the task of asking anyone and everyone if they knew Jackson.

Dylan was idly glancing at the array of boats in the harbour when he stopped so suddenly that Frank had gone on and was talking to himself.

"Look!" Dylan pointed as Frank doubled back.

"Bugger me!" Frank scratched his head in wonder. "Looks like you've found our man, Dylan."

People hadn't been calling Jackson a lucky man at all. They had been trying to be helpful by giving Dylan the name of his boat.

Or had they? The boat in question boasted at least fifty feet of sheer luxury. It was huge, obviously disgustingly expensive, and it gleamed smugly as the water lovingly caressed its sides.

"How much would this be worth, Frank?"

"If you've got to ask, you can't afford it."

That's what Dylan had thought. It must be worth thousands. It didn't look out of place, as there were several other similar vessels bobbing on the gentle swell, but such extravagance from an ex-garage owner from Dawson's Clough was surprising.

While they were ogling this treasure, thirty grands' worth of black BMW convertible pulled into a nearby parking spot. A 335i M if Dylan wasn't mistaken, and he rarely was when it came to cars. Boats you could keep, he liked to feel the ground beneath him, but he knew his cars.

Its driver jumped out and Dylan experienced the weird sensation of falling back in time. Fifteen years to be precise.

Matthew Jackson looked just as he had on his wedding day, as if he'd merely nipped home to change out of his finery before returning. He was tall and blond and, despite the faded jeans and thick baggy sweater, looked as if he should have been filming the next Hollywood blockbuster.

"Jesus," Frank murmured, and Dylan knew how he felt.

Smiling at them and revealing perfect white teeth, Jackson strode over to his boat.

"Good morning," Dylan said.

"English!" Jackson's smile was dazzling now. "Oh, what a wonderful sound. Here on holiday, are you? A pity the weather's not better for you." Without waiting for a reply, he nodded at the boat. "Admiring her, were you? A beauty, isn't she?"

"It certainly is." Dylan didn't refer to his car as a "she"—cars were too reliable to be feminine—and he had no intention of referring to Jackson's boat that way. And how in hell's name could you name a boat *Lucky Man* and then call it "she"?

"I've had her about a year now," Jackson said. "I

haven't taken her out much lately, but I come here most days to check on her. Fancy a look round?"

"Could we?" Frank asked.

"Gosh, thanks." Dylan tried to sound enthusiastic.

As Jackson rattled off the specification, insisted they feel the cream leather upholstery, marvelled at the vast sun deck, and told them there was little change from two thousand pounds for the TV in the lounge, Dylan couldn't help thinking that he was like a little boy showing off a new toy. Not that Dylan was averse to showing off his Morgan to anyone who showed interest.

Jackson went through that boat, pointing out every gadget, like a whirlwind. Much as Anita Champion would have. Yes, Dylan could imagine the two of them together. He could believe that Anita had fallen in love with this handsome, energetic, charismatic man.

"This is great—speaking English, I mean," Jackson said. "Do you have time for lunch? My treat. You must sample the oysters. They're the best in France!"

In the distant reaches of his mind, Dylan could hear Anita Champion laughing with delight as she tucked her arm through Jackson's and prepared to sample the best oysters in France.

Now, of course, was the time to tell Jackson that they'd come from England to see him. On the other hand, all that would do was take away the pleasure of the oysters. With a glance at Frank, he indicated that he'd break the news later. Preferably after the bill was paid.

They were ushered into a restaurant which, although it didn't look anything special from the outside and only had a dozen tables, was obviously The Place To Eat. Diners looked to be worth a few euros, and the prices were suitably steep. Dylan definitely didn't want to upset Jackson and get landed with the bill.

"So how long have you lived in France?" Frank asked as they waited for the promised oysters to be brought to their table.

"Twelve years."

"Any regrets about leaving England?"

"None at all." Jackson seemed to find that amusing. "I'm thinking of moving to the south coast, but I wouldn't want to go back to Blighty. The weather's naff and the roads are clogged."

"Tell me about it," Dylan said. "Your boat, what did you say it was again?"

"A Prestige 50."

"Here." Dylan took his boat ticket from his pocket and a pen. "Write it down for me, will you? The full spec. It's just that a mate of mine's into boats and he'll be pig sick when I tell him I've been shown over yours."

Smiling, Jackson wrote down the full spec of the boat, right down to the optional extras like the dishwasher.

"There you go." He handed it back to Dylan. "Tell your mate to start saving."

"Thanks. I will. He's an accountant, but an honest one. If he saved from now till they put him in his box, he'd still be a few hundred grand short."

"So what about you?" Jackson asked. "Where are you from?"

"Shepherd's Bush."

"But not you." Jackson nodded at Frank. "From that accent, I'd say you were from Lancashire."

"Spot on," Frank said.

"We haven't even introduced ourselves. Dylan Scott."

He extended his hand across the table and it was dutifully shaken.

"Frank." Probably a wise move not to mention his surname. As he'd been senior investigating officer on Anita Champion's case, the name might be familiar to Jackson.

"Matt Jackson. Happy to meet you."

Dylan knew then that the truth might as well come out now. Hang the oysters.

"You're kidding." He feigned amazement. "Matthew Jackson? Really?"

"Yes." Jackson frowned, as well he might.

"Originally from Dawson's Clough? Well, obviously, you are," Dylan said. "God, what an amazing coincidence. We've come here looking for you."

"Oh?" The smile faded a little.

"Well, I never." Frank was playing along. "Do you know, I bet Dylan here a hundred quid that we wouldn't find you."

"What are you wanting with me?" Jackson asked.

"It's a long story," Dylan said, "but we're looking into the disappearance of a friend of yours. You remember Anita Champion, I take it?"

"Yes, of course. Hang on a minute, I'm going to see where our food's got to. Usually you get good service here." Jackson was on his feet and marching across the dining area to a small counter.

Having spoken, in very good French, to the young girl there, he returned to his seat. "Sorry about that, but when you pay these prices, you expect a decent service. Now then, what were you saying?"

"Anita Champion," Dylan said. "We're looking into her disappearance and, as far as we know, you were the last person to see her on the night she disappeared. It was a long shot, we knew that, but we wondered if you could tell us anything. Besides, we fancied an expenses-paid trip to France," he added with a grin.

"Anita? Yes, I knew her. You'd know that, of course."

"You were at school with her, I gather?"

"Yes. As kids, we were even an item. I suppose you've been told that?"

Everything from Jackson was a question.

"Yes," Dylan agreed.

"So who are you?" Jackson asked. "Who are you working for? Police?"

"Good God, no."

"Her daughter," Frank said. "She had a daughter, as you'll know, and it's Holly who's asked us to look into her mother's disappearance. She's twenty-five now."

The oysters arrived and Dylan dutifully oohed and aahed. He couldn't say he was a lover of seafood, he was more passionate about pie and chips, but they were okay. Nothing on earth would persuade him to pay so dearly for them though.

For the main part, they were silent as they ate and Dylan wondered if they were giving Jackson time to invent a story.

He decided Jackson's time was up. "You know how it is when you're looking for a missing person. You find someone who saw that person, and they tell you that they saw her later with someone else. And so it goes on. The last person we spoke to, a chap called Colin Bates, who worked as a bouncer at Morty's for a while, said he saw her on that last night with you. Would that be right?"

"It would."

"And I suppose you're going to tell us that you saw someone else with her later?" Frank said.

"Nope. She went off to the ladies' and I got chatting to a load of mates. I didn't see her after that."

"How did she seem?" Dylan asked.

"The same as usual. Pissed. How do you mean?"

"Bates, the bouncer, said she was happy. Excited."

Jackson thought for a moment. "No more so than usual as far, as I can remember. It's a long time ago, Dylan."

"Don't I know it. How did you find out she'd vanished?"

"Sorry?"

"When and how did you realise she hadn't gone home that night?"

Jackson shrugged. "I can't remember."

"Oh?"

"You know what it's like in the Clough. Gossip spreads that fast, you can't remember who told you."

"Were you surprised? That she hadn't made it home, I mean?"

"Of course I was." Jackson signalled and the waitress scurried to their table. "Another bottle of wine, please."

"Are you okay drinking and driving over here?" Frank asked.

"It's a lot better than being in Blighty, but I'm not driving today. My wife's here, in Saint-Vaast, and she'll be driving me home."

"Very convenient. Where's home? Near here, is it?" Frank asked.

"Two kilometres down the road."

"Handy for the boat then? I can't tell you how envious

I am. Not that I'm ever going to be able to afford such a beauty. Still, a man can dream." Jackson was giving nothing away, and Dylan wanted to know how he could afford such a luxury vessel. "Are they any cheaper over here?"

"Not really." Jackson smiled. "You wouldn't get much change from half a million pounds."

"Half a million?" Dylan whistled in amazement. "You've got a better job than me then. Any vacancies going?"

Jackson laughed at that. "I've invested wisely over the years."

"Ah, so you don't work?"

"Only on my investments."

"And now I really am jealous," Dylan said. "I suppose you made a good healthy profit when you sold the garage you had in Dawson's Clough?"

"Of course. I'd built up a lot of goodwill and that's worth a lot. Well, it was back then."

Yet according to Harry Tyler, he'd let it go cheap for a quick sale.

"I don't want to get personal." Dylan fiddled with the stem of his wineglass. "But we did wonder if Anita's going off like that had anything to do with your decision to sell the garage. I know you can't take notice of gossip, but people thought you were close. Very close."

"Dylan!" Jackson waved a finger and laughed. "I was a married man."

"So am I." Dylan winked. "But Anita was some woman, wasn't she?" He lowered his voice to a whisper. "I heard that you were the love of her life."

"Whoever told you that?"

"Maggie. Maggie Gibson. Used to be Maggie Waters."

"Ah, Maggie the Mouse. I think you'll find, Dylan, that her bedroom floor is a foot deep in Mills and Boon romances."

"Probably." Dylan chuckled, as was expected, but he noted that Jackson hadn't answered his question. "So why did you sell up?"

Jackson shrugged. "It was all the rage back then. Everyone wanted to leave the rat race and live an idyllic life abroad."

"So they did. On the night Anita disappeared, what were the last words she said to you?"

"I can't remember." He laughed at the stupidity of the question. "It's thirteen years ago, for God's sake."

It was. But Anita hadn't gone home and, within in a few days, Jackson would have known that. When someone vanishes, or dies, people always—*always*—think back to the last time they saw that person, and the last conversation they shared. Given that the two had been close for several years, Jackson would have thought back to that last conversation on more than one occasion.

"She went to the ladies'," Jackson added. "Perhaps her last words to me were 'I need a pee.' Who knows?"

He was lying.

Or perhaps he wasn't. Perhaps he was a selfish, uncaring bastard who had forgotten all about Anita Champion. Maybe he lived by the motto out of sight, out of mind.

"That night at Morty's," Dylan said, "who else did she talk to?"

"Anita? Can't remember. She was anyone's for a free

drink. Now, I will say this for her, she could hold her drink."

"But you said she was pissed."

"She was drunk, yes, but no more than usual, and no more than anyone else."

"And you can't remember her talking to anyone but you?"

"No. And she didn't say much to me. Just hello and goodbye."

"But she didn't say goodbye, did she?"

"Not in so many words, but you know what I mean. We had a quick natter at the bar, she went to the ladies and I went to chat to my mates. That was all there was to it."

"I see."

"We also heard," Frank said, "that she had a bit of a thing going with Terry Armstrong. What do you know about that?"

Jackson's eyes narrowed. "Never heard of him."

"Really? He's a bit of a crook. He's from the east end of London, but he used to visit the area back then because his wife's family were there. He moved up to Lancashire about eight years ago."

"A crook? He's your main suspect then?"

"Suspect?" Dylan repeated. "For what?"

"For doing away with Anita." Jackson was definitely rattled.

"You think someone did away with her?" Dylan asked with a soft whistle.

"Who knows?"

The door swung open and Jackson's expression changed immediately. Dylan turned in his seat and saw a tall, slim dark-haired woman approaching them. She had sunglasses resting on top of her head.

"My wife, Francois." Jackson was on his feet, moving forward to kiss his wife on both cheeks. "Two English friends," he told her, "and I would love to chat longer, but alas."

Francois had no time to do anything but make a few polite pleased-to-meet-you noises.

"I hope we'll meet another time," Jackson said, "but now I must bid you farewell. We're already running late."

He took several large notes from his pocket, dropped them on the table and ushered his wife to the door. They were last seen striding across the road in the direction of the harbour and Jackson's BMW.

"Must have been something we said," Frank muttered.

"Must have. And what happened to his former wife, I wonder?"

"Traded her in for a foreign model, I guess." Frank let out his breath on a sigh. "He is a lucky bastard. A boat worth nearly half a million and a wife like that."

"Hmm."

"You didn't like him?" Frank asked.

Dylan had neither liked nor disliked him. Shallow was the word that sprang to mind. "It was a long way to come for that."

"True. But now we know where he is, we can get him checked out a bit. And find out what happened to the girl he married." He gave Dylan a knowing look. "Let's hope she hasn't done a disappearing act, too."

Frank had echoed Dylan's thoughts exactly.

"He reminds me of someone," Dylan said, "and I'm damned if I can think who it is."

"Oh?"

"It'll come to me."

"You've probably spent too long looking at his photo."

"Probably." Dylan pushed it from his mind. "And I've got a nice sample of his handwriting. It'll be interesting to see if the same hand wrote on Anita Champion's Valentinc's cards." He nodded at the cash on the table. "Do you think therc's enough there for another bottle of wine?"

"Sure to be."

As they formed their own opinions of Matthew Jackson, they enjoyed another bottle of wine at his expense.

CHAPTER TWENTY-NINE

THE FOLLOWING MORNING brought more blue skies and sunshine, and Dylan was happy to sit outside the small cafe, warm in his overcoat, and enjoy his croissants. He wasn't a great lover of French food, perhaps his palette wasn't sufficiently sophisticated, but he adored freshly baked croissants and could easily eat half a dozen.

The miracle was that he had a decent mug of coffee to go with them. The young waitress, on discovering that he and Frank were English, had asked if he wanted "tall coffee."

He couldn't understand why he'd imagined that bringing Frank along would have been an act of charity. It was saving him a great deal of time and effort. Frank had called his friends on the force, they in turn had contacted French officials and, early this morning, it had been confirmed that Jackson's former wife was alive and well and owner of this cafe in Cherbourg.

According to the young waitress, a girl whose English was as good as Dylan's French, Julie had left the cafe for a hair appointment and would return shortly. At least, that's what Dylan thought she'd said.

"Are you still planning to go back on the two o'clock ferry?" Frank asked, and Dylan nodded.

"I think so. Unless anything else comes to light."

Anything else? So far, nothing had come to light. He was no further forward than when he'd started on this case. He knew a lot more about Anita Champion, her friends and her habits, but he was no nearer to knowing what had happened to her.

A woman dashed inside the cafe, and Dylan thought it might have been Jackson's ex-wife.

Sure enough, seconds later she was there, pulling out a chair at their table and sliding into it.

"Two English gentlemen waiting for me." Her smile was warm. "How lovely!"

Her hair was longer these days, but the elfin features and large doelike eyes were just as Dylan remembered from the photo taken on her wedding day.

"Julie—Carrington?" According to Frank's sources, she had reverted to her maiden name. "I'm Dylan Scott and this is Frank Willoughby."

"Delighted to meet you both." She shook hands with them, her fingers long and slender. "How can I help you?"

Her face was heart-shaped, Dylan noticed, and her expression was open, friendly and genuine. He just hoped it remained so.

"I'm a private investigator." Dylan decided to come clean from the start. "My client has asked me to look into the disappearance of her mother, one Anita Champion. She lived—"

"Good heavens. That'll be Holly, won't it?"

"That's right, yes."

"Of course, she'll be grown up now, won't she?" She did a quick calculation. "She must be twenty-five. Heavens, that makes me feel old."

"She's working as a teacher now."

"Good for her. She was always a clever girl."

"Did you know Holly and her mother well?" Frank asked.

"Not really. My husband—ex-husband now—knew her better."

"Ah, yes. We had a brief chat with your ex-husband yesterday," Dylan said.

"Really?"

"Yes. He couldn't help, though."

"I don't suppose he could," she said. "It was a funny business, though. And if I were Holly, I'd want to know what happened, too. I can't begin to imagine how it must feel to be—abandoned like that. She had no one, did she? Well, an aunt and uncle, but it's not the same."

"Quite."

"I don't suppose I can help you either. You see—well, you'll probably know this, but Anita was Matt's girlfriend on and off for years. I was always jealous of her." She offered a self-conscious smile. "Anita was everything I wasn't. She was very beautiful."

In a far more understated way, Julie was beautiful, too. Deciding, however, that the words would sound insincere, Dylan didn't say so.

"I always wanted to get Matt away from her," she admitted with another of those self-conscious smiles. "I'd always fancied living in France, too, ever since—oh, I must have been twelve years old when my parents first brought me here on holiday. I thought it was a magical place. I still do. This—" she threw a proud nod at the cafe, "—is my dream come true." With a quick wave to the girl inside the building, she indicated that more coffee should be brought out. "It's chilly again, isn't it? Still, it will soon be summer and then we'll be complaining that it's too warm."

"No doubt," Frank agreed.

"You say you were jealous of Anita?" Dylan said. "Surely, that was before he married you?"

"And after. I could never understand, you see, why Matt wanted someone like me when it was obvious to anyone that he could have had Anita."

Dylan looked to Frank, hoping he'd make some suitable comment. He didn't.

"He probably wanted me because I was the first girl to turn him down." The grin she gave was childlike. "He asked me out and, knowing his reputation as a ladies' man, I said no. I think that was such a shock to him that he couldn't rest until he'd persuaded me to marry him."

"I'm sure that's not the case."

"You met his third wife yesterday?"

"Er, yes. Briefly." Very briefly. "His third wife, you say?"

"Yes. He met Juliet when we'd been living here about a year. From Julie to Juliet." She tried to make light of it but it must have hurt. "They married within a very short time and it ended about six months later. Then he married Francois. She's beautiful, too, isn't she?"

"She is." Dylan couldn't lie. "I'm sorry it didn't work out for the two of you."

"I have no regrets. We have two wonderful children, Jon and Toby, and I have the business. I love my life."

She anticipated Dylan's next question before he could ask it.

"Matt's very generous. He invested his money well and he's quite a rich man now. He won't allow me or the children to go without."

"We saw his boat," Frank said. "He certainly is a rich

man. He told us we'd have very little change from half a million."

"Boys and their toys," she said with amusement. "Yes, he's done well for himself."

"It must have been difficult when you first came to France, though," Dylan said. "I take it you didn't have jobs to come to? And your ex-husband didn't make a lot of money when he sold the garage in Dawson's Clough, did he?"

"Oh, but he did." She was surprised at Dylan's assumption. "He had it valued just after Christmas, realised exactly how much it was worth, and then sold it for a good sum in the New Year. That was 1998."

"But he must have had a mortgage on the premises," Dylan said.

"Good grief, no."

"Ah, that explains it then."

It explained nothing, other than the fact that perhaps Jackson had lied to her. The truth was that he'd taken out a hefty mortgage to buy that garage. He'd sold it at a bargain price and most of the money had gone straight back to the bank. Any remaining funds wouldn't have bought him a decent car.

"Matt came into a bit of money, too." A small frown marring her features. "It wasn't much, a winning bet apparently, but it helped. I remember we had an extravagant Christmas that year."

"What sort of bet?" Dylan asked.

"He'd been given a tip for a horse race."

"He's one lucky man," Dylan said, smiling. "Who gave him the tip?"

"Gosh, I've no idea. You'd have to ask Matt."

Dylan wasn't convinced. Was it possible that Jackson's

windfall hadn't come from an obliging horse, but from someone who paid well for jobs carried out neatly? Someone like Terry Armstrong?

"You've got a prime spot here, haven't you?" Dylan said as several more customers arrived for coffee and croissants.

"I love it."

"A friend of mine was thinking of opening a restaurant in France," Dylan lied, "but he couldn't get the hang of the system over here. Mind, he didn't have a clue about how to prepare his accounts in England, never mind France. Is it a lot more complicated?"

She laughed at that. "How would I know? I don't do any of that. I have an accountant who deals with all that sort of stuff. Maths was never my strong point."

So she was hopeless with money. It would have been easy enough for Jackson to lie to her about his financial status, if indeed he had.

All this speculation about Jackson's wealth was getting him nowhere. It was Anita Champion he wanted to know about.

"Getting back to Anita," he said, "can you remember the last time you saw her?"

"As clearly as if it happened yesterday. It was the day before she vanished. I'd been in Manchester, shopping, and when I got to the station, she was waiting for the same train back to Dawson's Clough."

"How did she seem?"

"Chatty. Friendly. But she always did. If she knew how jealous I was, if she had any idea how I longed for her to vanish off the face of the earth, she gave no indication. We chatted about the stunning Christmas decorations in Manchester and moaned about the lack of decorations in the Clough. I asked after Holly and she asked after Matt. The usual stuff."

"You got your wish then." Dylan watched her closely. "She seems to have done just that—vanished off the face of the earth."

Her skin turned such a deep shade of red that Dylan was half expecting his first case of human combustion.

"God, what an awful thing to say. I meant—"

"I know what you meant," Dylan said, and she smiled her gratitude.

"So you weren't at Morty's with your husband the following night?" he asked.

"No." She didn't elaborate.

"Why was that?"

"Oh, I rarely went. I've never been a clubbing sort of person. Besides, I had two young boys at home then."

"Of course."

She wasn't a clubbing type, yet she ran a thriving cafe in a bustling street in Cherbourg. That wasn't the action of a wallflower, was it?

"When your husband came home that night—the night Anita disappeared," Dylan said, "can you remember if anything was troubling him? Did he mention Anita? Did he seem bothered about anything?"

"Not that I recall, no. He didn't mention Anita, but he wouldn't, not to me. No, he didn't really say anything about it."

"I see." Dylan gave her his little-boy-lost smile. "And you can't think of anything that might help me?"

"I wish I could. As I said, I was always jealous of Anita, but I wouldn't have wished any harm to come to her. It's just awful to think of poor Holly abandoned like that." She brushed a crumb from the white tablecloth. "I remember the police asking questions at the time, and I really hoped they would find out what had happened, for Holly's sake, I mean. They never did, though."

"I'm hoping to be more successful," Dylan said.

"Gosh, yes, let's hope so."

"One more thing, did you know a man called Terry Armstrong?" At her blank expression, Dylan went on, "He only moved to Lancashire about eight years ago, but he made the occasional visit back then."

"No, I don't think I've ever heard the name."

"Don't worry, it was a long shot."

Dylan really would have to get some cards printed. As soon as he was back in England, he'd do just that. He'd stop at the motorway services and get some printed on the spot. For now, he tore another page from his notebook, wrote his name and phone number on it and handed it to Julie.

"If you think of anything, anything at all, no matter how insignificant you think it is, will you give me a call?"

"Of course I will." She took the page of paper, folded it in half and put it in the back pocket of her jeans. "I'm sorry I can't help you."

Dylan nodded. He was sorry, too.

He took his wallet from his pocket, but she pushed it away.

"This is on the house. And make sure you call again if ever you're in France."

Dylan and Frank promised they would, and she kissed them on both cheeks.

"Give my love to Lancashire!"

CHAPTER THIRTY

BY MONDAY, LANCASHIRE was hiding under another blanket of snow. So much for spring being on the way.

Dylan was paying another visit to the pub from hell, the Black Bull. It hadn't improved during his absence. Windows were still in need of repair, as were the seats, and it looked as if the counter was still awash with the same spilt beer. At least it was warm, though, and it was no mean feat heating a place this size.

With a pint in his hand, he sat at the bar, careful not to put his arms anywhere near it, and waited to see if Morty's ex-bouncer, Colin Bates, would put in an appearance.

Over the weekend, Dylan had compared the handwriting sample he'd obtained from Matthew Jackson with the two words written on the Valentine's cards Anita had cherished. He'd stared at them for two hours and still couldn't be one hundred percent certain they were written by the same hand. They were very similar, no doubt about that, but were they the same? He just didn't know. Not that it would prove anything one way or the other. Matthew Jackson made no secret of the fact that he and Anita had been an item. So he'd sent her a couple of Valentine's cards. So what? The fact that Anita had kept them must mean that the sender had meant a lot to her though.

Dylan couldn't help feeling that the key to all this

was Terry Armstrong. Matthew Jackson had come into some money, and it seemed likely that he'd lied to his wife about the origin of his little windfall. He *might* have won on the horses, but the only rich men in that game were the bookies. Besides, at the time, Jackson hadn't had enough money to place a substantial bet. No, a windfall had all the hallmarks of Armstrong.

Jackson's boat, as he'd been eager to point out, was a Prestige 50. A quick search on the internet had proved he hadn't been exaggerating when he said there would be little change from half a million pounds. He'd have to be a financial genius, and an incredibly lucky man, to invest a small sum of money and end up owning a boat like that.

Jackson was one of those rare beings who had no close family or friends. Come to think of it, his ex-wife, Julie, was the same. Both were only children. Matthew had parents who'd travelled around the country for years, and Julie had left home for university never to return. Both lacked the normal ties with home.

Dawson's Clough hadn't been home for either of them, he supposed. Their sons had been born there but it was no big deal for Matthew or Julie to up sticks and make a new life in another country without keeping in touch with old friends or neighbours.

Dylan would normally hear gossip. No one talked about the Jacksons, though, because no one had ever got close enough to either of them. Julie had said "Give my love to Lancashire," but there was no one in the town she'd grown close to or kept in touch with.

Tomorrow, he and Frank would pay Terry Armstrong another visit and they would question him about his relationship with Matthew Jackson. Neither Jackson nor his ex-wife had claimed to know Armstrong, but there had to be a link. Armstrong had to be involved in this. He had to be.

The door opened and banged shut. Dylan was in luck. And this time, Colin Bates was alone.

Bates nodded to him.

"Oh, yeah." Dylan put on his slurred voice. "Didn't recognise you for a minute, mate. I still haven't heard about that bloody job at Bannister's."

Dylan was wearing the oldest jeans he'd been able to find, brought from London specially for the occasion, and a jumper that he sometimes did a bit of gardening in. His trainers, old and with the sole coming loose, had run miles in their time.

"Where was it we met again?" he asked Bates, as the other man waited for his pint to be pulled.

"In here, last week."

"Ah, that's it. And before that, you were at Morty's." Dylan was proud of his drunken slur. "Christ, I had some times there, did I tell you?"

"Yeah." Bates handed over money for his pint and took the stool next to Dylan's. "Been in here long, have you?" He rolled his eyes.

"No, this is my first pint. I had a couple in the Vic, and then another in some dive down the road. Started a bit early." Dylan gave him his finest drunkard's grin.

"So I see." Bates took a long drink from his glass and didn't seem to mind that his elbow was resting in beer.

"Ah, Morty's," Dylan said. "Them were the days, eh?"

Bates shrugged at that.

"Tell you who I saw the other day," Dylan said. "Terry

Armstrong. Remember him? Yeah, you must. He used to visit Morty's now and again. Lived in the east end in them days. He's moved up north now though."

"Never heard of him."

"What? Oh, come on, you must have. Him and Anita had a bit of a thing going. That flash prat, Jackson, he knew him, too."

"Never heard of him," Bates said again, more firmly this time. "What about him anyway?"

Bates sounded genuine about not knowing Armstrong. On the other hand, he was curious about him.

"Just saying that I saw him the other day." Dylan tapped the side of his nose and, rather proud of his drunkard's impersonation, leaned toward Bates to whisper. "I did a few jobs for him back then. To tell the truth, I wouldn't mind doing another job for him. Easy money, if you know what I mean."

"No. What sort of job?"

"Ah, that'd be telling." He took a deep swallow of beer. "I wonder if Matt Jackson did jobs for him. Here you are, mate, I'll get these. I may as well have one more for the road." Dylan emptied his glass and banged it down on the counter. "Same again, love."

When their drinks were in front of them and Bates had muttered his thanks, Dylan said, "Jackson came into some money, you know. I bet the bastard was working for Armstrong. Sod it, I could have done that job. And I reckon we're talking big money, too."

"I never heard about Jackson coming into no money. When was that then?"

"Just before he left the Clough. About thirteen years ago. Moved to France."

"I knew he went abroad. Never heard about no money, though."

"Tells everyone he won a bet," Dylan said.

"Eh?" Bates laughed at that. "We tried to get him into a poker game once because we knew he'd be fucking crap at it, and the tosser kept telling us that gambling was a mug's game. He was too much of a wanker to win any bet."

"That's what I thought, which is why I reckon he was working for Armstrong."

"Dunno. Never heard of your man Armstrong."

"A good payer." Dylan supped at his beer for a few moments. "Jackson's wife was okay, though, wasn't she? Remember her?"

"A quiet, mousey thing, wasn't she? Can't remember her name."

"I can't, either. Yeah, she was a bit mousey, now you come to mention it. Was it Jane or Julie, summat like that?"

"Summat like that."

Dylan was getting nowhere and the beer was awful. As soon as he'd finished his pint, he left Colin Bates at the bar and walked the mile or so to where he'd parked his car. On two pints of that poor excuse for beer, he should be safe to drive.

CHAPTER THIRTY-ONE

"HE WON'T BE pleased to see us," Frank said.

"No change there then." Dylan put his foot to the accelerator and joined the motorway.

All he wanted to know was where Jackson's windfall had come from. Something or someone was responsible for a wealthy lifestyle that had Jackson showing off luxury boats to complete strangers, and Dylan very much doubted that a horse was responsible.

His money had appeared too close to Anita's disappearance for comfort. If Anita had fallen foul of Armstrong, and that wouldn't have been difficult, he would have wanted her taken out of his life. For good.

What better than to let the love her life, Matthew Jackson, do the dirty deed for him? Anita had trusted Jackson. She would have been his for the taking.

"He'll be threatening us with harassment," Frank added.

"So we'll be nice to him."

Dylan was soon stopping the car outside Armstrong's modest home. Not that the two cars on the drive, both top-of-the-range Mercedes, were particularly humble.

"His and hers," Frank said. "We might get to see Susie."

It was Susie who opened the door to them, and she came as something of a surprise to Dylan. He'd expected her to be younger whereas she was middle-aged. Her skin was pale and wrinkled, especially round the eyes and lips, and makeup was kept to a bare minimum. Blond hair was tied back in a ponytail and she wore a grey jogging suit. She was slim, but it didn't look as if she worked on that, and a cigarette was clasped between her fingers.

"Sorry to bother you, Mrs. Armstrong—it is Mrs. Armstrong, isn't it?" Dylan asked.

"Who wants to know?"

Good to see she shared her husband's welcoming manner.

"Sorry, I'm Dylan Scott and this is Frank Willoughby. We were passing and hoping for a quick word with Terry. Is he in?"

"You'd better come in." She stood back to let them enter, then yelled up the stairs. "Terry? A couple of blokes to see you."

Pad, pad, pad on the landing.

"Oh, it's you two." Armstrong paused to glare at them both before coming down the stairs. "Now what?"

It was obvious they weren't going to progress further than the hallway.

"Sorry to bother you, Mr. Armstrong," Dylan said, all friendly, "but we're trying to find Matthew Jackson."

"Good God, you're losing a few people, aren't you?" Armstrong laughed at his own joke. "First Anita, now this chap called Jackson. Remind me never to employ you to find someone."

"The thing is, we've heard rumours about this Jackson—you know him, do you?"

"No."

"Are you sure? He and Anita were close. *Very* close if you get my drift."

Armstrong's lips narrowed at that. Jealousy? "I don't know him."

"In that case," Dylan said, "we're probably wasting your time. It was just that he came into some money a few years back, not long after Anita disappeared to tell the truth, and rumour has it that the money came from you."

"It what?"

Dylan had touched a nerve. Armstrong wouldn't like people spreading rumours.

"Come in here." He clearly agreed with Dylan that the hallway was too crowded for a friendly chat.

Susie could be heard moving around in the room above the lounge.

"Now then," Armstrong demanded, "who's been talking about me?"

"That's just it, we don't know," Frank said. "We were in a bar in Accrington, asking about this Matthew Jackson, and you were mentioned. We didn't get their names."

"Why the hell not? And what the hell did they say?"

"Just that Jackson was living in France now. Well, we knew that anyway, but it's a big country to search, isn't it? When we said we wished we could afford to live there, they suggested we did a job for you. Said that was how Jackson had got his money."

"This Jackson bloke—tell me about him."

"Same age as Anita," Dylan said. "In fact, they had a thing between them from their schooldays until Jackson married and had a couple of kids. He took out a mortgage to buy an old garage on what is now Brightwell Industrial Estate. He was a good mechanic, by all accounts. Then, a month or so after Anita vanished, he came into some money, sold the garage off cheap, and took off with his family to France."

"A mechanic? What the fuck would I want with a mechanic?"

"We were hoping you'd tell us," Frank said.

"Then you're out of luck, Chief Inspector. I've no idea who the hell you're talking about."

Dylan took the photo of Jackson on his wedding day from his pocket and showed it to Terry Armstrong. Annoyingly, there didn't seem to be the smallest flicker of recognition.

"What sort of job is he supposed to have done for me?"

"We've no idea," Frank said.

"A big one, I imagine," Dylan put in. "According to rumour, Jackson lives like a king now—flash car, expensive boat, the works."

"I've no idea who he is, or how his name has been linked to mine. No idea at all."

"Then we've been wasting your time," Dylan said. "Sorry about that, Mr. Armstrong."

Armstrong grunted a couple of times as he showed them the door.

"That was a terrible thing, wasn't it?" Dylan said, just as Armstrong was about to open it. "Alan Cheyney's suicide. He was a tenant of yours, wasn't he?"

"He was. And yes, it was a shock. He had a bit of trouble a couple of weeks earlier, but I thought he was over that. He seemed okay about it when I visited him in hospital. Eager to get home, I thought."

"You visited him in hospital?" Dylan found it hard to keep the amazement from his voice.

"Took him some fruit." Smiling, Armstrong nodded. "He's a—*was* a good tenant."

"Rent up to date, was it?"

Armstrong smiled. "He'd paid it only that morning. In cash."

"A man of principle," Dylan said. "Making sure his bills were paid before topping himself."

"Indeed." Armstrong pulled open the door. "If you find out who's been spreading those rumours about me, you'll let me know?"

"You'll be the first," Frank said.

The wind was razor sharp as they dashed to Dylan's car.

"We should have come in your car, Frank," Dylan said once they were fastening their seat belts.

"Why?"

"Have you ever tried tailing someone when you're driving a Daytona Yellow Morgan?"

"I've never heard such a damn fool idea."

Dylan wasn't sure that he had either. But— "I bet Armstrong is on the phone as we speak. Either that, or he'll be leaving the house any minute. He didn't take kindly to people spreading rumours, did he?"

"Park up at the end of the road."

"I intend to." Dylan drove off and stopped the car in a lay-by on the main road. If Armstrong left the house by car, he'd have to pass them.

Without the engine running, the temperature dropped inside the car. That icy wind was rocking the vehicle.

Ten minutes passed. Then twenty. Thirty.

"I-spy with my little eye something beginning with *N*," Frank said at last.

"Newspaper?" Dylan was looking down at the foot well.

"Nope."

"New road sign?"

"Nope."

"Number plate." A lorry had parked in front of them.

"Nope."

"Give up."

"Nothing."

"What?"

"I see bloody nothing. Armstrong's sitting at home, Dylan."

Frank was right.

"I bet he's made a few phone calls though."

"So let's hope no one winds up dead!"

On that cheerful note, Dylan fired the engine and drove off. He drove slowly, though, and kept one eye on the rear-view mirror just in case Armstrong's Mercedes came into view.

CHAPTER THIRTY-TWO

THE MARITAL HOME was the same as ever. Bev, however, wasn't.

"What are you doing here?"

Dylan knew he wasn't the most observant of blokes when it came to women, but even he noticed that her hair had been cut and had very light blond streaks in it. She was wearing makeup, too. He couldn't remember her not reaching for a lipstick first thing in the morning, but today, and it was only eleven o'clock on a Saturday morning, she looked as if she was about to star in a Max Factor commercial.

"It's my house, remember?" Dylan wasn't standing for this nonsense any longer. Apart from anything else, it was damned stupid to be paying rent *and* a mortgage.

After three long days in Dawson's Clough achieving nothing, he wasn't in the mood for pandering to her sulks. He'd spent most of that time with Stevie, searching through all those newspaper cuttings for a link between Terry Armstrong and Matthew Jackson. He hadn't found one.

"Luke's not here," Bev said. "It's Tom's birthday so he's spending the day with him."

"I know. I do communicate with Luke, you know."

Dylan had spoken to Luke last night and he knew his son was going bowling and then to some fancy restaurant with his friend. Tomorrow, they would spend the day together, but meanwhile, Dylan was determined to talk some sense into Bev.

"Shall I come in?" he asked. "Or would you rather give the neighbours something to talk about?"

"Five minutes." She stepped back to allow him entry.

They walked into the kitchen where Bev stood, arms folded, with her back to the sink. She glanced at her watch, then at the clock on the wall, and then at Dylan. "Well?"

"Are you expecting company?"

"No." He wasn't sure if she blushed or not. "But I'm going out and I'll be late. I need to get on, Dylan. Can't this wait until tomorrow?"

"No, Bev, it can't. I want to know what's going on."

"Going on?"

"With you. With us. I want to know how long I'm expected to stand it in that blasted flat."

"What's wrong with it?"

"Everything, but that's not the point. I want to know how long it will be before we can forget all this nonsense and get back to normal."

She took a breath and glanced at her watch again.

"I've told you. It's over, Dylan. I can't live with you any longer."

"So are we talking divorce? Shall I go and instruct a solicitor, or would you rather sit down and talk finances now?"

He had, naturally enough, expected her to quake at the mention of solicitors and the D-word, but no. Credit where it was due, she was taking this strop all the way.

"I think we need to sit down and talk. But not now, Dylan. Really, I have to go out."

"Tomorrow?"

She nodded, but he could tell it was a reluctant agreement.

"Fine," he said. "I'll be back with Luke by sixish. We'll sit down then, shall we? Luke can join in and tell us how he feels about coming from a broken home."

"For God's sake, Dylan."

"What? A broken home is exactly what it is."

"We'll talk tomorrow." She looked at her watch again.

"Fine."

With that, he marched off. Two could play at this game, he thought, as he got in his car and gave the door a (gentle) slam. She would spend the day thinking he was serious about a divorce, and then wonder how she could climb down gracefully without making herself look ridiculous.

He had driven about twenty yards when a Nissan drove round the corner and into the quiet road, slowing to a crawl. The male driver was studying house numbers.

The Nissan pulled up in the exact spot Dylan had vacated. Dylan had to stop and turn around in his seat.

The man, carrying flowers, walked up to Dylan's front door and rang the bell.

He'd probably got the wrong house. Men took flowers to their wives if they'd been having an affair, or they gave flowers to their dying mothers, sisters or aunts. Yes, he must have the wrong house. Dylan put the Morgan into gear and slowly pulled away.

The next day, sitting in a draughty corner of McDonalds, Dylan did the unthinkable. He grilled Luke.

"Did your mum have any visitors yesterday?"

Luke poured ketchup over his chips. "Not that I know of."

"Did she have flowers in the house?"

Sadly, Luke had inherited Dylan's observational skills in the home. "I dunno."

"Has she seemed different lately?"

"No. Why?"

"When I called in yesterday, she kept looking at the clock. Then, just as I was leaving, some man called at the house. He was carrying flowers."

Luke's mouth, stuffed with burger, gaped. "You reckon she's got a bloke?"

"Ooh, I shouldn't think so." But Dylan didn't know what to think.

"She has been making me tidy up a lot recently."

"Has she?"

"Yeah."

"What? More than usual?"

"I dunno really."

Of course he didn't. Bev was obsessively tidy at the best of times.

"Well, we won't worry about it. I'll talk to her later and we'll soon get everything sorted out."

"I hope so. I hate it when you're not around, Dad."

Dylan ruffled his son's hair. "Me too. Don't worry, we'll sort it."

They were about to leave McDonald's when Dylan's phone rang.

"Hello?" As it was a foreign number, he expected it to be a mistake.

"Monsieur Scott?" a female asked.

"Yes?"

"Ah, *bonjour.* Um, my partner, say you call at house. You asked for the man, Monsieur Jackson?"

"Ah, yes, that's right."

"I know the *monsieur.* I bought this house from the *monsieur.*"

Before Dylan could explain that he'd already found the *monsieur,* she went on, "He live in Saint-Vaast-la-Hougue." She gave a tinkling laugh. "We call him Bond. If you had asked for Monsieur Bond, my partner, she would have known."

"Monsieur Bond?" Dylan suspected that, once again, a lot was being lost in the translation.

"*Mais oui.* A friend of mine, he call him James Bond. He thinks he work for, er, MI5. A lot of, er, gadgets. And a lot of money."

He certainly had a lot of money.

"Your friend," he asked, "who is that?"

"Pierre. He has small house near Barfleur. He knows Monsieur Jackson."

"Could you give me his number?"

"*Oui.* I have say to him that you will contact."

Dylan took down the man's number, thanked her for calling, and snapped his phone shut.

Then he opened it again and punched in the number she'd given him. There was no need to tell anyone he'd already found Jackson.

The call was answered and, no sooner had Dylan given his name, the man launched into faultless English.

"Yes, I was told you'd be calling, Mr. Scott. It's about Mr. Jackson, I gather."

"That's right. I understand you call him James Bond?"

"I do." The man chuckled. "One, because he likes his gadgets and two, because he has a different story for each day of the week."

"What do you mean by that?"

"He's told people he owned businesses in England." He was still finding it amusing. "He's told others he won the jackpot. I think he must be an undercover agent for your government."

"I see."

"A pretty lady might find out. He likes the ladies."

"Don't we all."

"Anyway, you're looking for him and I can tell you where he is."

Dylan had most of the details, but he made a note of Jackson's regular haunts.

Now what? he wondered as he closed his phone again. He couldn't expect Holly to fund another trip to France and, even if he financed it himself, there would be no point. He'd spoken to Jackson, and to his ex-wife, and found out nothing.

MI5 indeed. There were many possible explanations for Jackson's wealth, but employment by that particular agency wasn't one of them.

All the same, Jackson was involved in Anita's disappearance. Dylan was sure of it.

A pretty lady would find out.

The idea began to take form as Dylan drove Luke home…

"I'll make myself scarce," Luke said in a whisper as they arrived at the marital home.

Bev, Dylan noticed, didn't look worried about a

discussion centred on the D-word. He didn't see any flower arrangements, though. He'd known, deep down, that the stranger had called at the wrong house.

Today she was wearing much less makeup, and jeans and a sweater were the order of the day.

"Coffee?" she asked him as soon as Luke had legged it to his room.

"Please. Yes, thanks." That was a welcome surprise.

He wasn't sure how to broach this. With care, obviously. "It's half term, isn't it?"

"It is."

"Any plans?"

"No, not really."

"Bev?" Grovelling was his best option. "I could do with some help. Your help."

"Oh?" She sounded surprised and wary.

"Yes. It's to do with this case I'm working on."

She handed him his coffee and he told her all about Anita Champion. How she'd gone missing, how she'd been friendly with Terrence Armstrong, how Matthew Jackson had conveniently retired to France soon afterward, and how the man had more money than Croesus.

"Matthew Jackson is at the bottom of all this, I feel sure of it. So what I need is someone—well, not just anyone, obviously—someone who can act, someone attractive who can pander to his ego—"

"I thought you said he was in France." She frowned.

"He is. On the coast, quite close to Cherbourg. We could nail it in a couple of days."

"*We?*" It slowly sank in. "You want *me* to talk to this bloke?"

"Please, Bev. A couple of days, that's all. Hey, an all-expenses-paid trip to France. That can't be bad, can it?"

She was looking at him as if he'd arrived from Mars.

"You're asking me to go to France with you?" She spoke as she might to one of her slower pupils. "At a time like this, when we have so much to sort out, you expect me to go to France? With you? To talk to a complete stranger about another complete stranger who vanished thirteen years ago?"

"I thought it might give us time to talk things over. On neutral soil." He didn't want her thinking that the problems between them were unimportant. "And I really would appreciate your help, Bev."

"You're unbelievable. Absolutely bloody unbelievable!"

"That's why you love me."

"Pah." She picked up a place mat, only to return it to the same spot. "Neutral soil, you say?"

"Yes. On the boat, or in a swanky French restaurant." She was weakening, he was sure of it. "We can get our problems sorted out. Mum's here so she'll be able to have Luke for a few days. And I expect you could do with a break, couldn't you?"

She was considering it, and Dylan didn't know whether to be shocked or delighted. He was a little of both.

"Dylan," she said at last, "I truly don't want our relationship to go sour. We've had some good times and, for Luke's sake, I want us to stay friends. We need to sort everything out, obviously, but I'm sure we can do that without coming to blows."

Her expression, a mix of sadness and regret, took Dylan by surprise.

"Okay," she said. "Why not? You're right, it will give us chance to discuss things on neutral soil. Then, when we get back, we can get things moving." She gave him her all-pals-together smile. "When do you want to leave?"

"First thing in the morning?" Dylan was still trying to understand what she'd meant about getting things moving.

"Tomorrow? Oh, for—"

"Strike while the iron's hot, eh?"

"Okay."

He gained the impression she was humouring him.

"Great. Thanks, Bev, I appreciate it." He gave her a quick kiss on the cheek and wondered how long it had been since he'd kissed her. Too long. "I'll be here around sevenish. We can drop Luke off at my place on the way."

"Fine." She shook her head in a despairing sort of way. "I'd better get packing then."

CHAPTER THIRTY-THREE

BEV COULD SEE Dylan strolling along the street. He wasn't looking left or right, he wasn't acknowledging her, but she guessed he knew she was there, sitting by the harbour.

She still wasn't sure why she'd agreed to this madcap scheme, but she knew much credit should go to Dylan and his ability as a storyteller. Yesterday, for a few moments at least, she'd been caught up in the story of Holly Champion and the puzzling disappearance of her mother.

He'd played on her emotions, pointing out that Luke was the same age as Holly had been then. He'd forced her to think of Luke in the same situation, of Luke never knowing what had happened to his mother, of not knowing whether he'd been truly loved.

Yet the world was full of tragedy, and people vanished all the time. A huge proportion of her pupils came from broken homes. Many didn't know where their fathers were or, less often, their mothers. *Shit happens.*

As much as she sympathised with Holly Champion, her main reason for coming was the thought that, away from all that was familiar, she and Dylan had a good chance of discussing the future in a calm, reasonable manner. She'd thought she might finally convince him that their marriage was over, even make him see that it was for the best. Now, she was no longer sure that was possible.

Whatever argument she offered, he would simply say he loved her. If she pointed out the flaws in their relationship, he would act amazed, pretend everything in their world was rosy, remind her that all marriages had ups and downs, and then insist there was nothing fundamentally wrong between them.

"I love you, Bev," he'd say, and that, he thought, should be the end of it.

Perhaps she still loved him. She was no longer even sure of that.

He was one of those comfortable people it was so easy to be around. Or had been. For the past few years, ever since he'd been to prison, he'd been downright difficult to be around. He wasn't even comfortable with himself.

Where once he'd been a proud member of the police force, confident and happy, his dismissal from the force had left him bitter, resentful and lacking in self-esteem. She'd tried telling him he was the same decent, honest person, but it hadn't worked.

She might still love him, but she could no longer live with the bouts of despair, of self-loathing, drinking—

She'd called him a drunkard, and she regretted that. He didn't drink often. When he did, though, he quickly descended into depression. She wished he could accept what had happened and move on. If they went out for a meal or a drink, he would inevitably start talking about how life would have been if he hadn't been sent down.

She'd tried to talk to him about that on the ferry to France, but he believed he *had* moved on. He thought that this job, looking into the disappearance of Anita Champion, had given him purpose again.

"But what happens when it's over?" she'd asked him.

"I'll cross that bridge when I come to it."

Which translated as him waiting to see what landed in his lap. He would solve the puzzle of Anita Champion's disappearance—he wouldn't give up until he had—but then what? He would sink back into his despair and talk of nothing other than how life *should* be treating him.

She couldn't stand that.

The biggest problem, of course, was Luke. He adored his dad, always had. The two of them had been on the same wavelength right from the start. She hated the looks Luke kept giving her, the endless questions about when he'd see his dad, and when his dad would be home for good.

Round and round her thoughts went. She looked at Dylan and thought she loved him. When he wasn't around, though, it was as if a cloud had been banished from the sky. Life was straightforward and pleasant again. She wasn't constantly reminded of the way her husband had changed.

If she did love him, it was because he was easy to be with. Because he was—or had been—fun to be around. Because he could make her laugh when she was in the blackest of moods. Because she could trust him with her life. Because, even after all these years, sometimes, like now, she could watch him strolling along and fancy him like mad.

Yet she couldn't live with him. He got too down about life, and he dragged her down with him.

He vanished from her view and she strolled along

the harbour, pretending to admire the boats. Dylan had pointed out Matthew Jackson's boat to her, but there was no knowing if he would come anywhere near it today.

"He told me he stops by most days," Dylan had said.

"Most days isn't *every* day."

Still, she supposed she had nothing better to do and, away from home, she might be able to think more clearly.

If she and Dylan had a boat like the *Lucky Man*, perhaps things would be different. They could take off during school holidays and see a bit of the world. They would be able to relax, far away from the mundane of mortgages, decorating, gardening and ferrying Luke from one social event to the next.

But they didn't have a boat like that and never would.

She wished she could pinpoint the exact moment things had started to go wrong between them. Was it when he'd been accused of assault, and their every waking thought had been about the court case? Perhaps it was when he'd been locked up like a common criminal, so that she'd had to steel herself to visit him. Maybe it was when she'd tried to explain to Luke, only seven at the time, why his dad, his hero, was in prison. Or was it when they'd had to cope without Dylan's income…

The exact moment didn't matter, though.

After an hour or so of sitting on the harbour wall, she crossed the road and went into one of the many cafes. She had only intended to alleviate the boredom by getting a coffee, but she had crepes as well.

No, it wasn't boredom she was escaping. It was the thoughts that refused to be stilled.

On leaving the cafe, she walked up and down the harbour, keeping Jackson's boat in her line of vision at all times.

It was getting on for four o'clock, and she was thinking of returning to the hotel when she saw it. A black convertible pulled into a parking spot right by the *Lucky Man*.

She wondered if Dylan was watching.

The sight of Matthew Jackson, and it had to be him, had her wanting to laugh. "A flash, good-looking sort of bloke" had been Dylan's description. This man was *gorgeous*. She only wished her friend Lucy was there because he was every woman's dream. Tall, well muscled but not obscenely so, and slim. Faded jeans hung low on his hips, and a brown jacket in the softest leather covered a white T-shirt that clung to his broad chest.

She was only about ten feet from him, but he hadn't even glanced her way. He jumped onto his boat. He still hadn't noticed her.

"You're stunning," Dylan had said. "I have the feeling he'll chat to a beautiful woman."

Bev had been warmed by the compliment but now she knew how ridiculous that was. The man would have women hurling themselves at his feet.

Still, nothing ventured—

She walked forward and stood watching him for a moment.

"Hi!" she called out, and he straightened.

"Hi there!" He came forward and stood on the front of his boat, a hand lifted to shield his eyes from the sun. "What can I do for you?"

Another laugh tried to surface. It was probably nerves.

"You're English," she said. "What a relief. I've spent the last three days trying out my French and getting nowhere. Is this boat yours?"

"Yeah."

Dylan had been wrong. "He'll be showing you over that boat of his before you can say *bonjour*," he'd said. But Jackson was paying her no attention whatsoever. He was frowning, looked as if he a lot on his mind. Somehow, she had to win his attention.

"I've just bought a place on the coast. Provence," she said, "and, of course, my husband's after a new boat now. I'm not so sure, though, and as I keep telling him, it's my money. But I saw yours earlier, and I could probably get a liking for it. I love those leather seats."

"Provence, eh?"

"Yeah. Mind, it's not all it's cracked up to be. Everyone's a bit stuffy. Me, I like a laugh when I go out."

He smiled at that, showing off perfect white teeth.

"How much would this set me back?" She nodded at the boat. "A quarter of a mill? Half?"

"About half." He eyed her seriously for the first time.

"I suppose that's not bad, is it? I mean, you could almost live on it, couldn't you?"

"You could. So what brings you this far north?"

"We're heading home for a week, to England I mean, and my husband's visiting some old friends of his today. I'm killing time until the morning and I'm bored, to tell the truth. Mind, I'll let him have it if he has too much of the old vino tonight. He's supposed to be meeting me at the ferry terminal in Cherbourg in the morning."

"Would you like to kill some time looking round her?"

At last!

"Would I? Oh, wow! Yes, please."

He reached for her hand and she jumped down onto the boat. Nice hands he had, too.

Despite what Dylan had said, Bev knew she was neither stunning nor beautiful. Her ankles were too thick and her stomach wasn't as flat as it had been a decade ago. Added to that, her jacket made her look big round the hips. But she gained the impression that, even if she'd looked like a budding Miss World, he wouldn't have shown much interest. If anything, he was amused by her. Perhaps he'd had his fill of lovely young women clamouring for his attention.

He was engrossed in the specification of his boat now, most of which was going right over her head. He showed her the wine cooler. Bev knew nothing about wine, only that she enjoyed drinking it, but she suspected the wines cooling were of the best quality. He'd come a long way from the Lancashire mill town of Dawson's Clough.

"Join me in a glass?" he asked.

"What? Oh, I couldn't. I'm sure you have lots to do. I'm just being a nosy nuisance."

"Not at all. I'm taking her out for a quick run but another half hour won't make any difference." He took two long-stemmed wineglasses from a cupboard.

He was a showoff, nothing more and nothing less. Pleasing on the eye he might be, but she didn't warm to him.

He filled a glass and handed it to her. "Cheers!"

She had a quick taste. It was good, but she was too nervous to enjoy it.

Dylan had called her a terrific actress. That was nonsense. She was a good teacher, could bring out the best in her pupils, but her parts in the amateur dramatic productions she loved so much were only average.

"This is delicious," she said. "I'm taking a car full of wine back home tomorrow. Do you find that? If you don't go back with bottles of wine, your friends go a bit sniffy on you?"

"I haven't been home for years." He shrugged as if he never thought about it.

"And where is home?" She pretended to seriously consider the matter. "You don't have an accent that I can place."

"Probably because I've travelled around quite a bit."

"Really? That's nice. I didn't leave London until I was nineteen. Imagine that. So where did you come here from? I mean, what part of England?"

"Lancashire. A small town you won't have heard of."

"Try me!" She giggled as if it were some great game she'd invented.

"Dawson's Clough."

"Dawson's Clough," she murmured, trying to look thoughtful. "Dawson's Clough. Yes, I've heard of it."

"You're kidding me."

"No. I just can't think—" She narrowed her eyes into what she hoped was a suspicious frown. "A friend of mine moved to that area a few years back."

"Oh?"

"Yeah. Well, when I say friend, he's not the sort to have friends. I did a couple of jobs for him, that's all."

He took a long, slow swallow of wine. "Anyone I might know?"

"No."

He laughed at that, but it was a forced sound. "You could at least give me his name. I might know him. I lived in the Clough for years. I even ran a garage there."

"You won't know him."

"Try me." He was teasing her.

She smiled and rolled her eyes at him. "Terry Armstrong, if you must know."

"Really?"

The air around them seemed to crackle with tension.

"More wine?" he asked, and she practically thrust her glass in his face.

"Thanks."

"It's funny," he said at last, "bloody funny in fact, but it's twelve years since I lived in the Clough and I'd never heard of Terry Armstrong. Now, you're the second person to mention him in under a fortnight. How strange is that?"

"Oh? Who was the other person?"

"Some chap by the name of Scott. A private investigator, I gather."

"Christ, I wouldn't want to be in his shoes!" Bev chewed on her bottom lip. "Terry doesn't like people sniffing into his business. Mind, I think he's changed. Settled down now. The last time I spoke to him, about a year ago now, he was quite the man of leisure."

"So why's everyone so interested in him?"

"I don't think *everyone* is. He's got a reputation, that's all. He's done all right by me, though. If it weren't for him, I wouldn't be thinking of buying my Sam a boat. Do a good job for him, and he pays well. There's nothing wrong with that, is there?"

"Nothing at all."

Dylan was wrong. Jackson didn't know Terry Armstrong. What's more, he was suspicious now.

"One thing's certain," she said, "you don't get the sort of money that buys comfort like this from a nine-to-five job."

"No."

"You had a garage, you say, in Dawson's Clough? I bet you didn't make enough on that to buy this boat?"

"I didn't. Sorry, I don't know your name."

"Sylvia. And who are you?"

"Matt."

"Pleased to meet you, Matt, but now, I've taken up more than enough of your time." She emptied her glass. "I'll leave you to it." Her legs felt as if they might not co-operate. She couldn't remember the last time she'd felt so nervous.

"Why not come out on her with me?" he asked.

"What? Now? Oh, I couldn't. Really."

"Why not? You said you were bored. Just killing time, aren't you? I'll only be gone an hour or so."

What the hell did she say now? "Well—"

"As you're thinking of buying—"

"It's kind of you, really, but—"

"That's settled then. Pour yourself another drink while I get us moving."

He was gone and, unable to think of anything else to do, Bev poured herself a large drink.

As you're thinking of buying— He was suspicious. He probably knew she couldn't even afford the wine cooler.

Five minutes later, they were moving, very slowly, out of the harbour. She felt sick.

Dylan suspected this man of murder and here she was, alone with him, heading toward open sea.

What if her mention of Terry Armstrong had made him more than suspicious? What if he *did* know Armstrong? What if he thought Dylan was on to him?

She must pull herself together. She could act and she had a good brain. It would have to be enough.

She took him a glass of wine and was shocked by the bitterly cold wind whipping up the sea. Her jacket had been worn for effect rather than warmth, and she huddled deeper into it.

"You've got me worried." Not that she was going to let on exactly *how* worried. "If you see that bloke again, that private investigator, don't tell him about me, will you? I don't think Terry would like me telling people I'd worked for him. Anyway, it was years ago."

"It'll be our little secret."

"Why was he asking after him?"

"He came looking for me because someone I used to know in Dawson's Clough did a disappearing act. She just upped and left one night. It seems as if, after all this time, he's looking into that."

"Oh? How long ago did that happen?"

"Thirteen years."

"And what did Terry have to do with it?"

"Nothing. I don't know. As I said, I'd never heard of the bloke."

The harbour was getting further and further away.

"Well, whoever this bloke was, he'd better not come asking me about Terry Armstrong or where I got my money from."

He laughed at that. "People should mind their own

business. Tell them you had a lottery win. That's what I tell folk."

"Do you?"

"Sometimes, yeah. Not too much, mind, or all the begging letters will arrive."

"I can imagine."

Laughing, and looking as if he was loving the stinging wind on his face, he gave his boat an affectionate tap. "*Lucky Man,*" he shouted over the noise of the wind. "It's a lucky man who wins the lottery, eh?"

"So it is."

God almighty, the harbour was just a speck now. No way would she be able to swim back to shore from here.

The wind was pricking her eyes so that two tears escaped to her cheeks.

"There's a coat in the lounge," he said. "A big, thick one. Put that on before you freeze to death."

It wasn't freezing to death that was worrying her.

"Thanks."

Even with his coat zipped up tight, her teeth refused to stop chattering. At least it was bright red, she supposed. People would be able to find her body in the water…

CHAPTER THIRTY-FOUR

AT MIDNIGHT SEAN Ellis, one-time DJ and current drunk, was by the River Irwell. Only people from Dawson's Clough would call this piddling bit of water a river. At this point, on the northern edge of Dawson's Clough, it was possible to paddle through it, or even step over it if you didn't want to get your feet wet. Tonight there was a thin layer of ice at the edges.

Sean was sitting on a seat that he knew from memory had been donated by some woman in memory of her dog, Trudi.

"Thanks, Trudi!" He raised his almost empty can in a toast.

Having been refused a drink in the Legion, Sean had been on his way home. But he'd called at Asda and they'd been kind enough to sell him a couple of cans of Stella to drink on the way.

He'd had to stop by the river because his legs were objecting to the walk. Despite the cold, it was a pleasant enough night. Courtesy of Trudi's bench and a couple of street lights, it was a decent place to stop for a drink, too.

Before the Legion, he'd been in the Commercial. He'd hoped that chap might come in—what was his name? It bugged him not being able to put a name to a face.

Anyway, there had been no sign of him. No sign of anyone. The Commercial had been dead.

Sean had found his own drinking hole now. Dawson's Clough had put itself to bed for the night, no traffic moved and the trickle of the river was the only sound.

Tracy would have put herself to bed by now. Sean patted his back pocket to make sure he'd got his key. He had, but if she'd left her key in the lock, as she had a habit of doing, he'd be locked out again. Eventually, though, when he'd hammered loud enough for her to worry about what the neighbours would be making of it all, she'd let him in.

What the hell was that bloke's name, the one who'd been asking about Anita Champion? A funny name it was. He couldn't remember. He'd been a decent sort, though.

Dylan. Someone Dylan. Not Bob.

The thought made him laugh out loud. He could just imagine Bob Dylan supping a pint in the Commercial. The times certainly would be a-changing.

He wouldn't have minded talking to that bloke and having a drink with him. Maybe he'd even found out where Anita vanished to.

Sean wouldn't have minded buying Anita a drink. A good laugh, she'd been. Not like Tracy. He couldn't imagine Anita nagging anyone like his Tracy did. Nag, nag, bloody nag.

It was bloody odd how Anita had buggered off like that.

In the beginning, like everyone else, he'd assumed she'd gone off for the weekend with some lucky bastard she'd met. It wouldn't have been the first time.

The next thing, though, the police had been asking questions and her face had been on the telly.

As weeks had turned into months and then years,

Sean had forgotten all about her. Or, if he hadn't forgotten about her, he hadn't bothered to think about her.

It made you wonder, though.

That bloke, Dylan whatever his name was, had bought him *two* free drinks.

He'd been talking about Terry Armstrong, but he must have got that wrong. Anita hadn't known Armstrong. Not to his knowledge, anyway.

Over the past few days, Sean had thought a lot about that night at Morty's. He'd even remembered the dress Anita had been wearing. Red, it had been. He could see it now, swirling around her long legs as she moved. He could remember seeing Matt Jackson's hand on her arse, too.

The two of them had danced, although Anita had been too pissed for it really, and Jackson had persuaded her to sit down at the bar. Sean had been in his cage, playing music, watching everyone, watching Matt and Anita.

She'd been talking earnestly and Matt had been listening. For once she'd had his full attention. Usually, Matt would have been listening with one eye on the door to see if someone more interesting, influential or sexy had walked in. That night, he'd been spellbound.

Probably because Anita was so pissed. No doubt Jackson thought he'd be taken back to her bed.

Sean had put on some music to liven the place up a bit and, the next time he'd looked across at the bar, there had been no sign of either of them.

He'd assumed that Matt had dragged her outside, not that she ever took much dragging, and was shagging her.

"Lucky bastard," he muttered.

It was bloody funny how she'd buggered off into the sunset though. And if Sean were honest, he was a bit pissed off with her. It wouldn't have hurt her to say where she was going.

He tossed his empty can into the trickle of water that called itself a river and got to his feet, swearing as he slipped on the ice.

He yanked the ring pull from the other can and set off for home.

CHAPTER THIRTY-FIVE

"HERE." DYLAN PLONKED a large glass of wine in front of Bev. "This will make you feel better."

"I feel fine." This came through gritted teeth. "Well, considering I spent almost an hour with a bloody madman! Still, no change there, eh? I married one, after all!"

"You shouldn't have gone with him. For God's sake, what a damn stupid thing to do."

"And how was I supposed to get out of it?"

"You should have used your imagination."

"I already had. I used my imagination and told him I had all day and night to kill before I caught this bloody ferry."

Dylan wanted a beer but he had to drive them home. He stirred his coffee. "Still, no harm done, eh?"

"Huh!"

He wasn't sure if she was deliberately trying to make him feel guilty, but she was doing a damn good job. It had been stupid of him to involve her in this.

Getting on the boat had been a damn foolish thing to do, though. Anything could have happened.

Dylan had been watching from a distance. He'd sat in a bar, a glass of orange juice in front of him, smiling to himself when he saw Bev board the boat. Jackson would have been showing off the leather upholstery and boasting about the expensive TV. All had been going to plan.

At first, he'd thought his eyes had been playing tricks, but when he realised the boat really was moving away from the harbour wall, he'd been horrified. His first thought had been to phone her. He couldn't though. Unless she'd changed his caller ID to Bastard, Matthew Jackson might see that someone called Dylan was trying to speak to her.

Not knowing what else to do, he'd gone down to the harbour, his gaze on the boat that was now little more than a speck.

Just as he decided it was time to call the French police, he saw that the speck was a little larger. The boat was returning.

He watched, a whole host of emotions churning inside him, as Matthew Jackson helped Bev off the boat and, when she was on firm ground once more, kissed her on both cheeks. Dylan was so relieved that he could have kissed Jackson back.

He watched Bev stride away and, when Jackson was on his boat again, hurried after her…

The ferry carried them nearer home and Bev took a sip of her wine. Dylan knew she was still shaken. He wished for all the world that he hadn't involved her. It had been a crazy idea. As yet, he had no idea what he was dealing with.

Bev was convinced Jackson had been telling the truth about not knowing Armstrong. Yet he'd understood Bev's reluctance to say where her own fictional wealth had come from. If questioned, Jackson sometimes invented a lottery win. Why? Why lie? Of course, if the truth meant meeting your end courtesy of a single bullet from one of Armstrong's henchmen, it might make sense.

Dylan was becoming more and more convinced that Jackson, on Terry Armstrong's instructions, had killed Anita Champion. It was only a theory though. And that theory only existed because he had no better ideas.

To let his wife go off with someone who may or may not be capable of murder—

"I'm sorry, Bev. I shouldn't have involved you. It was selfish and irresponsible of me. Having said that, I knew you weren't in danger."

"For Christ's sake, you knew no such thing!"

The ferry made its sluggish way through the water as if they had all the time in the world. It was going to be a long and unpleasant journey.

"Thanks for coming with me," he said. "I appreciate it."

"Good. Because it's the last time, Dylan. Our marriage is over." Her raised voice had attracted the attention of a couple of passengers. "I mean it," she said, dropping her voice to a whisper.

"We'll talk about it some other time. When you've had chance to recover."

"I'm fully recovered. Not that there was anything to recover from. I'm perfectly capable of taking care of myself, you know." She clasped her hands around her glass as if it contained something warming instead of chilled white wine. "Okay, I was a bit nervous for a while. It did cross my mind that he'd twigged I was digging for information."

"I know, and I'm sorry."

"But he was fine. The perfect gentleman, in fact. I can see why Anita was so besotted with him. He's amazing to look at, he's charming, and he could be a lot of fun. I didn't take to him at first, thought he was shallow, but he's quite a man. I can't imagine him as a killer. I really can't."

Dylan had always respected Bev as a good judge of character, but he was convinced she was wrong this time. "What if there was a lot of money at stake?"

"I still can't see it. He and Anita had been friends for years, you said so yourself. I honestly can't believe he'd harm her."

Bev had another glass of wine and, when they moved away from the bar to the reclining seats, she soon dozed off.

Dylan's mind was too active for sleep. Maybe he'd got it all wrong. Perhaps Terry Armstrong and Matthew Jackson had nothing whatsoever to do with Anita's disappearance. Perhaps the answer was closer to home.

Everyone agreed that Ian Champion was a great bloke. He was one of those people constantly referred to as the salt of the earth. Dylan had gained the same impression. What if he was wrong, though? Champion had been, by his own admission, gutted to realise that Holly wasn't his. He must have been equally distraught to learn that the lovely Anita no longer wanted him in her life. He'd been settled with Anita, thinking he was made for life, believing that the two of them would raise children and grow old together with grandkids on their knee. Having Anita turn her back on him so completely must have been devastating.

But why would he wait so long before doing something about it?

What about Anita's sister, Joyce? She was a miserable, sour-faced, bitter woman. She could make something of herself in the looks department if only she'd try. A trip to a hairdresser, some makeup and colourful clothes would bring about a transformation. Yet it seemed to Dylan that she actually preferred to be plain, dowdy and downright miserable.

Was it true that she and Len hadn't wanted children? Or was it more likely that one of them hadn't been able to have them? Either way, Dylan would bet his life that Joyce had been jealous of Anita from the second she was born.

Perhaps she'd been jealous enough to rid herself of her sister's presence permanently.

As he stared at the grey water, he wondered how he'd feel if Anita Champion walked up to him and introduced herself. Despite everyone rattling off a whole list of faults, he had a feeling he would like her. An irresponsible woman, yes, but one who'd known that life was no dress rehearsal. She couldn't be blamed for grabbing what fun she could from life.

A lot of people had enjoyed Anita's company—her husband, her sister and brother-in-law, Sandra Butler, Yvonne Yates, Maggie Waters, Brenda Tomlinson, Bill Thornton, Alan Cheyney, Stevie, Geoff Lane, Colin Bates, Sean Ellis, Matthew Jackson, Julie Carrington, Terry Armstrong—yet no one seemed to give a damn about her.

Someone had killed Anita, he was sure of it, and those people were all suspects. Every last one of them.

CHAPTER THIRTY-SIX

MOORS PARK, DAWSON'S CLOUGH, wasn't an exciting place to be on a cold Monday afternoon. Having checked into his hotel and grabbed a quick lunch, however, Dylan wasn't sure where to start.

Something was bugging him about this case and he wasn't sure what.

The park was small but surprisingly well cared for. Tall iron railings kept dogs out of the children's play area. A lone duck sat on a pond, and further on a football pitch waited for action. All was neat and tidy although, after the great thaw, very wet underfoot. Dylan guessed that spring bulbs would soon be pushing their way to the surface.

He was sitting on a bench hoping for inspiration, and his surroundings didn't hold his interest for long.

What he needed to do was concentrate on Matthew Jackson, he was sure of it. Perhaps if he spoke to everyone again, this time asking the right questions about Jackson, he would get somewhere. But what were the right questions?

If he knew that, he wouldn't be sitting in a park risking frostbite.

Just as he was about to leave his bench, he saw the unmistakable figure of Stevie limping awkwardly, but quickly, along the path.

One question definitely needed answering.

"Stevie!"

His friend looked up, put up his hand, shuffled toward him and then sat beside him.

"It's another cold day," Dylan said.

"Yes."

"Stevie, what's your surname?"

His friend looked at him in surprise. "Greenwood."

"Stevie Greenwood." At least he'd solved one mystery.

"Steven James Greenwood."

Three words in a row. "That's a fine name, Stevie."

"Yes."

It would be good if Dylan could talk over his problems with Stevie, but that was out of the question. He'd bet Stevie could tell him a lot if only he wasn't so averse to conversation.

"Did you like Matthew Jackson?" Dylan asked.

"No." There was no hesitation.

"Why not?"

Dylan knew it was a mistake as soon as the words were out. Unless it could be answered with a simple yes or no, Stevie was a lost cause.

"He laughed at Anita."

"Oh? Why was that?"

Stevie shrugged. "Always did it."

"Because she liked him? Because she made it obvious?"

"Yes." Stevie's face creased in concentration. "Called her a whore. Hurt her."

Much to Dylan's surprise, they were getting a conversation going here. Stevie wasn't a lost cause at all. He might not waste time on idle chit-chat, but he was perceptive. Dylan very much doubted that Anita had told Stevie she'd been hurt. He would have seen it for himself.

"How do you know he called her that, Stevie?"

"I was listening."

"When was this?"

"Long time ago."

Obviously. "How long was it before she disappeared?"

"A year." Stevie thought a bit longer. "Maybe two years."

"What else do you know about him?" Dylan asked.

"Cruel. Dropped a cat from the bridge."

"Did he?"

"Yes. I took it home. Two broken legs."

Dylan shuddered at the mental picture of Stevie and his cat. Both broken. Both damaged.

"How long did it live?" Dylan dreaded the answer.

"Eleven years."

"Yes?"

Stevie smiled and nodded, then he rose to his feet. "Walking," he said.

"Be seeing you, Stevie."

Dylan watched him go, and the usual mix of sorrow and despair settled around him.

He wished the incident with the cat provided some sort of clue but it didn't. Boys will be boys, and many possessed a cruel streak. Dylan abhorred the mistreatment of animals but, for all he knew, Jackson had been haunted from that day to this by what he'd done. It didn't make him a killer.

Nothing would happen if he wasted time in the park, so he wandered into town. He spoke to a couple of shop owners, then decided on a pub crawl.

Dawson's Clough was deserted, though. After a couple of hours, he gave up on the day and returned to his hotel room.

Instead of going to bed, he dragged the chair up to the radiator and tried to get warm. All the while, a million thoughts chased themselves around his head.

Jackson had been the love of Anita's life. She would have confided in him, done anything for him, gone anywhere with him. In short, she would have trusted him with her life.

Most people agreed she had been drunk that night, and Dylan knew she had been drugged. Her tongue would have been loose. Things she might normally have kept to herself would have come spilling out.

Sean Ellis, esteemed DJ, had said she'd been pissed. Pissed and overexcited.

The club's bouncer, Colin Bates, had said Anita was pissed, too. He'd also seen her with Jackson.

What had he said about Jackson? That he didn't gamble? So much for the winning horse Jackson's ex-wife held responsible for her husband's lifestyle. So much for a lottery win, too.

What else had Bates said? That Anita had been talking about horses.

Drink, drugs, horses—

Unlike Jackson, who claimed to have won money on a horse, Anita was talking of *buying* one.

Dylan woke with a start to find that his arm was numb and his neck was screaming in agony.

Drink, drugs, horses…

"I wonder…"

CHAPTER THIRTY-SEVEN

THE FIRST DAY back at school was always chaotic, and today was no exception, so Bev thought she deserved a quiet lunch break away from colleagues and pupils. She decided to wander down the street for a coffee or maybe a spot of window shopping.

She was walking out of the main doors, well away from noisy pupils, when she saw the familiar figure of her mother-in-law striding toward her.

"Vicky? Is everything all right?"

"Yes, fine. I was nearby so I thought I'd see if you were around."

Relief that no catastrophes had occurred soon vanished. Vicky hadn't been nearby, Bev would stake her life on it. She'd want a chat, and the subject at the top of her list was sure to be the state of her son's marriage. Bev didn't want to talk about it.

"I was going to nip down the street—"

"Lovely. I'll walk with you."

"But I've got things to do," Bev said.

"We'd better get cracking then."

With a frustrated inner sigh, Bev gave in and fell into step with Vicky to walk down the drive away from the school. It was colder than Bev had realised and her jacket was a waste of time. It was all she had though because she hadn't planned on leaving the building until she drove home at the end of the day.

Her mother-in-law, on the other hand, was wearing knee-length suede boots, heavy skirt, long woollen coat, gloves and a hat.

"What's happening between you and Dylan?"

Vicky was a great believer in getting straight to the point, so the question didn't surprise Bev. She'd always liked her mother-in-law and didn't want anything to come between them, but she wasn't going to be made to feel guilty. Vicky thought Dylan was everything a man should be. He wasn't. He could be a total pain.

"At the moment, he's angry with me." She decided to concentrate on the immediate rather than the deeper issues.

"Nonsense."

"He is. I'm angry with him, too." She was furious, and still convinced she'd been conned into going to France with him. "Did he tell you what happened in France? The boat?"

Vicky shook her head.

"He wanted me to get close to a man he suspects of murder, and I did just that. I ended up being out at sea alone with him."

Vicky's frown deepened.

"It was fine," she said on a sigh. "But Dylan thinks I was a damn fool to get myself into that position, and I think he was a total bastard to involve me at all."

"Dear me. I had no idea."

Bev felt guilty now, and that was absurd. "It was nothing really. Just a stupid disagreement. Crying over spilt milk, you'd call it. I suppose we're both a bit—"

"Lonely? Stubborn?"

Bev was lonely, but that wasn't surprising. She and Dylan had been together a long time, so the separation was bound to involve a lot of adjustments. "You think I'm being stubborn?"

"I don't know, love."

It was so cold that Bev's teeth were beginning to chatter. She walked more quickly, hands stuffed in her jacket pockets. "Let's go for a coffee." Anything to get out of the cold.

The nearest cafe was less than a hundred yards away, and neither spoke until they were inside, away from the cutting wind.

As it was handy for the school, Bev knew it well and was used to the shabby interior. The scuffed tables and plastic chairs were off-putting, but the cappuccinos were delicious and the chocolate muffins impossible to resist.

Vicky had a decaffeinated coffee and a glass of water. Bev needed her chocolate fix.

"I know you're not the stubborn type," her mother-in-law took up the conversation again, "but I do think you need to sort things out. For Luke's sake, if nothing else."

"You're right. We do."

"And how can you do that if you're not even living in the same house?"

"I can't live him with." Bev wished there was an easier way of saying it. "He's changed, Vicky. He's—difficult."

"Prison changes most people, love."

"I know that but—"

"It took everything from Dylan."

"But it didn't. His wife, his son, his home—we were all right there, waiting for him. All it took from him was his job. Surely Luke and me are worth more than that?"

"Of course you are. You both mean the world to him, you know that." Vicky stirred her coffee. "What about his pride? His confidence? His self-respect?"

Bev couldn't answer that.

"You and Luke worshipped him," Vicky said. "Then, suddenly, he ends up behind bars like a common criminal. Worse, he's made to *feel* like a common criminal. How difficult do you think it was for him to come home and face you both?"

Bev knew all that, knew it had been hard for him. It had been awful for her and Luke, too. "He has to move on," she said.

"Of course he does, but he can only do that if he has the love and support of his family."

"I can't talk about it." Bev was annoyed to find that her voice was shaking.

"Okay."

It was impossible to offend Vicky, and Bev was glad. The last thing she wanted was any awkwardness between them.

"Where is he anyway?" she asked. "Back in Lancashire?"

"He was. But no, he drove home in the middle of the night, checked through some stuff that Holly Champion had given him, spent a few minutes on the internet and then left for France."

"France? What on earth has he gone back there for?"

"I've no idea. He said he'd explain when he got back."

Bev assumed he still had Matt Jackson down as a

suspect. But why? "Do you think he'll discover the truth about Anita Champion?"

"Of course I do. Dylan's no quitter. I know he won't give up until he has."

Smiling, Bev nodded. "Me, too."

The smile quickly faded. She had no idea what the future held in store. She might not be able to live with Dylan, but she was making a complete mess of trying to live without him.

She'd been on two dates with a colleague, just two, and that had ended in disaster. Paul had grown pushy, called her a tease—

God, what a mess.

CHAPTER THIRTY-EIGHT

DYLAN HAD DRIVEN past Jackson's home on his last visit to France, when Bev had been on that confounded boat trip, so the property came as no surprise. It was large but still managed to maintain a vision of quaint that the French are so good at. Old stone walls were painted cream, and the woodwork—doors, window frames and shutters—was a dark green. Despite its size, it was more country cottage than grand.

Today, though, probably because the sky was gun-metal grey and rain was lashing down, it looked less attractive.

Dylan parked his car on the driveway and ran to the front door. There was no bell, just a heavy brass knocker that, over the years, had left an indentation in the wood.

He recognised the slim, dark-haired woman who answered his knock as the current Mrs. Jackson. She recognised him, too.

"My husband isn't here," she said.

"That's a shame. I've come all the way from England to see him, too. When will he back?"

"I'm afraid I don't know. I'm sorry you've had a wasted journey." She went to shut the door on the heavy rain and on Dylan.

"He'll be back today, though, will he?"

She hesitated. "Yes. Later."

"No worries. I'll call back later. It's Francois, isn't it? We didn't have time to be introduced properly when we met. I'm Dylan."

He extended his hand, which, somewhat reluctantly he thought, she shook. He supposed he should have kissed both cheeks, but his affable manner had her relenting. Friendliness often bred manners, he'd found, and, still a little unwilling, she invited him inside.

"I'm sure Matthew won't be long." She spoke in exceptionally good English.

"It's not urgent." Like hell. "I don't want to disturb you so I can easily come back later."

"It's a pleasure, Mr.—Dylan."

It clearly wasn't. She was suspicious of him. Why? What had Jackson told her?

She ushered him into the kitchen, a vast barn of a room that managed to look homely. It was warm and, as all estate agent's recommended for a quick sale, filled with the delicious aroma of freshly baked bread. Lots of bright flowers sat on the window sills.

"You have a lovely home here," Dylan said.

"Thank you. Can I offer you wine?"

"That's very generous of you, but no." He needed a clear head for the coming ordeal.

"It's a real family home this, isn't it?" Dylan said. "Do you have children?"

"No. No, we don't."

"Ah, I have a boy. Luke's eleven. And they say the first eighteen years are the worst."

"Yes." She smiled politely and took a sneaky look at her watch.

Dylan chatted about the locale and the weather and, although it seemed like an eternity, it was only about ten minutes before a powerful car was heard pulling up outside.

Francois skipped to the window and looked out.

"Here is Matthew." She looked and sounded very nervous.

The front door opened and banged shut. "Who's is that Morgan—?"

Jackson stopped himself as he spotted Dylan. After the briefest of hesitations, there was a small smile. "Well, well. It's—"

"Dylan. Dylan Scott. And the Morgan's mine. Your wife was kind enough to invite me inside. I hope you don't mind."

"Not at all. Why should I?"

He took a step toward Francois, presumably to kiss her, and frowned when he saw her flinch. Dylan was right, she was very nervous.

"I offered him wine, but—"

"A little early for me," Dylan said.

"So what can I do for you?" Jackson asked.

"It's a bit delicate." Dylan had been seated at a large mahogany table but, as Jackson and his wife were both standing, he joined them. "It's about Anita Champion."

"I guessed as much. And?"

"It's about the night she disappeared. You were the last person to see her that night, weren't you?"

"No."

"Oh?"

"Well, it's pretty obvious to me that someone else saw her after me. People don't just vanish into thin air, do they? Someone else must have seen her."

"I don't think so. I think you were the last to see her. I think she told you something of interest, too."

"What?" He laughed at that. "Like what?"

"Who knows? I expect she was talking about horses."

A vein throbbed in Jackson's temple. Dylan was pleased to see he'd hit a nerve.

"I heard she was talking about horses that night," he said. "I expect she told you all about it. Told you that she was going to buy a horse for Holly. The girl was animal mad, wasn't she? Anita would have bought her a whole zoo full of animals if she'd been able to afford it."

"Quite probably, but as she couldn't even afford a bloody hamster, it's all a bit academic, isn't it?"

He was rattled. Good.

His wife was biting the skin on her finger.

"I think she could afford a hamster," Dylan said. "A horse, too. In fact, I think she could afford a whole zoo."

"What? She was a two-bit hairdresser, for Christ's sake!"

Dylan felt himself bristle on Anita's behalf. She'd had her faults, plenty of them, but she had deserved to lose her heart to someone better than Jackson.

"A two-bit hairdresser who enjoyed a flutter," Dylan said. "You've always believed that gambling is a mug's game, haven't you, Mr. Jackson? They tried, back in Dawson's Clough, to involve you in a poker game. But no, you believe it's only for morons."

"So?"

"So Anita was excited that night, wasn't she? Really over the top. She'd been drugged—" He smiled at Jackson's obvious surprise. "Oh, yes, her so-called friends had put something in her drink. But she was too excited to go home just yet. She was feeling ill, yet she had to tell you all about it, didn't she? She trusted you."

"She told me nothing!" Jackson spat out the words.

"You remember Colin Bates, the bouncer at Morty's?" He ignored Jackson's outburst. "She told him she was going to buy a horse. She wouldn't have told him how, though, would she? She would have told you instead. The love of her life. The man she believed she could trust."

"Matthew, please? What's going on?" Francois looked on the verge of tears.

"We're solving an old puzzle, Mrs. Jackson." Dylan gave her a kindly smile. "You see, back in 1997, your husband owned a small garage in a Lancashire mill town. He sold it cheap when he came into some money. Isn't that right, Mr. Jackson?"

"I don't have a clue what you're talking about."

"I'm talking about Anita Champion's lottery win."

"What?" An incredulous laugh.

"That was why she could make her daughter's dream come true and buy her that horse."

"You're mad," Jackson said, "and I think it's high time you and your farcical ideas left my house."

"It'll be easy enough to check up."

"Oh, yes? And how are you going to do that?"

Good question. And one for which Dylan had no answer.

Dylan had stopped at his flat to rummage through the pile of junk Holly had brought him. He'd seen two old lottery tickets and checked that the numbers were the same on both. They were. From that, Dylan assumed Anita would have used the same numbers week in and week out. Plenty of people chose birthdays or house numbers, so there was nothing unusual in that.

If she *had* used those same numbers, though, they would have netted her a cool two and a half million pounds on the night in question.

But how the hell was he going to prove it?

Yes, he could find out if the winning ticket had been bought in Manchester for that night's draw. He would also be able to find out who had claimed the money. Jackson wasn't stupid, though. He very much doubted if a Matthew Jackson had claimed on a winning ticket.

"There are ways. Well, thanks, Mr. Jackson—Mrs. Jackson. I'll leave you alone now."

The flowers were too exotic, their perfume too overpowering, and Dylan was feeling a little nauseous. Or maybe it wasn't the flowers—maybe it was Jackson.

The man was faster to the door and he stood in front of it, barring Dylan's way.

"You can't prove anything." He kept his voice low so that his wife wouldn't catch the words.

"You may be right there."

"I am right. You'll prove nothing because there's nothing to prove!"

Dylan leant forward until he was so close, Jackson would have felt his breath on his face. "I'll nail you for this, Jackson. If it's the last thing I ever do, I'll fucking nail you."

Jackson said nothing and, after a few moments, he moved aside.

"Thank you."

Dylan let himself out and returned to the Morgan. With luck, he'd catch the six o'clock ferry back to Portsmouth.

CHAPTER THIRTY-NINE

DYLAN STOPPED HIS car outside Verdun House and wondered what lay ahead.

He'd almost come straight to Holly's from the ferry, but sanity had prevailed and he'd checked into a hotel. After a quick meal, he'd phoned Frank Willoughby to update him, then crawled into his bed. He'd been asleep within seconds of his head touching the pillow.

Now he had to talk to her, and he wasn't sure how she would take it. She insisted she was prepared for bad news, and Dylan had told her often enough that he could give her nothing *but* bad news, but reality was always different.

She had the door open before he'd even switched off the engine. Knowing her, she would have been waiting at the window for hours.

He got out of his car and walked to the door.

"I've got the coffee on ready for you." She gave him a quick kiss.

"Ah. Thanks."

She asked about his journey and complained about the wet, windy weather as she took him inside and put his coffee in front of him. For all that, he could see that she was fit to burst with impatience.

"You said you had news for me," she said at last.

"Possibly." Dylan made himself as comfortable as he

could on the hard wooden stool in her kitchen. "And it's not good news, I'm afraid."

She nodded. White knuckles protruded from the over-long sleeves of the red sweater she was wearing. Her shoes were olive green and the heels were like six-inch nails.

"As I've told you, your mother was drugged the night she went missing. However, Stevie Greenwood saw her get into a taxi bound for Morty's. Several other people have confirmed that she was there. Everyone has agreed that she was happy that night. Overexcited. The DJ, Sean Ellis, confirmed it. As did the bouncer, Colin Bates. It was Bates who told me that she'd been talking about buying you a horse."

"A horse?"

"Yes." Dylan took a sip of coffee but it was too hot for comfort. "Of course, everyone laughed at her and put it down to the amount she'd been drinking. Now, the last person to see her that night was Matthew Jackson."

"And?"

"As you know, I've been to France to speak to him a couple of times. Bev, my wife, even went out on his boat with him to see what she could find out. Jackson owned a garage in Dawson's Clough and, shortly after your mother vanished, he sold it. According to the present owner, he sold it cheap for a quick sale. Jackson's story is that he made a good, healthy profit on it and has since been investing the proceeds wisely."

"So he's lying?"

"Yes." There was no doubt about that. What's more, Dylan could easily prove it. "When Bev tried to discover where his money had come from, she pretended to have a lot of her own. She also suggested that it had come from, well, let's say a less-than-honest source. Jackson suggested she tell people she'd had a lottery win."

Another sip of coffee. Holly was quite still, as if she was too enthralled to move.

"I saw Stevie again and he confirmed my opinion of Jackson. I don't like the man, and Stevie doesn't either. To my mind, Stevie's a good judge of character. Not that it has anything to do with it."

"Dylan, what are you saying exactly?"

"I'm getting to it. I was thinking of Jackson's sudden wealth and your mother talking about buying horses, and I began to wonder. I drove back to my flat and sorted through that pile of stuff you gave me, remember? There were a couple of old lottery tickets there that your mum—or you—hadn't thrown out. Your mum used the same numbers on both. Birthdays probably, something like that. Anyway, if she'd chosen those numbers on the night she vanished—and, obviously, I can't say if she did or not—but if she *had* used those numbers, she would have been worth two and a half million pounds."

All colour left Holly's face. A naturally pale girl, she usually had two spots of rose on her cheeks, but now she was ashen.

"Oh, my God." Her words came out as a whisper.

He gave her a few moments to recover before continuing.

"According to your mum's friend Maggie, Matthew Jackson was the man your mother loved. I don't know if that's true or not, but I believe she liked him. I think she would have trusted him. I think she told him she'd won the lottery."

"Jesus!"

"Quite. So yesterday, I went back to France to confront him."

"He denied everything?" she asked.

"Of course. But he was rattled enough to warn me that I'd never prove anything."

"Tell me about him." She wrapped her arms around herself, her gaze on the floor. "What's he like? Married? Where does he live exactly?" The questions came like bullets from a gun. "What did you say his boat was called? Does he have children?"

"Whoa! One at a time."

"Sorry."

He should have known there would be a lot of questions. Right from the start, Holly had demanded the truth, the whole truth and nothing but the truth. She had paid, both emotionally and financially, for the truth. She deserved it.

"Okay. Jackson came to Dawson's Clough with his parents and joined your mum's school. He's clever and good looking, and your mum and him went out together for a while. Then I gather he turned his back on her and married Julie. I don't think your mum got over him. I believe she loved him."

"I see."

"He and Julie had two boys, and he was doing quite well for himself. He was a mechanic and took out a bank loan to start up his own business. He sold it, at much less than its true value, just after your mother vanished, and then moved to France."

She nodded, taking in every word.

"Not long after moving to France, he met Juliet and married her. They've since divorced and, now, he's married to Francois."

"He's been married *three* times?"

"Yes. As I told you, he lives a couple of kilometres from St-Vaast-La-Hougue where he moors his boat, the *Lucky Man*."

"*Lucky Man!*" she scoffed.

She went to the sink and poured herself a tall glass of water which she drank straight down.

Dylan concentrated on his coffee, guessing she needed a couple of minutes for the news to sink in. It was impossible to tell how she was feeling, as all emotions were tightly in check. Dylan was glad of that—he didn't cope well with hysterical, weeping females.

She swung round to face him. "And you're not going to be able to prove any of this?"

"I don't know. A friend of mine, an ex-copper, is handing it over to the police. We'll see what they can do."

"Why him? Why not you?"

"Frank has more friends on the force. He's much further up the food chain, too. They'll listen to him."

"Right." She paced the square metre that was her kitchen floor. "So that's it then? It's all over?"

"We need to see what the force can find out. They'll be able to check where that two and a half million pounds ended up."

"I see."

"I'm sorry, Holly. Really, really sorry. I wish it could be better news."

Her expression softened. "Dylan, I wanted to know what had happened to her. And now I know she was killed for money. Killed by an old school friend, too. Someone she trusted."

"I have no evidence, but, yes, I think so."

Perhaps she was one of those who liked to shed her tears in private. She was certainly doing a good job of smiling through it all.

"I'll let you know as soon as I hear something," Dylan said.

"Thanks. And you'll send me your final bill? Or would you like me to pay you now?"

"Let's leave it until this is over, okay?"

"Okay."

Dylan left soon afterward, and she was still behaving as if he'd called in to borrow a cup of sugar. Perhaps he'd been wrong about her. Perhaps she'd known all along that something terrible had happened to her mother on that November night back in 1997.

All the same, it was with a heavy heart that Dylan drove away.

CHAPTER FORTY

"ANOTHER PINT?"

"Why not? Thanks, Frank."

Dylan was in the first really decent pub he'd seen since coming to Lancashire. Right on the edge of town, and almost hidden by surrounding houses, the Queen Victoria was easy to miss, and that would have been a pity as it had everything Dylan wanted from a pub—good beer, quick, friendly service, and no TVs or music blaring out. It was warm, clean and comfortable. In short, it was one of those pubs that made you reluctant to leave.

"Of course, it could be that you've got this all wrong." Frank put their pints on the table and sat down again. "There are a lot of coincidences, granted, but there's no hard evidence."

"Jackson's as guilty as hell. I'm sure of it. He as good as admitted it." Thinking back, and it was almost a week since Dylan had seen Matthew Jackson, he supposed that wasn't strictly accurate. Jackson had merely told him in no uncertain terms that he wouldn't be able to prove anything.

"We'll just have to wait and see then," Frank said.

Unfortunately, Dylan wasn't a naturally patient man. He would give a lot to be back on the force now, to have all the facilities at his disposal to look deep into Jackson's financial situation.

"They've got a lot on their plate at the moment," Frank said, "but they've promised to treat it seriously."

"They" was a slight exaggeration on Frank's part. Frank had passed on all Dylan knew to D.I. Graham.

"What's he like, this D.I. Graham?" Dylan asked.

"He's good. One of us." Frank took a sip of beer. "As honest as the day's long. His only problem is that he does everything by the book."

"Is that a bad thing?"

"No, but it means everything takes twice as long as it should."

Frank wasn't blessed with an abundance of patience, either.

"So what are your plans now?" Frank asked.

"I don't know." Dylan had only returned to Dawson's Clough because he wanted to be on the spot if any evidence came to light. It was pointless, not to mention expensive, to stay, though. "I suppose I'll go home, try and sort out my marriage, and carry on being an out-of-work bum."

Frank smiled at that. "If any of this can be proved, mate, you'll have more missing persons than you know what to do with."

"It's not really my cup of tea."

"Ah, that's where you're wrong."

Dylan frowned at him, not understanding.

"You've got a nose for this sort of thing, Dylan. And a stubborn streak. You won't give up until you've unearthed the truth."

Holly Champion had said something similar. That was why she'd employed him in the first place, because she'd believed he wouldn't give up. "It's not exactly exciting, though, is it?"

"Not until you get to know the person or persons involved, no."

Dylan knew what he meant. The thought of looking into the disappearance of Anita Champion hadn't appealed to him at all. In fact, if he'd been solvent, if Bev hadn't thrown him out, and if his mother hadn't moved in, he would have passed on it. It was only when he got a taste of Anita's life that he became fully involved.

"It was Terry Armstrong's involvement that intrigued me," Dylan said, "and yet it looks as if he didn't have anything to do with it."

"So it seems. Mind, there's a lot he *has* had something to do with. Murdering bastard!"

"Yeah."

They supped their pints, lost in their own thoughts.

"I expect I'll go home tomorrow," Dylan said, reaching a decision. "There's nothing I can do here."

"Don't worry, I'll keep on at D.I. Graham. I'll let you know the minute I hear anything."

"Thanks."

"And keep in touch, will you?"

"I will, Frank, yeah. You, too."

As he walked back to his hotel for the last time, Dylan made a silent vow to keep that promise. He *would* keep in touch.

He would sort out his marriage, too. He wasn't too blind to see that Bev was serious about it, but she'd come round, she always did. It had gone on long enough.

Surprisingly, he was going to miss Dawson's Clough. He'd begun to feel at home in the old mill town where people weren't afraid to speak to strangers. They laughed a lot, at each other and at themselves. They were blunt, speaking as they found, and Dylan liked that.

On that thought, he walked into the hotel and headed for the freezer that was his room. He wouldn't be sorry to leave the hotel. In fact, he had no idea why he'd put up with it for so long.

Apart from the room temperature, he supposed he'd grown attached to the old place. The service, in the main, was efficient and friendly, the food was wonderful, and it was handy for the town centre. It was just the blasted temperature. They'd promised to look into it several times, but nothing had happened. Given that the radiator was always too hot to touch, Dylan supposed there was little they could do other than installing another couple of radiators and lowering the ceiling by two feet.

He was tired but, when he was lying in bed with extra blankets for warmth, he couldn't sleep. His mind insisted on running through the last hours of Anita Champion's life. Every scenario was played out in full, bright Technicolor.

What if he'd got it all wrong? What if the police found evidence of a winning bet Jackson had made? What if, after leaving Jackson that night, Anita had met up with someone else?

Eventually, he drifted into a restless, dream-filled sleep. What seemed like minutes later, his phone rang. According to his bedside clock, it was just after eight o'clock, which meant that he'd slept for a solid six hours.

"Morning, Dylan."

"Frank?"

"I thought you might have left for London by now. Anyway, just thought you'd like to hear the latest. The boys in blue—the French ones—are going to question Jackson."

"Yeah? Excellent."

"That's not all. Apparently, just before selling his home in the Clough, Jackson had a new patio laid."

"Oh, Christ!"

"I know, I know. That'll be coming up later. I didn't get to speak to Graham, so I don't know what evidence they have, but they must have something if they're getting the spades out."

Dylan could only assume they had delved into Jackson's finances. Delved deep, too. Gone from one closed bank account to another.

"Let me know when you hear anything, Frank. I'm heading back home now. If I don't hear from you—well, I'll give you a ring tonight anyway."

"Okay. Drive carefully. Speak later."

Dylan dressed and went down to breakfast. Perhaps this meant he could stay in Dawson's Clough another day. But what was the point? The matter was out of his hands now.

It was time to go home.

CHAPTER FORTY-ONE

"TELL YOU WHAT, why don't we have a good fried breakfast?"

"A fried breakfast?" Even as he looked at his mother in astonishment, Dylan's mouth was watering.

"Don't look like that. I do eat meat, you know."

"I know, but it's a rare occurrence. You certainly don't *fry* it." He eyed her suspiciously. "When you say fried breakfast, do you mean sausage, bacon, egg—the whole works?"

"I do. I'll nip down to the corner shop and see what they've got."

He tried not to get too excited. His mother never cooked for him. She certainly never cooked "unhealthy" food.

He thought of calling Frank while he waited, but dismissed the idea. If there was any news, Frank would call him. They'd only spoken last night, and there had been nothing new.

Dylan was too restless to settle to anything. Anita Champion was unfinished business, and he hated that. All loose ends had to be neatly tied before he could move on.

His mother was back within fifteen minutes and, much to Dylan's surprise, she had sausages, bacon and tomatoes.

"We've already got some eggs," she said.

Dylan watched, speechless, as she set about cooking. He couldn't remember her tending a frying pan before. Most of her food was eaten raw and usually topped with yoghurt, nuts or seeds.

He had to ask. "What's this in aid of?"

"I thought it might do you good. You look—" She stopped trimming bacon rind to study him. "You look really fed up with life, love. It's unlike you."

He wasn't aware she'd noticed. "Life could be better."

"Beverley, you mean?"

"It would be good to be in my own home, with my own family, yes."

"When I last saw her, she looked a lot like you do now." She sighed. "I don't know why you two make such a meal out of marriage. I know I'm no expert, but it can't be that difficult, can it?"

Dylan smiled. "You wouldn't think so, would you?"

Bev was coming round to the flat this morning, and Dylan hoped they'd be able to sort things out. He'd sit her down and demand to know exactly what was wrong with their marriage. What she thought was wrong with it, at least. She kept insisting she couldn't live with him anymore. That was no help at all.

"One egg or two?"

"Two, please." It was the first time he'd smelled real food in this flat.

He was quiet as he ate, wondering if Stevie was having breakfast in Asda—unlikely, as he only seemed to eat there when Dylan was paying—and thinking he must do his final account for Holly. He could post it, but he'd prefer to hand it to her and say his goodbyes at the same time.

And then what would he do with his life?

Perhaps that was it. Perhaps he was feeling lost because he no longer had a purpose in life. Maybe Bev was right after all. Perhaps he was a loser.

His phone rang and, seeing who was calling, he flipped it open. "Anything new, Frank?"

"Yes, but it's not good. Christ, Dylan, you're never going to believe this."

"What?" Dylan was aware of an inexplicable feeling of dread. "What's happened?"

"Jackson's dead."

"Dead?" Of all the things Dylan had imagined, that wasn't one of them. "What happened?"

"I'm not sure. When the call came through, I was getting thrown out. I was being reminded that I'd retired. As if I'd forgotten. I know he's dead, that's all. Murdered. Stabbed, I think."

Dylan closed his eyes as the full horror sank in. What the hell had he started?

"At the moment," Frank said, his tone dry, "I can't think of a likely suspect, can you?"

"No." Hell and bloody damnation! "Unless Terry Armstrong had something to do with it after all."

"I don't think so. He's gone back to Florida." Frank sighed. "I might come up with a suspect later, Dylan. If I do, mate, I'll have to pass it on."

Dylan accepted that. "Give me—" He checked his watch and did a mental calculation. "Give me six hours, will you, Frank? You said yourself you didn't know the full story."

"Speak to you later." The line was as dead as Matthew Jackson.

Dylan sat for a moment, too dazed to move.

"Where are you going?" his mother asked as he pushed away his plate, got to his feet and grabbed his car keys.

"It's a long story. I'll see you later."

"But Beverley will be here soon."

"I know, but it'll wait. I'll phone her."

"That'll do a lot for your chances."

Dylan knew that, but he had things to do. And he didn't have much time.

Five minutes later, he was in his car. The one good thing to come out of all this was that, despite the exceptionally high mileage he'd been doing lately, his Morgan hadn't skipped so much as a beat. He tapped the steering wheel for luck.

He loved his car, but he was sick of driving. Traffic was bumper to bumper, and there were too many speed cameras to watch out for. The joy of driving had long gone.

All these thoughts went through his head as he drove. Far better to concentrate on the minutiae than let the full horror of Jackson's murder sink in.

A CARAVAN WAS offering hot drinks and he pulled into the layby.

"It smells like rain," the plump woman said as she poured weak tea from an urn.

"Ah." He wasn't sure if she was referring to the air or the tea.

"Milk and sugar's there, love." She pointed to the side of the counter.

"Thanks."

While she gave him change in the smallest denomination coins possible, Dylan added a drop of milk and three sugars to his mug.

Unwilling to discuss the smell of anything, he took his tea to his car. Steam misted the windscreen, but there was nothing to see so he didn't care.

He wasn't sure if he felt more upset or angry. The truth was, he was too shocked to feel much at all.

He should have spotted the signs, though. Holly Champion was bitter and, as it turned out, had every right to feel that way. Instead of living with a happy, laughing, fun-loving woman, she'd been incarcerated with Joyce and Len. Instead of joy, she had suffered the misery that was Joyce. Instead of living a life of luxury surrounded by horses, she bought her clothes from Oxfam.

But damn it, they had no proof of that. He'd made it clear to her that his theory was exactly that. A theory. Or had he? He'd been convinced of Jackson's guilt and Holly knew that.

With his excuse for tea finished, he returned the mug to its owner.

"Thanks, love. See you soon."

Dylan hoped not.

Back in his car, he sat for a moment. Then, with the windscreen clear, he set off for Verdun House. The miles were slowly eaten up and he was soon on those now-familiar narrow lanes in the middle of nowhere.

He should have phoned to let her know he was coming. She was sure to be working somewhere. He couldn't remember what she did on Saturdays. Did she work at the golf club?

He turned right into Blue Skies Caravan Park—

"Shit!"

He was too late. A police car was parked outside Holly's ridiculously named mobile home.

"Shit!"

Her door opened and two officers emerged with Holly behind them. Her arms were wrapped around herself like a straitjacket.

What the hell?

Instead of bundling her into the patrol car as he'd expected, the officers left her at the door, got in the car and drove off. Holly even gave them a wave.

She spotted him and ran to his car. As soon as he was out of it, she threw her arms around his neck and clung to him as if her life depended on him.

"How did you know?" Her voice was breaking.

Dylan had had dreams like this, ones where he turned up on the wrong stage with the wrong script.

"What did they want?" He nodded in the direction the patrol car had taken.

"You don't know? Then what—?" She looked at him, eyes swimming in pools of moisture. "They came to tell me about—" Her teeth were chattering. "They've found a body and they think it might be Mum. I have to prepare myself for bad news."

"Oh, Christ, Holly. I didn't know that. Where?"

"Dawson's Clough. At Matthew Jackson's former home."

Under that new bloody patio. Not so new now, of course. "Are you okay?"

"Yes. Yes, I'm fine." She wasn't. Her eyes were moist, her voice breaking at every word. "So how come you're here?" she asked again.

Dylan had raced to Devon, too shocked to feel upset or angry, just ready to shake Holly Champion until her teeth rattled. Ready to haul her off and have her arrested for murder.

No, that wasn't strictly accurate. He'd been ready to convince her that self-defence was her best option.

But now, looking at her—

"Jackson," he said simply.

"What about him?"

"You know he's been murdered?" He watched her closely, saw the last spots of colour drain from her face. "You didn't know, did you?"

Holly shook her head. "They didn't tell me. They just said I should be prepared for bad news and that someone would visit later."

She looked young and very vulnerable. Her emotions were under control, for the moment, but Dylan guessed she could fall apart at any moment. Wearing jeans and bright red shoes with the usual ridiculous heels, she reminded him of a child tottering around in her mother's footwear.

"Do you want to walk?" he asked, and she nodded.

Like a robot, she went back to her home. By the time Dylan had taken his overcoat from the car, she'd changed her shoes and locked up.

She slipped her arm through his and they headed for the beach.

"Who killed him?" she asked.

"I don't know. I thought..."

She waited for him to finish, then realisation dawned. "You thought it was me?" Her voice rose. "That's why you're here, isn't it? You thought I'd—what? Taken time off work? Travelled to France to find Matthew Jackson? Murdered him? Are you completely mad?"

"It crossed my mind. You're the only person I've spoken to, Holly. The only person who wanted him dead."

"Obviously not!" She snatched back her arm and shoved both hands in her pockets. Her pace increased, and Dylan's legs began to ache from the effort of walking on the pebbles as he kept up with her.

Then he saw the tears, one on each cheek, racing to her chin. They weren't tears for Jackson, or for Dylan's incorrect assumption.

"Holly!" He grabbed her arm. "I'm so very sorry about your mother."

She nodded but didn't look as if she trusted herself to speak. Several more tears ran down her cheeks, and Dylan pulled her close.

"I don't know how you could have thought I had anything to do with that man's murder," she said, when she was more in control.

"Sorry."

But if not Holly, then who the hell had put a knife into Jackson?

Or perhaps Frank had got it wrong. Perhaps they'd been talking about someone else and Frank had assumed— No, Frank wasn't stupid.

"I do want to thank you for finding out what happened to Mum," Holly said.

"I'm only sorry it's such awful news."

"I suppose I always knew it would be." She brushed her tears away. "Okay, perhaps I'd harboured a tiny hope that she'd spent the last thirteen years with amnesia, but deep down, I knew she was dead. In a way, it's a consolation to know she died happy. She didn't abandon me, I knew she hadn't. She died while believing she could buy me a horse."

Her voice cracked at the end and Dylan patted her arm.

"She did."

"Why the hell did she trust a man like Jackson?"

"Because she loved him."

"It makes her sound naive and stupid—she wasn't, you know. She wasn't the type to talk about money, either. She won a raffle once. The prize was small—only about fifty pounds—and I can still remember her telling me not to mention it to anyone. 'It's our business, not theirs,' she said."

"Winning fifty pounds is one thing. Winning a couple of million is vastly different. The excitement, the shock, the disbelief—it would be a lot for anyone to cope with." It was a problem Dylan wouldn't mind having, though.

"I suppose so." Holly kicked out at a few pebbles.

Given the excitement, and the fact that she'd been drugged, not to mention the alcohol consumption, Dylan thought Anita had done well to keep the news to herself for so long.

"It seems the only thing she did wrong," Holly said, "was to trust a man like Matthew Jackson." She drew a long, shuddering breath, her bottom lip quivered, and she burst into noisy tears.

Dylan held her close as the wind gusted and threatened to knock them from their feet. High above them, the gulls shrieked at the injustice of life.

"And damn it." She wiped her eyes on the sleeve of

her coat. "I *am* glad that bastard's dead. He killed my mother for money. That's all. Just money."

Two a half million wasn't *just* money, but Dylan didn't say so.

"He robbed my mother of her money, and he robbed me of my childhood. Because of him, I had to live with bloody awful Aunt Joyce."

Dylan smiled at the description and Holly laughed.

"Well, she is bloody awful. How Len puts up with her, I'll never know. She's mean, spiteful, miserable and—God, I know I'm supposed to be grateful to her, she reminds me on a daily basis, but I would rather have been left to walk the bloody streets!"

The laughter turned to tears and, once again, Dylan held her until she was more composed.

"I'm a wreck. Sorry, Dylan."

"You'll be fine."

"Yes, you're right." She didn't sound confident.

CHAPTER FORTY-TWO

"DYLAN!" BEV SHOUTED. "You're on the telly again!"

Somewhat reluctantly, as he was busy sorting through old Arsenal programmes with Luke, Dylan went into the marital lounge. He was in time to see his photo—looking slightly chubby, he couldn't help noticing—on the small screen.

"Fame and fortune, eh?" he joked, and she laughed.

"Fame, certainly. Perhaps the fortune will follow."

"Unlikely."

The screen was now showing a very frightened-looking Francois Jackson being taken into custody.

"What will happen to her, Dylan?"

"I don't know. She's claiming self-defence so, assuming she's got a damn good lawyer, she shouldn't fare too badly."

Dylan wondered if it *had* been self-defence. Francois was claiming that, after Dylan's visit to the family home, Jackson had confessed to killing Anita Champion for her lottery ticket. According to Francois, he was a foul-tempered man prone to violence. Funny that no one had mentioned such a trait to Dylan. He had allegedly threatened Francois at knifepoint with the same fate as Anita if she so much as breathed a word of his story to anyone. She'd been terrified, she claimed, a fight had ensued and she had accidentally killed him.

Dylan wasn't sure he believed her story. It was easy to

stab someone on TV and in Hollywood blockbusters. In real life it was extremely difficult to kill someone with a knife, and almost impossible to do it accidentally.

But Dylan had no sympathy for Jackson. Good luck to her.

"Will you have to go back to France?" Bev asked.

"I might be called as a witness. It depends on how things go, I suppose."

The story ended and the weather report came on.

"I'm proud of you, Dylan." Bev lowered the sound on the TV. "Luke is, too. We've got our own real-live hero."

Dylan didn't know how to answer that. He was no hero. Far from it. He'd been lucky in finding out what had happened to Anita Champion. Lucky that, even in death, she'd shown herself to be a creature of habit. Lucky that his brain remembered seemingly unimportant details, like Geoff telling him how Anita had always, but always, bought a lottery ticket and ten cigarettes, and how that particular week, she'd bought her cigarettes in Manchester. Dylan had known that, along with the cigarettes, she would have bought a lottery ticket. As someone determined to grab everything she could from life, she would have dreamed long and hard about the fun a lottery win would have brought. How could she have gone home that night when she'd been enjoying the most exciting time of her life? A lottery win. Unbelievable. A horse for Holly...

It was good to have his wife call him a hero, though. Far better than a drunkard and a loser.

"I never doubted you." Bev changed channels and settled down to the soap of the moment.

It seemed to Dylan that she'd doubted him constantly,

but he didn't argue. Instead, he left her to her programme and went back to Luke in the kitchen.

"Will you be a policeman again now, Dad?"

"No." Once you were an outcast, that was it. There was no way back in. Dylan didn't mind. In fact, he'd quite enjoyed being his own boss for a while. "I think I'll be a proper private investigator. Dylan Scott, P.I. It has a good ring to it, doesn't it?"

"Yeah." Luke grinned. "When I'm older, I can be your sidekick. They always have sidekicks who come to the rescue in the nick of time."

"They do."

They carried on sorting out the old Arsenal souvenirs—Luke could remember each and every game—until Bev joined them in the kitchen. She made Dylan coffee and sat at the table with them.

"Holly Champion is really pretty, isn't she?" she said.

"She's not a patch on her mother." Realising that sounded bad, he tried to make amends. "I mean, yes, she's lovely. Very pretty. Nice with it, too. But her mother was something else. She was gorgeous."

"A pity she didn't have a personality to match."

The sharp comment had Dylan looking at her in surprise. He realised belatedly he'd made a serious error. He should have said that, although Anita was gorgeous, she couldn't hold a candle to Bev.

Living with a woman, he decided, was on a par with running across a minefield. They were an alien breed.

"She liked to have fun, that's all." As ever, he had to jump to Anita's defence.

"So what about Holly?" Bev asked. "Will you keep in touch?"

"I don't know. Probably not."

They had kept in touch, and probably would until all this died down, but then there would be no need.

Confirmation had come through that the body found at Jackson's old home was indeed that of Anita Champion. No one had been surprised.

Dylan had taken Holly to Dawson's Clough, shown her around and introduced her to a few people. The most remarkable meeting, perhaps, had been with Ian Champion.

At first, Holly had refused to see him, but she'd relented just hours before they'd planned to leave Lancashire.

"I don't think I'll manage to be civil towards him," she'd said and Dylan understood that.

Within half an hour of arriving at the Champions' home, however, she had been drinking tea and bouncing young Chloe on her knee.

"You'll phone to let us know you've got home safely?" Ian had asked her as they were leaving. "And you'll come back soon, won't you?"

"I will."

People never failed to surprise Dylan.

"He's all the family I've got now," Holly had said.

That wasn't strictly accurate, of course. She still had her aunt and uncle, Joyce and Len. Dylan had to confess, though, that in her position he would do his best to forget those particular relatives, too.

What she didn't know was that her natural father was dead. When he and Frank had first met Jackson, Dylan had known the bloke reminded him of someone. It was his frown—the same expression that sometimes marred Holly's features. It wasn't Dylan's place to mention this, though. Besides, he had no proof, and some things were best left alone.

"Have you spoken to your Mum?" Bev asked.

"Not yet, no."

Dylan had switched his phone to silent as he didn't want anything intruding on his time with Luke, but he'd felt it vibrate at an incoming call a couple of times.

"I have. Their plane was an hour late, but they landed okay and were about to sit down to dinner in the best restaurant in Athens."

Dylan smiled at that, but he couldn't help wondering about the man brave enough to venture to Greece with his mother. Richard, according to his mum, was fun and adventurous. He hadn't hesitated when she'd suggested the two of them should go and paint Athens red.

More than anything, Dylan hoped the man lived up to expectations and the two became soul mates. A man in his mother's life would be bliss. She would be far too busy for anything more than a weekly phone call to Dylan. Sheer bliss.

"What's he like, this Richard?" he asked.

"I only saw him briefly, but I liked him. He's perfect for your mum. Quite handsome for his age, too."

"How old is he?"

"Sixty-two."

It wouldn't matter if he was as old as Methuselah. He'd spirited Vicky Scott to Greece and that was good enough for Dylan.

His phone vibrated again and this time, a quick glance told Dylan that it was an unknown number. Curious, he answered it.

"I'm sorry to bother you, Mr. Scott, but Frank Willoughby gave me your number. My name's Rob

Hunt, and it's about my daughter. She'll be twenty-two now. She vanished two years ago. You may have seen it in the papers. She set off for work one Friday morning and never came home again."

"What was her name?"

"Samantha Hunt."

The name meant nothing to Dylan. "And you're calling me because—?"

"I've seen you in the papers and on the telly. I want you to find my Samantha for me."

"It's not that—"

"I know, but as I say, I've been talking to Frank. He's a good friend of mine and he said that, if anyone can find her, you can, Mr. Scott. I'll pay whatever it takes."

"It's not about the money." Dylan could understand the man's pain, though, and, after all the hype on TV, he wasn't surprised that people believed he could work miracles. "Where do you live? Where did Samantha live?"

"She lived with me in Dawson's Clough."

"Can I call you tomorrow, Mr. Hunt?" Dylan asked. "I'll need to ask a lot of questions before I decide whether I can help or not."

"Yes, of course. Thank you. I'll look forward to your call."

As Dylan snapped his phone shut, he hoped Rob Hunt wasn't reduced to buying his clothes from Oxfam.

"What was all that about?" Bev asked.

"A man's daughter went missing a couple of years ago. He's a friend of Frank's and he wants my help."

"And will you help?"

Dylan shrugged. "I expect so."

"Of course you will." She reached across the table and squeezed his arm. "I'm so proud of you, Dylan!"

He basked in another moment of glory.

It was beginning to feel like old times, he thought with satisfaction. Luke went to bed at about nine o'clock, and then Dylan and Bev sat at the kitchen table and chatted about Anita Champion, about Lancashire, about Bev's pupils and Luke's schoolwork.

Dylan's phone vibrated, and this time, it was Frank.

"I've just spoken to your friend Rob Hunt," Dylan greeted him.

"Great. Thanks for that. He's a good bloke."

"I haven't agreed to anything yet, though."

"That's okay. Anyway, that's not why I'm calling. Sorry it's late, but I've only just heard."

"About what?"

"About the murder enquiry that's been launched by Lancashire Constabulary."

"What?"

"Alan Cheyney. Remember the bloke who hanged himself at his angling shop?"

"Of course I remember him. But it was suicide. They were sure of it."

"*They* were," Frank agreed, "but Cheyney's brother wasn't. He wouldn't let it rest, and he kept on at them about Cheyney's mobile phone. You see, he'd called him on it and chatted to him just before four that afternoon. Shortly after that, Cheyney supposedly hanged himself."

"So?"

"So they didn't find his phone with him, and Cheyney's brother insisted it would have been there. In the end, probably to shut him up, they got the phone records checked. You'll know how long that takes. Anyway—get this—Cheyney's phone made a call from the centre of Manchester around ten o'clock that night."

"Bloody hell! A walking phone, eh?"

For Bill Thornton's sake, Dylan was pleased. Bill had known his friend was made of sterner stuff. "Any suspects?"

"Funny you should ask," Frank said. "Cheyney was in debt, right? He owed his bank and he was way behind with his rent. He owed his landlord, our good friend Terry Armstrong, several thousand pounds."

Dylan knew that. "Yeah, but even Armstrong wouldn't kill a bloke for that."

"True. But he'd be mighty pissed off. He'd send a couple of his heavies round to remind him the money was due."

He'd certainly do that. A few cuts and bruises, a couple of cracked ribs—Bill Thornton had believed his friend had been beaten up by thugs who thought he had money on him. It was far more likely that Armstrong's men were responsible for Cheyney's stay in hospital.

"But murder? No, Frank, I don't buy it."

"Ah, but wait till you hear this. The lovely Mrs. Armstrong has come forward—frightened for her life apparently—willing to testify against her husband on condition the witness protection program works its magic."

"You're kidding me."

"Nope. She claims Armstrong's gone crazy. Christ, I could have told her that. The bastard's always been crazy." Frank chuckled at that. "It all started, she claims, when she met Cheyney at the golf club. He spilt his drink over her and Armstrong's mates saw her laughing with him. They took the piss out of Armstrong—said he couldn't keep his women, stuff like that. The next thing, Cheyney's dead."

"Come off it, Frank, that's ridiculous. Are you telling me that Armstrong was jealous of a bloke like Cheyney?"

Couldn't keep his women—

Perhaps it wasn't so ridiculous after all. Armstrong's first wife, Pam, had been murdered in the most brutal fashion because she'd had an affair with Tom Andrews. Her lover had been killed with a single bullet.

"Maybe it's not as stupid as it sounds," Dylan said. "After all, Armstrong's first wife—"

"Exactly. And Susie is frightened to death that she'll meet the same fate. The police have her in a safe house at the moment, and I hope for her sake it is bloody safe."

"And Armstrong's in custody?"

"Yes."

"Well, well. Keep me posted, Frank."

As Dylan switched off his phone, he was still trying to take in Frank's news. Was it possible that, after all these years, after all the terrible crimes he had allegedly committed, Armstrong would finally be brought to justice? And all because one of the most harmless men one could meet, Alan Cheyney, had spilt his drink?

"What was all that about?" Bev asked.

He told her all he knew of Alan Cheyney and, more important, his landlord, Terry Armstrong. "Armstrong was always heading for a life sentence. It was just a matter of time."

"Talking of time," she said, "it's time you went home."

Dylan's bubble burst and it no longer felt like old times.

However, he got to his feet, and checked for car keys, flat keys and wallet. "I'll see you on Saturday then?"

"Yes. Come whatever time you like."

"Okay."

He gave her a kiss on the cheek and was soon outside in the chilly air.

After a quick glance back at the house, a wave to Luke who, instead of being fast asleep, was at the window with a book in his hand, Dylan was reversing out of the drive.

It wouldn't be like this forever, though. Bev would come round. She always did.